Not Forsaken

Robin Colbert

ISBN 978-1-64349-787-7 (paperback)
ISBN 978-1-64349-851-5 (hardcover)
ISBN 978-1-64349-788-4 (digital)

Christian Faith Publishing, Inc.
832 Park Avenue
Meadville, PA 16335
www.christianfaithpublishing.com

Printed in the United States of America

Contents

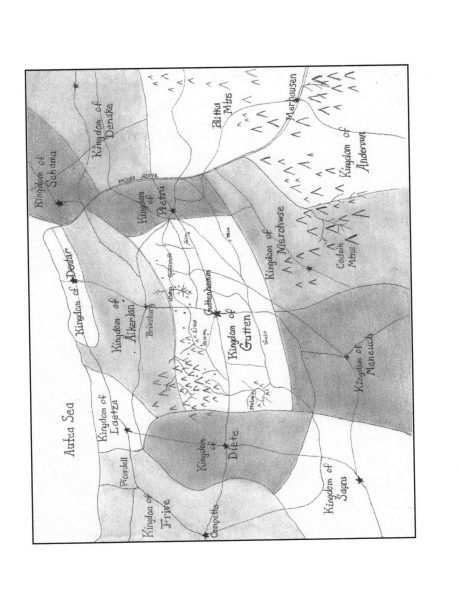

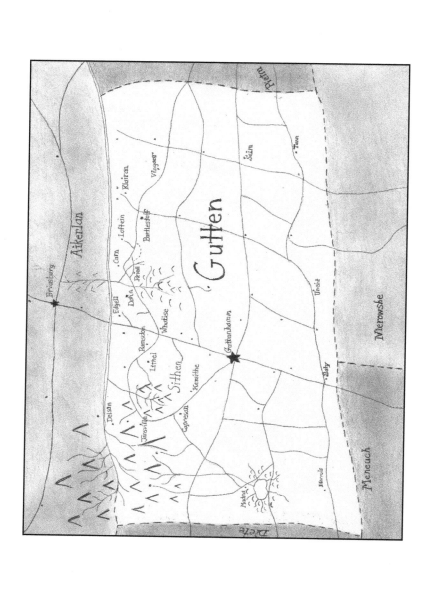

1

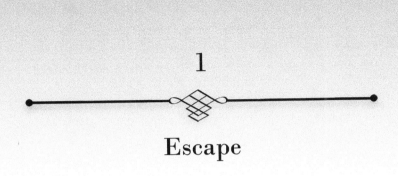

Escape

Gasping, she sat up in bed thinking she had heard a scream. The young lady waited for a moment, but when nothing unusual was heard, she laid back down and dozed off. A few minutes later, she was startled by the sounds of screaming. Quickly the lady fumbled in the darkness, shaking more and more as she dressed. Pulling her long hair away from her ear, she leaned against the chamber door and heard shouting and the distinct sound of steel striking against steel. Going to the window, she saw only darkness for the torches that had lined the lane were now extinguished. She knew for certain an enemy had infiltrated and the castle was under attack. Would it be safe to remain in her room to wait for help to come or should she go looking for it? She was not even sure which direction to go and her life may depend on a hastily made decision. Not knowing what to expect, she donned her cape and peeked into the hall only to hear another horrible scream, this time much closer and by the sound someone had met their Maker. With no hope of running, she looked around the room for a place to hide but it couldn't be too obvious. Dashing for the large armoire, she climbed inside, fluffed the clothes, and pulled the doors together. It was a tight fit. She could barely see through the keyhole but watched for movement. Suddenly she gasped noticing the door to the hall had not latched closed but had in fact swung wide open. It was too risky for her to crawl out of the armoire to close it now, so it would have to remain as it was. She could hear voices from the hallway and the sound of walls being hit as doors were thrown open. The lamps in the hall were still lit and now she could see shadows moving closer to her room. She held her breath as she saw the silhouettes of two men with swords in their hands.

"Look in there," one man said to the other. Cautiously the second man stepped to the doorway and took a glance around.

"There's no one. Let's move on."

"We should be ready to light the fires." The first man said as they continued going from room to room looking for victims. When she could no longer hear anyone, the lady quietly crawled from the armoire, carefully watching the hall. She had to find a way out of the castle or be burned alive. She peered into the hallway, and when she saw no one, she took off running toward the staircase. As she went past the other rooms, not a sound was heard and the lady's stomach turned as she knew all must be dead. Only an occasional sound of swords could be heard as she headed in the direction of the dining hall where a grand meal had been served only hours earlier. Seeing many shadows in the distance, the lady darted behind a large tapestry that hung along the wall. She could hear the men's armor as they walked and was glad they had stopped before coming too close. Wishing she could disappear into the cracks of the wall behind her, she listened to the men discuss the next phase of their plan. With a solemn sadness, they spoke of burning the castle, and making sure it was totally destroyed along with the occupants. Agreeing to a location to meet outside when the deed was finished, they each lit a torch and separated into pairs heading off in different directions. The two men that came in the lady's direction passed so closely that she could have reached out to touch them, and she was relieved that they were so engrossed in conversation that she was not noticed. Ready to make her escape, she slipped from behind the tapestry, and frequently looking over her shoulder, she stole down the hallway. Seeing a set of glass doors, she sighed with relief thinking she was saved. As she opened the door though, she suddenly realized she was *not* where she thought she was. These doors had opened into a chapel, not outside. Panic gripped her heart as in the next moment she saw the glow of torches coming down the hall. Desperately, she bolted into the chapel and staying low she searched for another door or even a window but her efforts were in vain. Ten feet off the floor was the sill of a stained glass window, but it was out of the lady's reach. As she turned, two men walked past the door and quickly she dropped to the floor, crouching behind a wooden altar. She heard one man call out in a German dialect.

"Wait, I thought I saw someone." She was thankful that her father had made her study the foreign language, but she would have rather heard the man say something different.

"We already searched this room, remember? It's a chapel and it was empty," the other man argued.

Not satisfied, the taller man replied, "You can go on, but I want to take another look."

With a sigh of disgust, the other man replied, "Suit yourself, Wilhelm. You won't find anything in there but shadows of the cross!" He stormed down the hall. Anxiously the young woman watched as Wilhelm drew his sword and stepped into the room.

This is it, she thought. *Without a miracle from God himself, I am going to die!* She tried to crouch lower not knowing what else to do.

"Who's there? Show yourself!" the man commanded in a deep voice, confident that he had seen someone in the shadows. A few seconds passed and then the lady answered him in German.

"I . . . I am unarmed and ask for mercy, my lord. Please spare my life. I am merely travelling through this kingdom and . . ." Her voice broke up. "Please, my lord, have mercy on me." Trembling, she slowly stood to her feet. The man was close enough that when he lifted his sword to her, its tip touched her chest. Suddenly she wished she had not been so rebellious about attending church and never surrendering her heart to God.

"What is your name?" the man demanded.

"Josephine Armand. My father is a nobleman in Picardell . . ."

"What are you doing here?" he asked, interrupting her and shifting on his feet anxiously. *Armand . . . Armand . . .* The name sounded familiar.

"I am returning from meeting a suitor and stopped here to rest. Please, my lord, I beg for mercy. I know nothing of this household or this conflict. Please have mercy on me. I am willing to be a servant in exchange for my life," she pleaded, although she didn't realize what she had spoken until she heard it with her own ears.

"I have no need of a servant," the man answered roughly.

"Please, my lord," she begged. Thankfully he had lowered his sword as the lady spoke, and she found herself taking a step closer to the man. His face was shadowed, so she could not see his reaction but she humbly dropped to her knees in front of him. With her voice quivering, she begged, "If you must kill me, then be merciful and kill me quickly." With tears running down her face, she pulled back her hair exposing her pale neck to him and lowered her head, for an easier execution. The lady did not look up as the man's sword came to rest upon her left shoulder. The few seconds that passed seemed like torturous minutes.

"Do you swear this to be the truth?" he asked. Wilhelm stood towering above her with his eyes piercing through the darkness as if to see into the lady's soul. Suddenly the light from the hallway reflected onto the stained glass window above the altar. The blood from the Savior seemed to glow a fiery red as it streamed onto the foreground of the scene. The man looked down at the lady kneeling before him. Suddenly, Wilhelm remembered that Renard Armand served at the court in Frive. He had an honorable reputation but was this young lady truly his daughter or just a skilled liar who knew of the nobleman? Wilhelm had to admit the lady's words gripped his heart. Was finding her beneath the chapel window a sign of divine intervention for him to spare her as she was truly innocent to the whole wretched affair? Her pleading no doubt was genuine but would he regret what he was about to do.

"Yes, my lord, as God as my witness," she replied with tears.

"I will spare you," he said, lowering his sword to his side. Slowly she stood to her feet with him still watching her carefully. Just because she wanted to live did not mean that she wouldn't get a wild notion to stab him or something. Josephine wanted to thank him for having mercy but how could she bring herself to show gratitude to a man who was a murderer. Remembering her vow of service, she humbly bowed.

"Command me as you will, my lord."

"Please," he said, motioning to her his disapproval. "That will not be necessary." He was interrupted by a loud popping noise from the ceiling above them. "We must hurry!" And he quickly took hold of her arm and helped her over the altar that stood between them. "It won't do to spare you the sword only to lose you to the fire. Stay close and follow me." They paused at the doorway noticing the hall was filling with smoke and ashes, and heat could be felt coming from above.

"Do you know which way to go?" Josephine asked as she pulled the hood of her cape over her hair.

"Yes," he answered as he pointed to the ceiling above them. She looked up to see flames breaking through. "Let's get out of here!" Wilhelm took off staying a few steps ahead of the lady but paused before every doorway to be sure an enemy was not lurking. They were halfway down the main hall when a threatening scream tore through the air. From a doorway just ahead charged a man swinging his sword wildly, and Josephine would have been killed had Wilhelm not blocked his attack. The man was very skilled and forced them back down the hall toward the raging flames. Josephine found herself not knowing what to do: caught in a nightmare that was only getting worse. Several times she tried to slide past the duel, but the other man would not allow it. He seemed determined not only to kill Wilhelm but her too. The fight went on, and they found themselves retreating into a smaller passageway. Then to Josephine's horror her back touched the wall behind her. In a matter of seconds, Wilhelm was against her and gave a deep groan, realizing it was a dead end.

Placing one hand behind him, he tried to guide Josephine's body in the direction he moved so she would not be hit as he avoided the other man's lunges. "I am sorry you fell into this mess." She could not believe what she was hearing, was he not fighting for his life and yet was apologizing to her. Suddenly the enemy made a sharp jab and Wilhelm was able to dodge it but the sword ripped through Josephine's cape, narrowly missing her flesh. She screamed in horror.

"All right, enough of this!" Wilhelm yelled as he charged forward. The unexpected move caught the other man off guard, and Wilhelm began to gain ground. In a few moments, their position had shifted so that they were edging along the length of the hallway. When there was enough room to slip past, Wilhelm said to Josephine, "Get out of here, I will be right behind you."

"But . . ."

"I said I will be right behind you!" he yelled. "I grow tired of this folly!" He was fighting with all that was in him and seemed to now have the upper hand. In a commanding voice, he added, "Wait for me at the entrance. Go now!" Without further hesitation, Josephine took off running down the hall. The heat from the flames was almost unbearable as she reached the foyer of the castle. Suddenly she stopped as she heard a gut-wrenching scream ring out. She hoped it had not come from her defender. She was indebted to him for saving her life for a second time that night. Stepping outside, she drew a deep breath of fresh air and then quickly retreated behind a nearby shrub a safe distance from the flames, for she could not risk being seen by the other man if he proved to be the victor of the duel. Impatiently she watched as the flames continued to spread, licking the massive columns along the porch. She could see the timbers giving way under the collapsing roof and second floor. Anxiously she peered around the greenery hoping to see some sign of life, but her stomach grew ill as she watched the castle burning. Where was her defender? He had bettered hurry if he was to escape. Or was it too late already?

"There you are," said a voice from behind, causing Josephine to nearly scream from fright. To her relief, it was Wilhelm. "Come. Let's get away from here." With a firm grip upon her arm, he pulled her toward the road.

"How did you get out of there?" Josephine asked as he quickened the pace.

"The hall was completely engulfed in flames so I had to go through a window. Which means, when we are far enough away from here to stop for a moment, I will need a favor from you." The lady began to pant as they were now at a slow run.

"If I may ask, where are we going?" To her disappointment, Wilhelm did not answer, and for fear of angering him she did not repeat the question. Suddenly he came to a stop and looked around as if for something in particular. Seeing his mark, he released her arm and headed into the woods. He paused and called to her.

"Follow me. The villagers will see the fire, but it is imperative that we remain hidden."

For a moment, Josephine hesitated but then obeyed him. She did not like the idea of being alone with a stranger, a murderer at that, in the woods, but what choice did she have? As they began to fight their way through the dense undergrowth, she questioned her decision again. Should she keep following him or when the chance came try to escape? A chill ran down her spine as she wondered if he would take the time to track her down and force her to go with him. But if she ran, she would be breaking her vow and would her conscience let her live with that decision? Who would ever know, except the two of them? It seemed odd, but this man's words and actions toward her seemed to be with honor for he had spared her life twice that night already. They continued making their way through the woods, and it wasn't long until Josephine was wishing she was in trousers instead of a dress. It seemed to snag on every branch and twig but thankfully the man was patient as she untangled herself. She was relieved when they came to the edge of a field. They crossed it and had reached the timbers on the far side when Wilhelm pointed out a sheltered place and said.

"We can rest here for a moment." He gathered a handful of twigs and pulled a flint from the pouch hanging from his waist and after a few minutes, a small fire was going. Josephine could not help but wonder what he was doing, for the night air had a slight chill but it was by no means cold. The purpose of the fire was revealed as he knelt beside the glowing sticks and lit the stub of a candle that he also took from his pouch. "Now I will require the favor," he said, turning toward the woman and stretching out his left hand. Josephine could see blood covering his knuckles. Earlier when he had asked for the favor, her heart had pounded anxiously as she had imagined the worst. By the looks of it he must be in terrible pain. "I can feel glass from the window in my hand," he explained, moving the candle closer. She knelt beside him and pulled a handkerchief from the pocket of her cape.

"It will be difficult to see anything for the blood," she commented in a meek voice. She had never been this close to a man except when she had danced. Switching the candle to his injured hand Wilhelm withdrew a canteen from beneath his chain mail. By the meager light of the candle he saw the lady's reaction for she assumed he was drinking liquor to dull the pain.

"It's only water. I promise you." He placed the container in her hand. As she unscrewed the lid she could not help but take a sniff and found he was telling the truth. "I don't drink," he added. Carefully she poured the water over his hand and he winced in pain. She positioned the candle for more light and brought his hand up closer to study it for fragments. She saw a glimmer in two places, and with a shaky hand, she reached toward the first one.

"I am not the one to be doing this." She said with an agonizing frown. "I don't think my fingers are strong enough to get a firm grip on the glass."

"Please, can you try?" he asked. There was no hiding her nervousness about the task but the man tried to reassure her. "You would have more experience with delicate matters than any of my men. Besides, it hurts already so there can be no more harm done." At his point, he saw a smile cross her face in the flickering of the candlelight. Perhaps he was on the right road to winning her trust. "Did I hear correctly that your name is Josephine?"

"Yes," she answered, trying to concentrate. She could feel the sliver between her fingernails and tightening her grip she gave a quick jerk straight up, which lifted the piece out perfectly. He gasped momentarily but with relief.

"One more?" he asked. She nodded and turning his hand to get a better view, summoned her courage to ask him a question this time.

"What may I call you? Will lord do, or is there another title that you prefer?" She was too busy studying his hand to notice how he looked at her. He was surprised that under such circumstances she had not shied away but was again pledging herself to his service. He knew she was afraid of him yet had enough control over her emotions to have pity and mend his hand without malice.

"Wilhelm will do," he said, and then groaned as Josephine's finger bumped the edge of the shard.

"I'm so sorry," she apologized.

"The piece seems to run under the edge of my ring, does it not? Can you help me slide it off?" She was hesitant to touch him after inflicting pain but he insisted. Very carefully, she removed the signet from his finger. She turned it in the light to see the details, but could not make them out.

"It's an eagle," he said, answering the question she had not spoken. "The crest of my family." Josephine knew how important the family signet was for she had never seen her father's hand without his ring. When her brother came of age, a replica was presented to him in a special ceremony.

"Let me put this on your other hand," she offered.

"Sorry, but it does not fit well upon any other finger. Just hold on to it for now."

"You should not trust such an heirloom to a stranger," she commented as she looked directly at him for the first time. She wished his hood did not shadow his face so she could have seen more than the man's chin and nose.

"Are you a lady of honor?" he asked.

"Yes," she answered him slowly, not sure what his next words would be.

"Promise me that you will not lose it and that you will return it to me when we reach the castle, and I will entrust it into your care." She wasn't sure how to take the compliment he was bestowing to her.

"Yes, my lord, as you wish. Did you say we are headed to a castle?"

"Yes, my family's," he replied as Josephine slipped the ring onto her middle finger where it hung loosely. She decided to put it on the chain of her necklace as soon as she had the chance. She lifted Wilhelm's hand toward the candle to survey where the last stubborn piece was lodged.

Josephine gave a tug on the shard but lost her grip causing Wilhelm to jerk with pain. She could not help but sigh at her failure and shaking with nervousness, the lady tried again.

"Have you ever been a servant to anyone before now?" he asked, watching Josephine move her head closer to study the point of entry. She shook her head to answer his question and then took hold of the piece again. Gently she pulled and slowly it slid out of his hand. "Thank you so much," Wilhelm said with relief.

"I'm glad to help you rather than hinder," Josephine said, looking up at him, again wishing she could see more of the details of his face. "Is it far to the castle?"

"Unfortunately, it's another full day's journey," he said, reaching for the canteen that now lay upon his knee. As he tipped it to his lips, she wondered who he was. She would guess him to be a nobleman, but why would a nobleman be fighting himself instead of sending servants to fight for him. Her heart wanted to believe him to be an honorable man, but the situation she had been delivered from made her think otherwise and Josephine found herself utterly confused as to which nature was the true Wilhelm. He attacked another castle, burning it to the ground and killing all inside, yet somehow he showed mercy to her. Her task completed, the lady stood to her feet and walked a few feet away to look up through the tree branches at the moon whose light had made their journey through the night much easier. Wilhelm rose and blew out the candle.

"Would you like a drink?" he asked, holding out the canteen. She took it from him and took a good swallow not realizing how thirsty she was. She wiped the corner of her mouth with her handkerchief and returned the container to him.

"Thank you," she said, fidgeting with the cloth "Oh, how silly of me." She realized she had not covered his wound. "Let me wrap your hand, so it will stay clean until you can see a doctor." Without a word, he stepped beside her and held out his hand. As she tied a knot in the make-shift bandage, Wilhelm gently reached to touch her arm, trying not to alarm her.

"We need to get moving or my brother will go back to Briasburg to look for me," he said. His words were not harsh, but Josephine found herself trembling. Sensing her anxiety, he said, "Please, don't be afraid of me. I know your first impression must be terrible, but if you will give me a chance, I will explain everything when we get to the castle. I promise I will not harm you in any way, nor will I let anyone else. I only ask that you have faith enough to trust me." Josephine wanted to, but it would be foolish not to exercise caution and stay fully alert to this man's every action. He let go of her arm and turned to put out the meager remains of the fire.

This time when they began to walk, Wilhelm changed directions, and shortly, they intersected a road. On the smoother surface, he went at a faster pace and she did her best to keep up.

"We should be getting close to the others," he said, glancing over his shoulder toward the lady.

"How many are there?" she asked.

"Twelve, including my brother and me." She was glad that he had humored her enough to answer her question.

"Was he the one you were speaking with outside the chapel?" she asked, panting in between words.

"You either have good ears or we have big mouths," he replied with a laugh.

"Perhaps, a little of both," she said, keeping her eyes to the ground trying not to stumble in the fading moon light. Suddenly he stopped so abruptly in front of her that she bumped into him. "Sorry," she said rather embarrassed, but to her surprise, he muffled a laugh.

"Whoa there . . . Listen . . ." He lifted his hands to his mouth and made a whistling sound like a bird. He was promptly answered with another but different sounding whistle, and then it was as if the woods leapt out at them. As Josephine started to scream, Wilhelm quickly turned and clamped his hand over her mouth. She watched as men clad in armor became visible.

"Who is that?" one of the men grumbled, pointing toward the woman with his sword. Slowly Wilhelm removed his hand from Josephine's mouth and answered.

"Put your sword away, Leopold. There's no need to be alarmed."

"What are you thinking dragging a woman along?"

17

"That is a story we should save for later," Wilhelm said, motioning to the others. "I see everyone's accounted for. Is there anyone wounded?"

"We can travel just fine sir," a man replied and lifted a bandaged arm.

"Let's head for home then. It's been a long night," Wilhelm said with a sigh as the last duel had taken more from him than all the other deeds of the night put together.

"Wilhelm," Leopold said, stepping in front of his brother. "Need I remind you that we were instructed not to leave anyone alive, not to mention bringing back any prisoners?"

"I know what orders were!" Wilhelm said, raising his voice. "Don't question my judgment!" In a calmer voice, he added, "She is the daughter of Duke Armand in Picardell of Frive. I know whose life I have spared dear brother." In shock, Josephine listened intently.

"We cannot afford for her to slow us down," Leopold grumbled.

"She's done fine so far," Wilhelm replied in her defense. Leopold took a step toward the lady and gave her a threatening push to show how weak she was.

"Leave her alone!" Wilhelm said, stepping in front of the woman to prevent his brother from pushing her again. Leopold mumbled under his breath and walked away. Wilhelm leaned toward Josephine and whispered, "Watch out for him—he can be pretty nasty when he's in a mood. Stay close to me, please." He hoped his brother would have been pleased that he had saved the nobleman's daughter, but alas, Leopold was his charming self. With a wave of Wilhelm's hand, the troop began to march down the road. Josephine turned her attention to staying close behind Wilhelm which proved even more difficult than it had been earlier. Finally she realized why she was struggling as all the men were at least a head taller than she was and it took two of her strides to equal one of theirs. There was just enough light for her to see Leopold turn to scowl at her over his shoulder. He was like a hawk waiting to swoop down and snatch up his prey. After an hour or so, Wilhelm slowed his pace to walk beside the lady. "How are you doing?" he asked.

"I'm managing," she replied out of breath. "I wish my legs were longer."

"I suppose that would help," he said with a laugh. "You are doing fine, even at a disadvantage. I am sorry for the poor reception from my brother. In his own way, he is just doing his job and protecting his family."

"Oh really?" she said. "I thought he was trying to be charming." At her comment, Wilhelm gave a loud laugh that caused the others to turn and look, but he didn't seem to mind. Shortly they crossed over a wooden bridge again being careful that no one heard their footsteps nor saw them. Wilhelm remained beside the lady as they continued on and daylight finally came. Briefly they stopped to rest near some fallen trees giving Josephine the chance to look at the few who had allowed their cape hoods to fall back upon their shoulders revealing their faces. They seemed like a respectable lot and most were polite in their conversations with each other with only Leopold grumbling. Before they took off again, every man put on his cloak and methodically pulled his hood over his head. Wilhelm warned Josephine they were not among friends and they had to shield their identity. Several times during the day they left the road hiding as travelers passed and twice to avoid walking through villages. It seemed to Josephine that the journey would never come to an end. As dusk began to fall, they left the road, but this time, they followed a well-worn path to a cabin. The old man living there knew they were coming and had provisions waiting for them. They sat at his table nearly an hour eating and resting their legs. Josephine wondered if they would be spending the night or continue on. Her question was shortly answered as Wilhelm called her away from the others.

"We must go on to be fully out of harm's way. Are you able to continue with us or would you rather . . ." The lady did not allow him to finish.

"I gave you my word," she said firmly. Wilhelm was pleased that the lady possessed the will power and strength to go on.

"Very well." He motioned to the others, and quickly they left the cabin and made their way back through the darkness to the road. The moonlight was not as bright as the previous night, so everyone pulled their hoods back as they could not afford to be hindered by the lack of sight. Several times, Josephine wondered if she was going to collapse but just as she was about to give up Wilhelm would suddenly come beside her. She wanted to tell him she was beginning to falter but just as she would start to she could visualize Leopold mocking her and changed her mind. They stopped only once to rest with Wilhelm letting her drink from his canteen again. They dared not sit for very long as all were reaching the point of exhaustion and she was told they would not arrive at the castle till early morning. As they began to walk again, the lady tried to keep herself awake by naming the neighboring kingdoms of Frive and their noblemen. They had walked south long enough that she would guess they were now in Gutten. The men had taken special care as to not disclose their destination and she wondered which brother's handiwork that was. Her mind wondered back to the castle at Briasburg. How long would it take for word to be sent to her family of its demise? Suddenly her heart seemed to skip a beat as she realized word would not be sent for her hired escorts would have perished in the raid, and she was not even supposed to be lodging at the castle that night. How long would it take for her father to go looking for her? Would he still want her to return home after her refusal of the suitor? She decided to dismiss the thought as it was not helping the state of her miserably aching body. Finally she saw the first glimpses of dawn approaching and Wilhelm came beside her again and cleared his throat. "In a few hours we will arrive at the town. The market is very busy in the mornings. Stay close to me."

"I will," Josephine answered.

"And when we get inside the castle, I will need my ring first thing," he added.

"Why don't you take it now?" she said, reaching for her necklace where it had been securely placed.

"No, my finger is still swollen. Wait and give it to me when we are there." He started to step away but then leaned toward her. "By the way, despite what you have seen, Leopold is a big flirt. When he finally decides you are not here to stab him in the back, he will be quick to make a move for you. I thought you should know."

"Oh," she commented. She was again surprised that the stranger was looking out for her. Curious to see how Wilhelm would react, Josephine added, "Does flirting run in the family?" There was just enough light for the lady to see a smile cross the man's face as he shrugged his shoulders.

"I don't know about that. Maybe you can give me your opinion later," he suggested as he pulled his hood up to cover his head again. He gave a whistle and the other men did likewise, and Josephine followed suit. She did not understand why these warriors of the night still wanted their identities concealed in their home town, but for whatever reason, their secret was to be kept to a select few.

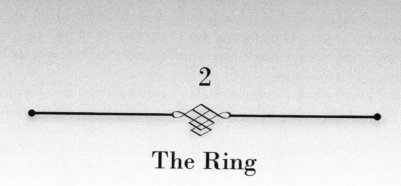

2

The Ring

Wilhelm had spoken correctly that the town would be busy that morning. As they made their way down the main street and approached the plaza, he turned to remind the woman.

"Stay close, I don't want to lose you in the crowd." Josephine looked up in time to see Leopold scowl at his brother's remark. His opinion of the lady was not hidden. As they began to work their way through the rows of vendors, Josephine stayed upon Wilhelm's heels. Suddenly Leopold cut in front of her, bringing her to a stop, but Wilhelm continued, not realizing they had been separated.

"Would you like to try some fruit?" Leopold asked sarcastically, shoving the woman toward a cart of apples.

"No, thank you," she said, trying to remain polite but knew his actions were intentional. "Excuse me. I need to catch up to Wilhelm." She tried to step around the man.

"Don't bother. Go home and forget about last night." He barked at her. "And forget about my brother too. He has more important things to do than lead you about."

"You don't understand," she pleaded. "He says whether I stay or go." With a grunt of disgust, Leopold gave the woman a push, knocking her hard into the cart. While she got her feet back under her, he slipped into the crowd. Frantically she tiptoed trying to see which direction he went but could not see the man at all. To her dismay, she could not see anyone wearing a cape as Wilhelm or his mercenaries had. She stood there for a moment, contemplating what to do. Should she abandon her quest and find a way to return to Picardell? But what was that worth? Her father had been unhappy with her for several months now, and she with him. Armand did not inherit his fortune but as a young man worked hard to acquire his holdings and his reputable position as duke. His wife and children enjoyed a simple but blissful life, not wanting for anything. Armand's social standing required frequent appearances in the royal court but only upon occasion did Laurie leave their children to be beside her husband. When old enough and schooled in proper etiquette, the children were allowed to accompany their parents on special occasions to the capital, Competta. Armand was of the generation that believed arranged marriages and long betrothals were best, but Laurie cautioned him that love would make the happiest home. Phillipe was studying abroad in Sapra when he fell in love. Natalee was from a noble house, which pleased Armand, and after courting for a year, they were wed. Arlene, however, was more trying of her father's patience. Being utterly beautiful, she never lacked for suitors but as she courted several gentlemen, not all were of notable character. A nobleman from western Frive made an offer for Arlene's hand that was not refused. A few months into the betrothal it was discovered that the suitor had pledged himself to three other ladies, preying upon their families' wealth to satisfy gambling debts. The engagement was broken, and Arlene was devastated, to say the least. A year later, she was blessed to meet a humble gentleman from the southern part of the country. Pierre's holdings were meager but he was determined to give Arlene the best. Relieved that a legitimate offer of marriage had been made, Armand granted his permission for the couple to wed. After the bad experience with Arlene, Josephine was not pushed toward settling down and she was allowed to travel with Armand as a personal secretary. She took every opportunity to further her knowledge of business and foreign policies and stayed upon her father's coat tails.

Unfortunately her hopes were crushed when she came into the room at her eighteenth birthday party. It took only one look around the room for her to know her father was hoping one of the dozen gentlemen present would catch her eye. Josephine was polite, dancing with each young man as was expected of her but she was not happy about it. The next morning when her father asked what she thought of the gentlemen, she tried to reason away her lack of interest but it was not well received and a heated argument followed. They left the breakfast table that morning at odds and spoke little to each other for weeks. One morning, it was announced that Josephine was to leave for Denske that afternoon with arrangements having been made for her to meet Duke Alfred, and if things went well, an engagement was to follow. Renard gave his daughter several reasons that Alfred had been chosen, but Josephine was furious and stormed from the room. Her mother tried to convince the girl that love still may be waiting for her as the young duke had been highly spoken of, and finally Josephine agreed to go on the journey, but it was more to get away from her father than to find a husband. Grasping at a slim chance, the young lady promised to keep an open mind and be on her best behavior but asked that the final decision be hers alone. Renard agreed but warned that if she refused Alfred, she might not like the outcome if it had not been for good reasons. With a long journey ahead, a better carriage and armed escorts were secured for the young lady to have adequate protection. After a week, she arrived in Denske and was warmly received. Alfred was handsome and seemed charming enough, but Josephine did not hold his attention for very long. He was more interested in flirting with the kitchen help than spending time with his bride to be. Finally Josephine confronted him concerning the matter, and the young man did not deny his need for attention from other women and could not promise that his desires would change upon marriage. He was bluntly told that she would not tolerate the infidelity, and they mutually agreed not to go through with the betrothal. Josephine had hoped Denske would be where she found love and happiness and satisfied her father. She knew Renard would be boiling mad with the refusal, and she was not eager to face him, dreading the encounter so much that she had entertained ways to delay the journey home. Willingly she detoured off the course her father had chosen, staying longer at a scenic town along the Mesra River. Her carriage was nowhere near where it was supposed to be that dreadful night and thus she had ended up at the Briasburg castle instead of the prearranged lodging. But now Josephine was caught up in a predicament much worse, having sworn her allegiance to Wilhelm, not even knowing who he was. In her heart, she wondered if she had found her excuse for not returning home.

What should she do now? She stood gazing across a sea of people. Suddenly her eyes fell upon the booth of a seamstress and she had an idea. She would need to disguise her appearance if she was to get close to either Wilhelm or Leopold again. Nothing she could do would ever convince someone that she was a man but she could easily pass as a peasant girl. Josephine approached the seamstress and made the woman an offer she could not refuse. Thirty minutes later, the young lady emerged, having traded her lavish dress and embroidered cape for a plain brown dress and dark-green cape. The deal had been so one-sided that the peddler gave Josephine several coins to compensate for the great loss the young lady had taken. Josephine had no doubt in her mind as to her next purchase. She wandered through the streets until she came upon a blacksmith. She couldn't be too careful after the last two days. The blacksmith was friendly and helped the young lady pick out a small but potent dagger. Not that she had ever used one but she was sure she could figure it out if the need arose. Josephine purchased the dagger and went on her way. As she worked her way back through the street in the direction the smith had pointed her, she finally came to a place where the town seemed to taper to an end. Before her lay a field that stretched roughly a mile before it began to slope upward to a sizeable knoll. At the top stood a castle. The young lady's heart sank as she realized getting inside was not going to be an easy task. She couldn't just walk up to the gates and tell the story of what had happened as no one would ever believe her. She wouldn't even be able to cross the field without being noticed, so a plan was needed before she got there. Could she pretend to be a new servant returning from the market? She would need to buy goods to carry in for it to look legitimate. She had begun to fidget with her necklace when she felt Wilhelm's ring catch on the buttons of her dress. Suddenly she had an idea. Returning to the market, she found a shop and purchased a sheet of parchment. Under the pretense of an emergency she asked the shopkeeper if she could use his writing desk and he obliged. Quickly she busied herself pretending to scribe a letter but actually left it completely blank and rolled it up. With a shaky hand, she dripped wax onto the scroll and stamped the seal using Wilhelm's ring which made the document look authentic from a glance. Thanking the shopkeeper for his kindness, the lady left and headed toward the castle. Gathering confidence, Josephine went to the gate, and as she saw two guards look in her direction, she took the initiative.

"Good morning. It's a lovely day, isn't it?" she said to the men trying to mimic the local accent. "I have a letter that needs to be returned to Lord Wilhelm." As she spoke, she handed the parchment to the guard closest to her. As he turned it in his hand he recognized the seal.

"It is his majesty's, but why hasn't it been opened?" he asked, looking the woman over with a sharp eye.

"I could not find the gentleman it was addressed to, but I have news of where he might be found. I was instructed to return the letter to Wilhelm personally if my task could not be completed," Josephine said, hoping that her lie sounded real. Convinced the guard placed the parchment back in the lady's hand.

"Go on to the foyer and ask for Karl. He will instruct you what to do." Josephine curtsied and began to walk. She was aggravated that she was being directed to go to someone else. The more people involved meant that she would have to continue the tale and the thought of that made her nervous. She decided not to ask for Karl and try her luck in a different avenue. She stepped into the foyer and asked the first servant she saw for directions to the kitchen. It was easy enough to find and bustling with activity. Quickly she explained herself and was told to hang her cloak in the breezeway leading to the courtyard and then help some of the maids with the preparation of lunch. In no time, she was chopping vegetables and listening to the gossip. A small town in the northern part of the kingdom had been attacked three days earlier. Most of the people had been killed, but the few that survived would bear scars the rest of their lives. Josephine found her stomach growing ill with each passing moment. The homes had been burned with the fields being set ablaze as well and the livestock slaughtered. Some of the servants present had lost family in the massacre. Josephine could not understand how someone would be so cruel to attack innocent people. The servants also spoke of a fear that was spreading across the region. Their faces bore the worry of awakening to the sound of swords and fires burning, and Josephine found herself trembling as she recalled her experience two nights earlier. She wondered if these people knew about the raid on Briasburg. Would they condemn it or condone it?

After an hour or so had passed with no mention of Wilhelm's name, Josephine slipped out of the kitchen. She didn't get very far when she was called to as she passed a doorway. Stepping into the room, she found an older lady scrubbing upon a washboard. Here the young lady was not as easily received as she was in the kitchen.

"What are you doing?"

"Uhh . . . the cook sent me this way to help." Josephine stuttered, almost slipping to reply in French as she offered an excuse.

"What's your name?" the woman demanded as she moved wet clothes into a nearby basket.

"Josephine."

"Well, dear, there's plenty to do. My name is Liza." She pointed to a large pile of laundry behind her. "Thursdays are the worst," she complained loudly. "I told 'em, 'Let's change the bedclothes on Mondays and table linens on Thursdays.' But would they listen to me? No! It all had to be done on the same day. Pooh!"

Josephine could understand why the white-haired woman was in a foul mood. The young lady wished she hadn't been noticed coming down the hallway, but then her conscience smote her as it wouldn't *hurt* her to help the woman. She might gain information while keeping from being discovered. She picked up a piece of linen and was beginning to lower it into a nearby tub when Liza yelled, "No, no. I will do the scrubbing. Here, go hang these on the line," and she pointed to a door that led outside. Josephine moved toward the basket of wet laundry.

"Yes, fraulein," she answered. The basket was much heavier than she was used to, and although she managed to make it through the doorway, she struggled to carry it beyond to the clothesline. To her relief, another young lady came to help.

"Hello, my name is Katrina," she said when the basket was sat down. The maid began to hang the clothes upon the line. "Are you new here?"

"Yes," Josephine answered.

"Just do as Liza says and you will be fine. Where are you from?" she asked as they each took an end of a blanket and hoisted it into the air.

"I used to live in Frive," Josephine answered. She guessed the maid to be just older than she and didn't mind how friendly she was. Josephine was struggling with the first clothespin when Katrina reached for another blanket. When no one was on the other end to lift it up, she saw the dilemma and smiling came to the lady's aid.

"You haven't hung out laundry before, have you?" and she demonstrated how to use the pin.

"It is rather obvious, isn't it?" Josephine replied as they reached for the next blanket.

"Uh huh. What are you really doing here?" Katrina asked, moving closer and lowering her voice as if a secret was being shared. "Did Leopold snag you?" Josephine almost dropped her end as she heard the man's name.

"You know Leopold?" she asked with surprise. Maybe she had stumbled onto someone who could help her after all. She was even more surprised when the lady laughed.

"Sure. I think every girl in the castle had encountered him one way or another." Turning red with embarrassment, Josephine realized what Katrina was implying and remembered Wilhelm's words of caution concerning his brother.

"Oh . . . It's not like that."

"I would hope that you know he's not serious about anyone, just always flirting," Katrina replied, ignoring the lady's denial.

"Please let me explain. I don't know him in a personal manner." She hesitated, not knowing whether to mention Wilhelm or not.

"Actually, I am looking for his brother." Josephine was not prepared for Katrina's reaction as she dropped what she had in her hand and gave an astonished look.

"What would you want with him?" she asked, fumbling to pick up the linen from the ground and shaking the dirt from it.

"I need to speak with him about a personal matter and I owe him a favor." Katrina's mouth opened wide and she shook her head. Suddenly Josephine realized what she must be thinking. She tried to explain herself. "Let me assure you, it is nothing like, well . . . you know . . . It is urgent that I speak with him and I don't know where to find him at this hour of the day." She gave a pleading look at Katrina as if asking for her input, but the maid quickly looked away and began to mumble.

"He's probably upstairs. But we are not allowed on that wing of the second floor because it's private chambers. Come, let us get back to work before we get into trouble." She nervously reached for the empty basket and took hold of Josephine's arm. "You should forget about Wilhelm. He's far too busy for trifle notions."

Refusing to give up, Josephine asked, "What about Leopold? Will *he* have time to talk with me?" Katrina didn't reply as they went inside, traded the basket and reemerged in the courtyard.

When they were out of Liza's sight, Katrina spoke up, "Leopold will be easy to find. He's never as busy as Wilhelm, but I wouldn't recommend going to him." She hesitated and then laughed. "I don't think he will want to do much talking, if you know what I mean." Josephine wanted to ask another question, but Katrina wanting to change the subject began humming a spirited tune. Taking the hint, Josephine focused on her task and began to ponder how to get to the private wing. Suddenly she noticed that the bedding on a far clothesline was dry. Could she take the bedding upstairs and if she was discovered use it as an excuse for being in the forbidden area? She continued working with Katrina until lunch, and they went to the kitchen and ate quietly. When they returned to the courtyard, they found the bedsheets were dry, and after taking them off the line, Josephine was quick to offer her help to Liza to remake the beds.

For a moment, the older lady hesitated but then with a smile she motioned for the young lady to grab a basket.

"You may come along, but remember, it is private chambers and you are not allowed without permission." They walked down the hallway past the kitchen and then up a narrow winding staircase. When they stepped out of the dark passageway, Josephine saw a wide beautiful hallway where elaborately carved tables adorned with fresh flowers lined the walls that were watched by stately portraits of ancestors.

Liza warned. "I could be in trouble for letting you come with me. So, remember your manners, please."

"Yes, fraulein. Thank you so much. It is lovely," Josephine added, acting as if she had never seen such a sight before. Even though the castle was not as lavishly decorated as the palace in Competta, the simple elegant beauty gave it regal splendor but focusing on her task Josephine began to ask. "Are all of these rooms bedchambers?"

"Oh no, not all of them. The rooms up to the junction where the hallways meet are bedchambers and thankfully only the beds that were used in the last week had to be changed," she added and then knocked on a door, and when nothing was heard, Liza went inside.

"Does the family entertain overnight guests often?" Josephine asked.

"It depends," Liza answered. Although the room was handsomely decorated, Josephine knew it had to be a guestroom for it contained no personal belongings. They stretched a sheet across the mattress and spread out a lovely quilt and plumped pillows before they left the room. They continued down the hall, making beds in several rooms that were similar to the first one. Liza stopped to explain that Josephine could not accompany her in the next room but instead asked her to get the linens from the chapel down the hall and then continue on alone with her duties to the next few rooms. Josephine felt her heart pound as she heard the word *chapel*, remembering her last time in the sacred place. Liza asked her one more time if she understood and when Josephine had repeated it to her they parted.

Slowly Josephine walked toward the chapel, and as she opened the door, she felt a shiver run down her spine. She sighed with relief as this room looked nothing like the one at Briasburg. Several paintings from the Holy Scriptures adorned the walls, and at the far end of the room, a cross was affixed to the wall with a pulpit beneath. With the pews blocking her view, she had already taken a few steps before the lady noticed that a man was kneeling at the altar. It seemed she had not disturbed him. She could hear his prayerful mumbling as she approached the pulpit to remove a basket of soiled handkerchiefs. She was carefully retracing her steps past the altar when her conscience burned within her. She should at least stop to thank God for sparing her life. Laying the basket on the first pew, she returned to the altar and knelt down. She had only said a few words until she found herself on the verge of tears, and quickly she stopped praying and rose to her feet. As she turned to leave, her eye caught a picture of Abraham offering up Isaac on Mount Moriah. How could a father be so willing to sacrifice his own son, she wondered, and her heart ached as she thought of her own father. He claimed he was only acting in her best interest by sending her away, but she did not agree. She felt betrayed with her life being sacrificed to his ambitions. Renard had always insisted the family pray together every morning, but since the heated argument, she had refused to join him and her mother for spite. She had never been one to seek after God, but after that day, she quit praying altogether. Josephine was so lost in thought that she did not notice the man at the altar raise his head to glance around. Suddenly out of the corner of her eye she saw him and apologized for intruding and stepped away. As she picked up the basket, she stopped to look the room over one last time and then left.

Josephine continued down the hall, and after tending two more guest rooms, she opened the door to a room clearly not used for visitors for it smelled of cologne and was much larger than the other chambers. A rack of antlers was mounted upon one wall, and she would venture a younger gentleman resided there by the personal affects scattered throughout. A display of weaponry hung upon the far wall and not a feminine touch could be found. Suddenly she wondered if the room belonged to Wilhelm. She would ask Liza when they met again. She had just stretched the sheet across the bed when she heard the door slam behind her. Startled she jumped terribly and turned to see who had come in and to her horror found it was Leopold. Quickly she turned back to her work knowing that if he recognized her it would not be good. She tried to compose herself, but she could feel his eyes upon her as he spoke.

"Hello there. You are a fresh face." Out of the corner of her eye she saw him sit down in an arm chair. Trying not to arouse any suspicion, she played to her role as chambermaid.

"Yes, my lord. Please permit me just a few minutes more and then I will be on my way."

"Take your time. There's no need to rush off," he said as he continued to stare. Josephine was relieved that he had not kept up the conversation as she was afraid her accent would give her away. Then she remembered the signet ring dangling from her necklace. Subtly she managed to tuck the chain into her collar and carefully she kept her back to the man as she worked. Finally she was done and turning to leave, she gave a respectful curtsy and headed for the door. To her dismay, Leopold was not willing to let her leave and beat her there.

"Will I be seeing you around the castle?" he asked, blocking her way of escape.

Keeping her head lowered and avoiding eye contact as was custom, she lied, "If it pleases you, my lord." She cringed as he lifted her chin and looked into her eyes. *Stay strong. Don't panic.* She could only hope he had not seen her face that morning, if he had . . . she dreaded to think of it.

"You are very beautiful," he said, leaning closer.

"Thank you, my lord. Ummm . . . Please excuse me, I need to return to work or Liza will bawl me out," Josephine said, interrupting him. He began to laugh and to her relief reached for the door.

"I will see you later then," he said, looking her over one more time before he let her slip out of the room. Quickly she headed for the back staircase, and when she was hidden in the darkness, she found herself stopping to lean against the wall. Her heart was beating rapidly. Wilhelm had rightly warned her about his brother. Still shaking, Josephine returned to the laundry where she discovered Liza was not back yet. The young lady knew she had thrown away an opportunity to find Wilhelm, but Leopold's behavior had caught her off guard and all she could think of was getting away from him. What if Leopold had seen his brother's ring dangling from her neck? If she dropped the chain inside her dress, it created an unsightly lump and she might be accused of stealing something, so she would have to put it back on her finger. Carefully she wound a stray piece of yarn around the band of the ring until she was sure it could not slip off her finger and turned the ring to face inward where only the smooth gold band could be seen from the topside of her hand. Putting on her cloak, she decided the only thing she could do was go in search of this Karl fellow. She would have to use the fake letter in hopes of finding Wilhelm, or maybe a better idea would present itself? She slipped out of the laundry room unnoticed and quietly stole down the hallway toward the entrance of the castle. The first room that Josephine was brave enough to enter was a parlor where she found a stately looking gentleman seated in a chair, reading. Upon seeing the lady, he laid the book upon a side table and rose to his feet.

"May I help you, fraulein?"

"I am looking for Karl," she said, trying to control the quiver in her voice.

"You have found him. What may I do for you?" he asked, walking closer and peering at her over his spectacles. She felt like she was being thoroughly examined in the few seconds that passed.

"I was to deliver this letter to a gentleman in the market, but if I could not find him, I was to return it to Wilhelm," Josephine said as she lifted the letter from her side and then lowered it again.

"I can see that he gets it," the man said, motioning for her to hand it to him.

"No, I cannot let you do that," she quickly said, stepping back as she did. She could not let him discover the parchment was blank on the inside. "It was urgent that I return it to Wilhelm's hand personally if I could not complete my task."

He was suspicious but to her surprise he said, "Very well, then. Follow me please." The man left the room and led Josephine down the hall and then up a very grand staircase. Opening the first door to the left, he motioned for her to step inside. "Wait here. It will be a few minutes." As he closed the door, Josephine felt as if the very air was being sucked from the room. Without a doubt, he did not believe her and now she was trapped. She began to pace the floor, trying to decide what to do next. If she left the room before the man returned, she knew the castle would be searched until she was found and then she would be thrown out, no questions asked. Like it or not, she would have to stay put and prepare for whatever happened. Walking over to a wall that was painted as a map of the region, she laid her hand upon her native Frive and closed her eyes. She wished that when she opened them she would be safe at home in her father's study. She opened her eyes and gave a sigh. She caught sight of the ring upon her finger. She thought back to how many times Wilhelm had mentioned that he would need it back as soon as they came to the castle. How long was it before he realized that she had been lost among the crowd in the town or did he even care? Then her mind wandered to Leopold. Perhaps he had lied to his brother that he saw her run away. But then again, maybe Wilhelm was concerned and had sent someone to look for her, or went himself. Josephine was so engrossed in thought that she did not hear Karl and Leopold as they came into the room. Suddenly the floor creaked and she turned around. As they approached, she gave a bow and they stopped a few feet away and took a moment to scrutinize the lady. Leopold recognized her instantly from his room and couldn't help but comment.

"So . . . I get to see you sooner than I thought I would." He gave a wave to Karl. "That will be all, thank you." The butler had a questioning look upon his face but could tell Leopold wasn't too alarmed by the lady's presence. As he began to walk away, Josephine realized she was about to be left alone with the young man again and uncomfortable with the idea she turned her back toward him pretending to look at the map upon the wall. Leopold took a few steps closer. "May I see this uhm . . . letter?" he asked and this time without hesitation Josephine handed over the parchment. He broke the seal and she heard a sigh as it was found to be blank. In a very serious voice, he demanded "What business do you have with my brother?"

Trying to sound calm and composed she answered him, "I need to speak with him concerning the other night." She did not look toward him but stared at the map.

"What do you mean, the other night?" he asked.

Mustering up what courage she could, she said, "The attack, upon Briasburg castle." Before she knew what was happening, Leopold had grabbed her arm and twisted it to turn her to face him.

"Who are you? A spy?" he yelled but not allowing her to answer he added "How do you know about Briasburg?"

"You're hurting me," Josephine cried out, trying to wiggle free from his grip.

"I asked you a question!" he demanded through gritted teeth.

"It is me, the lady that was found in the castle." She groaned in pain as tears filled her eyes. Now only inches away he looked into her face. "I am Josephine Armand." Still staring hard, he reached toward her and undone the pins in her hair, allowing it to fall about her shoulders. He gave a sigh as it was true. "Please, let go of my arm."

"Knowing your name does not explain why you are here. Are you spying for our enemy?" he questioned as she felt his grip loosen ever so slightly.

"I am no spy. Wilhelm knows why I am here. It is very important that I speak with him." She knew Leopold was not convinced. "Why don't you ask him about it?"

"Because I am asking you!" the man threatened. Josephine felt her face turning red. She was angry enough that she was about to argue with him when she remembered Wilhelm's defense of his brother. She took a few breaths to calm herself as she realized that she too would be vicious if anyone came against Arlene or Phillipe. She agreed to tell him anything he wanted to know if he would but sit and discuss the situation more civilized. Thankfully the man obliged her request but watched her like a hawk. Briefly she told how she came to Briasburg and her adventure that night but made it perfectly clear that she held no allegiance to Aikerlan or Gutten but to her native Frive. Leopold had listened quietly until she mentioned her debt to his brother, at which a nasty scowl crossed his face. "I think you should forget about this vow to Wilhelm. Arrangements can be made to return you safely home."

"I am sorry, but that will not do. I am not free to go until your brother gives me leave," she replied defiantly.

"You will do as I say," Leopold said, standing to his feet. He could tell by the look on her face that the young woman was not going to cooperate with him. "Are you always this difficult?" he said as she stood to her feet and came closer to him.

"I am about as difficult as you are," she snapped.

"Let me tell you something, my lady. I am the one who doesn't always play fairly. Most people are afraid of how unpredictable I am and what I might do." He was now very close to Josephine's face and with every word that he spoke he made her take a step backward. Suddenly she realized that she was against a bookshelf. Leopold gave her an impish grin. Normally he would trap a young lady and then follow with a passionate kiss, but this time he had another idea. He was still upset with Wilhelm for risking his life to save this stranger and then dragging her with them despite his opposition. He wondered if this woman would be the perfect way to get revenge with his brother and her too for being bold enough to defy him. "Nevertheless . . ." he continued. "You will be allowed to see Wilhelm and fulfill your debt to him." Josephine was shocked by his sudden change in attitude and wondered what he was thinking. "I will take you to his chambers." He offered his arm to escort her but she took a step back and shook her head. Only minutes early, he was trying to break the very arm he wanted to hold. Leopold gave a mischievous chuckle and said, "Follow me then." As they began to walk, Josephine's mind began to race. Several times she glanced over at him only to see a wicked little smile upon his face. Was he taking her to Wilhelm's chambers or was he taking her elsewhere to be held prisoner? When he was almost to the end of the hall, he stopped in front of a door to the left and was reaching for the knob when he said, "He is not here now, but he will return later."

"Then why did you bother to bring me *here* instead of taking me *to* him?" she asked in amazement.

"Just wait for him, and make yourself comfortable. He is in a meeting so it may be a while."

"But . . ." she stuttered before he interrupted her.

"This is his room so you stay here and wait for him. Those are easy enough instructions to follow, but can you do that?" She was about to protest when he opened the door, pushed her into the room, and as he was closing the door, added, "Just remember that it is your duty to please him, your master." He left her alone.

"Urrrr," Josephine said to herself. Leopold was so frustrating, and she would have enjoyed giving him a few words to send him on his way. As she took a seat in a nearby chair, she wondered how long it would be before the man came. After an hour had passed, she began to look around the room to spend the time. Leopold had rightly said "chambers" for the room was much larger than all the others she had changed linens in earlier that day. It appeared that the room was divided into two parts, but looking closer, she found the partition was not a wall but thick, heavy drapes. The first half of the room was more of a sitting area with a desk and a small breakfast table. A divan and chairs flanked a beautiful marble fireplace. Above the mantel hung a portrait of an older gentleman, with two young lads, one perched upon each knee. She wondered if the boys were Wilhelm and Leopold. As Josephine stepped to the second half of the room, she saw a large bed with four massive columns rising up to almost touch the vaulted ceiling. Thick curtains hung from the canopy for privacy. The bedspread and pillows were a deep crimson accented with gold cording and tassels. The colors reminded her of rubies in a crown of gold. To the left and right of the headboard stood matching armoires which carvings reflected those of the bedposts. To the far left stood a wooden screen behind which was a dressing table and cheval mirror. As she looked around she couldn't help but notice how neatly the room was kept with every little thing in its perfect place. The minutes began to pass rather slowly and impatiently the young lady began to pace. Hoping to escape the boredom, she strode to the window and looked out. The view included a stone veranda which held a handful of tables and benches and a small but neatly kept area of grass. Beyond the lawn she could see an elaborate hedge that was in fact a maze. Sadly no one came into view, and finally she decided to go and sit down as her feet were aching. It had been a long, difficult march and they hadn't stopped very long to rest since leaving Briasburg. She was also getting hungry again, but she hated to slip off to the kitchen and take the chance of missing Wilhelm. As she sat there pondering what to do, exhaustion began to creep up on her. She had only been asleep a few hours before the attack at Briasburg. Another hour passed by slowly and she would have guessed Leopold would have come to torment her. She shivered thinking about the encounter in the library. She decided to think of something more pleasant, but to her surprise, she continued to shiver. She placed a hand to her face and realized how cold she was. Her mind wandered over to the bed with its thick, comfy-looking blanket. She scolded herself for such a foolish notion, but after shaking a few more minutes, she gave a sigh and rose to her feet. She disliked the idea of being in someone else's bed, but she disliked being cold more and was growing sleepier by the moment. The partition would allow her to climb out of the bed before she was seen. Quickly she slipped off her shoes and crawled under the bedspread. As she stretched out, she found the bed even more comfortable than she had imagined. Embracing the warmth, Josephine gave into exhaustion. Drifting in-between sleep and consciousness, she could hear the crackle of a fire burning. Carefully she opened her eyes and remaining deathly still, she looked toward the fireplace. She watched a servant stoke the beginnings of a fire until it was burning brightly. Satisfied with his work, he placed a large log on the blaze, swept the hearth, and left the room. She was relieved her presence had not been noticed. Quietly she crawled from the bed and went to the fireplace to warm herself more. She was staring into the flames when from the hall she heard a clock ring out eleven times. She gave a deep sigh as she realized Leopold had tricked her again. *Well,* she thought, *this has to be someone's room and when they return I will insist that I speak with Wilhelm. I am tired of these games.* Returning to the bed, she carefully remade it and then went to the divan. There would be a lot less explaining to do if she was found there instead of in someone's bed, and at least she could rest until then. With a yawn, she lay down and was staring at the portrait above the fireplace when she dozed off.

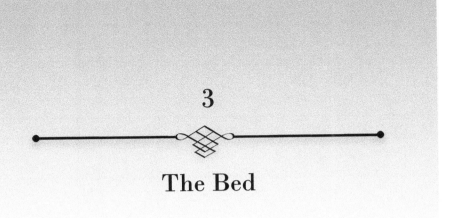

3

The Bed

Shortly after midnight, the door opened and Wilhelm stepped into the room. As he emptied the contents of his pockets onto the table beside the door, he sighed with relief knowing the day was finally over. That morning when he made it to the castle, he had quickly sought out his father to brief him on the status of the mission. He had hoped to steal a nap afterward, but the High Council had been called to meet early that afternoon and his testimony was needed. The session lasted past suppertime as several dukes were appalled that the strike on Briasburg had commenced and that assassination had been the key initiative. Even after the meeting had adjourned, some men stayed to privately discuss the matter with his father, but thankfully they backed the decision. It would have been a taxing day without coming from a battle and walking all the way home for secrecy's sake. Wilhelm was so tired that he didn't even reach to close the door of his room nor bother with a lamp since the light from the fireplace was enough to see his way to the bed. He folded back the bedspread and sat down. Aching all over, he pulled off one boot and let it slip to the floor with a soft thud. He had just begun to struggle with his other boot when he heard a noise. Looking up, he glanced around the room, and seeing nothing out of the ordinary, he finished pulling off his other shoe letting it drop to the floor. Startled again,

Josephine took another deep breath, which Wilhelm clearly heard. Cautiously he stood to his feet and slowly began creeping toward the divan. Upon seeing the woman lying there, he cried out in surprise.

"Good heavens!" Hearing his voice, Josephine awoke but still half asleep, stumbled to her feet. "What are you doing here in my room?" Wilhelm demanded as the woman moved around to the far end of the divan, keeping the furniture between her and the man, as there was no mistake that he was angry.

"Qu'est-ce que c'est?" Josephine asked, rubbing her eyes.

"What?" Wilhelm asked.

"Excusem-moi?" she said. Suddenly she realized she was speaking French instead of German and correcting her error she began again. "My lord, Leopold brought me here to these chambers to await the return of his brother Wilhelm. Forgive me for falling asleep while I was waiting. I . . ." She was still so groggy-headed that she couldn't think well enough to explain herself, and the man looked terribly upset for her intrusion so thinking it was best, she headed toward the door to leave the room.

"Hold on, I am not finished speaking with you," Wilhelm said as he followed her. He was not about to let this woman leave until he had answers. "Why did Leopold bring you here to wait?"

Not knowing whether to trust this man or not, Josephine decided to stick with her story. "I am a new servant, and Leopold wanted to be sure Wilhelm met me."

"He what?" he interrupted himself as he spoke out loud. "Meet here? What did he say exactly?"

"He said to make myself comfortable while I waited for Wilhelm and to remember that a servant's job is to please their master," Josephine answered, still not realizing in whose presence she now stood or that she had been the crucial element of a prank. Wilhelm on the other hand was starting to piece together what his brother had done.

"Was you to be my mistress for the evening?" he asked with a sarcastic tone; not able to think of another reason the lady would have been brought to his chambers to wait for him. The suggestion infuriated Josephine, and forgetting her manners, she quickly turned and took a swing at the man's face. His reflexes were fast though and he caught her arm before she made contact.

"How dare you imply that I am a . . . I will be no man's mistress, thank you!" She felt herself blush all over, not for trying to hit the man, but from embarrassment over the implication. Now she knew why Leopold was so eager to leave her alone to wait for his brother. Wilhelm released her arm as she continued on a rant. "That little rat, he set me up! If I could get my hands around his neck, I would . . ." At that moment, Josephine's manners caught up with her as she realized she had insulted Leopold in front of this stranger. Quickly she tried to make amends. "I'm sorry. I'm just so upset."

"No need to apologize. He can be quite annoying at times," Wilhelm agreed.

"This is such an awkward situation and I should leave. It's urgent that I find Wilhelm anyways."

"Why, may I ask?"

"I need to return something that belongs to him," Josephine said, attempting to walk through the doorway.

Taking hold of her arm to prevent her from leaving, the man asked, "What is your name?"

Turning her gaze to the floor, the lady nervously replied, "Josephine."

Wilhelm sighed with relief, knowing why her voice sounded familiar to him. "Would *it* happen to be a ring?" he asked. She looked up at him in surprise.

"How did you know that?" she questioned.

Carefully he reached for the hand that he had seen the lady place the ring upon and answered, "Because the ring belongs to me." Josephine stood there dumb struck. Instead of her finding Wilhelm, he had stumbled upon her. She wasn't the only one staring though as he was looking the lady over long and hard for their hoods had concealed their faces by day and the darkness by night. Finally, he could see the one whose life he had spared, and she the one who had spared her life. After several moments, Josephine broke the silence with an apology.

"Please forgive me for not finding you sooner. I . . ." She could not finish her statement, as she was not sure even what to say.

"You could not have known *what* I looked like. Did you even know *who* you were looking for?" he asked. He could only guess the obstacles she had overcame to finally make it into the castle and end up in his chambers. The same determination she had demonstrated during the journey back had spurred her onward until she had found him again.

"Not really," she admitted "Please, I do hope that I have not inconvenienced you by not returning your ring earlier." Wilhelm was pleased to hear the sincerity in her voice.

"Well, not too much. I needed it once this afternoon, but I had father use his seal instead. He asked me where my ring was and I explained about the glass shards and assured him it was safe," he said with a smile. "I see that I have spoken correctly." He still was looking the woman over but then he stopped. "Now that we are not in harm's way and secrecy is not vital, let me introduce myself. I am Wilhelm Von Strauss." Josephine could see a hint of hesitation cross his face. "Prince Wilhelm of Gutten." Slowly she began to smile. The announcement did not seem as a total shock but rather it explained so many little things that she had found herself wondering about. "My lady, would you mind sitting?" He motioned toward the divan. "I would like to hear how you found me with so little to go on."

Still shaking from being abruptly awakened, Josephine started to accept the offer but then refrained saying, "My lord, I do not think it would be right for me to remain in your chambers. Where I am from, it is not proper for an unmarried lady to be alone with—"

The prince interrupted her, and as he did, he motioned toward the hallway. "If you choose to stay, the door will remain open and two of the king's guardsmen are standing near the library as we speak. Shall I call for them to come closer?" At his words, she begged him not to bring further embarrassment to her nor chance his reputation to such a scandal. She would agree to sit with him but only under the auspice of keeping adequate distance between them. Smiling the prince accepted the terms, and they each sat down on opposite ends of the divan. She had not gotten far into the tale until she stopped to stare. In her mind's eye, she was trying to connect the man before her with the voice and actions from the previous days. He was as tall as she had thought but didn't seem as stout as he had without the chain mail and cape about him. His hair was brown and his eyes were dark but full of kindness, not what she had expected to see in a warrior. Her voice had suddenly faded and noticing how she was studying him Wilhelm couldn't help but ask, "I do not look as you had expected?" Josephine quickly looked toward the fireplace as it seemed he had read her thoughts.

"No, not exactly. I envision warriors as rough-looking rogues, not princes. The voice is the same but . . ." She looked back at the man sitting before her. "I will admit it was much easier speaking to you in the darkness." He smiled as he thought how unreserved she was with her opinion of him, seemingly unhindered by the invisible crown upon his head.

"If you would rather we can step out onto the veranda for you to finish your tale," he said jokingly with a smile. His appearance may have seemed different to her, but the beautiful young lady he saw matched the voice he had heard in the darkness.

"No," she said softly, embarrassed by her statement. It was an awkward moment that she was not entirely prepared for. Trying to recover, she asked "Shall we start over again? Good evening, my lord." And she extended her hand to shake his. To her surprise, he took her hand.

"Good evening, my lady. It is a pleasure to meet you." As their eyes met, Josephine felt herself blush. "Will you entertain me with details of your day, my lady?" Wilhelm released her hand and she began to tell of her adventures. When she explained what Leopold had done to her in the market, Wilhelm said he would be mentioning it to his father. When she told about her arm being twisted in the library, he rose to his feet and began to pace in front of the fireplace. Finally her story came to an end with her being brought to the prince's chambers.

"Oh, he's in for it," Wilhelm ranted. "A little teasing here or there but roughing you up is not excusable. And then to have you wait here for me like a wench . . ." He let out a sigh of disgust as Josephine rose to her feet.

"Don't be rash," she pleaded. "I'm not saying that what he did was right, but don't do anything that you will regret on my account."

"I can't afford to do things that I will regret, even when someone deserves it," Wilhelm commented as if irritated that due to his position he had to keep his temper under control. Suddenly Josephine's stomach growled loudly and embarrassed she turned away covering her face with her hands but she couldn't help but laugh.

"Did you bring a bear with you?" Wilhelm teased.

"I'm sorry. I'm just so hungry," she whispered

"When did Leopold leave you here?" he asked.

"Midafternoon?" she replied.

"You didn't have supper?" he asked. She shook her head and he moaned in disapproval.

"Let's get you something to eat, come on," he said, motioning for her to follow him.

"I can manage," she argued. "I know my way to the kitchen."

"What? How can I get something for myself if you don't let me go too?" he teased. They were almost to the door when Josephine realized that she was not wearing any shoes.

"Wait, I have to get my boots," she said coming to a stop. Wilhelm looked down and gave a funny look as he too had nothing on his feet.

"I will get both of ours," he offered starting to step away. "Which end of the divan are yours at?" She headed to a chair and managed to squeak out a response.

"I slipped mine off beside your bed." He turned to look at the woman, but she had intentionally ducked her head. He wanted to ask how her boots ended up across the room but he didn't, curious to see if she would divulge the information on her own. The prince returned with two sets of boots, but Josephine's conscience was burning fierce and she could take it no longer. "I hope you will not be upset with me. But while I was waiting for you I got cold. The fire hadn't been built yet and . . . oh yeah the servant didn't notice me . . . and I was so tired . . ." She paused searching for the right words to soften the impact of what she was about to admit but found none. "I crawled into your bed and fell asleep!" she blurted out. "I know I shouldn't have but I was so cold and tired."

Cautiously she watched for his reaction but she was shocked by how he responded. "I understand. Don't worry about it." She watched as he pulled his boots on and then said, "Let's go raid the kitchen." She was amazed that he was not upset, but actually Wilhelm was relieved that no one had found the lady in his chambers. He knew Leopold would have given almost anything to see his brother's face when he found the lady in his room. And then, if she had in fact been found asleep in the bed, what an uproar it would have been. Yes, the relief of a bad situation having been avoided was more upon his mind: relief and revenge. Wilhelm paused at the door to be sure the guards were not facing in their direction, and when the coast was clear, the pair headed to the servant's staircase that Josephine and Liza had used earlier than afternoon. They had only descended a few steps when Wilhelm tried to insist that the lady take hold of his arm to prevent her from stumbling in the darkness but she declined.

He took hold of her arm anyways at which Josephine couldn't help but comment, "Do you ever take no for an answer?"

"Not usually," he replied. His remark was not meant to sound threatening, but the lady found herself feeling uneasy. He was the prince and had the right to do as he pleased even if it was against her wishes, including taking advantage of her upon the dark staircase. Would anyone hear her pleas at this hour of the night? She found herself saying aloud what she was thinking.

"My father would have a fit if he knew I was alone with you!" She had stopped and was trying to slide her arm from his hand when she heard him laugh.

"Would he object to you being alone . . . with a prince?" Wilhelm teased, securing his hold upon her arm.

"You have not heard the speech that I have. Father said never to be alone with a man unless his ring is on your finger." With her statement, Wilhelm burst into laughter, aggravating Josephine immensely, as she was being very serious.

Trying to regain his composure, he said, "He has no reason to worry. You have my ring upon your finger!" and then he began laughing again.

"I don't find that amusing," she said, jerking her arm loose and starting down the stairs again alone.

"Wait, hold on," he pleaded now trying not to laugh. "I'm sorry, I couldn't help myself. Stop. Wait!" He reached out in the darkness trying to find her. He caught up to her and somehow took her by the hand, pulling her to a standstill. "I apologize." He could feel her trembling. "Do I make you nervous?" he asked.

"Yes," she admitted. "A little, after all, your brother's reception was not pleasant."

"Let me clarify a few things. My family built this kingdom upon morals and honor, and I stand for those virtues as well. Let me assure you that I will never give you a reason to be afraid of me. I would like to earn your trust. I am sorry that I have made you feel uncomfortable. Please forgive me for doing so." He paused, hoping to hear a response but none came. Finally Wilhelm broke the silence. "Enough talking, let's get some food in you before you faint." As they entered the kitchen, he motioned her to sit at the table while he went to a cupboard. In a few minutes, he presented a plate filled with fruit, cheese, and bread. She was invited to eat as he retrieved glasses and filled them with water. Wilhelm joined the lady and to her surprise ate as much as she did.

"Didn't *you* eat supper?" she asked as she popped another grape in her mouth.

"Yeah, but haven't you heard that growing boys have to eat?" he said, getting up to refill their glasses.

"I didn't think boys were sent off to assassinate people and burn down their houses." she remarked as he sat down opposite her again.

"Well, my mother still thinks I am her little boy. On the other part . . . you are sadly mistaken." Although he had been smiling, Josephine saw the prince's countenance change when he mentioned the latter. The tone in his voice also became icy cold which she did not like.

"Well, if you are just a boy, I would hate to see how tall you are when fully grown." And with the statement, she stood to her feet and gathered up the dishes and took them to the sink. She was reaching for a pitcher of water to begin washing them when Wilhelm interrupted her.

"Don't trouble yourself, the servants will tend to it in the morning," he explained.

"Yes, but I was that servant this morning," she said sarcastically.

"You won't be doing any of that again in my castle, if I have anything to say about it," he firmly replied, stepping beside the woman and removing the pitcher from her hand. He let out a sigh. "We need to discuss this vow you made." He looked at Josephine and then gave a nod as he gave in to her wishes and began slowly pouring water from the pitcher onto the plate the lady still held in her other hand. The prince began speaking again. "You have created quite a dilemma for me."

"How so?" she asked as she washed the glasses.

"Just hear me out," he said as he sat down the pitcher and reached for a towel to dry their hands upon. "How would it seem for a nobleman's daughter to come to my kingdom and become a kitchen servant in my household? It would not be good for relations between our countries now would it?" They began to walk back upstairs while continuing the conversation.

"No, I suppose it wouldn't be right. Would you rather that I break my vow and return home?" she asked.

"I believe that God holds us accountable for our every word, and I would not force you to go back on your promise. We just have to find a way to honor it, more appropriately." As he explained, Josephine got the impression that he was more a man of action rather than just sitting on a throne sleeping behind his royal robe.

"Do you have a suggestion, then?" she asked.

"Maybe you could return to Frive as our ambassadress?" he said as they came to the top of the staircase. Carefully Wilhelm spied out the guards and then quietly they stole to his room again. "What do you think?" he asked once they were safely inside. Now back where the firelight shone upon her face, he could see she was disappointed. "You don't care for the idea?" She wrinkled her face. "Perhaps, something else?"

"The position is wonderful, but it's the location that does not suit me," Josephine admitted.

"Should I dare ask why?" Josephine could not turn fast enough for him not to see the look upon her face. She walked around the far end of the divan and sat down and began fidgeting with her hands. He came and sat down and waited, not knowing whether to say anything or not. Finally swallowing hard, she began to tell of the difference of opinion that had escalated to the point that she had been sent away and was not in a hurry to return to Picardell, now or ever. She tried to be vague, but the relationship was over as far as the lady was concerned.

"I know that you want to distance yourself from your family, but you know the situation won't go away on its own," Wilhelm said. Josephine stared blindly at the fire, not wanting to hear another lecture of how this was her fault for not wanting to marry and do as society dictated. In fact, the truth was that she wanted to pursue her own interest, marrying for love with her husband supporting her endeavors as much as his own. She would not settle for being a boring wife spending all her days at the beckon call of a boring husband. Wilhelm saw the stubborn look upon the young lady's face and leaned to one side to catch her gaze as he added, "You can love someone while disliking their ways, as in the instance of my brother. Everything about us is opposite. He is not exactly evil, but mischievous to a fault, as you have discovered. Sometimes I would like to ring his neck for childish pranks and being irresponsible. One time when I was praying, the Lord spoke to me and reminded me that I was here to love my brother, not to judge him. When Leopold does things like he did to you today, I have to remember what God has shown me and show mercy upon him. He may not deserve the kindness but—"

"I understand what you are saying," Josephine said, interrupting the prince. She was much too angry to act civil toward her father let alone reconcile with him. Hoping to change the subject, she asked for the prince to tell of his day.

"Moi?" he said, pointing a finger to his chest.

"Oui monseignnuer," she answered with a smile.

"By the way," Wilhelm said, speaking German again, "you deserve to be complemented on your language skills."

"Thank you, but I owe that to my father and a patient tutor," she replied, standing to her feet and stretching. Suddenly she turned and looked at the prince and asked, "Are you avoiding my question about your day?"

He laughed as he answered her, "My day was not nearly as interesting as yours. When I got here, I sent someone to look for you in town although I had no worthy description to give them. Then I met with father." As he spoke, Josephine walked around the divan not wanting to sit down again just yet. He watched her carefully for a reaction. "Then, I went to the chapel to pray." She turned and looked at him very surprised.

"You were in the chapel today?" she asked.

He nodded, smiled, and replied, "Yes, this beautiful lady came and knelt beside me at the altar. I must admit it was the shortest prayer I ever witnessed but I guess even the little ones count with God."

Josephine, deciding she would turn the joke on him, slipped her hands down over the back of the divan as she pretended to still be ignorant of the lady's identity. "Did you get a good look at her?" she asked as her finger tips touched the edge of a small pillow.

"I said she was beautiful, didn't I?" he answered still smiling.

To his surprise, her countenance suddenly changed, and in a rougher voice, she said, "You mean to tell me that I was right there beside you and you didn't even speak up to let me know it was you!" And without any warning, she snatched up the pillow and hit him across the chest. "I wasted my whole day looking for you and you were the man in the chapel?" she yelled, not being loud enough to be heard from the hallway but still being dramatic.

Amused, he moaned as if he was in pain but then burst into laughter. "Honestly, I didn't know it was you until I saw your face a while ago." He pleaded and then as if from nowhere the lady was hit with a pillow. Startled she almost let out a scream but tried to muffle it. "*Shhh!*" he said, still laughing. "I'd hate to explain if someone found us." He stood to his feet with both taking a few more ill-aimed swings before a truce was called. They returned to the divan, and Wilhelm began to tell about his day. Sadly it only took a few minutes before Josephine's exhaustion began to creep back upon her, and now sitting still, she began to doze off. Wilhelm was quick to confess it had been a long day and suggested they turn in.

"Just tell me where I should sleep and I'll be off," Josephine said, rubbing her eyes.

Taking advantage of how groggy she had become, the prince replied, "Turn to your left, take six steps . . . well, that would be twelve for you, and then lay down." The lady had already taken two steps while counting aloud when she caught on to where he was directing her to go.

"Oh no, I told you. I am not that kind of lady," she argued.

"No, no," he said, now rather embarrassed. "That's not what I meant. Only one person at a time is allowed in my bed."

"I am not taking your bed either," she protested.

"Yes, you are. Listen to me, first the guest rooms would be terribly cold and this room is warm. Second," as he spoke he raised his eyebrow and gave her an unusual look. "I would rather the guards not see you come waltzing from my room at this hour, so I insist that you remain here tonight and *I* will go to another room. It will be much less complicated that way." She was shaking her head. "Do I have to make it a royal decree for you to obey, my lady?"

Holding up her hand and turning it to catch the light, she smiled and said, "Not without this, my lord." Although they had spoken of his signet ring, it had not been given back to him. Reaching for her hand Wilhelm gently slid it from her finger, yarn and all, shaking his head and smiling as she had the advantage over him.

"Please, don't argue with me about using my chambers tonight. In the morning, I will send someone for you. The dress you are wearing will not do for a lady at court, but that will be taken care of as well. You will do as I have asked?" he said as he strode over to the fireplace. She mumbled that she would and then watched as he placed the ring inside a small wooden box upon the mantle. "My finger is still too swollen to wear it just yet." He turned around and began walking toward the door. When he had taken hold of the knob he said "Thank you again for returning my ring. Good night, my lady." And with a bow, he shut the door.

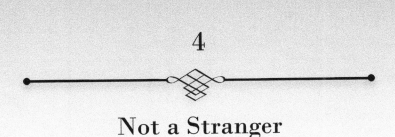

4

Not a Stranger

Wilhelm began walking down the hallway toward the guest wing. When he approached the junction of the hallways, he greeted the night guards who were making their rounds. To his relief, they did not question him being up at the late hour but merely went on their way. When he came to the first guest room, he couldn't help but look over his shoulder to be sure he was not seen as he crept inside. He did not light a lamp and carefully made his way to the bed. It was indeed cold, but he had been colder he thought to himself as he pulled the blanket up over his shoulder. He did not fall asleep quickly for his mind kept straying back to the lady he had left. He found himself smiling as he remembered how she had spoken so boldly, at ease in his presence. He enjoyed listening to her, the way she explained herself, even the sound of her voice was pleasant to his ears. He was thinking of her long dark hair and lovely smile when he dozed off. The next thing he knew, there was a pale light coming through the drapes as morning was approaching. Carefully he remade the bed and hoped it was to Liza's standards. Having been with the family for years she would notice the slightest little thing out of place and would report someone was slack in housekeeping. Not able to return to his room to change, the prince tucked in his shirt and ran his fingers through his hair. The current state of his appearance could not be helped, and he had more pressing matters concerning Josephine to deal with. Quickly, he headed for his father's chambers but found the king and queen had already went to the private dining room for breakfast. He had hoped to inform them of the lady's presence as early as possible to avoid any awkward situations.

As he entered the dining room, his parents looked up to greet him, but upon seeing his rumpled shirt, his mother asked, "Wilhelm, is everything all right?" Before he could answer, he saw his brother seated next to her, grinning from ear to ear.

"I believe he had a late night, Mother. Didn't get a lot of sleep, brother?" Leopold commented. Before they knew what was happening, Wilhelm came around the table, and threw a punch, knocking his brother backward out of the chair he was in. The queen screamed and the king stood to his feet, yelling for Wilhelm to stop at once. Thankfully Leopold had landed on the floor and slid backward on the tile just enough to give him a few spare seconds to get to his feet.

"If you ever pull a stunt like that again, I will—"

He was interrupted as his father stepped in between the two, and facing Wilhelm, he cried out, "What is this about?"

Coming to his senses, Wilhelm stood still and took a deep breath. Leopold stayed back as he said, "It was just a harmless prank, Father." Wilhelm glared at his brother as Agatha took hold of her older son's arm, trying to calm him down.

"I daresay!" Wilhelm yelled. Thoughts of hitting his brother raced through his mind yet again. Looking at his father, he added, "I returned to my chambers last night to find a young lady waiting there for me." Agatha gasped and Hubert turned and gave Leopold a stern look. "And that's not the half of it. She is the daughter of the duke of Picardell in Frive."

Hubert turned to look at Wilhelm and exclaimed, "What is she doing here in Guttenhamm?"

"Now that is none of my doing," Leopold explained. "That is Wilhelm's fault for not following your orders, Father." At his words, Wilhelm again felt his temper flare up. The king turned back to look at his younger son.

"I think you should both take a seat and let's get to the bottom of this, and quickly I might add." Scowls were exchanged but finally the two younger men began to move toward opposite sides of the dining table. "Now, tell me from the beginning," Hubert said, nodding to Wilhelm to start talking. His eldest son had not mentioned a word of the young lady being spared at Briasburg nor of her returning with the Elite Guard to Gutten. Wilhelm watched his father's expressions, knowing that he was not pleased that the details had been omitted from the briefing the day before. Leopold on the other hand fidgeted with irritation as his brother spoke. Wilhelm went on to explain that Josephine had pledged herself to his service in return for her life.

All four had managed to calm down enough to eat breakfast, and as the plates were being taken away, Wilhelm turned his attention to his brother and said, "Do you remember a few years ago when we went to Competta?" Cautiously Leopold nodded. "We attended a grand ball at court with the lords and ladies of the kingdom coming out. Armand was the man who was always at the king's left hand."

"Taller fellow, with a spindly mustache?" Leopold asked.

"Yes, that's him. Do you remember how he took time to introduce us to each of his children in such a formal manner?"

"Is it the older or younger daughter that is here?" Agatha asked as she began to remember the scene which Wilhelm spoke of.

"The younger daughter, Josephine. She wore a deep purple gown if I recall correctly and stayed close to her father no matter where he went."

"Oh yes," Leopold said with a laugh as he could picture the girl in his mind. "When it came time to dance, I was stuck with her. She was horrible and kept stepping on my toes."

"Actually," Wilhelm interrupted, "she was an excellent dancer."

"How can you say that?" Leopold asked with a puzzled brow.

"Because I paired with her next and she never missed a step. I asked her why she was having a difficult time with you, and she admitted to intentionally stepping on your toes because you were holding her too close for comfort." And with the comment, both

Hubert and Agatha burst into laughter. Leopold made a face at his brother. "*She* is the one that is here," Wilhelm said.

"Where is she now?" the queen asked.

And before he realized what he had spoken, he answered, "She's asleep in my bed." All eyes turned upon him and Leopold gave a snicker. Trying to make it sound less incriminating, Wilhelm quickly added, "I insisted that she use my chambers as a fire had already been built, and I went to a guest room.

"Got proof of that, brother dear?" Leopold chided as he rose to his feet. Wilhelm started up as if wanting to take another swing at his brother for the statement, but his father caught him by the arm and he settled back into his seat again. Leopold excused himself, but when he got to the door, he couldn't help but pause to add, "I guess that *would* explain why you look so rough."

"Heed my warning, little brother," Wilhelm said "Stay away from her. Do you hear me?"

"Loud and clear," he answered sarcastically. "If I didn't know otherwise, I would have to think you were defending your territory." And with a sly grin, he left. The king bid Wilhelm to pay no mind to his brother as they all knew he was only out to instigate a fight. Hearing the clock strike on the hour, they stood to their feet. Hubert declared the matter needed more discussion, but for now, he had affairs of state to tend to. Wilhelm too had business but he asked a favor of his mother.

"Would you mind helping with Josephine?" he pleaded. "I know you are busy, but after what she's been through the last two days, I would rather not pass her to just anyone." She nodded. "I made her promise to sleep in." He began to smile. "We talked late into the night." They began to walk together, the queen holding on to her son's arm.

"I'll take care of her, don't worry. Is she still as pretty as she was four years ago?"

"Even more so." Wilhelm had answered the question before he realized his mother had asked purposely to see his reaction. He shook his head at her and smiled. "No meddling, Mother. I won't allow it." Coming to the bottom of the staircase, she gave her son a wide smile, and he kissed her on the forehead and they went their separate ways. As Wilhelm went toward the council chambers, he passed by a large mirror and had to stop to take a second look. The man in the reflection looked rather rough, out of sorts was a better description. Although he had gotten a few hours' sleep, the dark circles under his eyes told otherwise. He was glad it was only the foreign affairs committee meeting and not the whole High Council. They would not be as understanding of his appearance.

Hubert had called for a second meeting to discuss the raid on Briasburg. Waging war on a neighboring kingdom was not something he took lightly and needed the council involved as much as possible. Recently, there had been some discord about what to do with the situation at hand and when to take action. During the last year, a band of marauders had been causing trouble in the region. At first rumors of small skirmishes were considered tales but then as more and more incidents happened, it could not be dismissed. Finally, officials from surrounding kingdoms held a summit to discuss the violence. The mayhem always seemed to be traced back to the princes of Aikerlan. Word was sent asking King Airik to attend the meeting, but he instead sent his youngest son Maximillian. When questioned about the incidents, he denied involvement, even when identified by witnesses. He then let everyone at the meeting know that such accusations would only lead to further conflicts between the kingdoms. King Hubert boldly let the young prince know that injustice would not be tolerated and compromise was not an option.

Wilhelm vividly remembered the look on Maximillian's face when he walked to King Hubert's chair and snarled as he leaned toward him, "Thank you, now I have no doubt where you stand in the matter."

The implied personal threat infuriated Wilhelm, and he was rising to his feet when his brother took his arm and whispered, "This is not the time, nor the place. We will deal with him later."

Sadly, within the next month, reports of robbery and unexplained house fires plagued Gutten's northern region. The High Council knew the time of peaceful negotiation was over. But then something happened that they would never forget. A troop of Gharda musicians was travelling through the region, holding concerts at larger villages and cities. They had performed in the amphitheater at Guttenhamm and then consulted King Hubert as to the best route to take heading north to Schama. The king explained the touchy situation in the region and advised that the troop go a more southerly route before heading on northward. The chief musician was quite upset explaining that they needed to arrive within the month and could not afford the delay. The king spoke with them at length hoping to persuade them to heed his advice and finally they agreed to do so. Hubert suspected they were not intending to fulfill their word but merely said so to appease him. His fears were confirmed a week later when news came that they had been murdered not one day after leaving Gutten's borders. The royal family was very disturbed with the loss knowing how many children were with the troop. Recently, the enemy had grown bolder with attacks upon surrounding kingdoms becoming a weekly occurrence. The council knew action was needed but insisted that war with Aikerlan should be the last option.

The meeting that morning went along smoothly to Wilhelm's relief for he was having terrible trouble focusing. Part of his problem was the lack of sleep but part of it he owed to the lady in his chambers. As the meeting adjourned, Wilhelm followed his father toward their offices, desperately wanting to know what the king thought of the situation. Hubert could tell by the look on his son's face that he was perplexed. When they were alone, the king asked what was on his mind. The prince sat down in a chair and didn't answer and let out a sigh instead. The king took his place behind his desk and asked if it had anything to do with the visitor upstairs. Wilhelm glanced toward the ceiling.

"Yes, it does," he answered as he sank back into the chair. "I don't even know where to begin, let alone what to *do* with her." He was thinking about what to say when he suddenly sat straight up in the chair and added, "And when you meet her you will understand." And then he sunk back again.

The king was amazed at his son's reaction to the lady's presence but then a thought occurred to him. "Tell me what you already know about her and maybe it will enlighten us how to proceed." And with that, Wilhelm began to describe how fluent Josephine was in their language and how well her manners were concerning not only intruding into his chambers but the skill she had used to locate him with so little information. He assumed that she was well studied as her father would have required a formal education of his children because of his position in Frive. He also conveyed how easily she had adapted to her surroundings, learning quickly what needed to be done and had the determination to stay the course despite fatigue. "I wonder if she would be interested in the commerce position that we have open." Hubert thought out loud. "No one has applied since Duke Callin retired, with all the unrest upon the people's minds. I would think she knows plenty about it since her father excels in that field." Wilhelm agreed and they began discussing minor details. She would be given a small office just down the hall, a salary would be provided and access to transportation with a personal guard to travel with her as needed. Her responsibilities would start out small, staying local in her dealings but then would grow to encompass the kingdom.

"Father, would you object to offering her a room here in the castle?" Wilhelm asked.

"To be honest, Wilhelm, I would not feel comfortable with her staying anywhere but here. This is a delicate matter having her in our employ and for her own safety it needs to be thus. I would not see Armand allowing her to live out on her own either." At the mention of her father, Wilhelm's countenance fell.

"She does not care what he thinks at the moment. 'A parting of ways' was in order she said," he mumbled.

"Son, is it that serious between them?" the king asked. Wilhelm nodded. With a sting, he remembered when he wore the look of disgust toward his father as she did. Feeling the need to describe Josephine's conflict at home, he told the king what he knew. When he was finished, both sat in silence for several minutes contemplating what to do.

Finally the king spoke, "I will write to Armand letting him know that his daughter is safe. I will also carefully explain that she has mentioned a difference of opinion and that I am prepared to offer her a place to stay until she is ready to return home and I will be writing again in the next few days with more details. Is there anything else?"

"That will do for now. The sooner her family knows she is alive and well the better. I am curious though to see what she thinks of our offer," Wilhelm said, standing to his feet as he began to walk about the room. "She does not hold back with her opinion." He thought of her comments to him during the night. Hubert raised an eyebrow as he saw a look in his son's eye that he had never seen before.

"All of this will have to be handled carefully," the king stated, watching his son. "Having a young lady residing under the same roof with two young men . . ." Wilhelm turned his gaze toward his father.

"I think you should be reminding Leopold of such things, not me, Father." But he could not conceal a smile as he thought of Josephine. "I will admit she has caught my attention but that was totally unavoidable as you have heard."

The king stood to his feet and joined his son. "Yes, of course," he replied.

"Father, I know you will be sending a letter to Armand but would you mind if I wrote him as well?" Hubert tilted his head as a puzzled look crossed his brow and Wilhelm explained, "I feel personally responsible for Josephine's well-being and . . ." He took a deep breath, recalling a scene from his past. "I can relate to her circumstances. It is important to me to see their relationship restored." Hubert patted his son on the back and gave his permission. They walked to the door, and when Wilhelm had taken a few steps down the hall, the king called out to him.

"You did remember the council dinner party tonight, didn't you?" The words brought Wilhelm to a standstill and he turned and looked at his father. He had not remembered and was *not* looking forward to it either. "We will see if our guest still knows how to dance," Hubert added.

"Or step on toes?" Wilhelm said as he turned and went into his office. He sat down at his desk and took out a piece of parchment with the royal letterhead upon it. With great care, he began to write a greeting but then at a loss for words, he laid the pen down. If it were *his* daughter alone, so far from home, having been through a near death experience, what would convince him to let her remain abroad? Would anything assure him enough to let her stay? Resting his elbows on the desk, Wilhelm covered his face with his hands and began to pray. After several minutes, he reached for the pen.

My noble Duke Armand,

I am pleased to inform you that your daughter Josephine is alive and well here in Guttenhamm. I cannot begin to imagine how distraught you must have been hearing that Briasburg castle was destroyed. I want to assure you that she is not being held against her will. She may leave at any time and I will personally escort her into your loving arms. I would like to ask your permission that she remain here with my family. Although the circumstances that brought her to us were extreme, I feel that the Lord has placed her in our hands for a reason and I would not be so bold to ask this favor if I did not feel His guidance in this matter. She has privately mentioned to me the details of her journey and failed betrothal. She was sincerely disappointed that it was not a suitable match but more than anything wanted to please you. Please do not judge her harshly for mentioning a difference of opinion and I can assure you she has not dishonored you in any way. When she is settled in, I will encourage her to write and I have faith that the hand of the Lord will move upon her heart to do so. Please feel free to correspond often and I look forward to hearing from you. Again, I take full responsibility for her welfare, and I give you my word that I will protect her as I would my own flesh and blood.

Sincerely
Wilhelm Von Strauss, Prince of Gutten

A few minutes later, he reemerged from his office with the letter and headed to find Karl. The butler deserved a proper explanation of the visitor, and the prince hoped to stave off any rumors before the lady made another appearance about the castle. Karl would also be the one sending the two letters by courier, and Wilhelm wanted to stress the importance of a fast delivery.

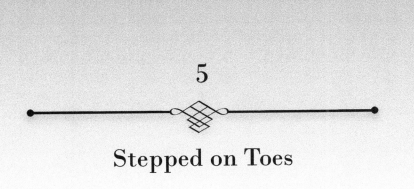

5

Stepped on Toes

Several hours had passed since Agatha left Wilhelm, but the queen had wasted no time preparing for their unexpected visitor. It wasn't that the family didn't have guests stay at the castle from time to time but this situation required more thought. With the young lady bound to feel displaced, Agatha was determined to make her welcome. A room in the private wing of the castle would be best to keep Josephine closer to the family not only for companionship but safety for should they have other guests, especially gentlemen, it would better for the lady's door to be farther down the hallway. There were a handful of rooms to choose from, but Agatha couldn't help but pick the last one on the right side of the hallway. It had been years since the queen's sister and husband had come to visit and used the room, but Cherice had always remarked that the windows afforded a romantic view of the sunset. The queen laughed to herself as she remembered her sister's words as she opened the windows to let fresh air in. Antoni came and built a fire, left and then returned with a pitcher of water for the basin and fresh oil for the lamps. Liza had been called, and when the man had left the room again, the older woman could not contain her curiosity about Josephine's behavior and the queen was quick to explain the dire situation the young lady had been involved in. Her behavior would be excused and her true character would be determined going forward. A carriage was then called for as the queen knew she would need to purchase a few dresses from a local shop as the ball was that evening and the seamstress did not have enough time to work a miracle. Assuming that she would only need to pick the color of the gown, the queen thought her trip to the village would be quick. But, when the shopkeeper asked for the size of the lady, Agatha was at a loss. She had not even given a thought to Josephine's height or her figure. After much debate, she choose several dresses of various sizes and colors and assured the shopkeeper that the ones not needed would be returned later that day. Agatha climbed back into the carriage and headed to the castle.

Disappointed with her lack of knowledge of her guest, she decided to pay her husband a visit. He was in his office studying over papers when she walked in. She greeted him, and then pulling a chair closer, she sat down beside him.

"What brings you here, my dear?" he asked with a chuckle. He could tell by the twinkle in her eye that she was up to something.

"Well . . . I was wondering what you thought of our guest?" she asked.

Hubert stroked his beard as he looked back at the papers on his desk and replied, "I haven't met her yet. Have you?"

"No. I wanted to speak with you first," Agatha answered.

"Knowing Armand, she will be a proper young lady, well-mannered and smart as a whip." He shuffled the papers before him.

"Wilhelm would add beautiful to that list," the queen said with a smile.

"Were those his words?" Hubert asked. "Or yours?"

"Well, not his exactly, but . . ." she mumbled.

"Then don't read into the matter," the king said, interrupting his wife. "We promised our sons that we would not get involved in such matters." He held up his hand for her to hold her comments.

"I won't," she answered. "But you should have seen the look in his eyes when he spoke about her."

"I have seen plenty, Agatha." The last word was meant as a reprimand, but she thought she had seen the hint of a smile cross his face before her name was spoken.

"Has he talked to you about her?" she wondered if her husband knew more than he was letting on.

"We discussed a suitable position for her. Wilhelm seems confident in her abilities, and we are hoping that she will agree to it."

"Anything else?" the queen asked, hoping her husband had more to tell.

"Nothing that I am at liberty to say," he said with a grin as he knew his wife was digging for information. The queen rose to her feet with the king following suit and walked her to the door. "Off you go." She had taken a few steps when he added, "I would like to have Josephine attend the dinner tonight."

"Yes, darling, I thought as much," she said, turning to face him. "And with your permission, she will walk out on Wilhelm's arm, as *Lady* Josephine Armand." The king shook his head and smiled.

"That will be fine," he said and went back into his office. He hoped neither Wilhelm nor Josephine minded, but he wondered how they would act toward each other.

It wasn't that Wilhelm was against the idea of finding a bride and settling down, but he had chosen to consume himself in the affairs of state. The younger prince on the other hand enjoyed socializing among the ladies but refused to commit to a relationship which had earned him a less than desirable reputation. Thankfully he had refrained from anything beyond flirting, but the family worried temptation might lead to a disgraceful situation. Leopold's carefree attitude had become a sore subject between the brothers and that he seemingly had to be the center of attention or at the least his presence be made known. Wilhelm however was completely opposite, not wanting to be out front in public but satisfied to fade into the background behind his father. Wilhelm had often remarked to his father that his brother was his strongest ally when he was not wasting his energy on whims. Both sons were intelligent and resourceful and physically had grown to be cunning men of arms.

As Agatha finally came to the door of Wilhelm's chambers, she found herself anxiously pausing. She was terribly curious about the young lady that had been through so much but also had caused her sons to quarrel. Should she mention that she was queen at the start or wait until after the young lady was settled in her new room? As she knocked softly on the door, she decided to wait. Hearing no answer, she let herself in. She walked across the room and stood staring for it was shocking to see a woman lying in her son's bed.

"Dear . . ." she said quietly. "Dear, I hate to wake you, but it's afternoon and we have a lot to do before supper time." Josephine took a long, deep breath and started to stretch. Suddenly she remembered where she was and sat straight up. The daylight blinded her eyes but she shielded them as she turned toward the queen. "I am Agatha. Wilhelm tells me your name is Josephine."

"Yes, yes, it is," the young lady replied in a shaky voice. Quickly she added, "Please tell me he explained how I came to be in his room."

Agatha smiled. "Yes, he did." She reached to take hold of Josephine's hand. "Do not worry, he has explained it very well, and for your peace of mind, Wilhelm would never be involved in anything of the other sort." At which, Josephine returned a smile. "He did mention that you would be in need of a dress."

"Please don't bother, I can make do with the one I have until—"

She was not allowed to finish as the queen stated, "Nonsense. The daughter of Renard Armand will not be seen at the dinner party tonight in rags!" She was offering Josephine a hand to climb out of bed when she saw the surprised look on the young lady's face. "He did not mention the party? Well, no doubt there have been other things on his mind. Come. Let's get you to your room." The queen quickly took the lady across the hall as Josephine attempted to argue that she could not go to such a thing, being a stranger and not knowing anything about the kingdom. Agatha however explained that she knew otherwise of how capable the young lady was and could not refuse the invitation. The furniture in the room was of a deep cherry wood with mauve upholstery upon the chairs and bedding. The marble fireplace was not as large as the one in Wilhelm's room. A very large window was centered on the far wall with an excellent view of the grounds.

"This is too nice for me to use. There must have been a misunderstanding. Perhaps Wilhelm didn't explain that I was to be . . ." The queen knew Josephine's next word would have been *servant*.

"A guest of the royal family," Agatha said, finishing the statement. "I chose this room especially for you."

Josephine apologized if she had offended, at which the older woman assured her she hadn't and announced that a bath had been drawn and then they should choose a dress for the evening. She was taken to the last door of the hall where to her surprise Katrina was waiting. Both young ladies began to laugh, and Agatha left them stating she would be back shortly. Swearing the maid to secrecy, Josephine told Katrina the truth of her search for Wilhelm, including the details of the awkward night she had spent in his chambers. Washed and wrapped in a thick robe, they returned to Josephine's new room where they dried the lady's hair by the fireplace. Agatha came and apologized for the long delay for she had changed her clothes as well. Josephine was in awe of the dress the older lady now wore. With a smile, Agatha opened an armoire to reveal the garments she had purchased earlier that day.

"Let's see about a dress for you, dear." After several had been tried on, one of a deep blue was chosen that reminded Josephine of the sapphires in her grandmother's favorite pendant. The velvet dress had elegant white lace that fell from the elbows to adorn the sleeves and also accented the square neckline. Katrina had just finished helping Josephine into the dress when Agatha's lady in waiting, Patreece, came to do Josephine's hair. As she sat down in front of the dressing table, Josephine felt a twinge of nervousness. She was not accustomed to being fussed over especially since she was no one important. She wondered about the dinner party. What would she say? Would there be formal introductions like at court in Frive? How would she be announced? Would it be a small gathering or would all the lords and ladies of the land be attending? She felt her stomach growing uneasy. Patreece and Katrina were excused, and for the second time that day, Agatha grew anxious worrying that Josephine would be upset with her not mentioning that she was the queen. Knowing they would be late if they did not leave immediately, Agatha took the younger lady's hand and started for the door.

"The king is waiting for us just down the hall." As she reached to open the door, Josephine gave a questioning look but did not ask what the older lady meant. "We will be announced first and then you and my son," Agatha added and at the last word Josephine's mouth fell open and she could not contain her curiosity.

"Your son?" She swallowed hard in disbelief and then repeated her question. "Wilhelm is your son?"

"Yes, dear. After all you had been through, he didn't want anyone but me helping you today. Please forgive me for not telling you from the start, but I was afraid you wouldn't accept my help if you knew I was the queen." Josephine's head was swimmy for a moment and she reached for the wall. "I am sorry and I hope I have not disappointed you." Josephine laid her hand across her stomach and drew several breaths to calm her nerves.

"A lot has happened in one day," she commented. "I am not sure what to think of all of this."

"I can't imagine," Agatha said as voices were heard from down the hall causing both to look up. "I hate to rush you, but the king is waiting for us and we don't want to be late." The queen took Josephine's hand and they began to walk. "As I was saying, Wilhelm will be announced and then you. You will also be seated to his right at dinner. Do you understand?" Josephine said she did. When they were closer, Hubert saw the ladies and greeted them. He took his wife's arm, kissing her cheek and then introduced himself to the young lady. He expressed how pleased he was to meet her and that the next morning they would discuss details concerning her stay in Guttenhamm. Not wishing to delay the dinner the three began walking toward the staircase with the king explaining to Josephine why the dinner was being held and various attendees she would see that night. The young lady was obliged that he was taking the time to prepare her for the event. They were at the top of the steps when she heard Wilhelm's voice behind them and they turned to see him hurrying down the hall in their direction. Josephine was standing in the shadow of the king, and the prince did not realize she was present until he was almost to them. When he saw her he came to an abrupt stop. There was no mistaking the look upon his face as he was stunned by Josephine's appearance. The king and queen exchanged glances, and Josephine found herself blushing as the young man addressed her.

"Josephine . . . Good evening." He gave a smile and then tried to turn his attention to his father. "Sorry, I am late." The king just gave a smile and began leading his wife down the steps. Wilhelm hesitated awkwardly for a moment and then asked Josephine if she would accompany him to which she agreed. The next few minutes were spent nervously clinging to each other's arm as they were introduced and then began mingling among the crowd. The prince was pleased with how Josephine was handling the questions addressed to her and was in fact turning the conversations to her advantage, learning about the guests. Several times he left her side and made a few rounds through the crowd by himself. On one such occasion he stopped to talk with his father who scolded his son for abandoning the young lady. Wilhelm was quick to assure his father not to worry because she was doing quite well without him hovering over her. When dinner was announced, Wilhelm rejoined Josephine and they were seated at the king's right hand. The meal was uneventful which gave much needed relief to the lady as she was starting to feel overwhelmed trying to remember the names of all she had spoken with. After dessert, the guests began leaving the table making their way back into the ballroom where the orchestra had started playing softly. The queen was commenting to Josephine about another lady's dress when to their surprise Wilhelm turned and asked Josephine to dance with him. She obliged and together they went to the center of the floor. The young lady was very self-conscious but only for a moment as when they began to dance Wilhelm asked if she was enjoying the evening. Then he began to tell more about the people she had met. So absorbed were they in their conversation that they had not realized the dance had ended until the others began to clap. They bowed to each other and returned to where the king and queen were standing. As the music began again, Josephine heard her name and turned to see Leopold, now bowing as he requested the next dance. She felt a lump rise up in her throat, and she swallowed hard, hesitating to answer him. She was afraid to take his hand, but she was more afraid she would offend his family if she didn't. Reluctantly she raised her hand, stretched out her fingers and ever so gently he laid his hand under hers and led her onto the floor. She knew she was shaking, but couldn't get control before she felt his hand slide about her waist. Summoning every ounce of courage she had, she looked up into his face.

"Please, do not hold me so close," she stated as the pair began to sway to the music.

"My lady, I believe I have learned that lesson since the last time we danced," he said as he looked into her eyes.

"The last time?" she asked, her eyebrow rising.

"We danced together at the royal ball in Competta several years ago. You kept stepping on my toes because I was holding you too close," he said as he watched for her reaction.

She looked away for a moment, and then returning her gaze to him, she asked, "That was you?" Suddenly she couldn't help but smile thinking of how she had treated the annoyingly eager, young man.

They twirled about for several minutes before Leopold began to speak again. "I would like to apologize for my behavior toward you." Josephine had to look up at him again as she doubted he was telling the truth. "We were in a hostile environment and the security of my kingdom was all that I was thinking about," he explained.

She very shrewdly asked, "And what about leaving me in Wilhelm's chambers?"

Leopold twisted his mouth, making a strange face as he admitted, "That was childish of me." She guessed that would be as close to the truth as he was going to confess to. "I have heard that you will be staying a while so I want to make peace with you." She felt her eyebrow rising in disbelief again. "I would rather not have us at each other's throats anyways."

He only wanted to make peace because he was afraid she wouldn't be won over by his charm, she thought. She almost spoke her mind before she bit her lip. She did not trust him for one minute. She agreed to be civil and then before she was required to say more the dance ended and she excused herself and left him standing alone. She looked for the queen and quickly returned to her side. The third time Josephine muffled a yawn Agatha whispered to the lady that she should go upstairs and retire for the evening. The queen assured her there would be plenty of opportunity to meet the people when she was better rested. Discreetly Josephine excused herself and had already climbed the grand staircase and made it to the start of the private wing when she heard her name being called. She stopped and turned to see Leopold coming to her.

"My lady, I was hoping for another dance." As he drew near, she was reminded how much taller he was than her. Her heart began to race as she knew his following more than likely meant trouble. "Did I tell you how beautiful you look this evening?" he asked as he leaned toward her. She felt the hair on the back of her neck tingle.

"No, you didn't and thank you. Sorry, but good night," she said. She turned and began walking again, hoping that he would not follow. He let her get a few steps ahead before he caught up to her and took hold of her arm to stop her.

Quickly he came around to face her and said, "Your dress is the same color as your eyes." She was caught off guard by his comment and even more so by his actions as he reached to touch her face. Josephine turned her head and would have stepped away, but he held her arm firmly.

"Let go of me, Leopold," she demanded. "I don't like what you are doing."

"You are even prettier when you're cheeks are flushed," he commented. She had closed her eyes, but suddenly she realized his face was near hers, near enough to kiss her easily. She turned and looked at him, and with her free hand, she reached up to slap him, but he caught her hand in his. "Now, now. None of that," he said. "It wouldn't do for me to go back downstairs with your handprint across my face now would it?"

"Then kindly let loose of me!" she demanded. She glared at him, noses almost touching. He leaned his head as if he was surveying where to plant a kiss when she added. "Just you try it again and I will scream."

"No one will hear with the orchestra playing," he replied with a grin.

"No one but me!" a voice boomed from down the hall. Josephine felt Leopold's grip loosen and thought she heard Leopold mumble as he stood upright. She could now see Wilhelm marching toward them. "I believe you should let go of the lady." The look the older prince wore was terrible, and the tone of his voice made Josephine shudder.

To her surprise, Leopold sarcastically answered his brother, "You seem to drop by at the most inopportune times and spoil my fun." The man looked at Josephine and gave a wicked smile. "I guess we can resume this conversation later in private, my dear." He released her just as Wilhelm came within an arm's length and began to walk. When the two brothers passed each other, the friction was as if two huge boulders had slid against each other down a hillside. When Leopold's shadow had disappeared down the hall, Wilhelm asked if the lady was hurt. She assured him she was fine and excused herself to her room. Wilhelm watched until the door was closed, and then returned downstairs.

6

A Difference of Opinion

About seven o'clock the next morning, the queen awoke Josephine to start her day. As she dressed, Agatha filled her in on what few things transpired after the lady had retired for the evening. As they were walking to breakfast, she also gave the lady her schedule which included meeting with the king, the seamstress and later with the queen for a meeting of the ladies of court. Josephine did not disguise her displeasure at the mention of such a gathering and she caught a sharp look from the queen at which she offered an apology. Agatha just shook her head smiling as she was finding Josephine to be very opinionated for one so young. She did however mention that she expected the young lady to use her manners and be as impressive as she had been the night before.

Breakfast proved awkward as she tried to avoid eye contact as Leopold repeatedly glanced in her direction. She noticed the brother's glare at each other several times, and she wondered if words had been exchanged after she was in her room the night before. She was glad when the meal was over and all rose to go about their business. The king motioned for her to follow him, and as they walked toward his office, he asked about her father. She couldn't help but feel apprehensive as he closed the door behind them as she was reminded of when she was called into her father's study for misbehaving. As he invited her to sit with him he explained her well-being was his first priority and he needed to know more about her to help him with the other task at hand. She found talking to Hubert very easy and nothing that he mentioned aroused concern or fear, even when he asked about the conflict with her father. He explained that she would not be allowed to perform any service that would be condescending of her family's status but he did have a position of employment in mind that would allow her to help his family and give her the opportunity to continue in an area that she was skilled in already. She was to reside at the castle, as their ward and would be respected as a member of the family in all areas concerning the staff and people of the kingdom. She would also have access to the resources of the crown for her business purposes since travelling would be necessary. At the mention of a small salary Josephine protested but the king persisted. She would also be interviewed by certain council members, and more details would be given, but there was no hurry to place her in the position. The excitement with which the king spoke made Josephine want to embark on the adventure. Their conversation came to an end when Karl interrupted to announce the king's next appointment had arrived.

Happy with how the meeting had gone, Josephine returned to her room for her fitting. The seamstress by no fault of her own got on the lady's nerves pretty quick. The more measurements that were taken the more Josephine thought about frilly, tight fitting dresses that she had seen at court in Frive. The young lady detested the favoritism and bribery her father had witnessed while serving the king. When her mother would accompany him to Competta, she was under such pressure and scrutiny that Armand done his best to excuse her to remain at their home with the children. Josephine's patience had run out and she was asking the seamstress how much longer it would be when the queen came into the room. She could tell by the look on the young lady's face that she was irritated. A list of apparel was made as the seamstress finished up and then the queen and Josephine went downstairs to prepare for their meeting.

The queen introduced Josephine and explained that she would be staying at the castle for an extended period of time. The ladies were rather surprised and a few whispers were heard. Josephine hoped her being upon Wilhelm's arm the evening before had not doomed her to the notion that they were a couple. Thirty minutes after the meeting began, brunch was announced and all retreated to the formal dining hall where a buffet had been set up. Josephine had allowed the others to go ahead of her and was waiting at the end of the line beside the door when she felt a gentle tap upon her shoulder and turned to find Wilhelm. Staying hidden in the shadow of the doorway, he whispered to ask how things were going then slipped away. The queen had just adjourned the gathering and good-byes were being said in the foyer when Karl came to Josephine to let her know she was needed by the king.

As she stepped into the office, she found several men waiting. Josephine was politely asked to sit down with Hubert explaining that the council members that were present wanted to interview her. Nervously she agreed and the next hour flew by as she was asked about involvement with her father's business and what she knew of current commerce trading and aspects of that field. The lady's composure improved as time went on and she knew more than what the members had guessed. Equally impressive was the manner in which she answered when she was not familiar with the subject for she declared she would have to rely upon the wisdom of men like themselves in those cases. She was told an answer would be given to her by morning, was dismissed and retreated to the library. Josephine had dreamed of such a position. Was she a candidate? She thought as she stood in front of the map wall. Or were the men only being polite to her? She did not have experience of her own to brag about but had only accompanied her father. She was nervously pacing when Agatha came to take her to the town to select fabrics for her dresses and pick up some other personal items. When they were on the way back to the castle, the queen asked about the interview, and with elation Josephine began to tell what had happened. There was no doubt that the young lady was interested in the position, but the queen secretly hoped the men kept an open mind under the circumstances.

When the carriage pulled up at the castle, the ladies saw a small wagon like one used to transport prisoners. Josephine cringed as she wondered what it was doing there. The areas of the castle the lady had seen seemed so pleasant but were there rooms that were otherwise? She knew the palace in Competta had lower levels, not only servant quarters but dungeons where the condemned were held. Yes, there was a prison in the city, but her knowledge was that nameless prisoners were sent to the palace. Josephine had always imagined scenes of torture and death but now she had to wonder if Guttenhamm was no different. Her heart raced as she and the queen were helped from the carriage. She watched to see if Agatha seemed apprehensive by the presence of the wagon but the older lady merely smiled and continued in conversation. They were halfway up the staircase when shouts could be heard which made the ladies stop in midstep.

Josephine could feel the blood drain from her face and Agatha must have seen her turn pale for she took hold of the young lady's arm and said, "Let's hurry on. We must freshen up before supper." They were almost to the top of the stairs when the cries were heard again, and Josephine couldn't help but stop to look over her shoulder. A man in ragged clothing, held at the elbow by two soldiers was being drug toward the door. The man was still calling to those down the hall and a few seconds later she could see the prince walking in his direction. The other men stepped into view and she could clearly hear what Wilhelm replied.

"I will hear no more. Take this filth to the garrison," and before anymore was said, the queen tugged at Josephine and the ladies hurried on. This time, the queen took Josephine to her own chambers. Agatha called for Patreece who began to fix Josephine's hair as the queen changed. Katrina brought another dress for Josephine and helped the young lady into it while the queen's hair was done. The servants were dismissed, and the queen was deciding on jewelry when she noticed Josephine had gone to a window and was staring off in the distance. Agatha asked for an opinion, and when there was no answer, she went to the young lady's side.

"Is the scene downstairs what is on your mind or something else?"

Josephine continued to look into the distance but answered quietly, "Downstairs." She hesitated but then added, "I didn't like what

Wilhelm said." The queen gently laid her hand upon Josephine's arm.

"He speaks with authority that makes one tremble, doesn't he?" Josephine turned to look into the queen's eyes.

"And how can he speak that way and the next moment put his hands upon me ever so gently while we are dancing?" There was a pain in her voice as she spoke. "I am confused, which is the real Wilhelm?" she asked.

"Both are, my dear," Agatha replied. She could see fear in the young lady's eyes as well as tears beginning to well up.

"I don't understand," Josephine mumbled as she turned her gaze to the floor. "He sounded so terrible downstairs. I cannot look him in the eye after hearing such things." The queen remembered how pleased her son was that he could speak to Josephine so freely and her with him. She thought of how he was smiling when he described her, now the bond that had been felt was on the verge of being broken.

"Josephine, I suggest that you speak with him after supper and tell him how you feel."

"How could I say such things to him?" the young lady questioned as she looked at the woman again.

"Just explain it like you did to me. Has he not been reasonable when you have spoken together?" the queen asked and Josephine nodded that he had. "But don't just tell him how you feel, but ask him who the prisoner was. I have a feeling he won't hold back from you, as long as his father has not forbidden him to speak of it, he will confide it in you. His responsibilities involve more than looking handsome at dinner parties." She turned the lady about to face the room, looked her over and they began to walk toward the chamber doors. "And . . . you will have to learn to trust his judgment, my dear."

The crown entertained three dignitaries and their wives as guests for supper that night. For protocol, Josephine was seated farther down the table which came as a relief. The conversation with the queen still weighed upon the lady's mind, and she planned on taking the advice. After a brief visit in the parlor good-byes were exchanged so the guests would not be travelling late into the night. As the family made their way upstairs, Josephine found herself trembling as she second-guessed her decision. They were almost to the library when she noticed the queen whisper to the king, and they suddenly excused themselves for the night. Josephine came to a standstill as if frozen, and Agatha must have looked back for she called out from down the hall that the lady wished to speak with Wilhelm alone in the library. Josephine blushed as both princes turned and looked at her. Leopold gave a bow and walked away leaving his brother standing alone. Josephine took a deep breath trying to find the courage to speak. It was obvious to Wilhelm that she was struggling, and so he motioned toward the library and thankfully Josephine's legs obeyed because her mouth wasn't cooperating. Quickly she headed for the map wall and waited nervously until the prince came beside her.

"I have not seen you at a loss for words until now. Something is weighing heavy on your mind," he said, trying to make her laugh. She managed a smile and then began to brag on how well he was treating her and the whole family for that matter. She had seen a merciful, compassionate side of him, the stately prince that had been at the council dinner and the gentleman that had danced with her. All the while as Josephine spoke Wilhelm listened closely, but he could tell by the look upon her face that the lady seemed in anguish. Finally Josephine began to explain it was as if she had come to know two completely different men. The man that night who had shown no mercy upon his victims until he came to her was the same one whose cruel words that afternoon made her heart melt within her. The lady was standing still until that moment, and then she stepped closer to look him in the eyes. Suddenly she demanded answers from him, and at first, he said very little to defend himself which only upset her more. Several times it was as if he started to reveal something and then changing his mind, mumbled that she just did not know what all was involved. She provoked him to explain himself, and again, he started to and then stopped and turned away. This time when he turned back to her she was not prepared for his reply. The words were sharp and stung as he explained that the situation was dire for them to attack Briasburg and how could she think him so inhumane to slaughter people. Was this her opinion of him? Before she could answer him, he continued rambling about being responsible for the lives of his people and how could she understand being thrown into the middle of such chaos. Then stepping closer, he began to whisper, "How dare you judge me? You have so much to learn. When you have seen such filth walk about, destroying innocent lives, they do not deserve to crawl upon the earth to beg mercy from those they have taken everything from!" He had stopped with his face only inches from hers, and she had begun to cry as she stood stubbornly defiant before him. "You want answers?" Wilhelm looked deeply into her eyes. "I will give them, but are you strong enough to bear them, I wonder?" Suddenly he came to his senses and was ashamed for yelling at the woman before him. He swallowed hard as he knew he could not take back the words he had spoken in his anger at her accusations. His outburst had done more to hurt than help. But she had not fled before him and why she hadn't he didn't know. Could he trust her with the truth of all that was happening in the kingdom? "I want you to accompany me on a trip tomorrow morning," he said calmly and watched as Josephine's eyebrows grew serious.

"Why would I ever go anywhere with you after?" Her voice broke off as the pain of seeing him so angry with her began to move her again and the lady let her gaze fall to his shirt. "How can I trust you? I do not know you." The prince found himself reaching for Josephine's arm, and just before he took hold of it, he stopped short, knowing she would not let him touch her.

"I understand and I am sorry. I am but a man and have a temper, especially when it comes to certain things. Please, I beg you to consider going with me. I need to show you something that will explain far more than words can ever tell." The lady had stopped crying and seemed to be shaking less. She glanced up at him for a split second and then looked downward again. "We would not be alone. There will be at least a regiment travelling with us. I cannot undo my behavior tonight but please let me attempt to explain better." He was pleading so earnestly that neither realized he had in fact taken her arm. Despite all her unanswered fears, Josephine could not help but believe him. There had to be more to the situation than she had seen and at the least she would have another piece to the puzzle that was unfolding before her. She also needed to know more of the kingdom before she agreed to remain in Guttenhamm regardless of how inviting the position seemed.

"I will go with you," the lady whispered. Relieved, Wilhelm took a long deep breath.

"I will have mother see to the things you will need on the trip." He took a step back and let go of her arm. "And we should turn in as we will have a very long day ahead of us." The prince started toward the door with the lady a few steps behind feeling better but not enough to walk beside him. They continued down the hall to their rooms, and as Josephine was stepping through her doorway, she heard Wilhelm say, "Thank you for coming to me with your concerns. It means more to me than you know."

7

The Village

Just before dawn, Agatha came knocking at Josephine's door. She laid out a simpler everyday dress and instructed the young woman to braid her hair for she would be travelling by horseback. She also recommended an extra pair of stockings for warmth and to take the heavier cloak from the armoire, just in case.

"Wilhelm is already downstairs making final preparations. There's not enough time to sit down to a full breakfast, but I am sure the cook has something ready for you." The queen was starting to leave the room when she gave her a hug and added, "Be careful today." Josephine suspected that Agatha knew where Wilhelm was taking her. When the young lady came into the kitchen, the cook was placing hot muffins in a basket on the table. Josephine poured herself a glass of milk and was just sitting down when Wilhelm strode into the room.

"Good morning," he said, taking a seat across from the lady. "Sorry to get you up so early, but we have several hours of riding ahead. And"—reaching for another muffin—"a lot to do before we return home. The horses are being saddled." He seemed to be in a good mood. She watched him eat and wondered where they were going. Wilhelm could tell by her quietness that she was still upset with him from the night before but he figured curiosity would overcome her and she would start asking questions. When he had eaten his fill and she still hadn't spoken, he decided not to volunteer any information until they reached their destination.

A soldier stepped to the doorway. "We're ready your majesty," he announced and then nodded toward the lady. Simultaneously, the prince and the lady rose to their feet and started away from the table.

"You didn't eat enough to feed a bird," Wilhelm commented, pointing toward three muffins that still lay upon her plate. "Why don't you wrap them in a napkin and take them along."

"That's not necessary. I am fine," she stated but he insisted.

"You really should take them with you. You will think you're starving before we have a chance to eat again."

"I will be . . ." She started to say *fine* through gritted teeth.

But the prince stopped and in a stern voice said, "Take them, or we won't even leave the kitchen!" With a snarl, the lady retrieved the muffins and stomped past the prince. So much for his good mood, she thought. If she was hungry, it was her business, not his. Wilhelm followed her down the hall toward the foyer but as they neared the stairs Karl called to him from above.

"My lord, your father needs to speak with you." The butler sounded anxious as he spoke. Wilhelm began climbing the staircase, leaving Josephine and Captain Vaughn alone. A few minutes passed until a terrible commotion was heard upstairs. Nervously Josephine shifted upon her feet. Suddenly they could recognize Wilhelm's voice and goosebumps rose on the young lady's arms. Vaughn politely made an excuse to step outside, and Josephine joined him. The morning was very cool and crisp, and she found the other soldiers assembled in rank already mounted and awaiting their commander. A few minutes passed with no sign of Wilhelm and already beginning to feel cold, Josephine slipped back inside to wait. Things were not any better as she could still hear shouting every little bit, then suddenly all grew quiet and she heard a door slam. Footsteps could be heard, and looking up toward the staircase, she saw Wilhelm coming down the stairs alone. His face wore an ugly frightening frown. As soon as his feet landed on the foyer, he asked the lady if she was ready to leave, and without glancing toward her as she answered, he walked on outside.

Josephine followed him to find that two wagons were now waiting, stacked high with crates. Wilhelm greeted his men and then led her to a mare, and helped her into the saddle. She thought she heard him apologize for not asking the lady if she could ride well, but his head was turned away and she dared not have him repeat himself. Quickly he mounted his horse, gave the signal, snapped his reins, and they headed for the gates. When the main road was reached, the riders brought their horses to a gallop, leaving the wagons far behind. The company skirted the edge of Guttenhamm and headed northward. As they rode through the countryside, Josephine noticed a heavier frost had fallen in the night. She was reminded of her father's words as he planned her trip east.

"You are to stay a few weeks at Alfred's home. Then you both will return to Picardell before the snow falls. You may even beat the first frost," he said with excitement. The suitor would meet her family to discuss details of the betrothal and marriage, and then he would return home until spring when he could travel again. Josephine caught herself making an ugly face as she thought of Alfred and hoped none of the soldiers saw her. As they continued to ride, Josephine wondered if the winter was harsher here in Gutten with the mountain range in the west emptying onto a large plain as the land turned to the east. The air that morning was colder than what she was used to when riding and it did not take very long for the lady to wish she had done a better job pulling her cape tight around her neck. Several times she attempted to adjust it, but with the terrain and the speed with which they rode, she was not successful. Finally they came to place where the road ran straight, and she was able to fix the cape how she wanted it. Still they rode on, and just when Josephine thought she could take the stinging cold upon her face no longer, she looked up and through blurry eyes saw Wilhelm wave his arm. The regiment came to an orderly halt. They were poised at the crest of a hill, overlooking a valley with the road descending quickly among the rocky crags. To her surprise, Wilhelm brought his horse alongside hers and gave orders for the others to proceed ahead.

"I need a word with you before we continue," he said in a serious tone. Josephine hoped an explanation of the shouting she had heard before they left the castle was about to be given.

When the last soldier had passed by and their conversation could not be heard by the others, the prince began, "*This* is where we are going." As he spoke, he pointed to the valley that lay before them. Josephine gave him a bewildered look. "Six days ago, a thriving village stood here."

"What?" the lady asked, looking hard, barely able to distinguish the crude shapes of buildings in the distance. "What happened? How?" Wilhelm did not answer for a moment but carefully searched for words. So much depended on the explanation and he could not afford to allow his anger to take control.

"It was destroyed by King Airik's sons." He felt his eyebrows tense up as Josephine looked at him, shaking her head in disbelief.

"Airik . . . of Briasburg?" she asked. "Why would his family do such a thing?"

"They were consumed by the thought of conquering. This is not the only village his sons have pillaged and burned, Josephine. My father has met with leaders from Pietra, Roland, Denske, who have all been plagued by Airik's lust for power." He could not hide the anger in his voice as he finished. As she stared in the distance, Josephine's mind began to race back to Briasburg castle. The king had gladly taken her in, offering her the crown's resources for her journey homeward. She had visited with him during the afternoon and was introduced to each of his sons that night at supper. She had even danced with several of them following the meal before they had visited in the parlor and then turned in for the night. She felt lightheaded as she could not grasp what had happened. Had the princes been in this valley only hours before she arrived at Briasburg? Hadn't they come down to dinner with smiles upon their faces?

"But if King Airik wanted more land for his own, why would he destroy everything that lay upon it?" she asked.

"If he displayed his might by wreaking havoc on smaller villages, then maybe the larger ones would be too afraid to resist his army. He actually let some of the villagers go without hunting them

down. As if he needed witnesses to spread fear of what he could do."
Josephine understood Wilhelm's reasoning but the sight before her
was almost incomprehensible.

Trying to piece it all together, she asked, "Was this the village
your servants were speaking of?" She turned to look at Wilhelm once
more and he nodded.

"It makes me ill to know how many innocent people died when
they traveled into Aikerlan and to think that Airik let you make it all
the way to his castle," Wilhelm said with concern. "And to take you in
as if it were peaceful times. I am convinced the king had plans for you."

"And why on earth would he be concerned with me?" Josephine
asked, glancing back toward the valley.

"Perhaps you were to be a bargaining chip with Frive?" The
prince shrugged his shoulders. "Unless Airik needed you for something, I have no doubt he would have killed you." Josephine shuddered
at the possibility in his words. "When we return to Guttenhamm, ask
my father to show you the chronicles of the High Council and it will
prove what I have spoken as truth."

"So . . . you attacked Briasburg as revenge for this village?"
Josephine asked, pointing in the distance. Wilhelm was quick to
answer.

"*No!* No, it was not for revenge. Sometimes measures have to be
taken that are not pleasant," he said, trying to explain.

"Are you sure you are not offering an excuse?" Josephine asked
with a glare. Wilhelm shifted in his saddle. Obviously he needed to
explain a different way.

"Let's say as a child you do something wrong and your father
punishes you. Is it wrong for him to do so?" he asked.

"Of course not," Josephine answered, trying to follow the
prince's thought.

"It is his responsibility to correct you even if you think he's
just being mean. But, in fact, your father loves you enough to do
what is necessary for you to know right from wrong so you will be
a better person. Airik was told what was right and what was wrong,
and this is the choice he made. He chose to take countless lives and
planned to destroy more. He had to be stopped and that unfortunate

lot fell to my brother and me to carry out." He lowered his head as he spoke and sighed. He wasn't sure he had convinced the lady, but they needed to ride on.

"Come, enough talk of things that I wish were different. Let's get on down into the valley. We have to take it slow though as the rocks here are shifty." He nudged his horse and the lady followed suit. When they had reached the bottom of the hill and it began to level out, the prince warned. "I am not sure what we will find. It may be gruesome. The families may not have buried their dead yet. I just don't know for sure." With his statement, Josephine felt weak. The only time she had seen a dead person was in a funeral procession. Her life had been rather sheltered, and she had not experienced very much in the way of hardship until the past week. Wilhelm saw the look on Josephine's face and part of him wished he had not brought her with him, yet he knew with her strong will she would not have believed his words alone. With sadness, he spurred his horse onward to what was left of the village. Piles of rubble that used to be homes lay all around with charred pieces of wood scattered among stone foundations, and only one short length of a wall was left standing. All the soldiers had already dismounted, and were searching through the rubble in search of bodies except for the four who were to ride on to the next village to let survivors know supplies were on the way. As Josephine dismounted, she noticed a fire had been started near the lone wall, and she went to warm herself. Only a few minutes later, Wilhelm came carrying her saddle.

"A seat for you, my lady," he said, placing it on the ground. He pointed to the wall. "This should keep the breeze off you."

"Did you bring me all this way to *watch* you work?" she asked. "Or am I allowed to help?" She saw him smile as he stood back upright.

"When the wagons arrive, you can direct them to distribute the supplies," he said as he went to the fire and stretched out his hands to warm them. "Will that work, my lady?" As she stepped beside him, she asked if he was implying that she was bossy, but he teased that he only knew she was assertive enough to keep his men in line. It felt good to laugh together after such tension had been between them since the night before. Within an hour, Josephine spotted visitors coming along the road, and her heart was moved with compassion as the villagers drew near. An older man wore a blood-stained bandage around his head, and a younger man's face was severely bruised and his left hand was wrapped in dirty rags.

Compelled to call out to them, Josephine said with a quivering voice, "Good morning."

The older man stepped closer to her and in a gruff voice replied, "We were told the king was sending supplies. Where are they at?" The harshness was frightening and the lady was at a loss how to answer him.

She felt a reassuring hand rest against the back of her arm as the prince spoke up, "God bless you for coming." A smile crossed the peasants' faces and they bowed in respect. "The wagons will be here shortly. Come, warm yourselves by the fire." He motioned to them. Josephine watched as Wilhelm sat down on the ground with the people, and they began to tell what had befallen them. One man described the raid so vividly that Josephine had to walk away as the details were more than she could stand to hear. She had just regained her composure when she felt a gentle tug at her skirt. She looked down to see a young lad and crouching she asked what he needed. He told her that he was hungry. Looking into his sweet blue eyes, she guessed he couldn't have been more than three years old. Suddenly, she heard the familiar creaking of wagon wheels and looked up to see that supplies had arrived. She explained that she would have something for him in just a few minutes and then took hold of his little grubby hand.

"You are so cold!" she cried out. "Where are your parents?"

"Father is there," the child said, pointing to where several men were now standing by a wagon.

"And where is your mother?" she asked. The little boy's face went blank, and he just stared solemnly at her.

"She's gone," he said quietly. Josephine asked him what he meant, and he just repeated the words again.

"Gone where?" she asked. When he answered this time, his face wrinkled up in frustration.

"The bad men took her away. Father says I won't be able to see her." Suddenly Josephine understood what he was too young to comprehend. The young lady swallowed hard fighting back tears. She glanced around not knowing what to say or do. Wilhelm had just unloaded a crate and turned at the right time to see the lost look upon Josephine's face. Quickly, he went to the lady, and when he was beside her, the lady whispered to him, and without hesitation, he reached down and scooped the boy up in his arms swinging him around.

"Hello there, young man," he said as the boy grinned. The prince glanced toward Josephine. "Henri, our field cook is starting a soup, but it won't be ready for a while yet. Let's get you closer to the fire so you'll be warmer." And with that, he playfully swung the boy along as he walked making the child giggle with delight. Returning to her saddle, Josephine sat down, and Wilhelm lowered the boy onto her lap. Quickly, the child looked up at Josephine to remind her that he was still hungry. His little voice tore at her heart strings and she felt a tear slide down her cheek. It caught Wilhelm's attention, and he was reaching to catch it when she noticed him about to do so and checking himself he quickly withdrew his hand. "None of that, we don't want to upset our new friend," he said, putting the focus back on the boy. Suddenly Josephine began to laugh.

"How silly of me for not remembering sooner," she said, reaching into the pocket of her cape. She pulled out a cloth unfolding it to reveal the three muffins from breakfast. The little boy looked up at her with a smile and started to reach for one but then hesitated. "Go ahead. You can have them all if you like." He didn't need to be told twice for he grabbed a muffin and began to gobble it down. She looked up at Wilhelm who not only was watching the boy but her as well. He didn't say a word but the prince knew she was thankful he had insisted that she bring the muffins along. Giving her a wink, Wilhelm stood to his feet and left her and the boy.

When the last crumb had been eaten, the lad climbed off Josephine's lap and scampered away. The lady stood to her feet and watched him until he had rejoined his father. Then she looked for Wilhelm who was giving orders near the wagons. When he saw her approaching, he stopped to introduce her and announced that she would be instructing them further concerning the supplies. At first it made her nervous to be placed in charge, but it didn't seem to bother the men at all. Within a few hours, there was a meager but steady stream of people coming to get supplies. She wondered how she had ended up in a foreign land, handing out food to villagers whose homes had been destroyed. Morning turned into afternoon and then into evening until finally all the wagons were empty. By that point, attention had turned to removing the debris from where homes once stood with the foundations barely visible under the piles of charred rubble. It was urgent that structures be rebuilt before winter fully set in. A line had formed to pass pieces along to deposit in a more suitable location. With her previous task finished, Josephine had tried to help but no matter where she stood, the soldiers would not pass a piece to her. She had just about given up when Wilhelm came to her aid.

"Are they giving you a hard time?" he asked. With a wave of his hand, he motioned for her to follow him. They walked toward the front of the line. "I'm sure no offense was meant, but with some of the pieces being rather heavy, they were only keeping your best interest in mind." He turned and offered a hand to steady her as they climbed up into a pile of stone and boards. "Start here. I know you will only pass something you can handle." He smiled. Josephine unbuttoned her sleeves to roll them up as she thanked him. "It is a dirty job, but if you are willing—"

Before he could finish, she had reached for the blackened end of a board and passed it to the man closest to her. As she reached for a brick, she realized Wilhelm hadn't moved but was watching her.

"Is there something wrong?" she asked, reaching for another piece of rubble.

"No, not at all," he replied and turned his attention to the work at hand. He couldn't help but wonder about this young lady that he had saved. She had come with him that morning because he had demanded that she do so, but she had not volunteered to help for the sake of public display. He knew her family's social status would have forbid her to be elbow deep in grime, yet the compassion she felt for these strangers would not let her sit by the wayside. She was definitely different than any young noble lady he had ever known. Just before sunset, the prince called to her, and as they stepped away, he began to explain. "We are hours from being done." He looked as if he was thinking hard about something and reached up, running his fingers over the whiskers upon his chin. He glanced at her and added, "I can send you back to Dahn to spend the night. You should make it just after dark."

"And what about the rest of you?" she asked as she looked toward the line of men still passing rubble to the outskirts of the village.

"We will probably spend the night here and return home tomorrow."

"Perhaps I should just stay. As you said, there is still a lot to do." She didn't like the idea of having no shelter, but she hated the thought of being sent away if others were staying.

"I don't know," Wilhelm replied. "It will be rough."

"I know that," she said. "Are you letting me stay then?"

With a sigh, he answered, "You can, but I hope neither of us regrets the decision." She gave him a smile. "And we'll see if you're still smiling by morning." She gave him a smirk and shook her head. Was there something he wasn't telling her, or did he just think she wouldn't fare well?

As darkness fell, torches were lit so they could continue working. Finally, Wilhelm called the workers closer to him. He said they were done for the day and thanked them for their efforts. Henri had supper ready for all, and campfires had been built for the soldiers to sleep around. Josephine followed Wilhelm as he went toward the fire beside the lone wall. She welcomed the warmth and flexed her cold stiff fingers near the flames. The prince stepped away for a moment, but when he returned, he was carrying blankets. He knelt and prepared places to sleep by the saddles. Her heart dropped in disappointment. She knew he said they would be spending the night outside but somehow she hoped to be under a canopy. She had just sat down on her saddle when Henri brought food to them. As she ate, Josephine watched the men shuffle around the makeshift camp, and she knew this was not the first time they had been out together.

Wood had been brought close to keep the fires burning through the night and the men started settling down with their saddles and blankets.

She was watching them quietly when Wilhelm interrupted her solitude. "I should have made you go on to Dahn," he said, and she turned her gaze toward him. "This is as good as it gets."

"It'll do," she lied, trying to make him feel better. "Besides, you gave me a choice."

"It was against my better judgment," he replied. He stood to his feet for a moment and readjusted where his saddle was and then spread his blanket out again. "I was not expecting the temperature to drop so quickly." Josephine moved from where she was sitting upon her saddle to the blanket lying in front of it.

"If you didn't want me to stay, then why did you let me?" she asked as she tried to smooth out a wrinkle that lay to her right. She wasn't getting rid of it, and suddenly Wilhelm leaned in her direction and reached under the blanket and removed a stick. She smiled at him. "And you have already guessed that this is a new experience for me. It's not that I haven't slept outside but in a wagon a few times, and in the barn, and once in a stack of hay." She heard laughter as Wilhelm leaned back against his saddle.

"If I were to guess, you like adventure?" The grin he wore was almost irritating for the lady couldn't tell if he was complementing her or criticizing her.

"Why *did* you let me stay?" she asked again as she leaned against her saddle. The prince sat up as he looked at her.

"Because I knew you wanted to help and I needed it. I admire that you are trying to make the best out of a rotten situation," he added. "I only hope you will forgive me for being selfish and keeping you here to sleep on the cold, hard ground." By the light of the fire, she could see how serious his face was. Suddenly she could hear the faint sound of wolves howling.

"I will forgive you as long as you promise not to let any wild animals eat me in the night," she said as she turned her back to the prince and pulled her blanket up over her shoulder. He agreed and bid her good night.

She lay there listening to the fire crackling and all the unfamiliar sounds. She retraced her day in her mind, desperately trying to fall asleep. She could feel her arms and legs starting to ache from riding and handling the debris but thankfully only the side of her that was against the ground was cold. Her mind wandered to Wilhelm, and she wondered if he had fallen asleep yet. She needed to roll over, but it would be awkward if he was still awake. Finally she could take it no longer, and she began to move. Before she was settled, she noticed his eyes were open.

"Can't sleep either?" She nodded, and after rising up on one elbow, he added, "I don't mind being outdoors, but this feels rather exposed." He was whispering quiet enough that the crackle of the fire was louder than his voice.

The lady wiggled closer and commented, "I can barely hear you." Motioning for her to raise up, the prince took hold of the edge of her saddle and pulled it closer to him. Josephine rested back against it again.

"Sorry. We need to keep it down. If my men can rest, then let's not disturb them. Is there anything I can do to make you more comfortable? Perhaps a lullaby?" Josephine saw a sly grin cross his face and shook her head, smiling. Suddenly an eerie howl was heard and the lady shivered with fright.

"How close is he?" she asked quickly.

Very calmly, Wilhelm whispered back, "He's far enough away not to worry. The watchmen would not let them get too close." The young lady was not yet convinced as another howl was heard. "And remember that we have a nice fire." Wilhelm watched as Josephine leaned closer to him. "And he has to eat how many men before he gets to you." At his last words, the lady looked at him and gave a faint smile.

"I'm sorry. It just frightens me so." She offered, now sitting not an arm's length away from the prince. He glanced down and then looked back at the lady.

"But . . . it isn't proper for you to spend the night *this* close to me." Wilhelm assumed she would move away at his statement, but she didn't and just looked at him wide-eyed. "Tell you what, let me put old Trusty between us and call it good."

Josephine gave a questioning look and asked, "Who or what is Trusty?" The prince turned, picked up his sword and brought it to rest upon the ground between them. "Oh, I see," she replied now amused. "No one can come between a man and his sword, eh?"

"Well, a man has to keep his standards you know," he replied. For a moment, both seemed embarrassed, and Josephine for a split-second considered moving until the wolf howled again and she glanced at Wilhelm nervously.

"I will not be the start of a scandal nor put a blemish upon your honor." She said with a quiver in her voice, but trying to be brave, she pulled her blanket to the side to move.

Wilhelm reached for the lady's arm and whispered, "Nothing of the sort would happen on account of you. Lie back down and let's get some sleep." Josephine glanced at the sword one more time as another wolf howled answering the first one. She closed her eyes tight and began to relax knowing she was safe where she was at.

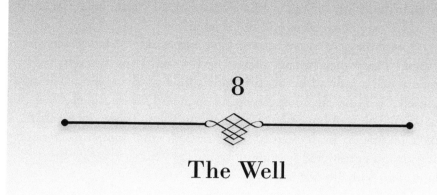

8

The Well

When Josephine awoke the next morning, it was just before dawn, and she could hear the occasional chirp of birds. She looked in Wilhelm's direction and found him to still be sleeping and was a bit startled as she realized they were very close to each other. She tried to sit up without waking him but was not successful as he heard her and opened his eyes.

"Good morning," he said quietly. She answered him but was preoccupied with her blanket that seemingly had her unable to move freely. "What is wrong?" He glanced down and realizing how close they were asked, "Which one of us crossed the line?" Josephine glared at him for he seemed quite amused.

"This is not funny," she stated. "What if someone sees us?"

"My question is, *where* is my sword?" the prince asked feeling under his blanket. "It was special made from Damascus steel, and well, we have been through a lot together me and old Trusty." Josephine stopped struggling with her blanket and gave him a mean look. He was about to laugh and then changed his mind as she was terribly upset. "May I?" and without waiting for an answer, he slid his hands under her blanket lifting her slightly into the air. He drew out his sword and let her plop to the ground. Josephine turned red and looked away from him. She didn't know whether she was more embarrassed over her being the guilty party or him moving her about the way he had. "It's a wonder you slept with such a bulky thing under you," he said as he stood to his feet. He offered her his hand to help her up. Reluctantly, she took it but could not bring herself to look at him. "We'll be heading back home when everyone is saddled up." He bent over and picked up his blanket from the ground and shook it out. He tossed it over his shoulder before he reached for his saddle. "Let's see if Henri has a morsel to tide you over till we get to Dahn." She followed him to where the horses were tied up. Just before he got to his mare, she pulled the blanket from his shoulder and spread it upon the horse's back for him. He secured the straps, and then the pair returned for her saddle and done likewise. They could hear the others stirring and occasionally laughter erupted.

"They are in a good mood," Josephine commented as she patted her horse while Wilhelm adjusted her stirrups.

"It's a wonder after sleeping on the ground." Finishing, he began to stroke the horse's mane. "The ground seemed harder than I remembered. I have a new appreciation for my bed," he said with a laugh.

"Well," Josephine said, deciding to make light of the awkward situation that morning. "Old Trusty was quite comfortable, perhaps you should give it a try?" Wilhelm leaned to see the lady's face and found her smiling at him.

The two started back toward the others and were stepping over a pile of rocky debris when suddenly Josephine felt the ground give way beneath her. As she felt herself falling, she gave a blood curdling scream. In the next instant, she plunged into water cold enough to take her breath. She resurfaced coughing and spitting out water and began wildly swinging her arms. She began to panic as she did not know how to swim. Looking upward, she could not judge the distance to the top. There was just enough light for her to see a rocky wall in front of her, and she tried to make her way toward it. By her guess she had fallen into a well, a deep well for that matter. She could barely move as her skirt was clinging like ropes to her legs, and with fear taking hold of her mind, she was sinking more than she thought she was going forward. Suddenly in the midst of the splashing, her fingers touched something and she grabbed hold of a protruding rock. As she took hold of it better and quit flailing about, she could hear Wilhelm desperately screaming her name. When she answered, she heard him say, "Thank God," with relief. Josephine looked upward again and could see shadows moving in the blinding light.

"Josephine, are you hurt?" he asked urgently. She thought for a moment and then told him no. She could hear other voices but could not understand what they were saying. Leaning into the opening, Wilhelm yelled to her, explaining that the well was deep and they were looking for rope. He also told her it would be a few minutes and to hold on to the wall.

"Wilhelm," she desperately pleaded, "I can't swim."

"Don't worry about swimming, just hold on to the wall," he answered, trying to encourage her. She looked back toward the opening and saw shadows moving away from the rim. A commotion was heard as the men's voices rose. She could make out Wilhelm's voice among them, and she felt sorry for whoever was at the mercy of his wrath. She cringed as she wondered if he was angry with her carelessness, getting herself into such a predicament. When she was pulled up to safety, would he scream at her like he had two nights ago? Waves of panic flooded over her again as she realized she might not even escape the well to face him. Fighting back tears of anticipation, she tried to convince herself a rescue was only moments away. She heard a shifting sound from above and looking up saw shadows again at the opening. Wilhelm yelled down, "Still holding on? We don't have anything long enough yet. I have sent men out in every direction. At the worst, they can bring rope from Dahn, but as you know, that will take a little while. I have also sent word to my father to be ready for us. That is all we can do for now. Try not to be afraid. We are here and most of all God is with you." Light filled the opening once more as she was left alone.

God? she thought. Would God still be with her after she had turned her back against Him? Her heart sank knowing how determined she had been of late to keep Him out of her thoughts. She had refused to join her family at church and had begun breaking commandments right and left. She refused to honor her parents' wishes, becoming a selfish rebellious person bent on getting her way. Her thoughts were consumed with the hatred of her father and revenge for her being sent away to find a husband. How could a holy God tolerate her enough to be with her in this deep, dark place? She had begun to cry as she knew she deserved even to die for the heartache she had brought to her family. Her streak of self-pity was interrupted by the sound of arguing from above. She could not hear well enough to understand what was said, but someone had dared to challenge Wilhelm's authority. Suddenly all grew quiet save the sound of the rocks shifting as someone approached.

"Josephine," Wilhelm yelled.

"Yes?" she answered.

"They have found some rope, but it doesn't look very strong. We are going to test it before we try it with you." She could hear more shifting at the surface and then he continued, "I need you to do something very important for me." He waited for her acknowledgement and then explained, "Using your legs, I need you to feel around and be sure there is nothing sticking up in the water, no debris that is."

Not wanting to turn loose of the wall, she replied, "I went under quite a ways and there was nothing."

To her surprise, Wilhelm snapped back at her excuse, "Just do as I said!" He gave a sigh as he had lost his temper with her yet again. Trying to sound nicer, he repeated himself. "Please just feel for anything in the water. I know you are afraid to let go, but it is very important. Go ahead." Josephine stretched out her leg and began probing the water. Carefully she eased herself along the wall until she had made a full circle. She could tell she hadn't reached fully into the center so summoning her courage she pushed out away from the wall. Her skirt clung to her again and she struggled making a commotion. Retreating to the wall she steadied herself and kept trying until she was sure the center was clear. She yelled back to Wilhelm that she was finished. She wasn't sure whether she had done as he requested out of obedience or fear of angering him further.

"That's fine," he replied and she could hear other voices again. "Now keep yourself as close to the wall as possible. If the rope breaks, I don't want to fall on you."

"What?" she shrieked. "Oh no! No! You are not coming down here. Please . . . don't. Don't risk it. Just lower the rope and pull me up."

"Just stay close to the wall," he replied, ignoring the lady's pleas for his safety. She flattened her body against the wall, knowing his mind was made up. He was stubborn and arguing at this point was a waste of breath. Josephine looked up one more time to see Wilhelm's shadow as the men began to lower him into the well. The lady closed her eyes and held her breath as she could hear the rope creaking. Wilhelm was about halfway down when suddenly a sharp ping was heard. He cried out and she opened her eyes just in time to see the prince plummet into the water. Josephine was not able to turn her head away fast enough, and the splash drenched her face. She was wiping her eyes when Wilhelm surfaced close by.

"Whew! Now isn't this a refreshing temperature," he said, swimming over to her.

"That is not funny!" she yelled at him. If she could have managed, she would have held him under for frightening her. Wilhelm looked up toward the men poised on the edge of the rim and assured them he was fine but to hurry. Carefully, he edged up to the lady and touched her arm.

"Now that I am here with you, how are you really?" he asked very softly with concern. "Are you hurt?"

Mumbling she replied. "Why on earth did you risk your life coming down here?"

"Because I was worried about you." He paused for a moment and added, "And I did not want you to be alone." His words struck the lady's heart. "You needed to be reminded of something." He looked at the lady as best he could. "God promised that He would never leave us nor forsake us." As the shock of seeing him falling through the air wore off Josephine could not control her emotions and began to sob. Wilhelm put his arm around her, and she clung to his shoulder crying.

Maybe God loved her after all? she thought. The small measure of faith she had left grew as a glimmer of hope seemed to shine in the distance. Josephine stopped crying and leaned away from the prince and apologized for being so emotional.

She had turned and was reaching for the wall when the prince asked, "So you can't swim?" He turned and began to glide through the chilly water.

"No, I'm afraid not," she said sheepishly. She was almost jealous of how he seemed to be enjoying the swim.

A few moments later, she changed her mind when he said, "Aha, just what I was searching for." Burning with curiosity, she asked what it was. "There's a ledge just wide enough for you to stand upon." He invited her to come to him, and even though he wasn't very far away, she was not about to let go of the rock she was clinging tightly to. Suddenly he realized she was too frightened to move, and he dove into the water again and came up beside her. "We have nothing but time on our hands, let me teach you how to swim," he offered.

"Not today," she replied firmly.

"It's not hard, come on," he pleaded, reaching for her arm.

"I said no!" she protested as he gave a tug. "Besides, if I make a mistake, you will only yell at me." He let go of her arm to slap the water. He let out a sigh before he began to talk.

"I am sorry that you think so. At least let me help you to the ledge. It will make it easier on you." She wanted to be stubborn and refuse him, yet she knew her hands were aching already and her arms were beginning to tremble. As she reached out, Wilhelm gently slipped his hands under both of her arms and drew her through the water slowly as to not frighten her. When they made it to the other side, he held her steady and she could tell he was searching for the ledge with his foot.

"Here it is," he said, sliding to one side to allow her to take his place. "You should be able to feel it." The young woman tried to find the outcropping but with no luck.

"Is this the right place?" she asked, moving for him to trade with her. Almost instantly, the prince found it and directed her to where it was. She tried again but could not find it. Worried that he was irritated with her she apologized. Suddenly a thought occurred to her.

"Here," she said, moving to the side. "You stand on the ledge and make sure you are standing up straight." Reaching for his shoulder, she moved closer to him, but as he straightened himself in the water, she began to realize his foot was much deeper than hers had been. Carefully she eased herself farther down until her chin was level with the water's surface. She pointed her toes and felt something near the wall.

"Wilhelm. I can't reach it flatfooted."

"Oh," he said with disappointment.

"It was a good idea," she commented. She was so relieved that she had a legitimate reason for not finding the ledge sooner. Suddenly they felt a cold draft as a gust of wind blew down into the well and Josephine shivered hard.

"I have another idea," Wilhelm said optimistically. "Let me stand on the ledge and you can rest between me and the wall. It might keep the breeze off you too. What do you think?" he asked. The idea was not a bad one, but Josephine found herself thinking about his temper. "Josephine?"

"I am not entirely comfortable being so close to you."

"I give you my word I would never do anything dishonorable. Surely you know that. Do you not trust me?"

"Trust you?" she blurted out. "You have lost your temper so many times today that I . . . I thought my opinion of you had changed until you began yelling at everyone. I don't know you well enough . . . I'm not comfortable with you acting one way one minute and another way the next." To her surprise, the prince did not say a word. She had guessed he would have interrupted her at least to dispute her accusations, but he remained quiet.

In a calm voice, he finally spoke, "We might as well get this cleared up before we go on." He paused for a moment, but then without asking permission, he moved closer to her. "First though, I need to get you situated where you can rest while we talk." She started to resist him, but with authority he said, "*Stop* questioning my every action. Just trust my judgment and *stop* arguing with me. I would *never* do anything to hurt you." He gave a grunt and then added, "This is why I am upset with you." Josephine swallowed hard as she knew he spoke the truth. Without another word, she moved toward the wall and let him do what was needed. Feeling terribly guilty, she began to apologize.

"I'm sorry. I am not purposely challenging your authority." The prince did not reply but found the ledge with his foot and then slid his arms around her waist and leaned closer to keep his balance. He rested his hands behind her against the rocks of the wall and her weight shifted as he held her up. Gently he began to speak to her again.

"I do not ask for you to agree with my ways, but I will ask that you respect me enough to do as I say. I realize that I am not your sovereign prince, but you must stop testing my authority, at least in front of my subjects." Josephine lowered her head shamefully. "And what is this about you not knowing what kind of man I am?" The lady already felt like she had been called out for her behavior and his words were strapping her to the post to be whipped.

"You have explained why you were angry with me, but why were you yelling before they lowered you down?"

"My men didn't want me to take the risk. Several were offering to go in my place, but I just couldn't let them do it. They were doing their best to persuade me as they should, and, yes, I lost my temper with them. Well, I actually think I lost it when I called for some rope and they couldn't find enough." The prince gave a sigh. "As much as I try, I don't always exercise enough self-control, especially when someone could get hurt." He hesitated and then added, "I was very worried about you." The tenderness with which he spoke made Josephine blush and she hoped the darkness had kept her secret. "If you have other questions about me, please ask them."

She thought for a moment and then said, "Yes, before we left the castle, when Karl came for you." She heard Wilhelm grunt as if he had been punched in the stomach. He shifted on his feet and took a long deep breath before he began.

"I will admit that I was very upset. I am still upset. I am passionate when it comes to my people being in harm's way, and I will never apologize for that." By the length of the pause in between sentences, it was apparent that he was having difficulty finding the exact words he wanted to use. "Airik's youngest son Maximillian was not at the castle when we attacked, so he is alive and unscathed." Josephine thought back to that night. The man had walked her to her room and when he said good night, had warned her to lock her door. When they parted, it was very late. Why would he head off somewhere at that hour? Wilhelm continued, "He is as full of evil as his father, maybe even more so. Our troubles have only begun."

"So where is he at now?" she interrupted.

"Rumor says he is staying deeper into his kingdom, closer to Montoise, plotting revenge. I am sure he will come after my family with everything in him. It's only a matter of time before he comes for us."

"Could he attack us here?" she asked with concern. "Now?" She could not fathom the young prince doing such things but she could not deny the ruins that lay on the surface above them.

"It is a possibility, but not likely I'd say. So now you know why I lost it when I heard that he was alive." The lady listened closely as he explained himself further. "I knew my people would need supplies, and there was a risk involved but it had to be done. Actually"—looking as best as he could into her eyes—"you were in danger by coming with us."

"Then *why* did you ask me?" she asked him bluntly.

"Because it was now or never if I was to prove to you that I am not a murdering scoundrel. If I waited to show you, then it would only give Maximillian time to mount an army and the risk of showing you these things would be greater. The devastation you have seen speaks better than my words ever could. I only hoped it would clear my name before you. I take no pleasure in what has happened or what is to come. Josephine, I am not a thief or murderer. Yes, I have taken men's lives, but believe me when I say I have no glory in those deeds. The Bible says that "God is not mocked. Whatsoever a man sows, that also shall he reap." The people in this village were good, kind people who obeyed the laws of my kingdom. They did not deserve this. But King Airik went looking for trouble. He sowed seeds that could only lead to judgment and death. Even still my heart grieves knowing that he would not repent of his ways and turn from this evil." So moving were Wilhelm's words that the lady felt goosebumps as he spoke. Suddenly, a pang of conviction pierced her heart. Lately she had been like this king choosing to willfully sin with no signs of repentance. Wilhelm must have sensed her anxiousness for he suddenly turned the conversation toward her. "It was not by chance that we have crossed paths." A tear slid down Josephine's cheek as Wilhelm spoke softly. "If God had not quickened my heart, I would have slain you in that chapel. Even in the woods, the Lord was dealing with me to speak with you. Let me assure you I have never had my signet ring off my finger since it was given to me, let alone entrust it to someone else. God has placed you in my care for a reason, and right now you need to know that He is here waiting for you to return to Him."

"But I have been so rebellious. I have turned my back on Him . . ." Her voice broke off. "And my father."

"But God loves you and will forgive you when you ask Him to." The prince was silent giving her time to think about what he said. Then he began to pray out loud, uninhibited by her presence. "Lord, we come before you in a time of need. Lord, Josephine needs forgiveness. There are things in her life that has separated her from you, impurities, sin . . . Lord, I know your mercy through salvation can cleanse her from all unrighteousness." Wilhelm leaned his head toward her and whispered, "Just ask Him. Let His love and peace come into your heart again." At first she was mumbling so as not to be heard, but then it became a whisper as she began to feel a change come over her. She could feel God's presence like she had never known before, and at that moment, she forgot Wilhelm was with her. She was thanking God for showing mercy to her when suddenly she heard the prince's voice as he was praying beside her. She became quiet at which he asked, "Are things better between you and Father?"

"Yes," she concluded with a smile. "With my Heavenly Father, that is."

"Don't worry. I will be here with you to help improve things with the earthly one." She gave a sigh and he added, "God has brought you here for a reason. I say we let Him work on your father's heart as He has yours." Wilhelm was right for it had been a long time since she had felt at peace with God. Suddenly a voice was heard from above them.

"My Lord, we have rope!"

"Thank you, God!" Wilhelm whispered. "One half down and one half to go. We need to get you home before you catch your death in those wet clothes."

"Yours are as wet as mine," she replied defensively, not liking the implication that she was the weaker of the two.

"That's true," he admitted, hearing the tone of her voice. "We still have a battle ahead of us." Above them came another shout as rope was lowered, and they waited patiently until they heard it hit the surface of the water. As Wilhelm swam out to get it, Josephine had to smile as she realized he had held her the entire time instead of the short periods as he had intended to let her arms rest. Quickly he came back and began securing the rope around her for the ascent. As he worked to loop it under her arm and then tie it off, he teased about her long beauty soak coming to an end. The prince gave the signal, the rope's slack began to tighten and Josephine's body began to rise out of the water. She couldn't help but close her eyes as she went upward, and as the light became brighter, she opened them again to see the outline of the men come into focus. Two men positioned themselves at the rim to take hold of her when she was hoisted clear of the opening. They quickly untied her, wrapped her in a blanket and lowered the rope again to retrieve Wilhelm. Henri tried to lead her to the fire but she wouldn't budge until she saw the prince was safely above ground. Wilhelm headed toward the fire as well, giving orders as he walked. Most of the men were to stay to finish their task, but a small party would accompany him and the lady back to Dahn. Despite the setback, the mission still had to be completed. About a half hour later, horses were brought and the few that were leaving mounted up. It did not take very long for Josephine to realize why Wilhelm had referred to the trip home as a battle. The temperature was not at the freezing point but was terribly cold nonetheless, and they were riding along at a good pace which made her face sting with pain. The lady had pulled up her hood and lowered her head to shield her eyes, but it didn't seem to help much. Suddenly Wilhelm gave a signal and everyone slowed until they came to a complete stop. Turning his mare around, he brought his horse alongside Josephine's.

"I'm going to move you." The young lady gave a questioning look although she was sure her face was too cold to let him see her full expression. "You are leaning quite a bit, and it wouldn't be pretty if you fell off your horse." Part of her wanted to insist that she could make it, but she remembered her promise and didn't protest. A thinner man spoke up and offered to let her ride double with him. As he approached, the prince dismounted and then lifted her easily from her horse. Wilhelm let the lady's feet touch the ground long enough for Rupert to ride up close and then Wilhelm lifted her up. Another man took the reins of Josephine's horse and the troop started moving again. She found herself dozing off several times, and Rupert told her to lean back against him, which she willingly did. Her next memory was arriving in Dahn where her and the prince boarded a carriage to ride back to Guttenhamm. She remembered hearing Wilhelm coughing while she slept. When they arrived at the castle Leopold was the first one to reach the carriage and found Josephine leaning hard against his brother's arm. The younger brother helped them inside. Josephine made it to the foyer but suddenly she stopped and stood very still. Wilhelm turned in time to see her face go pale and he caught her. She had not completely lost consciousness but could only whisper his name as he lifted her into his arms. He gave a groan as he took a deep breath and then began to climb the staircase. She mumbled something about her lungs burning, and he agreed that his were too. Leopold offered to carry her, but when Wilhelm refused he ran ahead and opened the door to her room where the Queen was waiting inside with the bedspread turned down and pillows stacked up. Wilhelm carried Josephine to her bed and gently laid her down. For a brief second, she opened her eyes to look at him and he smiled and said, "We made it." She closed her eyes and then was asleep. The queen moved to the far side of the bed and was climbing up beside the young woman as Wilhelm stepped away. Hubert had just came into the room when he heard Wilhelm take a stifled breath. Suddenly Leopold lunged to catch his brother as he collapsed onto the foot of the bed.

9

A Handful of Coins

The next morning both Wilhelm and Josephine were with fever, and by that afternoon, pneumonia was setting in. The queen couldn't say which one of the two was more troublesome as both were uncooperative about remaining in bed and kept asking about the other's welfare. During the next few days, servants were placed at the patients' bedsides to keep them still. The doctor visited several times and assured the family that as strong-willed as the patients were it would only be a few days before they fully recovered. The third night, the fevers broke and rest finally came to the castle.

Just before dawn the fourth morning, Josephine awoke to a strange tapping sound. At first she thought it must be a bird at the window, but it seemed to be coming from outside her door. The noise stopped for a few seconds and she had just closed her eyes when she heard it again. The pinging sound was not like anything she had heard before. All grew quiet and then it started again but this time she heard her name faintly called from the other side of the door. Carefully she slid her legs over the edge of the bed and let them touch the floor. Seeing her robe draped over a chair across the room, she stood to her feet. Her legs were weak, but she managed to walk ever so slowly to the chair. She sat down for a moment while she donned her garment and tied the belt around her waist. She heard the tap at the door again and smiled, wondering who was doing such a thing. Slowly she began to walk and had just reached for the door knob when she distinctly heard Wilhelm call her name. The lady opened the door and saw coins scattered on the floor and looked up to see the prince. He was leaning heavily against his door with something clenched in his hand. When he saw the lady he smiled.

"My lady, can you come out to play?" he asked, and Josephine couldn't help but smile in return.

"At such an early hour, my prince?" she answered. He nodded and she began to walk toward him. By the time she made it across the hall, her head was spinning. She reached for the doorframe to steady herself and meagerly he took hold of her arm.

"We are a pitiful pair," he said. As they slowly made their way back inside his room, he explained that he was coming to see her when he became light headed and dared not go further. He couldn't think of a way to get the lady's attention that wouldn't wake the whole castle until he saw the coins on the table beside his door. He hoped that she would hear the sound and would be well enough to come to him. As they took a seat on each end of the couch, they started to laugh at their situation which made both begin to cough. As their spell subsided they rested their heads against the divan for they were too weak to hold them up any longer. They could only talk a few minutes at a time before the coughing returned and finally Wilhelm looked at Josephine and said, "It is good to see you." The lady agreed, raising her head up long enough to give him a smile. It didn't take very long for both to doze off.

With the fevers having broken in the night and Wilhelm and Josephine sleeping soundly, no one thought to check on the invalids any sooner than the usual time that the royal family stirred in the morning. When Katrina went to the young lady's room and found it empty, she was in a panic and went running to the queen's chambers. The king had already risen and had stepped onto the balcony while his wife was getting dressed and two servants were tending to things within the chambers. Upon hearing Katrina cry out that Josephine was not to be found, Agatha took off toward the young lady's room and likewise the other servants were close behind. The scurry of activity had caught the attention of the guard who was at the junction of the hallways and two men servants who were tending lamps. Coins were seen scattered on the floor but was paid no mind as the entourage stepped into Josephine's room to look around. Suddenly a thought came to Agatha, and she went back to the doorway and looked toward her son's room where she saw the door open wide. She motioned to her husband, and together they crossed the hall. The king looked toward the bed where he could see the bedspread pushed to one side, and then he glanced toward the divan. It took only a few steps for Hubert to see the top of Wilhelm's head but Agatha hurried on into the room. She gave a sigh of relief as she saw Josephine draped upon the right end of the divan's armrest and Wilhelm leaning against the left one. Both were sleeping so soundly that they didn't stir as the servants filed into the room behind them. Quickly the king turned and put a finger to his lips signaling the others and then motioned for all to leave the room. Not a whisper was heard among the staff, but patiently they waited for their master to address them.

The king closed the door to the room and clearing his throat, began to speak, "As you all know, Wilhelm and Josephine have been extremely ill these past few days and yet have constantly inquired of each other's welfare." He glanced at Agatha who offered him no thoughts as to how to continue. "I would ask that nothing be said to them about . . ." He couldn't find the right words to use so he started again. "As you have seen, there was distance between them and the door was left open." He hesitated as he was not sure whether to forbid the servants to speak of the incident or beg them not to read into the matter. He was interrupted before he could decide.

"My liege, your son is an honorable man. We have seen nothing here this morning that would make us think otherwise," Louis said, and the others nodded in agreement. The king thanked them for understanding and asked for help to get Josephine back to her room as he opened the door again.

The next few days, the pair were allowed to venture as far as the library for a few hours at a time. To Josephine's relief, the king had not disclosed anything of the mishap at the village to her family.

Hubert had however received a response from Armand that correspondence had been received. Josephine had passed her interview for the commerce position and would be given more specifics in the next week as to what the job would entail, should she agree to it. While recovering, Josephine spent more time getting to know the servants, and Katrina was allowed to stay by her side as much as she wanted. For the first few days, Wilhelm remained with her in the library, and then as he felt better returned to his office. The only drawback to the elder prince being absent was that Leopold took the opportunity to sit with the lady. He had apologized a second time for his behavior, but she trusted him about as far as she could throw him. She had to threaten him several times about sitting too close to her upon the divan, and he would move further away and then a few minutes later would edge back closer. He seemed determined to know more about her, and she was suspicious about whether he was merely curious or trying to gain something to use against her. Finally, she made a bargain that she would answer a question, but he had to answer one in turn from her. He thought it to be entertaining, and the lady was relieved that he was being reasonably civil.

A week after the fever had left, Josephine felt like her strength had returned, and she was taken downstairs and shown a small but adequate office to use and then the king explained the position he was offering. The previous Commerce director had retired during the summer and although the economy was doing well he would rather fill the position to ensure prosperity. The lady had a working knowledge and the particulars concerning the kingdom would be learned during the winter in lieu of the busy spring and summer harvest season. Josephine was thrilled with the idea but admitted she thought herself inadequate for such a responsibility. Hubert assured her she would not be alone in the task and time was on her side. He pointed out that the position would make her an active member of the High Council with voting rights. He watched as her countenance became very grave. Never before had a woman been on the council, and she would receive criticism for it. She would have to be strong and not lash out, but rise above the voices and hold to her integrity.

For a moment, the king wondered if Josephine was going to change her mind as she looked deep in thought but then she spoke.

"If you truly think I know enough to get started, I will accept the position. On the other hand, being a part of the council seems an incredible task, but if it will not come back against you . . . then I am willing to take it on." With a pleased smile the king answered.

"I hoped you would."

By the next week, Josephine was wishing she could have feigned that she was still sick. The king had assigned her a schedule which included meeting with several local businessmen. Hubert was not kidding when he said that she would have to be strong. At the first meeting in the town hall, the men commented under their breath as she was introduced by Karl and she laid out a plan before them. The businessmen refused to answer the lady's questions with one man openly mocking her suggestions. Josephine found herself fighting her temper not to raise her voice demanding that they respect her, but finally she announced another meeting would be held in two days and adjourned the gathering. She was unusually quiet when she returned to the castle, and when asked how her day had been, she just mumbled that it was interesting. The king would have asked her to elaborate but was interrupted with the news of another skirmish along the border. Not that the lady wanted something to be wrong but she was glad the conversation went elsewhere. The next day she accompanied the queen to the town and the trip proved to be a nightmare for the lady. She was stared at and whispers were exchanged as she walked down the street. She had just stepped into a backroom with a shopkeeper to view items when they overheard several women discussing how she was mistress to the prince and how the young lady had been given a position on the council to cover for her deeds, being an ignorant foreign girl who knew only how to do one thing. The shopkeeper was horrified and apologized but the lady was numb with shock and tried to excuse herself. The man was helping her back to the carriage when the queen saw them. She could tell something was wrong, but Josephine would only say that she was tired and begged her majesty to finish her errands while she rested in the carriage. Reluctantly, Agatha left the young lady but questioned the storekeeper. The gossipers had already gone on their way and were nowhere to be seen along the street. The ladies returned to the castle where Josephine retreated to her room. When the queen was alone with the king, she told him what had happened. Karl was called for and asked if anything was said to that effect in the meeting at the town hall the day before. He said no rumors of that nature had been brought up but that the lady received a very cold reception and asked the businessmen to meet with her again the following day. The butler was thanked and dismissed, and the couple began to discuss the accusations and disrespect. If they intervened, it might give the wrong implication, as if she was favored by the family or that she was incapable of defending herself in a position of authority. It was agreed the matter would need careful consideration.

The next day, Josephine awoke with dread in her heart as she thought of meeting with the businessmen. Would they show up to ridicule her, or would they show up at all? One thing for sure, she wasn't going to utter a word of the matter to *any* of the royal family. She didn't know how, but she *had* to gain the respect of the people. After breakfast, everyone went about their tasks and the lady called for a carriage and left for the town. Not to her surprise, no one came to the hall at the appointed time. Disappointed yet in a small measure relieved, she left and decided to stroll through the street. At first she started to go down the usual avenue that she had frequented with the queen, but then fearing an encounter with one of the absent shopkeepers, she turned down a side street. By appearance the shops seemed less impressive, but she found them to be stocked with quality goods at a more reasonable price. As she browsed, an idea occurred to her. These merchants had not been invited to her meeting but perhaps they would be interested in her proposal. Being a stranger she might frighten them away with such talk but not if they first came to know her personally and not as a businesswoman. Josephine spent the rest of the day and the next going from shop to shop visiting with the owners. If she spied anyone working behind the counter or in a stockroom she made a point to inquire about them and introduce herself. Although the progress seemed insignificant, no doors had been shut in her face and the common people were warming up to her nicely. The third morning, she was working her way along another street of outdoor vendors when she happened upon Duke Giovanna. She called to him, and he waved and came to where she was standing. After greeting the lady, he inquired what she was doing in that part of the village as most ladies of court shopped along the main street. Suddenly Josephine found herself confiding that she had encountered resistance and was searching for a way around the obstacle. The duke was not surprised that she had run into opposition but encouraged her to continue in her efforts. He promised to do what he could to influence those he had dealings with and bid goodbye saying he would see her later that afternoon at the castle. He was out of sight when she fully understood what he meant. She was so consumed with her undertaking that she had forgotten that the High Council was to meet at four o'clock that afternoon and then have dinner at six. Quickly she headed back to the castle for she knew the queen would be wondering where she was.

Carriages were already beginning to fill the court, and as Josephine suspected, the queen was anxiously waiting for her return. She was helped into a dress and hurried off downstairs. She was thankful that she didn't have enough time for her nerves to get worked up more than they were for the thought of being with the High Council scared her. Wilhelm was waiting outside the chamber doors and as he led her inside he whispered that the only thing she needed to do that day was acknowledge that she was present when her name was called for role. She received a few glances from gentlemen as she passed by but no one spoke to her. When "Lady Armand" was read she answered only to hear gasps and receive looks from the men sitting nearby. The sound of chairs shifting was heard as many tried to see where the voice had come from but the sentinel continued on with the next name on the list. After the opening formalities and the business of the court had begun Josephine wished she had brought paper and pencil. She knew from reading the Chronicles of the Council that the proceedings were well outlined but being new she also wanted to document descriptions of who was presenting motions to aide her memory. To her surprise Duke Cusall called on her to stand as he introduced her as Duke Callin's replacement as

Commerce Director. Before she could be seated, the sound of grumbling could be heard and she forced a smile as she pretended not to notice. She was rescued from the awkward glares when Duke Dentiel asked to take the floor to present a proposition for a bridge over the Polosin River. The topic drew the attention away from her, and relieved, she sank back into her chair. When the meeting adjourned Josephine wondered if she should run for the door, wander through the crowd, or just remain seated and wait for the others to leave. As she tried to make up her mind, she couldn't help but notice that most of the men were purposely looking the other direction when they passed by her. She was glaring at the worst offenders when the dukes from her interview came near. They expressed how they were looking forward to her serving with them, and she in turn thanked them for the opportunity. The king and princes followed up the procession as they all slowly made their way to the ballroom. A handful of men asked the king for a word in private and the rest of the council joined the ladies who were waiting until dinner was announced.

Unbeknownst to Josephine, Duke Giovanna was very displeased by the reception the lady had received from the merchants along the main street. He wasted no time conveying his opinion to the king with Duke Cusall and Duke Heinds listening closely. Although King Hubert remained quiet as the other men commented his countenance reflected their sentiment. Finally the king spoke, letting them know Josephine had not disclosed the matter to him. Giovanna had expected no less as she was a very determined individual to which Heinds pointed out that is what he liked most about the young lady during the interview. All agreed that a little help might be needed to overcome certain obstacles. At this point, the king said he could not intervene to sway support unless it was extremely dire. Giovanna then asked with his majesty's permission to try an idea concerning the young lady. Hubert trusted the duke's judgment and gave him liberty to do as he pleased, and the four men walked on to the ballroom. Dinner was announced shortly thereafter, and Josephine was seated as she had been at the first dinner, next to Wilhelm. When the meal was over, all returned to the ballroom, and much to her annoyance, Leopold was the first one to ask her to dance. Reluctantly she agreed. To her surprise, he was a perfect gentleman and gave no reason for her to be upset with him on any count. She actually enjoyed the conversation with him. She wondered if he was truly turning over a new leaf or whether he was merely plotting mischief again. Several dances later, she was rescued from the floor by Wilhelm who after they had taken a turn about the room, asked if she would like a glass of punch. They had just refreshed themselves when Giovanna came to them. He nodded respectfully to the prince but turned his attention solely upon Josephine.

"May I be so bold as to ask two things of you this evening, Lady Josephine?" he inquired. Both the lady and the prince gave a puzzling look.

"Yes, my lord. I will do my best to oblige you," Josephine answered.

With a smile, he said, "First, I need you to trust me. Second, I will need you to follow my lead." The young lady desperately wanted to ask questions but didn't get the chance for the duke took her arm and led her across the room to where several men were standing. He introduced her, and then to her surprise, he asked her a very direct question about trading goods within the kingdom. Politely she answered him, and had barely finished when Duke Cusall directed a question to her. She replied and then asked him a question in return. Suddenly Duke Heinds joined in the conversation expanding upon the topic and asked the lady more questions about what she would do concerning the matter. The prince had followed the pair across the floor and was standing behind the lady listening. Suddenly Giovanna made a comment that made Wilhelm cringe, and shockingly the duke asked the lady to give her opinion. The prince desperately wished he was standing where he could have made eye contact with her to signal it was a controversial subject and to be wary. Josephine began to speak, but it was only a moment before she was rudely interrupted by Duke Graham. He disagreed and explained to her why. Several others chided in and when the prince would have changed the subject, Josephine instead spoke up that she had found it otherwise. Her words clashed upon their ears, but not dismayed by the looks upon their faces, she continued on. It was at this time that

Karl came to the prince to say that he was urgently needed by the king. Wilhelm did not want to leave the lady in the midst of such a battle of words, but he knew his father would not call for him on a whim, so he stepped away. As Josephine began to mention detailed accounts of times, places, amounts, and goods, she saw the councilmen look at each other in disbelief. Graham asked where she had gotten this information, and boldly she told them that Duke Callin had left a ledger with more than adequate information. Quickly she questioned them asking if the details were correct, and reluctantly they admitted it was true. She concluded her argument and then hoping to change the subject asked Giovanna about a topic much less controversial. The duke caught the hint, and the conversation was directed away from the lady.

When Wilhelm came near his father, he had expected to see a worried frown upon his face, but instead, he was smiling as he looked upon his subjects.

"What did you need, Father?"

"I need for you to remain here with me a few minutes." He leaned to see around his son, looking across the room and asked, "How is Josephine faring?"

Wilhelm scowled at his father. "So you are aware of what is taking place?" he asked. "They are gnashing at her and you have pulled me away to *let* them do it?"

Hubert returned his gaze to his son and in a serious voice, quietly said, "Giovanna has brought a matter to my attention, and the crown cannot interfere. He has my permission to do what is needed."

"At her expense?" Wilhelm asked, concerned.

"She is strong and will be fine."

"And if she's not fine, then what, Father?" He turned to look across the room where it seemed the conversation was still taking place. "Will she know how to handle those men or be brave enough to stand up to them?" He turned to look at his father again.

"She didn't back down with you, and I believe she won't with them," the king concluded. The words stung as Wilhelm thought back to his argument with the lady a week earlier. His countenance fell, and the king guessed what was upon his son's mind.

"I would give anything to take back the things I said the night we argued," the prince confessed. Hubert laid his hand upon Wilhelm's shoulder, and then the pair turned to watch the crowd in silence.

Josephine was glad the conversation had shifted from attacking her philosophies to other things. She was relieved when Leopold came to her and asked if she would dance with him. When they were on the floor and his arm was around her, he instantly knew something was wrong.

"Josephine, you are trembling. Are you all right?" he asked. She looked up to see genuine worry upon his face, and she couldn't keep the truth from him. She explained about the heated discussion she had been rescued from and thanked him for doing so. He assured her not to be alarmed as the gentlemen she had named could be quite cantankerous. His description of them made her laugh and to her surprise, he told her more about the men she had just left. When the dance ended, he asked if he could call upon her again later in the evening, and she was starting to agree when she abruptly retracted her answer.

"I very much enjoyed our conversation, and, yes, I would . . . No . . . maybe we shouldn't," she added as she nervously looked around the room. Not willing to be turned down, he reached for her hand to ask why not. "Things are bad enough without adding to any rumors that I . . ." Her voice broke off as she had let more slip than she planned to.

"Oh, I see," he said. He let go of her hand but stepped close enough that she could hear him whisper, "Don't want them to think you are my mistress too?" The look she gave made him prepare to be slapped across the face.

"Is there anyone that hasn't heard that rumor?" she squeaked with despair. She felt her face turning red and looked at the floor. "Have I done something to warrant these accusations? Is it something I have said or my clothes? I don't understand." Leopold had thought the lady was a threat to the kingdom, his family, to his brother, but not anymore. He had watched her the past two weeks and had come to the conclusion that she was merely trying to figure out where she belonged in a world that she didn't want to be in. Not only did she not want to be there, but after the confrontation minutes earlier, it seemed the world didn't want her there either. As he held her, he realized how fragile she could be despite her tough talk and boldness. The only real threat the lady could ever pose was to his heart.

Very gently, he answered her, "You have done nothing, nothing but show up." His words caused her to look up at him. "You stood beside Wilhelm at the ball and beside him at dinner and danced with him." He gave her a reassuring look. "That is all you are guilty of. No lady has ever done that before, and people have talked. Pay them no mind, just let it go." Josephine looked at him and smiled as she knew he was right. He bowed to her, and then she watched him slowly walk away. She never would have thought Leopold would be the one to lift her burden.

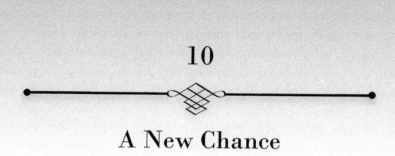

10

A New Chance

The next few weeks, it seemed that all Josephine managed was to keep her head above water as she consistently faced opposition from the well-established, wealthier businessmen. Duke Giovanna confirmed her suspicions when he came to call on her one afternoon. He had met with the proprietors and presented them with a well-outlined agenda that would increase their pocketbooks. They were quick to rave how wonderful it was, and he made a point to ask several times if it was as good as they claimed it to be. They were alarmed when the duke unfolded the bottom portion of the document to reveal it was penned by the Lady Armand and bore the king's seal. Giovanna let the businessmen know that opportunity had knocked, and when they refused to open the door because she wore a dress instead of pants, the lady went elsewhere. A stiff warning was also given that Lady Armand was a council member as well as the director of commerce and their actions were being watched by the High Council and the crown. Giovanna apologized to the lady for the narrowmindedness but assured her that when the lesser known merchants began to reap the reward of her labor, the others would be seeking her out.

After Josephine had visited each business within Guttenhamm several times, she began to venture to the neighboring villages that were within a few hours' ride. The reception was again mixed, but the lady learned not to mention her title until the people knew her better. The people in her father's circle were not friendly and too much talk about anything other than business had been discouraged. There wasn't a need to know the people for *who* they were, but it was different here. Of course, some people just turned their nose up toward her or walked off leaving her standing alone, but that was not always the case. The commoners were very excited about the lady's agenda and asked her to return often. The more she saw the people, the more she became attached to them.

Although it was part of her duties, it concerned Wilhelm when Josephine traveled outside Guttenhamm. He had scolded her several times when she returned later in the afternoon than he liked and was appalled that she would venture out alone. In her defense, she reminded him that she was an excellent rider and capable otherwise, but he was not convinced that she could fend off a robber or a wild beast. He stopped just short of challenging her to prove herself and thankfully so because she would have miserably failed. He pressed her to promise him that she would not go out alone, but she would only agree to take more precautions. The thought of limitations annoyed her, but the truth was that she had not felt safe. She was good with a horse but being thrown was the least of her worries and her dagger was virtually useless unless someone was very close and it could be wrested from her easily.

It was upon this situation that Leopold found his opportunity. Having overheard the latest disagreement between his brother and the lady, he came to Josephine and offered his services to teach her how to not only use a sword but to defend herself otherwise. He cautioned that it would have to be kept secret between the two of them. Her heart leapt at the thought of retaining her independence, but she didn't want her eagerness for him to help her to be misunderstood. Through a lengthy conversation, she made the young man promise to be professional in his dealings with her, and when he had agreed, she accepted the offer. Leopold spoke with the blacksmith about meeting in a backroom of his establishment as often as their schedules permitted. The sessions proved very awkward at first. Leopold would instruct her in a stance, and she would attempt it unsuccessfully and he would explain again and then finally have to physically move her arm or leg into the correct position. She was greatly aggravated at how slowly she caught on, but Leopold didn't seem to mind and was enjoying the time alone with the lady. After a handful of meetings, she began to improve, and when he would attempt to come close to her, she could fend him off. Hand-to-hand combat also proved interesting as thoughts of slapping Leopold's face would cross Josephine's mind as pretending to be attacked forced them into very close quarters. Several times when he pinned her where she couldn't move, she thought he was going to kiss her but he retained his composure. During practice one day he slammed her back against the wall and held her arms at the wrists high above her head. "That was not fair!" she cried out as he had cheated in order to get the upper hand.

"Never let your guard down. I could have just stolen your virtue or have taken your life!" he said as he let go of her allowing her arms to drop suddenly. She could not forget the look in his eyes. He stepped away and retrieved both of their cloaks, and told her it was time to return to the castle. The younger prince didn't say another word to her the rest of the night until they were all walking to their rooms to turn in. He asked for a word, and when they were alone, he apologized for sulking at her the whole evening. "I just want you to understand why I was so upset with you. It's not a game. When you go riding off on your own, it is a matter of your virtue and your life. I don't want harm to come to you." Josephine was almost dumbfounded by his words. Despite his immature flirting, he truly cared for her and was serious about keeping her safe.

"I understand." She hesitated and then added, "I appreciate the patience you have with me. All the time you have spent and what you are doing means a lot." She had just finished when he leaned toward her and kissed her on the cheek. It was a quick but gentle peck, and he didn't linger but bid her good night and excused himself.

It was about this time that the queen asked Katrina to be Josephine's lady in waiting. It seemed strange to the young lady as Josephine considered herself Katrina's equal, not her superior, yet Katrina was not offended by the request. She was excited to be the lady's personal servant and reminded her that she had been helping her every morning and evening already. The most notable difference was that Katrina's wardrobe changed from plain dresses to fancier ones. As far as proper etiquette, Katrina was a quick learner and filled her role perfectly. Josephine asked Leopold to train her friend, but after the first session, he declared she knew plenty. For a short time after her parents had been killed Katrina had lived in precarious situations where she had learned how to defend herself. Thankfully she was recommended to the palace where she was taken in and had remained ever since. Upon hearing that her lady in waiting was travel ready, Josephine did not hesitate to take her with her on her rounds. She knew Wilhelm would have a hard time making her remain in Guttenhamm with two that could wield a sword. The plan was a working well until it abruptly came to a halt one day.

Several of the servants along with Josephine and Katrina went together to the town to buy goods for the castle. They were walking along when suddenly Liza slowed down. The older lady dismissed it as being tired, but Josephine had noticed the lady had grown pale and insisted she sit down for a while. The young lady sent the others on ahead except for Katrina. A few minutes passed and Liza said she was refreshed and stood to her feet to continue on, but the young lady noticed the older woman's eyes looked strange and she could see beads of sweat upon her brow although it was cold outside. Josephine asked for Liza to let Dr. Stehle examine her before they returned to the castle and Katrina ran to get him. By the time they returned, Liza was feeling weak again, and it took but a moment for the doctor to insist that she come to his office. As they were helping her to the carriage, she collapsed, losing consciousness. Josephine guessed that it was the lady's heart. At the clinic, Dr. Stehle administered medicine and said the patient needed to remain there with him. Liza had suffered a minor heart attack and precautions had to be taken to keep her from having another one. As they walked outside, Dr. Stehle asked Josephine to visit him again that week as he wanted to discuss an important matter with her. The queen was moved to tears upon the news and most of the staff was upset. By Dr. Stehle's order, Liza should not receive visitors as it would be too much excitement for her weak condition. It was decided that Katrina would remain with the housekeeper at the clinic until the doctor released her from his care. And so it was that Josephine was minus her closest companion.

Two mornings later, snow flurries were in the air but it didn't last. Josephine was told the winter precipitation would come and go and not to take it seriously for another month. Then snow would fall more frequently, and would remain on the ground till February. The temperature would gradually get colder as well. As excited as she was for a real taste of winter, as Picardell's was mild, she dreaded the thought of staying indoors for any length of time. For now, she just pushed the thought aside as the flurries melted away and focused her efforts on building her repertoire in the kingdom.

Josephine did stop by the clinic later in the week to see Liza, who was resting comfortably, and to inquire what the doctor wanted to speak with her about. The gentleman began by commending the young lady for her speedy diagnosis that had in fact saved the older lady's life. Josephine tried to dismiss her actions as nothing worthy of mentioning, but he did not agree.

The lady was looking at shiny instruments upon a tray when the older man asked, "How are your sewing skills, my lady?" Josephine stopped and looked at him. The question caught her by surprise, but she had no doubt the doctor had been around her enough already to know she was not a typical, proper lady.

"I guess I can sew fair enough," she answered him, not able to imagine why he would ask her such a thing. Suddenly the door flew open and three men came rushing in with the man in the middle bleeding heavily. His arm had been sliced open by a piece of metal while they were repairing a building. Dr. Stehle instructed them to place the patient on the examining table while he washed his hands and returned to them. Josephine had stepped back along one wall to give the men plenty of room, but suddenly she heard her name called as the doctor told her to wash and assist him. Without hesitation, she did as she was told and began handing him the instruments he requested. As he cleaned the wound, he explained that the two gentlemen who normally assisted him were checking on patients. The doctor sutured the wound and after giving instruction concerning changing the bandages he sent the patient and his friends on their way. He asked Josephine to remain a little while as he again turned the conversation to sewing.

"I can sew, but I don't like to." She caught the doctor give a sly grin at her reply.

"So the sight of blood doesn't bother you?" he asked as he took a seat at his desk across the room. She could tell he was leading up to something, and after a few minutes, he began to tell that he wanted her to think about training with him, as an extra assistant. There were times that catastrophes occurred that left him short-handed, and he thought she would do the job nicely. And he somberly added that in the event war broke out, the need for trained staff would be dire. She agreed to consider his request, and would let him know within a week. As she was turning to leave, she commented with a mischievous smile.

"It does me good to know those tedious hours I spent learning to embroider pillows could be put to better use," Dr. Stehle agreed and invited her to come and see him again. It took only a day for Josephine to return to his office to give her answer as she greatly wanted to become a part of the doctor's team. She did remind him that she had other responsibilities that she had committed to. She confessed that the royal family might think it too much with her other duties, so the two agreed it would not be openly mentioned unless the need arose.

And so it seemed that for every good day Josephine had, she was rewarded two bad ones. The harder she tried, it seemed the worse it turned out, and then out of nowhere, she would have someone approach her with an opportunity as Dr. Stehle had. A few weeks later, Josephine happened to overhear Wilhelm telling the king his business the following morning was a distance away and he wouldn't return until after dark. With Josephine having visited all the local merchants she needed to travel farther from the town to continue her rounds. It irritated her to ask for help, but she swallowed her pride as she knew the prince would prevent her from journeying north without a military escort. Seeing an opportunity, the lady asked the prince to give her safe passage. He was pleased by her asking but was hesitant to approve of the journey to Lithel alone. Finally, he agreed and the next morning the party left at dawn. When they parted where the road turned off to Lithel, Wilhelm reminded her to not only be safe but to be back by three o'clock or else he would come looking for her. She didn't know which bothered her more, asking for his help or being threatened as if she was a child. She reached Lithel within an hour and quickly made her rounds among the traders and then headed on toward the foothills, for she had the notion to visit an establishment that served as both a mercantile and hunting lodge. She knew it would take more time to ride there than to update her records, but she had promised the old couple that ran the place that she would return at least once before winter set in. Finally, she came to a clearing and saw the massive cabin up ahead. As she rode up to the porch of the main building, she dismounted and tied her horse to the post. She heard whinnying from the direction of the stables and turned to see several steeds lined up at the feeding trough. Stepping onto the porch, she knocked on the door and called out the names of the proprietors. When no answer was received, she tried the knob and let herself in.

"My lady," Rebekah exclaimed. "We were not expecting you out this way." She motioned to a lad to come to her side from across the room. Josephine smiled as she went to the fireplace and began to remove her gloves to warm her hands. Rebekah whispered to the boy and sent him outside. Nervously the older woman watched the door as she came to the lady's side and took her cloak.

With a quiver in her voice, she asked about the ride and the weather and then finally Josephine asked, "Rebekah, is everything all right? You seem on edge."

The older woman sighed and then gave a smile. "Yes, my apologies. Johann's customers today are a bit temperamental, that's all. You know how people can be with business, wanting their way, their price," she explained.

"Oh, yes, I saw the horses. It makes me happy that business is well for you," the young lady commented. Suddenly the front door opened, and Johann stepped inside, quickly shutting the door behind himself. He bowed to the lady and then apologized as he needed a word alone with his wife. The old man's face was red, and Josephine would have been worried except for what Rebekah had already said about the visitors' mood. Josephine was courteously led into the kitchen where a cup of coffee was poured for her while she waited. When Rebekah returned to the other room, she found her husband nervously peering out the window, a frown upon his face.

"What are you going to do?" she whispered as she came near.

"There is only one thing I can do. Give them what they want for that price." He glanced out the window again. "They won't kill us until we are of no use to them, and right now they need us."

"I don't like this. Can't we leave or at least send for help?" Rebekah asked still whispering.

"I told you they have been watching us. I am sure they will leave a man here this time, especially since . . . Of all the days for her to show up." He shook his head and glanced toward the kitchen. "I am worried what they will do to her."

"Maybe they won't think anything about her being here. What they don't know—" She was interrupted by her husband.

"They saw her ride up and watched her until she was inside. Just now they were looking her horse over. They are not stupid. They know the mare is from the king's stables."

"Then what should we do? Do you think they will take her with them?" she asked with a shudder.

"I don't know. Wait," he said as he saw someone coming to the porch. "Keep the girl in the kitchen and have her help you. I will tell them you are making lunch for them. Just keep her out of sight," he said no more as he went to the door and hurried outside.

Shaking, Rebekah returned to the kitchen and asked the lady to help prepare the meal. It did not take much for Josephine to agree as she was so excited that the couple had a larger than normal crowd.

Outside, Johann greeted his visitors again.

"Lord Oskaar, my wife and I will accept your offer. To extend our hospitality, she is preparing a meal for you and your men and it will be ready within half an hour, if you are able to wait." As he spoke, he prevented the man from moving closer to the door. The old man's actions were not subtle and not well received.

"Johann, if I did not know better, I would think you didn't want me going inside." As the man spoke, he turned in the direction of his men and gave an evil-sounding laugh.

"My lord, I will do anything you want me to so long as her ladyship is not made aware of the situation and is kept out of this matter," the old man begged, causing Oskaar to turn and look at him.

"And who is this lady?" he asked. Johann hesitated for a moment but knew they would drag it from him if he refused to answer.

"Lady Armand, my lord. She comes once a month to check on our trading business as she does all who buys or sells within the kingdom. Please, my lord, keep her out of this matter. She doesn't have to know you were here. She will be on her way shortly I am sure. Please . . ."

"She is of no significance to me. Whether or not—"

Suddenly a voice was heard from among his men.

"But she is to me." All turned as a man clad in black from head to toe stepped forward. "Is this Josephine Armand that you speak of?"

"Yes, it is, sir." The man in black motioned to Oskaar who quickly went to him. They whispered a few moments, and then Oskaar walked back to the porch.

"Her ladyship must remain in the kitchen and be kept ignorant of my men and our dealings. My lord also wishes to observe the lady without her knowledge. Is there a way for that to happen?" Johann glanced toward the man in black, wondering what the strange request meant but nodded to him. "You may go and tell them we will come in shortly." With a wave of his hand, the visitors turned and went back to the stables, all except for the man in black. Johann wasn't sure whether to be relieved by the sudden change or be more alarmed than ever for Josephine. Quietly he led the man behind the cabin, taking him to the door of a storage room just off the kitchen. The lady could be seen through the spaces between the boards of the wall. Johann excused himself and went through another door into the kitchen and promptly asked to speak with Rebecca alone again. Josephine was stirring a pot of soup upon the stove and didn't look up. Johann explained the situation at which his wife was equally disturbed but agreed they were not in a position to do anything but follow the orders. The couple stepped back into the kitchen where Johann began to explain that he would prefer that Josephine remain in the kitchen instead of attending the visitors.

"Johann, I am not so high and mighty that I cannot help serve your guests," she said as she loaded plates onto a platter.

"No, my lady, it's not that at all," he said, nervously looking in the direction of the storage room. "These men are of the rougher sort. Hear them now as they are coming in." He hoped to convince her to remain out of sight. Deep voices could be heard mingled with laughter as heavy footsteps echoed, and chairs were moved as the men were sitting down at the tables.

"I have been around men that lacked manners," she said as she filled a pitcher with fresh water from the bucket and took it to another platter.

"Not like these, my lady. I must insist you remain here in the kitchen." Josephine stopped what she was doing and looked at the old man. She could not bear to go against his wishes. He tilted his head as he looked at her. "Have pity on an old man who thinks highly of you. I would not allow my own daughter to be looked at as these men would do. You should not be subjected to such things."

"All right," she said slowly. "I will stay here. But I need to leave within the hour and you must realize that I will have to leave the kitchen then whether or not they are still here." She warned him with a smile. As the couple began to make trips in and out of the room to serve their guests, Josephine called for the lad to fetch her ledger from her saddle bag. A few minutes later, the boy returned and placed it on the table. Josephine went to the sink and began to wash dishes as she waited on Rebekah. Several minutes passed before the older woman returned seeming flustered, but Josephine guessed she had been haggled by the guests.

"Rebekah, if you can spare a few minutes, I need to do what I came here for." The woman agreed and sat down across the table from the lady. Josephine began to ask questions and record the figures not noticing the older woman look toward the storage room every little bit. Rebekah had just poured another cup of coffee when she took the young lady's hand.

"Josephine dear, why did you venture this far north? I mean, with all the unrest, were you not worried something could happen to you?" As she finished speaking, she found herself glancing at the wall again. Josephine smiled and squeezed the woman's hand.

"I have not come this far *entirely* alone," the lady replied at which Rebekah gave a soft gasp. "The prince had affairs in Ramsdon this morning, and I took advantage of his trip and joined him. Of course he wanted to know what my business was and I told him I needed to make rounds in Lithel."

"Why Lithel is a good hour away!" the older woman exclaimed. Her mind raced to the man watching them, afraid that Josephine had revealed too much. The young lady would be easy prey for him, but what could she do or say with the stranger watching their every move?

"Yes, I know," Josephine said, rising to her feet. "And it doesn't need to get back to the prince that I was here." She pushed her chair toward the table. "Speaking of which, I need to head back or he will come with a regiment to look for me. And it would be terribly miserable to ride all the way back to Guttenhämm with him upset with me." She laughed as Rebekah stood up.

"I beg you not to do such a thing again. There are men who look to take advantage of ladies upon the road," the older woman pleaded as she desperately took hold of the lady's arm, realizing she was about to leave. "Please stay a little longer, at least until they have gone." Josephine stopped and gave the woman a look. It was not like her to act this way.

"Is it that these men should not see me, or am I not to see them?" she asked bluntly. Rebekah stepped back with surprise. "What business have they with Johann again?" Nervously the older woman looked toward the door.

"I didn't ask, he just . . . Sometimes it is better not to ask," she said in a whisper turning her gaze to the floor.

"But it is *my* business to do the asking," Josephine replied. Suddenly the older woman tightened her grip upon the lady's arm.

"Please . . . don't ask. If you must go, then leave quickly. Go and don't stop to look at anyone or anything until you are safe in Guttenhamm. Just get on your horse and go about your business." Josephine pushed Rebekah back to see her face. There was a wretched paralyzing fear in her eyes. Suddenly as the difference between night and day, the older woman's countenance changed and she broke into a wide smile and shook her head. "I am so sorry, my dear. Don't mind this old woman and her foolish worries. I've heard one too many stories by the fire lately for my own good. Those men may be rough around the edges, but they will not harm you." She began to walk almost pulling Josephine along as she took her from the kitchen and walked into the other room going past the men who were still seated at tables. Josephine didn't have time to look at them as the older woman moved her along quickly, talking as they went and only took a breath when they came to the lady's horse. "Do go on now and don't make his majesty worry about you. He won't know you were here. Your secret is safe with us. And I am sorry if I frightened you." Johann was a few steps behind them carrying Josephine's cloak and ledger and hurried to catch up to give her a boost into her saddle. Rebekah added, "Thank you for coming to see us today. But please, don't chance the weather next month. I will keep good records and let you know all that has happened come spring. Promise me now that you won't risk it." Josephine gave her word and said goodbye. She was confused as to what had made the woman act so strangely, but maybe it was just foolishness as she said. Josephine couldn't help but feel like she was being watched though and before the cabin was completely out of sight, she slowed down enough to turn and look over her shoulder. She saw the lone silhouette of a man in black standing just in front of the porch.

The young lady had stayed much longer than she planned and found herself riding hard to make it back to Ramsdon in time. She hoped that Wilhelm had not gone to Lithel early to look for her. She sighed with relief when she rounded the last bend and found his party as she had left it that morning.

"I was beginning to wonder," he said as she brought her horse to a halt.

"Does anything ever go as I plan?" she replied. "It is five till according to my watch."

"Yes," he said. "But three o'clock was an hour past when I would have liked to have returned." Wilhelm turned and motioned to his men.

"Then next time tell me the real time I should be back by," she quipped as she turned her horse in the opposite direction. She saw him give a sigh and then shake his head as he began to smile.

"I wanted to give you a little more time since you did ask for my protection."

Ah, she thought, *so, he was intentionally being difficult with me but more importantly my plan to appeal to his weakness worked.* "Well, thank you," she said. "I appreciate it more than you know." And with that, he motioned again and they all headed home.

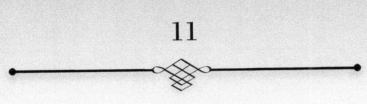

11

Old Friends

A month had passed since Liza's spell with her heart. The older lady had finally been released from the clinic but on the condition of light duty. Katrina remained by her side, only helping Josephine in the mornings and evenings until Liza was stronger. It had been a typical day in Guttenhamm with Josephine visiting businesses to record information concerning sales and the demand for goods. About four o'clock in the afternoon, she called it a day and headed back toward the castle, but as she crested the long hill leading up to the royal residence, she saw an unfamiliar but stately carriage at the main entrance. Visitors were commonplace so she didn't think too much of it as she turned her horse toward the stables. She was glad to be back and looked forward to getting warm again as although the snow of last week had melted quickly, the bitter chill in the air had remained.

Josephine was just making her way across the gravel road and onto the lawn when she noticed two men standing upon the back terrace but did not recognize them as anyone she knew. For a moment, she thought about changing her route and going back to the front entrance to avoid the strangers but then curiosity took hold and she remained on her course walking straight toward them. The closer she came, she could tell they knew each other well by how they leaned toward each other as they spoke and they were very aware that she was coming toward them. She was almost to the steps when they called out to her.

"Good afternoon, my lady," the taller one said. They bowed to her and she curtsied.

"Good afternoon, gentlemen. How do you do?" she answered.

"Fine, very fine," the shorter of the two men answered as Josephine began walking toward the door that opened into the dining hall. "We have not had the pleasure of making your acquaintance." He reached for the doorknob and motioned the lady to enter ahead of him.

"Yes, I was thinking the same," she replied. It seemed the young man was familiar with the castle and where the door led.

"I am Rhys and this is—"

"Liam," the other man interjected, and Josephine respectfully nodded to him. "And you are?" he asked as the three stepped into the dimly lit room.

"Josephine Armand," the young lady replied as she kept walking toward the far end of the room, forcing the gentlemen to have to follow her to keep the conversation going.

"It is apparent you are acquainted with the residence." Rhys pointed out as he tried to slow the lady by stepping between her and the fast approaching doorway.

"Yes," she said and paused as she could go no further. "This is my home, thank you." She attempted to step to the left of the gentleman to go around him. Not willing to let her pass just yet, he stepped to block her and with a grin upon his face laughed as he spoke.

"We have known this family all of our lives and have visited Wilhelm and Leopold throughout the years and yet we never knew they had a *sister*," he said with emphasis upon the last word. If he had not been smiling from ear to ear and trying to be so friendly, Josephine would have taken offence to him preventing her from continuing on, but as it was, she returned a smile.

With a mischievous laugh, she replied, "Who said I was their sister?" The second man had stepped beside the other as she spoke and at her words he gave a hearty laugh. Suddenly she could hear the voices of servants from the hall and her sense of duty returned.

"Gentlemen, it would be nice to visit with you both, but I am on an errand and short on time." She had hoped her words would have caused them to step aside allowing her to pass, but as they exchanged glances, she knew it would take more to move them. "Will you be staying for dinner tonight?" she asked, taking hold of her skirt and swishing it forward as she cautiously lifted her foot to take a step.

At these words, they both answered, "Yes."

Seeing her moment of opportunity, she added, "Very well, I shall see you then." To her relief they parted, stepping aside to let her pass.

Rhys spoke up, "We are looking forward to it, my lady." And he bowed as she quickly hustled on to the hallway. She could feel their eyes looking her over. This kind of attention would have infuriated her a few months ago, but now she only found herself blushing. She hurried on to her office and when inside, she shut the door tightly. She let out a sigh as she wondered who these men were as she could not recall any mention of family by those names. She sat down at her desk and began filing away her papers from the day, but her mind kept drifting off. The visitors seemed to be close in age to that of the princes, and they were equally as handsome. Because of their apparel and manners, she would guess them to be of nobility and not hesitating to stop her would include having authority to some degree. Military ranking could be ruled out as the carriage at the entrance would have included guards and the gentlemen's jackets would have born some type of markings. Finishing her task, she left her office. Supper was at five-thirty that evening, and it was a quarter till five already. She had just cleared the top of the staircase and was headed toward the private wing when she noticed the two gentlemen and the princes standing just outside the library. They were so engrossed in conversation that they didn't notice the lady approaching. She could hear bits and pieces of what was being said with laughter mingled in. She was almost upon them when Wilhelm saw her.

"My lady," he said, which caused the others to turn in her direction.

"Good afternoon," she replied. Again she was torn between remaining to find out who the strangers were and heading to her room to get ready for supper.

"I hear you have met Rhys and Liam," Leopold said as full attention was given to Josephine. She felt herself blushing as she was not expecting the four of them to look at her in the manner they were.

"Did you complete your task, my lady?" Rhys asked as he stepped forward and reached for her hand. Surprisingly she lifted it to him.

He was just about to kiss it when quickly she pulled it back and replied, "Yes, yes, I did." She swallowed hard as she slipped her hand completely from his grasp. "I must again apologize as I cannot stay. I am sure her majesty will not allow me at the supper table looking disheveled." And at the mention of the queen, she looked toward Wilhelm. She caught a sly grin cross his face as he knew she was trying to wiggle her way out and needed his help to escape.

"Yes, my lady, that would be true." He took a step back and gave an exaggerated motion for her to move along.

"You will be at supper tonight then?" Liam asked as Josephine began to walk away.

"Most assuredly," she replied, not daring to look back at them. She was almost to her door when she heard the four begin to laugh.

The men had watched the young lady hurry down the hallway, and when he thought she was far enough away not to hear what he said, Liam spoke, "If that is disheveled, we are in for a treat tonight."

At which comment, Rhys added, "She is lovely . . . Absolutely lovely . . ." The words spoken were not offensive or belittling of the lady but struck both of the princes in a way they could not explain. Having the lady residing with the royal family had been an enlightening experience. Leopold's affections had been declared for the lady on numerous occasions pledging to wait patiently for her to reciprocate his feelings. The failed efforts had forced him to take a more serious approach not only with Josephine but his responsibilities to his family and kingdom. Josephine was pleased with the changes she saw but still exercised caution as he had moments that romance overtook him. Wilhelm too had taken an interest in the lady but tried to convince himself that it was on a professional basis and they were merely friends. He had to admit that her presence beside him offered the perfect excuse to keep husband-hungry ladies at bay although rumors had circulated concerning the pair. In the past, the heir to the throne had been careful not to remain close to other ladies during social events to avoid misunderstandings, but he also had not found a lady who held his attention as Josephine had. Perhaps it was the lady's thirst for adventure or that she shared interest in the same topics as he did or maybe it was that she was not afraid for her opinion to differ from his. He treasured the fact that she saw beyond the crown and spoke to him as an ordinary man when they were in private chambers. As hard as he tried not to, he often caught himself stealing glances of the lady and watching with admiration as she went about her work. She had humbly risen to her new station in life, always helping those around her and was content to remain supportive behind the scenes, not having to be the center of attention. Both princes enjoyed the lady's company and suddenly felt the need to defend her.

"A word of caution, my friends," Wilhelm stated quickly. The brothers turned their attention toward the princes.

"Yes," Leopold added. "She bites." The puzzled look on their faces at his comment was genuine as they could not match the statement to what they had seen of the politeness of the lady.

"Yes, and she will not hesitate to leave the print of her hand across your face," Wilhelm said as he took a few steps in the direction of his room.

"And she hits hard enough that it hurts," Leopold said, reaching up to rub his face as he recalled the kiss he had tried to steal from her.

"By experience, you both know this?" Rhys asked at which all four burst into laughter. Nodding to each other, they parted ways to freshen up before going downstairs to eat.

Supper proved to be enlightening to say the least. Although they had never been mentioned before, Josephine discovered Rhys and Liam were the best of friends with the princes and would come to visit for a week or more several times during a year. When the meal was over the group migrated across the hall to the parlor where in a matter of moments the men had made themselves comfortable, sinking into the chairs, resuming conversation again. Rhys and Liam's parents were chatting with the king and queen, and all seemed to be enjoying the evening. Josephine thought it was nice to see the royal family not discussing business or affairs of state. Not too much had been said in Josephine's direction, but she wasn't minding as she was learning so much just listening to the others. Suddenly she heard her name and sat up straight, as she had sunk into the couch she was on.

"Josephine," Wilhelm said as he rose to his feet. "Would you mind if we moved our conversation to the veranda?" As he finished speaking, he came to where she was and offered a hand to help her to her feet. The other young men had risen to their feet and were moving toward the doorway.

"The veranda sounds fine to me," she answered. "If you want me to tag along."

She had just moved past Wilhelm, but he gently took hold of her arm, and leaning toward her, he softly answered, "I wouldn't have asked if I didn't want you with us." They had worked together for several months and although because of Wilhelm's height it was common for his whisper to fall upon Josephine's ears, this time the hair on the back of her neck tingled as he spoke. As he wound her arm through his, she wondered if he had done it on purpose. They walked outside together where they found a fire had already been built in the pit upon the far end of the stoned terrace. They were almost seated when Josephine decided it was too cold for her.

"If you will permit me, I think I need my cloak from the foyer. Shall I get all of yours as well?"

"Yes, thank you. We will get situated," Wilhelm answered as he and Liam reached for each end of a bench and moved it closer to the fire. Leopold and Rhys picked up several chairs and moved them closer as well. Josephine watched them for a moment and then turned and retraced her steps inside. When she reached the foyer, she found the men's cloaks but hers was missing. With a sigh, she headed up the staircase as she knew Katrina must have returned it to her room. She hurried along only concentrating on not tripping on the cloaks in her arms. She was three steps down the stairs when she abruptly came to a halt as she realized Rhys was standing in front of her. He put his arms out to keep her from falling.

"I wondered what happened to you," he said with a smile as he steadied her.

"I had to retrieve my cloak from my room. I'm sorry I almost knocked you over. I wasn't paying attention." Very carefully, he lifted the garments from her arms and laid them over his shoulder. The lady started to take a step, but he didn't move and as she looked at him she realized he was detaining her on purpose. "Shall we rejoin the others?" she asked.

"Yes," he replied, but making sure her eyes were fixed upon his he added. "If you will but answer me one question." At that moment, Josephine knew his question was personal because of the way he looked at her. It made the young lady turn her gaze from him and she felt her face growing warm as she blushed. She heard an unfamiliar waver in her voice as she spoke.

"Nothing personal, I hope." And as she finished, she looked back into his eyes searching for what secrets they held.

"Well . . ." he broke off and looked away to give a laugh. "Well, maybe there were two questions that I wanted to ask you." And he returned his gaze to hers. Josephine could not help but smile at his gesture. The innocent way he was flirting had not offended her, and she was enjoying his attention.

"You know," she replied with a playful air, "personal matters of the royal family are *not* to be discussed." She tried to sound matter-of-factly.

"Uh, yes, I know this," he answered as he shifted on his feet. He was pleased that she seemed flattered by his actions thus far.

"First question?" she asked.

"How is it that you are so beautiful, my lady?" Josephine had supposed his questions would be something of the sort but she found herself laughing aloud.

"Oh my." When she could make a straight face again, she asked, "And second question?"

Rhys continued to shift on his feet as if nervous and finally began to explain himself very slowly and in a pleading tone. "In conversation earlier this evening, I learned that you are not related to the Von Strauss family." He hesitated as both smiled at the apparent truth. "And also that you are not married nor betrothed." Josephine felt the smile begin to leave her face as he continued. "With great humility, I want to ask . . ." his voice broke off as he watched the reaction upon the young lady's face and he could feel her beginning to pull away from him. She knew she shouldn't, but she dreaded what he might say next. "My lady, before I go further." He stopped in midsentence and let out a sigh. "Before I get my hopes up, I just want to know if you are even remotely interested in getting to know me better." Suddenly Josephine realized that she had closed her eyes. Could he be merely asking permission to speak with her instead of jumping to drastic things like courtship? When she opened her eyes, she found he was staring at the floor, as if afraid of what her answer would be.

She was not expecting his insecurity, and softly she answered him, "Rhys." He looked up at her. "You seem like a respectable gentleman." She hesitated as she searched for the right words. So many thoughts crossed her mind in those few seconds. She could hear Wilhelm reminding her that she was at liberty to do as she pleased while residing in Gutten, which included entertaining suitors as she so desired. He had encouraged her to have her own circle of friends that had nothing to do with affairs of state. One day, she would find herself enjoying the company of a true gentleman to the point she would find herself not despising all men as she had in the past. Could it be true, was she longing to know more about Rhys? She had to admit she was attracted to him, and she was not upset by his forward actions as she was in the case of Leopold. Even now, standing here with him, she did not want to slap him nor run away. There was only one other man who she had been this comfortable being close to. "Perhaps." She heard herself whisper, and she bit her lip softly.

"Perhaps is good," he replied. For a moment, she felt as if he was subtly moving toward her and then she realized that he really was. The fear of him kissing her caused Josephine to panic, and she quickly stepped to one side and blurted out.

"They will be missing us. Shall we return?" Her reaction caught the young man off guard, and he did as she asked. He would have liked to have taken her hand as they walked back but was afraid to after startling her. Things might not have gone exactly as he hoped, but he was satisfied that she hadn't given him an all-out no. A few minutes later, they were back on the veranda where the others were standing beside the now blazing fire. Josephine saw Wilhelm shoot her a concerned look as she stepped to warm herself, and Rhys sat down on the bench. She had stood for quite a while by the fire just listening to stories of boyhood adventures when Wilhelm called to her as he moved to the couch.

"Come sit down, you are making me weary." He patted the cushion. "I would stand but I might end up pinning your skirt tail down." Without a second thought, she joined him on the couch, but when she looked over at Rhys, he had a strange expression upon his face. She and the prince had ridden in the carriage together so many times that she was used to being close beside him. Once while on a longer trip with the king and queen, she had slept against his shoulder most of the way home. Suddenly she wondered if it bothered Rhys for her to be so close to another man. She pretended that her skirt was rumpled, and she rose up to adjust it and sat down again placing several inches between them this time. The prince, totally unaware of her dilemma, had already rejoined the conversation. She listened closely and was starting to understand what subject they were talking about when to Josephine's dismay, Wilhelm stretched his arm out behind her across the top of the couch. She held her breath as she looked toward Rhys who had noticed where the prince's arm now lay. Just when Josephine thought her situation could not get any more awkward, Wilhelm turned his attention to her.

"I haven't had the chance to ask how your day went."

How my day went? she thought. *Really? Did he have to ask me now, right now?* She felt herself fidget as she glanced toward Rhys whose eyebrows were now raised. Quickly she answered Wilhelm.

"My day went well, thank you." She hoped it was enough that he would resume visiting with the others.

"Oh," he replied. "That's good." Josephine was growing anxious. Why did she go and sit down beside him anyways. Why hadn't she sat next to Rhys? He was the only one on the bench and it was closer to the fire than she was now. She was still scolding herself when suddenly Wilhelm leaned toward her, their faces within inches of each other. "Are you warm enough, Josephine?" he asked in a soft voice. "I can move you closer to the fire if needed." Suddenly she felt horrible for wishing she wasn't sitting beside him as he was only looking out for her.

She smiled and answered him, "I will let you know when I get cold." He gave a smile and turned his attention back to the conversation. Although she may have wanted to move beside Rhys, she just could not do it, thinking how loyal Wilhelm was to her. If Rhys was truly interested in a relationship with her, he would have to try again on another day as she was resigned not to betray Wilhelm's friendship that night.

The stories continued on for hours with much laughter and joyous memories being shared. Josephine was glad that she was not pulled into the storytelling for although she had been adventurous anything the lady had done paled in comparison with what these four had been through. Leopold had just started a tale about the old cemetery north of Guttenhamm when Josephine closed her eyes as she pictured the scene he was describing, having been at that very place a month earlier. The next thing she knew, Wilhelm was calling her name softly as he gently rubbed her hands.

"Josephine, wake up long enough for us to walk to our chambers." Slowly she opened her eyes to see him leaning toward her. He had noticed her drifting off and had intertwined their arms to keep the lady from falling forward as they did when sleeping in the carriage. Thirty minutes had passed before the others decided it was time to turn in. So much for not looking like she was attached to Wilhelm, she thought. She heard Rhys's voice.

"Here, let me offer you my arm, my lady. I can help you to your chambers." At which he came and stood in front of her. To her surprise, Wilhelm pushed her up toward the man and then rose to his feet.

"Keep a tight hold of her so she doesn't fall," he instructed.

"Yes, sir," Rhys replied as if he had just won a prize and smiled at Josephine who was now clinging to his arm. Maybe the night turned out all right, she thought. The five were rather quiet as they went upstairs. Liam said good night and went to his room while the others went on down the dimly lit hallway.

Rhys and Josephine had just reached her door when he spoke, "I hope you had a pleasant evening."

"I did," she replied, looking up at her escort.

"I am looking forward to the next few days." He added, to which the lady agreed. "Although the company is good, I hope our schedules can afford some time together . . . alone." She could tell he wanted to say more, but whether it was just how to say goodnight or something else he was struggling. Suddenly she wondered if he would kiss her. The thought almost made her ill yet part of her was curious. Would the fear of a man kissing her finally be laid to rest? How would she know unless she let him do it? Suddenly Josephine decided it was too soon to do anything of the sort, and she let go of his arm.

"Perhaps we can," she replied. "Thank you for helping me to my room. Good night." Rhys took the hint and bowing bid the lady good night and strode back down the hallway. Josephine stood there for a moment watching him and was just stepping inside her chambers when out of the corner of her eye she saw Wilhelm's door close.

Morning came only too soon for the family and guests and with the late night it seemed a chore to make it to the breakfast table. The king and princes were a few minutes late, and Josephine could tell by the looks on their faces that something had happened. After everyone had eaten and they were leaving the table, the king exchanged glances with Wilhelm and then the prince asked for a word alone with Josephine. Another skirmish along the border had been reported and he and Leopold would be leaving in the next few minutes. He asked Rhys and Liam to go with her on rounds that day as he would be taking all available soldiers as several scouting parties were needed. Trying not to seem too pleased with the sudden turn of events, the lady assured the prince that she could make the arrangement work.

Josephine had contemplated postponing her rounds until their guests had left, but now she could spend time with them while not getting behind in her work. It seemed Rhys had staked claim to any affections the lady would have and although Liam was free with flatteries toward Josephine it was not with the same intentions as his brother. Though not entirely alone, the time spent that morning had helped the lady learn a lot about Rhys with the nervousness from the night before having faded. Deciding to eat lunch in the town, Josephine picked her favorite restaurant to entertain her guests. The sight of the lady with the strangers drew attention, and although she explained to the hostess that they were the princes' friends, she still received glares from the kitchen. It made her remember the first few times she was with Wilhelm in the town with all eyes watching to see if she truly was his love interest. Her mind returned back to the present, and she smiled at Rhys who was sitting across the table from her. They should finish the rounds in time to walk together upon the grounds of the castle before supper. They were leaving the restaurant when Rhys took her by the hand and asked for her to spare a few minutes before she resumed business. He gave his brother a look, and Liam excused himself to a shop across the street.

They had barely begun to walk when Rhys began to talk. "There is something I feel I must ask you about," he said gravely. Josephine could feel her eyebrows rising as she anticipated it to be another personal question. "Something that I have noticed." He stopped walking. She wished he hadn't for depending upon the topic, she might not want to look him in the eye. "You and Wilhelm and Leopold are close, are you not?

"Yes," she replied, tensing up.

"Like brothers and sisters?" he added, turning toward the young lady as she feared he would.

"Yes, of course," she said, managing a smile.

"You and Leopold," he said, watching her face.

"Yes . . ."she answered and smiled again. *What is he wanting to know?* she wondered, looking hard at him but trying to seem relaxed.

"And you and Wilhelm." His voice trailed off as he spoke, and he raised a questioning eyebrow.

"What do you want to know, Rhys?" she asked bluntly. "We are all very close." And with that, she looked down and fidgeted with the buttons on her dress.

"I have just noticed things said and done between you and Wilhelm that would make a man think otherwise."

"Otherwise how?" she questioned, now feeling her face blushing with irritation. Rhys expected the response and wished he didn't have to mention it but he needed to know if she had feelings for the prince before he fell harder for the lady.

"Like your feelings toward each other are more than that of a brother for a sister." And as he finished, he let go of the lady's hand and took a step back to give her space. She wanted to deny the allegation yet the truth stung so badly that all she could do was stand there. She knew her feelings for Wilhelm were different that those she had for Phillipe, but she was not madly in love with him. She was determined not to destroy her day with Rhys with a poor choice of words just because her relationship with Wilhelm was complicated.

"Let me explain," she said and cleared her throat, preparing for what she expected would be a lengthy statement. She glanced away looking down the street as she searched for words but suddenly she noticed an old man being pushed. Immediately all her attention was fixed upon the scene unfolding as she recognized the man as Hartle, the fruit vendor. Quickly she looked to Rhys. "I hope you are good with your sword," she stated as she pointed down the street, and before he could reply, she began to run in that direction. In shock, it took a moment for Rhys to react, and then he broke into a run to catch up to the lady. "Excuse me!" Josephine said, stepping precariously close to Hartle who had just been shoved again by a rough-looking man. "Is there a problem here?"

"None of your business." The man barked as he started to reach for the older man.

"It *is* my business," Josephine said sternly as she stepped forward placing herself between the two. The taller man was not pleased by her actions but withdrew his arms as he yelled in the lady's face.

"He owes me four more!" He glared at the vendor, leaning to the left to see him better as the lady was partially blocking his view.

Afraid to turn her back to the rough man, she asked Hartle to explain what was going on.

"He paid for two, miss. Only two, not half a dozen," he replied.

"Why you old—" Before he could get the next word out, Josephine boldly interrupted him.

"That will be enough," she yelled. "You have what you paid for, now be on your way." At this point, she took a step toward the man letting him know that she was not intimidated by his threatening. He was tall but thin with a scraggly beard reaching to his chest. He seemed well dressed but the dirt that covered him from head to toe let the lady know he had traveled for many days to reach Guttenhamm. If Josephine had not been in the town surrounded by familiar people, she would not have chanced her luck with the stranger, but she felt she could win this battle. The man was not in a mood to back down especially to a woman who had just embarrassed him in public. He had just turned his hand and was lifting it to backhand her across the face when he saw Rhys coming to the lady's defense with his hand upon the hilt of his sword.

"My Lady Armand, shall I place him under arrest?" Rhys asked in an official sort of tone. Liam was only a few steps behind his brother and his sword was drawn. The stranger lowered his hand as he realized the men were prepared to defend the woman.

Josephine spoke up, "No need. It was a simple misunderstanding. He is about to be on his way." She motioned for the man to go on down the street. The crowd that had gathered seemed to part, and the man grunted loudly and glared devilishly at the woman before walking away. The townspeople began to scatter and returned to what they had been doing before the scuffle. Josephine turned her attention to the old man who was relatively unscathed but badly shaken up and fearing the stranger would return for revenge. The lady assured him she would alert the guard to keep an eye out for the man. Rhys and Liam had remained nearby shocked by Josephine's boldness to confront the menace and were not pleased to have come so close to using their swords. When the lady was finished comforting Hartle, the young men insisted they return to the castle.

Hardly a word was spoken on the ride back, and Josephine wondered if she had alienated Rhys by not answering his question. Thankfully the awkward silence was short lived as the queen and Lady Gehrett met them upon the veranda and asked about the trip to town. Glances were exchanged and Josephine was quick to steer the conversation away from the incident. The princes had returned only minutes earlier and the young men excused themselves inside. Josephine was relieved as she was ready to separate from Rhys for a while as he had given her plenty to think about. The queen invited Josephine to join them on a stroll through the gardens, and as the lady stepped onto the lawn, she sighed thinking about how her day had turned sour. She only half listened to the conversation as she contemplated a plan of recovery as they walked farther away from the veranda. The ladies had made it past the green used for sport or horse events and were about to reach the second section of the flowers known for its blooming bushes when they heard voices from the veranda. The women waved as they caught sight of the men. Josephine could not concentrate well enough to come to a solution for her dilemma with Rhys and had decided it would have to wait when she heard a strange noise that sounded like animals moving through the tall dry grass. Suddenly barking was heard and she turned to see the commotion only to behold three dogs running toward her and the ladies. Even from a distance, she could see they were dreadfully thin and had a wild look about them. She watched as they crossed the farthest green and kept coming closer. A fear gripped her heart as she realized the dogs were headed straight toward them.

"Get behind me ladies, now! Hurry," she cried out. "Don't move, or speak." She pleaded, knowing there was no place to seek shelter. Quickly the queen and Lady Gehrett done as they were told and the trio began to edge backward as fast as they could while facing the approaching animals. The watchful eyes of the princes had noticed the dogs as they came across the green and without a second thought they had taken off running toward the ladies, drawing their swords as they went. Josephine could hear a noise from the direction of the veranda but dared not look away as the dogs came to a stop only a few yards from her. The largest of the three stepped out in front of the other two and was snarling as he began to slowly creep closer. Josephine watched as he crouched lower.

This is it, she thought. With every ounce of courage she could muster she screamed, "Run!" to the ladies and then took hold of her skirt tail and swished it as high as she could causing the dog to lunge toward her. As it dove at her its teeth sunk deep into the fabric, jaws locking tightly with the dog not able to turn loose. The animal was growling viciously as Josephine fought against it, managing to kick back at its body while trying not to fall down or be wounded by its paws. At some point she had begun screaming for Wilhelm, which was just enough commotion that the two other animals had not yet came forward to attack her. The few seconds that passed seemed like minutes when suddenly she heard a yell, and from her right, she saw the glimmer of steel coming down upon her attacker. The animal yelped and fell limp pulling her forward, but Wilhelm's quick reflexes kept her from falling. As he steadied her with one arm, he cut the front of her skirt to free her from the dog's jaws which were still tightly clamped upon the fabric. As she buried her face into the prince's chest, she could hear the yells of Leopold as he quickly done away with the other two strays. She could hear the voices of the others as they approached, but could not raise her head from Wilhelm. She was sobbing horribly when she felt his hand upon her cheek as he bent over her pressing his face against hers.

"I've got you, Josephine. I've got you," he said as he let his sword fall to the ground beside them. Without any hesitation, he put his arm under the lady, lifted her, and not waiting to speak with the others, headed back to the castle. When they were inside, Josephine apologized for the trouble but was sternly hushed. The prince carried her upstairs, and when he had placed her upon the couch in the library, the lady tried to apologize again but this time he placed his finger upon her lips. "Stop," he said. Ever so tenderly, he moved his hand from her lips to her cheek and began to wipe the tears away. "Don't think that for one moment I would want to hear you call out any other man's name but mine." Before she could say anything, he leaned his head toward her until their foreheads touched. The way she felt at that moment was not like anything she had felt before.

Neither spoke as he held her close and did not move until the others came into the room. At the sound of his mother's voice, Wilhelm rose to his feet and left Josephine in Agatha's care saying there was something he had to do as he hurried out of the room past Rhys and the others.

With the help of the maids, Josephine was ushered to her room, carefully undressed and examined by the queen. Even a scratch upon the skin could mean a cruel death for the lady. With great relief, they found only the lady's dress was marred by the attack. Word was relayed to the king who was waiting in the hallway who then went to tell the others the good news. Josephine was promptly redressed and tucked into bed. She asked to be left alone, but the queen wouldn't hear of it and Katrina offered to stay with her while she rested. No sooner had the door closed when Josephine began to cry, as did her lady in waiting as she climbed into the bed to comfort her friend. In a little while, Josephine was fast asleep with Katrina still holding on to her hand.

Wilhelm's mind had immediately returned to the dog. The prince would not be at ease until he had examined the animal to see if it was rabid. The thought too had crossed Leopold's mind, and he had followed his brother back outside. Two of the guards were looking the animals over when the princes returned to the green, and after a few minutes, all agreed the telltale signs were not visible. No foaming at the mouth or blood was upon the dogs' greasy coats from other recent attacks. From the boney carcasses they guessed starvation had driven the animals mad. As Wilhelm and Leopold strode back to the veranda, they did not utter a sound with their thoughts now only upon Josephine. The stories of horror flooded their minds as they stood staring blankly toward the gardens. A few minutes passed before the king emerged from the castle and walked quickly to his sons.

"Your mother said there is not a mark upon Josephine's body," he stated very loudly. Wilhelm was so overcome that he had to sit down in a nearby chair. He leaned forward and dropped his head to cover his face with his hands.

"She is all right," he repeated to himself. "Not a mark." Hubert and Leopold smiled to each other, and with a bow, the younger prince excused himself and went inside. The king walked to where his son was sitting and gently placed a hand upon Wilhelm's shoulder. Hubert knew that Wilhelm's feelings for the young lady ran deep and the brush with death weighed heavily upon his son's emotions.

Just before supper, the queen awoke the lady and Josephine agreed to make an appearance if not a word of the incident was mentioned. About halfway down the staircase, the young lady began to shake. The food had already been blessed when the pair entered the room. The young men started to their feet, but the queen bid them to remain seated as Josephine took her place beside Wilhelm. The king was mindful to keep the conversation steady to avoid any awkward silences hoping to calm nerves. Although she was still rattled, Josephine was glad that she had joined the others. She had laid her napkin on the table between her and Wilhelm and was reaching for her glass when her sleeve brushed against the linen causing it to move toward the edge of the table. She felt it shift and attempted to recover it but Wilhelm's reflexes were quicker and he caught the napkin as it started to fall.

"I've got it my lady," he replied as he placed the napkin back upon the table. As he did however, he rested his hand gently over hers. As he let go of the piece of cloth, she felt his fingers slide in between hers and he glanced her way. She smiled and flexed her fingers farther apart, allowing him to get a better hold of her hand. As if afraid of drawing attention, the pair remained still as they pretended to be listening. They dared not look at each other for fear their thoughts might be revealed. A few minutes passed and then Josephine felt Wilhelm ever so subtly lift her hand under his and slide it back toward them and then move it under the tabletop. As their hands disappeared from view, he took a better hold and then he looked at Josephine and gave a tender smile. It was almost as if his eyes were asking if she approved and with a smile, she gave his hand a squeeze. Sinking back into her chair, she sighed as the calm that only Wilhelm could bring began to settle upon her.

12

The Mill

"Meet me downstairs tomorrow morning at seven o'clock," Wilhelm demanded.

"What for?" Josephine quipped in return, still upset with him for rebuking her.

"We need to take a trip, so be ready to ride," he added, and not giving her the opportunity to start arguing with him again, he excused himself.

The next morning, Josephine asked Agatha if the prince had let her know where they were going.

"I have no idea, my dear. And when I offered to have a lunch prepared for the road, he refused me," the queen answered. One thing the queen had learned was not to be concerned over the frequent disagreements between the lady and her eldest son. Tempers would flare, but within a day, they were so miserable that they sought each other out and reconciled the matter. When the ladies went downstairs, they found Wilhelm waiting and he motioned for Josephine to follow him outside. The tension emulating from the prince made her nervous. She desperately wanted to know where they were heading or at least how long they would be gone but dared not ask. As they rode past the garrison in Guttenhamm, the lady noticed four soldiers fell into line behind her and the prince. Wherever they were headed, the prince felt they would need an escort. The longer they rode, the more Josephine wondered about the trip. Did the outing have to do with business or the latest argument between the two?

Her mind went back to the day before. The morning had gone smoothly for the lady as she had visited several villages to the east of Guttenhamm and had managed to make it back before three that afternoon. She was particularly pleased as Leopold had reminded her at breakfast that they could meet at the blacksmith's if she made it back early enough. Although the younger prince had taught her basic sword play, he suggested that they keep meeting as often as they could for she would learn more by practicing. Josephine had made it to the blacksmith shop and had traded her dress for a tunic and pants when she heard Leopold call for her. She stepped out of a stall to answer.

"I was beginning to wonder if *you* were the one detained this time," the lady teased as lately their schedules had not allowed them to meet but once a week.

"I almost was," he announced as he came closer. "I stopped by the garrison. The new recruits were dueling and asked me to show them some moves." He watched as the lady finished braiding back her hair.

"Oh," Josephine commented as she tucked her pants inside her boots.

"Yes." The prince hesitated and then asked, "You wouldn't want to try your hand against them, would you?" The lady stood up straight and gave a questioning look.

"Me? No, I don't think I am ready for anything like that," she answered. She had assumed the duel had been mentioned for her to watch not participate.

"I think you are," Leopold answered as he sat down on a nearby bucket. "You won't have confidence until you fight someone other than me."

"Dying is not the way I want to find out that I fail the test, Leopold," she said bluntly.

"I would be there to stop your opponent *before* you got hurt," he pleaded.

"Then what would be the point in me trying?"

"I was just asking if you were up to it. Honestly, I think you can do it—at least the first round for sure," he added. He could tell the lady was considering it for she began to pace back and forth across the room. Suddenly she stopped and turned toward him.

"But when they see I am a woman wouldn't they go easy on me?" Josephine asked.

"No," he said, standing to his feet and walking toward her. "Because . . . They have to wear a masked hood and a vest of chain mail. They wouldn't know any different unless you were to cry out. You'd just be a small, young man." He paused as he could see the temptation was getting too great to overcome. "Will you give it a try?"

"How do you talk me into such things? Promise me that you won't let someone kill me," she said.

"Upon my life," he answered. "Wilhelm would kill me if you even so much as get a scratch." They both laughed at the statement as they knew he was right. Leopold borrowed a hood from the smith and when Josephine had put it on the pair headed for the garrison. The soldiers were still in the yard, some practicing with swords and spears but a few were gathered around the corral watching the duels. Leopold called to Captain Bernhardt explaining that he had a friend from the village that wanted to practice with the recruits. Bernhardt joked to the prince that the young man might ought to wait a few years to try his hand, but Leopold suggested the lad at least be given a chance for being brave enough to ask. With a sigh, the captain agreed and pointed to where a vest was draped over the boards of the corral. As Leopold helped the chain mail over Josephine's head, he reminded her not to go easy on her opponent. Josephine was so nervous that she almost called out to the prince before they even began. Suddenly she thought about Wilhelm and how angry he would be if he was told she was sword fighting at the garrison. Too involved already, she decided she would have to win at least the first round in order to bow out. A yell was heard as Bernhardt called the match to begin. The lady looked across the corral and to her relief a young man similar in size to herself stepped forward. He gave a yell and swinging wildly, came at her and without a second thought she began her footwork as she engaged him. Very carefully she watched the next few minutes, studying his actions, for although she was defending herself quite well she would need to change tactics if she was to win the round. For a moment, the lady pretended to falter stepping awkwardly to the side, but then to the young man's surprise, she quickly began to turn the tables and within a few minutes pinned him against the fence. She almost slipped and asked aloud if he wanted to surrender, but thankfully she remembered her façade and instead made a lunge with her sword coming to rest flat on his shoulder near his neck.

"Mercy! I surrender to you," he yelled. Immediately those who were watching began to clap, and Josephine lowered her sword and turned to bow to the prince. Quickly the lady made her way across the corral and had begun to climb through the boards when Leopold came to her side.

"Please, go another round." Josephine shook her head, but the prince blocked her escape and said, "Come now, don't tell me that wasn't easy work for you." She looked up at him. "And don't tell me you didn't enjoy it either." The lady gave a sigh for he was right.

"And if I go another round . . . will you let me stop then?" she whispered as he took hold of her arm.

"I would only stop when I was beaten," he replied. "And that way, if the day ever comes that you face a true enemy you will know how to fight for your life." Leopold's words made Josephine think back to Briasburg and Edgell. She had never faced such things before, and she would have reacted better and been calmer if she had been more prepared. She lifted her leg back through the boards and placed her foot inside the corral once more.

"You are such a bad influence on me," she commented.

Leopold smiled. "That's my girl . . . Uhmm, good job." He covered his error and turning, called out, "Bernhardt, do you have anyone willing to challenge my young friend."

An hour passed with Josephine winning three more duels. Each opponent she faced grew harder but the lady was enjoying herself far too much to care. Leopold coached her in between rounds, pointing out mistakes so it would not cost her later and things seemed to be progressing well. Shortly after the second man was beaten, the other soldiers in the yard turned their attention to the corral, but Josephine kept her focus and was not distracted by them. The men were amazed that the newcomer was talented enough to best the last man who had been twice his size. The fourth man that stepped up to the challenge was not a novice, having been a soldier for more than a year and Leopold seemed to be fully aware of the fact. The prince was not sure the lady would be able to defeat the man, but he needed to know how she would react when pressed hard. As Bernhardt gave the signal and the match began, Leopold casually slipped through the boards into the corral, and discreetly slid his sword from its sheath just in case he had to stop the duel. He knew Josephine was losing her strength and this opponent was much stouter than she. Several times the lady was backed into a corner and Leopold took a step in her direction, but Josephine managed to hold her own and by mistakes of her opponent, she worked her way through the close call. Finally, Josephine made several quick moves and her sword came to rest on the soldier's chest, and she was named the victor. She motioned to the prince, and when he was at her side, she whispered that she was done for the day. Leopold turned to the crowd that had gathered and asked the men to give a round of applause. Josephine waved and started to leave the corral, but several of the recruits climbed inside, wanting to shake hands with the winner. Bernhardt was not far behind calling out to Leopold that he wanted to be introduced to his young friend as he would be pleased to have him join the guard. Neither Leopold nor Josephine had anticipated such a response, and Leopold was growing anxious to get the lady away before her identity was discovered. Suddenly a familiar voice was heard and the soldiers parted to let someone through the crowd. Josephine looked, and to her horror, it was Wilhelm. With everything inside her she wanted to run, yet couldn't. She took a deep breath and looked around hoping to spot Leopold to help her out of the situation. About the time he caught sight of his brother, it was too late.

"Well, young man. That was a fine display of swordsmanship. Who taught you?" Wilhelm asked.

Before Josephine was forced to answer, Leopold spoke up, "I had the honors." Wilhelm turned and gave his brother a look of surprise.

"Well then," Wilhelm said, looking back to the newcomer. "I am pleased that you have survived with *him* as your tutor." The men gave a hearty laugh as the prince bowed in respect of the accomplishment. Josephine had hoped that was all Wilhelm had to say, but her eyes fixed upon him slowly drawing his sword as he continued, "You done well . . . but how will you fare against one more skilled?" Josephine thought she was going to faint as he lifted his sword and signaled for the duel to begin. She stood staring at him in total shock not knowing what to do, when suddenly he came at her. "You should never give your opponent the opportunity to do as he will," he yelled as the lady took a step to the left to avoid being stabbed in the chest. Part of her wanted to call out to him but then part of her was afraid to let him hear her voice. She didn't have time to dwell upon the thought as Wilhelm began a full attack, and she found herself struggling to remember her foot work. She heard Leopold yelling a position he had taught her, and quickly she responded and began to hold her own. It only lasted for a moment as Wilhelm seemed ten times stronger than the other men, and with every time she blocked, she thought she was going to lose her grip and her sword fall to the ground. She could only hope that Leopold would see the look on her face and stop the fight, but then she remembered she was wearing the hood. Finally, she felt the boards of the fence against her back which brought some measure of relief as she knew the end had to be near. She thought Wilhelm would have lightened up knowing he would soon be declared the victor but he didn't, and in fact came at her harder still. Desperate now, the lady took a risk and lunged suddenly at the prince. It caught him by surprise, and he took an ill-aimed swing lodging his sword in the top rail of the fence. The error gave her time to slip past him, and none too soon for when he pulled on his sword, the rail splintered to the ground where she had been standing. The lady had made it back to the center of the corral and was panting for breath, watching as Wilhelm began to walk toward her. Suddenly Leopold stepped between the two and began to talk.

"I hate to interrupt, but I want my friend to live to see another day, dear brother. Let's hear it for the prince and our brave newcomer," he concluded, and the men began to cheer. Wilhelm gave a bow toward the crowd and Josephine followed suit. Henri's loud voice called out that supper was ready, and the soldiers took off in the direction of the dining hall. Josephine had just ducked under the fence when she felt someone take hold of her vest.

"Wait, I want to see the face of the man that fought so bravely today," Bernhardt said, turning her around.

"Yes, as do I," Wilhelm said as he came near.

"Not today," Leopold replied, coming up behind the two men. As soon as the words were spoken, a thought crossed Wilhelm's mind. He reached for the hood and pulled it off the lady. Gasps were heard as Josephine stood before them not uttering a word. Wilhelm took a step back and looked toward the ground and took several deep breaths and no one had to guess if he was angry.

"Wilhelm let me explain," Leopold said, but his brother just held up a hand for him to stop. Bernhardt was not sure what to do, expecting that he was in trouble for not being observant enough to realize a lady had fought against his men for the last hour and a half.

Finally the captain spoke, "My lady, I am not sure whether to be pleased that you have beaten my men or frightened that I was so careless to have let you take the risk. But you were very brave to test your skills, especially considering they were much larger than you. I must admit you do a fine job with a sword and have the endurance needed for battle."

"For battle? Captain, the lady does not need any encouragement for such things. Josephine, what on earth were you thinking? You could have been hurt or . . . I was not taking it easy on you, one wrong move and I would have run you through."

"It is not her fault," Leopold interrupted. "I put her up to this."

"And you . . ." Wilhelm said, turning to face his brother. "How could you *do* such a thing? So is it true—you have been training her?"

"Yes, I have. Even if we were not on the brink of war, she cannot be confined to Guttenhamm all of her days and needs to know how to defend herself. Today was a test to see how she would do," he explained, stepping between Wilhelm and Josephine.

"There will be no more of this. How could you take a chance of her being hurt?"

"Despite what you think, I was waiting on the inner side of the corral all this time with my sword drawn in case she faltered. Do you think I would *ever* let her get hurt?" At this point, Josephine expected to see the brothers exchange blows and not able to deal with it if they did, she climbed on through the fence and began to walk back toward the blacksmith's shop. Bernhardt was waiting as she came back outside now wearing her dress.

"Captain, please forgive me if I have offended you, for it was not meant. Leopold and I both are at fault but it was as he said, the best way to test my skills under duress. Are the princes . . ."

"They are still arguing, my lady." He glanced in the direction of the garrison and then back at her. She had untied her horse and was walking it along the street. The captain boosted her into the saddle and as she was turning to leave, he said, "Not that I could say in front of his majesty, but you did *very* well. I would gladly let you ride with my men, not that I would want it coming to that if you understand me." Josephine thanked him for the compliment and rode back to the castle alone. The princes arrived about a half hour later, and the mood at supper was horribly tense. The king and queen didn't have to guess the three were upset with each other. After supper, Josephine managed to slip upstairs before the others but did not go to her room and instead went down the back staircase and left the castle and headed toward the stables. She had been brewing over the situation for more than an hour when she heard someone climbing the ladder into the loft where she was hiding.

"Before I climb the rest of the way up, you are there, aren't you?" Leopold asked quietly.

"I am," Josephine answered, relieved that it was the younger of the two brothers and that she had company. He came and sank down into the hay beside the lady. "How did you find me?"

"I figured you was returning your sword to its hiding place and took advantage of the quiet," he answered.

"What a mess this turned out to be," she said with a solemn look on her face.

"Wilhelm is just overreacting," Leopold said, relaxing back against the hay. "You should have heard him after you left."

"I don't want to know," she answered, glancing over at him. "How can you be so calm about all of this? I still have a fight ahead of me."

"Years of battling it out with him, I suppose. He had no right to treat you that way, concerned for your safety or not."

"Well, I am not looking forward to when he catches up with me. It makes me ill when we argue."

"Then don't," Leopold said, sitting up and moving closer. "Just stay away from him or stay close to me and I won't let him . . ."

"That won't work. Besides, I won't run away from him and it's better for me to just . . ." Her voice broke off in midthought as the dread of facing him took her focus. She swallowed hard and added, "I might as well go to him and let him speak his mind. It's better than hiding in the loft for a week." Leopold shook his head in frustration at the lady's stubbornness. He was convinced he could speak to his father about what happened and that the king would forbid Wilhelm from confronting the lady. Leopold let out a sigh as he realized the determination Josephine possessed was one of the qualities he liked most about her.

"If that is your decision, then I won't stop you, but only if you let me go with you," he replied. Josephine didn't like the idea but finally agreed as Leopold would not let her leave the loft until she had and the worst part of her day still lay ahead. Together they went back inside in the castle and found Wilhelm sitting in the library as expected. The rebuke that followed was fierce and Leopold found himself gripping the chair arm several times to keep from going across the room and decking his brother for speaking to Josephine like he was. Wilhelm scolded the lady for not only being reckless but falling prey to every whim suggested to her. The comments did not sit well with the lady, and she in turn defended her actions joining the prince as he stood by the fireplace. For several minutes, they spoke with raised voices, Wilhelm accusing that she was trying to prove her worth through careless actions that could cost her life and Josephine reminding him that her life was her own to do with as she pleased. The two were standing within an arm's length of each other when they both fell silent as they were too angry to find words. As Wilhelm stood there glaring at the lady, he suddenly realized the foolishness of letting his temper take control of him. All the concern he felt toward Josephine had been lost in the fact that he had not made her understand why he was upset but had in fact now driven her further away from the truth. Clearing his throat, he informed the lady that she would accompany him on a trip the next morning and quickly turned and left her standing by the fireplace alone. Not feeling like the issue had been resolved, Josephine attempted to follow him that night but Leopold caught her at the doorway and prevented her from pursuing his brother.

She hoped Wilhelm had considered the argument as a stalemate for it had upset her enough already, but here she was, riding with him when she didn't want to speak with him for at least a week after such a heated argument. Finally, the group turned off the main road and then after another good length of time, came to a village. She recognized a few establishments as she been there before. To her amazement, the prince turned his horse up a narrow path. Still they rode on, winding through the brush and then through the grass again as they began to ascend a hill. As they came to the crest, she could see a mill with foothills in the distance.

It is business, Josephine thought as she saw a swift stream flowing. She sank into her saddle with relief as it meant there were no repercussions from the evening before, and Wilhelm had brought her to meet the proprietor. As they rode closer, she saw a garden spot and several smaller outbuildings. Another, broader road was beyond and she wondered which town it led to. When they stopped, a soldier helped her dismount while Wilhelm greeted a man who had come to meet them. She watched the two walk along a path, laughing as they talked. They came to a stop and looked toward the woman and although she could not hear what they said she knew they were speaking about her. When she drew near, the prince introduced her and then motioned to the soldiers. They could do as they pleased for the next hour and were dismissed until then. To the lady's surprise, the mill keeper bowed and bid them a good afternoon and left the two standing on the path alone. As the man walked away a feeling of dread came over Josephine. Perhaps this was not a business trip after all.

"We need to talk," the prince said as he offered her his arm to walk with him. The tone of his voice reminded her of her father's when she was in trouble, and she couldn't help but feel so weak next to Wilhelm as she thought back to the duel. Trembling, she took his arm and they walked into the old building. They could only take a few steps before they had to stop to let their eyes adjust to the darkness. Josephine could hear the sound of water as it poured into the paddles of the mill wheel and the whirring growl of the grinding stone. Wilhelm began to lead the lady across the building, passing sacks filled with grain. She had the general idea of how a mill worked, but she found it intriguing as they moved closer to the inner workings. Wilhelm could tell she was curious and began to point out certain details. This was the side of the prince that the lady preferred to be around, not the critical one she had butted heads with the evening before. Wilhelm found himself wishing he did not have to deliver what was weighing so heavily upon his heart. He surveyed the room until he saw what he needed.

"I am sure you have guessed that you were brought here because of our conversation yesterday." Josephine let go of the prince's arm and kept walking but purposely kept her back to him. She wasn't exactly pleased with how the week had went herself. She had pushed herself too hard during her rounds and returned after dark three evenings. Wilhelm had confronted her the first time and she had rudely replied that she was capable of defending herself. The king and queen had not uttered a word about her late arrival but she could tell they were terribly worried. Another day she had come upon a scene of injustice and had tried to intervene with help being rejected. On the third day she happened upon an elderly man being robbed and not having her sword, she could do nothing but get shoved to the ground trying to defend him. The old man was severely beaten and after securing care for him it was well past dark and she still had to journey back to Guttenhamm. Because of her appearance there was no hiding that something had transpired, and Wilhelm again condemned her foolishness for travelling alone. She had expected the king to at least scold her but he didn't and his silence was worse punishment. The queen followed the lady to her room where Josephine collapsed in her arms crying. Every effort she made seemed to be plagued by trouble that she was not looking for but seemed to follow her. Agatha reminded the young lady that sometimes things do not go as we want but not to be discouraged for when the tough times come we have to walk by faith and lean on God to see us through. Josephine appreciated the support, but the part about faith in God made her conscious burn. The following evening had ended with her and Wilhelm arguing and saying things she regretted. So far, neither of the two had apologized for their words nor actions that night, and here they were miles from home and she knew it would be a tumultuous day yet again.

"Something has been weighing heavy upon my mind and I will not be released until I have delivered it. Please, I ask that you listen and let me explain fully before you interrupt." The prince began to walk about the room, and it seemed both were moving in a circle as he spoke. "Lately there are things that I have noticed that bring back memories—memories of some unpleasant times." Josephine knew by the pacing that the prince was struggling to express himself. "When we don't surrender to God's will, it causes strife in our life." Josephine's eyebrow rose as she glanced across the room at him, wondering where his speech was headed. "We find ourselves fighting a power that we cannot win against." He went to a nearby table and picked up a crude looking pitcher. She wondered if it had been made by a child because of the bumps and lumps she could see even from a distance, and it appeared lop-sided. The prince carried it across the room for the lady to see it better. Not all the disfigurements were part of the original clay but some had been added after the piece had been initially fired. As Wilhelm turned the pitcher in his hand, she noticed tiny sparkles in the dim light resembling colored pieces of glass upon the surface. Upon closer inspection, she thought the piece even more hideously ugly and wondered why the prince was taking the time to show it to her. Finally Wilhelm began to speak again. "Let's say this is my life." Josephine looked at him with surprise. "Would you agree that it is functional? After all, it will hold water, won't it?" The lady nodded but didn't say anything as her curiosity grew. "Although it seems functional, it really isn't how God intended it to be. See here, this one edge is much lower than the other so it can't hold as much as the Master would like it to. Perhaps the rim started out level, but there is evidence that pressure was applied forcing it down. And see these rough pieces on the outside, they would cut anyone who brushed up against them, so the pitcher couldn't be placed near anything delicate. You might have noticed the original part was good and smooth, but something happened along the way when things began to cling to the outside. Perhaps these things were not even noticed at first. What about the pieces of glass? They seem to be added on purpose, willfully but not gracefully. They didn't add to the functionality, but someone wanted them on the pitcher and didn't consult the Master. Yes, it is truly an ugly piece to behold." Wilhelm turned the pitcher being sure the lady could see the flaws very well. "And so it becomes with our lives. We were created by God, for the purpose He designed for each of us. Somewhere along the way, we begin to interfere with His plan. Sometimes it's just that we don't understand His will for us. Our ideas of how we want life to be gets in the way of His plan. Sometimes it's that situations come along with enough force to crush our hope, seemingly knocking us out of His will." Wilhelm pointed to the top of the pitcher, tracing the warped edge with his finger. "But what I have found is that we tend to find other things that we attach ourselves to that we want for our lives more than we want the Master. So we bring things upon ourselves trying to cover up what His plan is. He has a plan and knows the end from the beginning, being the Author and Finisher of our faith—our Creator." At that point, Wilhelm pointed to places where the glaze had been applied too thick, causing drippy globs to form. "Truly nothing can hide us from the Lord, not people, not material possessions. He sees through the outer things and inside to our heart. And"—now pointing to a bit of glass protruding from the pitcher's surface—"no matter what we add to our life, it won't replace what we are truly missing." Josephine was soaking in the comparisons made when the prince strode over to a table and picked up a hammer. "But God is longsuffering and full of compassion, not willing to leave us in such a pitiful state. He knows we cannot serve Him with these other things hindering us. He loves us enough to do what He must." And without warning, Wilhelm struck the pitcher with the hammer, startling the lady. A small piece fell to the floor. Josephine was not sure whether it was the sudden violence that disturbed her or the meaning of the words he had spoken. "So He allows things to come our way until our will desires His will." Suddenly Wilhelm struck the pitcher again and another piece fell off. "God cannot let anything that is not of Him remain." As the prince swung again, Josephine's heart began to race. "Anything that is not of His will: possessions that we desire but are not part of His plan for us. Possessions that seem good but would weigh us down—would end up hindering us, causing us to stray from Him. Money, land, fame, titles, relationships, even things that are good and true can come between us and God. He loves us enough *not* to allow us to cling to it. Out of love, He has to strip everything away until it is only us and Him. When it comes down to it, that is all that matters. We have to get to the place that He is all we cling to." The prince swung the hammer again, and another piece crashed to the floor in front of the lady.

"So you are saying God takes good things from us?" Josephine asked as the idea tore at her heart as she thought of things she had lost in the last year of her life.

"He allows them to be taken away from us according to His will. The Lord giveth and the Lord taketh away. Blessed be the name of the Lord," he said, letting the hammer fall again. Josephine was at the point her nerves could not stand hearing the sound of the pitcher being broken again.

"I don't understand," she cried out.

The prince looked at her and answered, "His thoughts are not our thoughts nor are His ways our ways." He started to let the hammer drop again but the lady cried out.

"Stop! Please . . . I cannot bear to hear the sound." And as she turned her back to him, she began to weep.

"The Master desires that we are in His will above all else, not conforming to things that will harm us or leave us destitute. He alone knows what we are to be. God shapes us while we are young, soft, malleable, but if we choose not to be molded, He does not force us. We can choose to submit to His will or He is forced by His love to chip away anything that doesn't belong."

"And then?" the lady asked as Wilhelm came close behind her.

"Everything is stripped away until only pieces are left behind, pieces that cannot be made into anything of its own doing." Josephine turned to see that Wilhelm now had only the handle of the pitcher and a few broken shards that he had caught in his hands. "Even then, most times they must be crushed." He began to step backward, nodding for her to follow. He led her to the massive grinding wheel and carefully placed the pieces in his hands upon the stone. The lady watched them disappear as a crushing sound was heard. "And whosoever shall fall upon this stone shall be broken, but on whomsoever it shall fall, it will grind him into powder.

"Into powder? Destroyed then?" she pleaded. "What good could come of this?" She could not control her emotions any longer, and for a moment, Wilhelm wondered if he would have the strength to continue.

"Not destroyed entirely," he replied. "The Master knows what He is doing. He started in the beginning with nothing, but from the dust, He made man a living soul."

"But how could He crush someone completely, taking away everything that is held dearly, leaving nothing but ashes in place of . . ."

"Everything is not gone. It's only ready to be remade," he said as the wheel came full circle and he scooped up the powder in his hands and placed it in a bowl and then walked back to the water wheel where he added a few drops. Carefully he began to stir with his fingers until a soft claylike lump was produced. "Now it's ready to be formed into what the Master desires. The clay is submissive to His will, His ways, wanting only the plan the Master has for its life. You can never know Him unless you are broken before Him. You can never be healed unless you are in need of a physician. You can

161

never know His strength unless you were first weak; know His hope unless you face disappointment. You can never be filled until you are first empty. The Master's eye is always upon His work, He never abandons it, never forsakes it. There will always be choices knocking at your door, but the only one you need to pay heed to is how to submit to His will."

"How can I do that? It feels like everywhere I turn, the battle is against me. At times it's the villagers, the weather, my family, my bad luck," the lady said as she returned to the prince's side.

"Then stop fighting," he declared, causing her to look at him in shock. She shook her head, not understanding what he meant. He stepped up to explain. "Stop fighting what He has allowed to come your way." She looked away from him, but Wilhelm took hold of her arm. "You never chose to be born to Renard and Laurie Armand nor did you choose to be born a woman instead of a man. You didn't want to go to Denske nor fall into trouble at Briasburg. You never chose to be rejected by the snoody businessmen in Guttenhamm." Josephine turned her head back to the prince. "Try as you may, you cannot change certain things in your life. There will always be things out of your control. You think you are fighting against people and circumstances, but it's God who has allowed it. So really you are fighting against Him, and you won't win that battle and all you will do is make yourself miserable." The lady closed her eyes as she did not want to hear anymore. While he spoke, it was as if all the times her heart had been broken seemed to press upon her at that moment and she thought she was going to suffocate. She didn't want to hear that this was what God had chosen for her. Why would He let her go through so much? Suddenly she heard a sound and opened her eyes to see that Wilhelm had dropped more broken pieces upon the grinding wheel.

Was it true? Had she refused to place her life in God's hands? Down in the well she had felt God's love for her and repented of her sin. She had willingly gone to church with the royal family every week and felt things were better. She was grateful to be alive and no longer thought of serving God as drudgery. She was excited for several weeks knowing how much God cared for her but then her enthusiasm began to wane. She still faithfully attended services but it didn't seem the same and her thoughts were rarely upon God unless she was at the church. She had given her heart to Him while shivering in the cold water that day in the well, but had she given Him her life? Did she honestly think she was in control of her destiny or that she would do a better job with it than Him? She had felt the gentle tug upon her heart of the Master's hand but had chosen to ignore it. Was He trying to lead but she wasn't willing to follow? Her heart ached within her as she realized the struggle going on inside was greater than that around her. She was so busy trying not to conform to what society demanded that she had fallen in a trap, being forced to do things she never wanted to do or was capable of. How many times had Wilhelm reminded her to stop living for someone else because that road only led to misery? How often had she met herself coming while she was going to please others? It was as Wilhelm had said. She was trying to prove her worth when God made her who she was with her own talents and gifts. She had to let go of everyone else's idea of what she could be and most of all hers. The only thing she could do was surrender it all to Him, falling at His feet broken and asking to be made again. She cried out to God.

When she came to herself, she was leaning hard against the table where Wilhelm had laid the hammer down. She wiped her eyes and looked around but saw no one. For a while longer, she walked about the mill, thinking about everything the prince had said but more what God had spoken to her heart. She could no longer look at where she had been or what she had been through the same any more. It was all part of the Master's plan designed just for her. She chose to surrender everything to Him including the painful memories that had wounded her heart. By His grace, she would overcome them and not let the sharp pieces of resentment or bitterness mar her life. Finally, she took a deep breath and headed to the door. The prince and the guardsmen were visiting across the garden with the mill keeper. As soon as Wilhelm saw the lady, he started in her direction. He had not wanted to leave her, but he knew that he had poured out his heart and God needed to speak to her next. As the prince came closer, Josephine began to smile and Wilhelm gave a sigh as he knew she had spoken to the Master.

13

Secrets

"And here we go again," yelled Wilhelm with disgust. The rain was now coming down in a torrent bringing the riders to a halt. "Let's head toward the Plyler place." Lightning flashed in the distance. They turned their horses and began to move, but slowly. Between the rain and her hood being pulled forward to shield her face, Josephine could barely see. Weeks earlier, Wilhelm had approached the lady with a proposition she could not refuse. Any business either of them had outside Guttenhamm would be carefully scheduled for them to travel together therefore fulfilling several purposes. Wilhelm wanted the lady at his side as he secured alliances within the kingdom. The king thought the dukes may feel threatened if his son spoke with them alone but Josephine's presence would cast a different light, softening the visits. The lady would be tending her commerce affairs and with winter settling in, she would not be allowed to travel outside Guttenhamm otherwise. With the prince at her side the people were reminded that the lady was endorsed by not only the crown but the council. The arrangement had worked not only to calm tattered nerves, but trust had built toward Josephine. The only hiccup in the plan seemed to be that every time her ladyship accompanied the eldest prince trouble befell them. After the first few incidents, Josephine tried to bow out but the prince only teased that she should be drug along and made to suffer in penance for all that had transpired already. The truth of the matter be told, the lady's particular skills had come in handy more than once to get the company out of a bind. Even with winter descending upon them, the enemy had continued to plague the northern villages, and the High Council had taken measures to secure the people by placing soldiers throughout the affected areas.

Early that morning, the troop had left for Kensithe. It was the third trip within a week that Josephine had made with both princes and their escorts, and here the nine of them were, upon the road in a cold, hard rain. The lady wondered how far they still were from shelter as she tried to lift her hood up just enough to see the horse in front of hers. Finally they turned off the main road and onto a small lane hedged in by trees whose branches tore at the riders. They hadn't gone very far when they were stopped by a tree which had fallen during the storm. The men were forced to dismount and gave their reins to the lady in case the horses got spooked. Each man took a branch and slowly dragged the tree away from the road. Suddenly a crashing sound was heard and the sound of someone crying out. The young lady rose up in her saddle but could not see through the branches and the heavy rain that was falling. Several yells were heard, and then the men remerged from the woods. They mounted and continued down the lane. When they came to the Plyler cabin, Leopold and Vaughn went inside to speak with the widower, and when they returned, Leopold helped the lady from her horse and took her inside the small but cozy dwelling. Several minutes later, Vaughn and Wilhelm stepped inside, but the moment Josephine saw their faces, she knew something was wrong. Wilhelm went to a chair near the fireplace as Vaughn came to the lady.

"Wilhelm is hurt and will need you to tend his arm." Josephine felt herself go numb from head to toe, and she must have turned pale for Vaughn took hold of her arm and asked if she was all right. It was as if the wind had been knocked from her with the words she dreaded most falling upon her ears. "My lady." Josephine drew several short breaths as her senses began to return. Quickly she went to the prince's side where he was attempting to remove his cloak. Wilhelm assured her that he was fine save a gash in the upper part of his right arm. The lady turned toward the other soldiers who were now inside and asked for her saddle bags to be fetched and some water. Then she suggested the prince move his chair closer to the fire for better lighting while she worked. When he was seated again, he took her by the arm and told her there was something urgent he needed to discuss *before* she began to tend to his wound. She was sliding his uninjured arm from his jacket sleeve and politely said they would talk after he had been taken care of. She let the jacket fall from his other arm only to reveal a blood-soaked sleeve. Josephine stood up straight and prepared herself to see the worst. One of the guards had just laid her bags on the table, and she was opening them when Wilhelm caught hold of the lady's arm again but this time with a firm grip.

"This cannot wait," he said. The desperation in his voice caused her to stop and look at him. He was equally as serious. "We need to discuss secrets."

Josephine's face grew warm as she asked, "What do you mean? Is this about Dr. Stehle?"

"Not exactly but, yes, I found out," he replied, still holding on to her arm.

"How did you find out? Did he tell you?" she questioned.

"I happened to see you coming out of his clinic one day and I pressed him until he told me why you were there."

"Pressed him? Wilhelm," she scolded.

"I was worried about you," he offered. "You were already distancing yourself from me, and I thought perhaps you were not feeling well. Maybe I was meddling. But I was worried. Anyways, that is not what I needed to speak with you about." The prince gave her a serious look.

"Wilhelm, you are still bleeding. Can't it wait until later?" she pleaded.

"No, I'm afraid it can't. I have to tell you something, something that may affect your opinion of me forever." As Josephine looked hard into his eyes, she saw a pain that was frightening.

"What could possibly . . ." She couldn't finish her statement.

Wilhelm motioned to his brother, and in his official tone, he said, "We will need a few moments alone." The others left the room as their lord had commanded. Josephine was now so nervous that she left where Wilhelm was seated and went to the far end of the fireplace and began to stare at the flames. The prince rose to his feet and went to stand behind the lady. "I need you to listen to what I have to say."

"You should sit back down," she pleaded, but neither moved toward the chair. "Please . . ." She turned to look at his blood-stained sleeve. "And I ask that you have pity upon me. Your being wounded has upset me enough. Tell me what you need to another day . . . when I can bear it." She looked up at him and he stood there somberly, considering what she said.

Quietly he returned to his chair, and as she followed him, he said, "There are things in my past that I am not proud of, things that I terribly regret, things I wish I could change." Josephine began to unbutton his shirt.

"All of us have regrets," she said as Wilhelm helped her with his left hand.

"But not to the degree that I speak of," he replied as he looked up at her face once more. "Once you thought me a murderer and it tormented me so that I could not rest until I had proven to you that I wasn't."

"Why are you bringing this up?" the lady asked as she moved in front of the man and reached to remove the sleeve from his uninjured arm.

"For weeks now I have wanted to tell you of my past and have been too afraid to do so."

"Afraid? Afraid of what?" the lady asked, stopping what she was doing.

"Afraid that our relationship would never be the same again," he answered. "I was afraid the truth would be too much." He paused as he fought to keep his emotions under control. Would she think less of him for what he had done? Would she be disgusted and leave Guttenhamm? But if she chose to remain, would their relationship be forever damaged? Wilhelm drew his mind back to the lady in front of him. "But I trust you enough to reveal my darkest secrets."

At his words, Josephine felt her head swimming and she didn't want to listen anymore.

"Please, don't," she begged. "You don't have to tell me anything of the sort."

"Yes, I do," he answered. "If not tonight then it would be another one, but I will have to tell you everything." Josephine looked away. Why did he think he had to tell her? Didn't he understand she didn't want to know something that could change the way she felt about him. She was frightened enough already. The prince took hold of her hand and pulled her close. "I know it will be difficult, but I have to share this with you." She could not look at him, and suddenly Wilhelm knew it was pointless for him to say anything else. "Please look at me." Josephine hesitated and then did as he asked. "I never wanted to upset you and I would never do anything to hurt you." She bore no expression on her face, trying to block out her emotions. "I will let you address my wound." The lady took a deep breath and continued where she had left off. Carefully she reached over the top of his head and brought his shirt where she could gently slide it from his wounded arm. The gash was about six inches long and an inch deep and needed stitches. Wilhelm sat silently as he watched her dip a cloth in the bowl of water. She wrung it out and still standing directly in front of him she began to wipe blood from the wound. When the rag was red, she rinsed it and returned to clean his arm again. This time the lady stepped around Wilhelm's knee to his side and had just made one pass over his arm with the cloth when she suddenly stopped. He looked in time to see Josephine's mouth open in shock as her eyes studied what she saw. The lady took several quick breaths in a row and then Wilhelm felt her hands touch his back. Gently she traced the marks with her finger and then withdrew her hand as if she had been caught in the act of a crime. Her eyes met the prince's and she wanted to say something but dared not.

"Ask me," Wilhelm whispered as he watched a tear slide down the lady's face.

"What . . . How . . ." she could not find the words as her mind raced in different directions. Before she knew what was happening, Wilhelm pulled her close to him. He leaned until their heads touched so that neither could see the other's eyes as he began to explain, keeping his voice low.

Seven years ago, he decided he wanted his own path in life. He had the notion his father was nothing more than a tyrant, and he wanted no part of the throne nor the political arena. The people didn't need him, and he didn't need them either. He had decided there was no such thing as justice, and he was done with everyone and everything. Knowing his father would never willingly let him leave or abdicate the throne, he devised a plan to get away, asking his father to let him study abroad. Finally Hubert agreed but with the condition that someone would go with him. The plan worked and when the prince was a safe distance from Gutten, he turned his path in an entirely different direction. For the plan to work, Wilhelm cut all ties with his home and denounced his name. Reality was quick to plague him, and within a month, troubles came. One might call it bad luck, but in hindsight, he knew it was Providence that had buffeted him from every side. He found himself scraping by to survive and ended up with a rough lot of men sold to work in the fields until their debts were paid. One night, a handful of their group broke into the storehouse and stole some of the goods. The prince knew of their plans but did nothing to stop them. When the field master discovered the loss, he pressed them as to what happened, and one of Wilhelm's friends ratted out the others. The next morning dawned to find his friend hanging from a rope in the barnyard. The prince was beside himself and confronted the thieves and a fight broke out. The field master heard the scuffle, and fingers were pointed to him as starting the ruckus. Still upset about the whole incident, Wilhelm got in the master's face mouthing to him. The master did not hesitate to have the prince apprehended and taken to the post to be whipped. The prince's loyal companion begged Wilhelm to reveal his identity, which he wouldn't do and then tried to get the master to let him take the whipping in his place but was refused. Wilhelm took his lashes—five for starting the fight and five for questioning the master's authority. While the prince spoke, Josephine wept.

"Oh, Wilhelm, how much it must have hurt," she mumbled.

"It was horrible, but it did not compare to the first time my mother saw my back," he continued, explaining that his companion nursed his wounds and they labored another month until they paid their debt. Through much prayer, he humbled himself to the mighty hand of God, and the pair returned home. He did not speak of where he had been or what had happened and using the excuse of finding God while he was away he kept to himself except for being present for business. His father knew that he was not at Casborough but if he knew exactly where the prince had been he had never disclosed it. Wilhelm done his best to conceal his scars, and several months had passed before he accidentally took his shirt off in front of his parents. When his mother saw the marks, she cried out, running to him and asking questions which he would not answer. "The look on her face, Josephine . . ." The prince's voice was muffled as he choked back tears. "I could have been whipped ten times over and it not been as punishing as her weeping over me, nor you." He leaned back and lifted the lady's chin to look in her eyes. "Seeing the anguish upon your face over mistakes that I made."

"Did you tell them what happened?" she asked.

"No. I was too ashamed. How could I tell them that I was so blinded by my selfishness that I was willing to throw away everything including their love for me? The very values that I disowned and denounced were the very ones that I clung to the most. It would have broken their hearts if they knew what I had done and been involved with."

"What did your father say that day?" the lady asked.

"He didn't say a word, which may have been harder to bear than if he had forced me to tell him. He has never brought it up, and I cannot bring myself to tell him. Only one other person knows the truth besides you," he concluded as he let out a sigh and closed his eyes, leaning his head against the lady's once more, relieved as the burden was lifted from his shoulders.

A thought came to Josephine and she whispered, "It was Vaughn that went with you, wasn't it?" Wilhelm opened his eyes and smiling nodded his head that it was.

"You know me better than anyone." He leaned back to look deep into her eyes and searched for her thoughts as he asked, "Can you forgive me?"

"There is nothing to forgive," she replied.

"Yes, there is," he said firmly. "I did not want you to make the same mistakes that I made, only to wake up one morning to despise who you have become. So . . . I badgered you, thinking I could force you to change and go down a different path." He swallowed hard as tears welled up in his eyes. "I could not stand by and watch you destroy yourself and the relationships with those you loved dearly. So what did I do but let my old nature rise up in frustration and lose my temper with you at every opportunity." Wilhelm shook his head. "I cannot begin to make amends for how horrible I have been to you. All I started out to do was protect you from heartache. Please, there is so much that needs forgiven." Josephine reached toward his face and gently laid her hand upon his jaw. The humbleness of regret shone from the prince's eyes and the lady's heart was moved with compassion.

"How many times have you forgiven me?" she asked with a tender smile as she slid her hand over his beard. Josephine dropped her hands from his face and down to the prince's wounded arm. "Will you please let me take care of you?" He gave a smile.

She had just threaded her needle when the others came back inside. While she worked, she thought about what had been said. So many little things he had said in the last few months suddenly made sense. Several times, her hand wandered to the stripes upon Wilhelm's back. The prince pretended not to notice but continued speaking with his brother. He was not accustomed to the touch of a lady's hand, but he knew she was coming to terms with what she had beheld. Her curiosity gave him hope that he had not frightened her away and he was sure that she would have more questions for him.

When Wilhelm's arm was mended, Josephine spoke with Mr. Plyler, and an hour later, they had made supper for all the men. The rain had not let up, and it was agreed the company would spend the night at the cabin. As they made their pallets on the floor, the guard began their travelling ritual of telling stories in front of the fire.

Josephine's saddle was placed in middle of the room between both of the princes. Just before they laid down, Wilhelm asked Vaughn to bring him his sword. When it was in his hand, he promptly turned and presented it to the lady. She gave a wide smile and carefully laid it on the floor between them. She heard Leopold mumble behind her, and suddenly she wondered how it would go with the younger prince sleeping next to her. It had seemed that lately his affections for her had waned, but she recalled how passionately he had professed his love for her and she was a bit nervous as this would be a first. As the others quieted down, Wilhelm stretched out lying on his side facing Josephine. By the look on the elder prince's face, the lady wasn't sure whether it was to favor his wound or to keep a watchful eye on his brother.

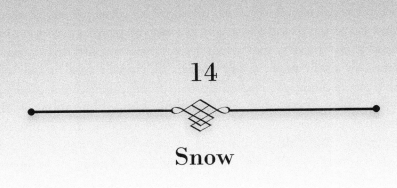

14

Snow

"It's time to leave," Wilhelm whispered toward Josephine's ear. He had walked close behind the lady as she was tending to a patient's wound.

"I am almost finished," she replied, not looking away from the man's shoulder.

"That was what you told me thirty minutes ago," the prince whispered again.

"Thirty minutes ago it was a different patient," she said, still focusing on her work.

"Don't make me hog-tie you to get you out of here," he said, reaching for a bandage on the table and handing it to the lady as she started to turn for it. Two minutes later, she was finished and the patient rose to his feet, thanked the lady and left the clinic. After Josephine had washed, Wilhelm helped her with her cloak and they bid a good evening to Dr. Stehle who was not yet ready to leave. Taking a lantern the pair stepped out into the night and headed to the inn where they were staying. Several inches of fresh snow blanketed the ground, and more was coming down as they hurried along.

As they warmed themselves by the fireplace of the inn's great room, Josephine began to think about the last few weeks. It was no secret that the lady was looking forward to when the snow would fall, and with the first considerable accumulation, Josephine spent most of the day outside. She was not alone however, for business had almost come to a standstill which allowed the princes time to enjoy it as well. By the next day, schedules resumed but it didn't dampen Josephine's excitement. Every couple of days, a few inches fell, and when enough was packed down, the carriages were traded for sleighs. She was reminded that travelling outside the capital would be contingent upon the amount of snow coming down and the temperature. After the second week of snow blanketing the ground, Dr. Stehle came to the castle requesting that Josephine accompany him throughout the kingdom for more training while trading was slow. It was not that his medical team was lacking, but if war broke out, he wanted the lady to be his personal assistant attending to the king's guardsmen. From her actions thus far, he knew she was able to bear the responsibility, and her skills were added to every time they worked together. He had noticed that Josephine's presence among the wounded brought comfort and hope of better days ahead. As long as the doctor traveled south, the crown did not insist that a greater presence of the guard go with the lady but when they went northward, at least one if not both of the princes accompanied the pair. Most of the time, Katrina stayed behind at the castle, not only because of the nature of the outings, but because Josephine did not want her lady in waiting out in the weather. Travelling had proven risky and several times the group had to alter plans staying longer in a village or stopping at a residence along the road for shelter because of the amount of snow falling. If Wilhelm was along, Josephine didn't mind the delay, but when he wasn't, the lady found herself rather lonely. They had formed several habits during the past few months that they were in no hurry to break. Every morning, they met and went to the chapel to pray and read the Bible. Josephine was fluent enough speaking German, but she had found several passages of scriptures hard for her to read. The prince had been quick to offer his help and in the evenings the two would retreat to the library to pour over selections while sitting side by side on the divan. Hours were spent reading aloud in both languages as they enjoyed each other's company. As the friendship grew they began confiding in each other and shared details of their day as soon as they were together. Now accustomed to each other's presence, the first time Josephine remained at the castle while both princes went on a two day mission, the young lady found herself anxiously watching for their return. By lunchtime of the third day of their absence Josephine ran out of things to keep her busy, even helping the servants until she retreated upstairs to wait. The king and queen had joined her in the library and all were reading when the trumpets were heard announcing the princes were returning. Josephine was almost to the staircase when she saw Leopold clearing the last step. She gave him a big smile, and without warning, he scooped her into his arms and swung her around. Both laughed as he let her feet touch the floor again.

"You are not hurt, I see," the lady said as he planted a kiss on her cheek. She laughed again and pushed him away. "You ornery thing!"

"I am fine, dearest," he teased.

"And your brother?"

"He is slowly climbing the stairs," Leopold added, acting as if he was going to try for another kiss.

"No more of that," Josephine stated. "If I wasn't relieved that you were safe, you wouldn't have gotten by with what you have." Before he could reply, Hubert called his son's name and Leopold let loose of the lady and went to speak with him. Josephine turned and watched as Wilhelm came closer. "Are you hurt?" She took a few steps down to meet him.

"No, just worn out," he answered. She took his hand as if to help him with the last few steps, and she in turn stepped up backward.

"Don't stop on the stairs, you might fall," she said as they made it to the upper landing. To her surprise, he leaned and kissed her cheek.

"My token for being allowed to pass, my lady." Not yet drawing back, he added, "I have missed you." Josephine found herself blushing as both smiled. He stood upright again and winding her arm through his, they walked on to the library. She wanted to tell him that she had missed him too but just couldn't after the unexpected gesture. An embrace from him held more significance than meager flirting.

The sound of rattling as dishes were gathered up from a nearby table brought Josephine's mind back to the present. The evening was far spent, and after a light supper, the prince and the lady walked to their rooms to turn in. Wilhelm reminded Josephine that he would be leaving at dawn as part of the scouting party. They would return in a couple days unless they came across trouble. Dr. Stehle had been informed that the medical outpost would remain at the village until the prince returned and then together all would head back to Guttenhamm. As anxious as Josephine was to return to the comforts of the castle, she dreaded being cooped up but had faith that the doctor would invite her to join him so her solitude would not last long. The next morning after the scouting party had left, Josephine and Dr. Stehle headed to the clinic. The village of Seim had enough residents to keep the lady occupied as far as patients and there was plenty of news concerning business dealings. Thankfully she had made rounds with her ledger the first day they had arrived for she could not have retained her focus at the clinic otherwise. In the prince's absence, Josephine was allowed to work much later with the doctor than he would have allowed. The second morning at breakfast, the young lady mentioned to Dr. Stehle that she would be stopping by the mercantile on her way to the clinic to order more medical supplies that the clinic seemed to be running short of. The pair walked down the street together, and then the doctor went on while Josephine made her stop. With her errand completed, the lady left and hurried on down the main street.

"My lady, a word please," a voice called out. Josephine came to a stop and glanced to the right to see a tall man lurking at the edge of the street.

"Sir, I do not know you. You have mistaken me for someone else," she said, wishing she had kept walking. The man took a step forward and as he spoke again it made the hair on the back of the lady's neck tingle.

"You are Josephine Armand," he replied in a serious tone. "A mutual friend requests that you help a friend of his in need." The man began to move quickly toward the lady causing her to step back. She had started to turn, hoping to run from him, but someone grabbed her from behind and placed a hand over her mouth silencing her cries. She was pushed toward an alley between the buildings until they were hidden in the shadows where they would not be easily noticed by a passerby. "Do not scream and he will remove his hand. Do you understand?" Josephine gave a nod and felt the hand slide away from her mouth but only to take hold of her arm firmly. "We will need you to come with us." Josephine did not hesitate to answer him.

"I would rather not do anything of the sort, friend or not."

"We have to insist," the taller man said.

"You are frightening me," she pleaded. "Just let me go on my way."

"Our intentions are not to frighten you or harm you, but our friend may die if you do not help him." The man waved his hand, and footsteps could be heard and Josephine saw men moving farther down the side street. The man turned her to the side. "I apologize, my lady, but you must be blindfolded," the taller man said. "Cooperate and you will not be bound nor gagged."

"No!" Josephine said in a whimper as she watched the man who had a hold of her arm pull a cloth out from under his cape. "Please don't," she begged, not knowing what the men were truly about to do with her. Struggling against him was useless, and she knew it would only make matters worse at this point being at such a disadvantage, so she turned her efforts to gathering as much information as she could as the blindfold was secured. "If the man's life is truly in the balances, then let me go for the doctor as I am but training as a nurse."

"My lady, you of all people know that we are on the brink of war. Not many can be trusted."

"Then you are with my enemy?" she asked as the hooded man began to walk, guiding her as they went.

"Not necessarily. But due to eyes and ears being everywhere and rumors of the enemy lurking in every corner, how can one know who is friend or foe in times such as these."

"Then how do you know that *I* can be trusted?" the lady asked as they came to a stop.

"Because you are honorable and would never let a man perish over foolish ideas. My friend will carry you so as not to chance you falling . . . or being able to find our location again." Josephine expected to be picked up and tossed over the man's shoulder like a sack of feed, but instead she was carefully lifted up in his arms. A few minutes passed and she could tell they were going around obstacles by how her kidnapper swayed to the left or right. She had determined with her vision obstructed to do her best to obtain clues to where she was being taken. Voices could be heard and occasionally a rumble or whiny of a horse but nothing distinguishable. Finally, the first man announced that they had arrived and she was sat down. The blindfold was removed to reveal she was in a room with blankets draping three of the walls. A man was lying in a bed and even from a distance blood could be seen soaking through his shirt with his upper chest at the right shoulder bearing a nasty gash. The first man explained the wound had only been washed, and a simple bandage applied but a lot of blood had been lost on the journey to Seim. Josephine asked for water, bandages, and more light as she reached for the man's tattered shirt. Out of the corner of her eye, she saw the glimmer of a knife blade beside her and gave a gasp as the sight startled her. Quickly the hooded man flipped the knife so that the blade rested in his palm as he silently offered it for the lady to use. Regaining her composure, Josephine took it from him and cut away the shirt. She asked for thread or horse hair to use for sewing and trying to be discreet Josephine slid a needle from the bottom edge of her petticoat. She had started keeping a needle or two there just in case she was separated from her medical pouch and was caught in a bind. Carefully the lady washed the wound and sterilized her needle in the candle flame and then began mending the unconscious man. The hooded man remained at her side, assisting as she instructed him but never saying a word to her. Several times, Josephine attempted to get a better look at his face, but he recognized her efforts and managed to turn his head just enough that all she saw was his coal black beard. Even when the lady asked him questions, he did not answer but the taller man spoke for him. When she had done all that she knew to do, she covered the man's wound with a blanket and asked for clean water to wash her hands. As it was brought, Josephine tried to look around the room, but the two men seemed to know her intentions and came and stood close by, preventing her from seeing too much.

"Where are we?" Josephine asked. The first man smiled and looked toward his friend.

With a laugh, he replied, "You are a brave one, aren't you?"

"I would say *you* are the brave one for not hiding your face from me like your companion has."

"I have no reason to hide from you. I am not from here nor will I ever be in these parts again once I see this man home. I am a friend of a friend you might say. Friends don't have to hide their faces."

"Must you only speak in riddles?" Josephine said with a glare, frustrated that every effort she had made to learn something of these men had been blocked.

"Better than to speak lies," he answered. The patient moaned, and as Josephine returned to his side, she begged that he be taken to a real doctor for better care. The first man was quick to answer. "That option is not available to us."

"He has lost a lot of blood, and there is greater risk of infection with the wound being as it is. He needs more care," she argued. "Surely you can trust his life to a doctor."

"It's not that the doctor could not be trusted but how would you suggest getting this man to Dr. Stehle? We would be seen by the villagers, and what then? Many lives depend on it *not* being known that he is here."

"Then he is a man of great importance?" Josephine asked.

"Is every life not important my lady? Would you have saved him if he were of noble birth or let him die if he was a lowly peasant?" Before she could answer, he spoke for her. "His station matters not to you. You, Josephine Armand, have regard for every man. You hold the respect of the people and the crown of both friends and enemies alike." He paused. "So I have heard." The statement was meant as a compliment, but the connotations were unnerving for the lady. Would her reputation be such that her character was known beyond Gutten? The thought of her name being mentioned at her enemy's table bothered her. The pressing question however still remained to be answered. Was she standing in the presence of a friend or an enemy? Nervously she lifted the blanket, checking the patient's wound, and to her relief, the bleeding had virtually stopped. The lady covered the man again, and as she turned, she saw the hooded man pulling the blindfold from his cape again. Her heart began to race as he stepped toward her.

"Please," she said. "I won't tell just . . ."

"It is for your own safety as well as ours," the taller man said, reaching for her as she had shrunk back from them. "We are sorry." She closed her eyes trying not to panic. When the blindfold was secured, Josephine was picked up again, but this time, it seemed the way they traveled was rougher. Finally her curiosity forced her to ask.

"Where are you taking me for this is not the way we came?" To her surprise, she heard several men give a muffled laugh and mumble remarks to each other. Suddenly all grew quiet and the man carrying her came to an abrupt stop. He turned sharply and then ducked under something. The suddenness of his movements caused the lady to gasp at which he pressed his lips to her cheek.

"*Shhhh*," he said in a quiet but deep voice. She could hear other sounds that she recognized as from the main street. It seemed they were outside, as the edges of the blindfold appeared brighter, but then maybe it was just her imagination. A few minutes more passed and then she heard the taller man whisper that it was clear to move. They walked some more, and this time, when they stopped, she was let down from the hooded man's arms.

"You are back where you were earlier. Say nothing of this to the doctor, but that your errand ran long," the taller man said as the blindfold was untied.

"And how do you know I was on an errand?" Josephine asked curtly.

"Shall I describe in detail what you have done the last two days here in Seim or shall I mention the two days you spent in Winfalle or the three days before that in Terkulla?" The lady could feel the blood drain from her face as the man told of where she had been. "You will say nothing of this," he demanded.

"I cannot promise that," she replied but then wished she hadn't said anything as he stepped closer to her and with a threatening look added.

"Can your conscience bear someone dying because of you? That is what will happen as my friend will not survive being moved too soon. If any of my party are discovered, it will result in bloodshed, whether they be friend or foe. Do you understand what I am saying?" The defiant part of Josephine wanted to speak up, saying it was better for the truth to be known, but the reasonable part of her wouldn't let her do it. Like it or not, she knew the man's words held truth. The wounded man would die, and there could be the unnecessary loss of life as there were not many guardsmen in the village with the prince being gone to arrest her kidnappers. But what if the man was implying that if she reported the incident that people close to her would be hurt? Yes, her kidnapper had the advantage, and if she didn't agree to his demands, she doubted she would be set free either.

"I will do as you have asked for now, but I cannot promise that it will be kept from the prince."

"Fair enough. That will give us a day's rest for he is not expected until tomorrow afternoon, or am I mistaken?" the man asked with a smile, gloating over the fact that he knew the lady's affairs. He took hold of Josephine's arm and led her to the edge of the street. "Go on now. Don't look behind you. We have kept our end of the bargain, you keep yours. Say nothing and all will go well." He edged back into the shadows.

Josephine began to walk almost in a daze, as she thought about the man's words. It had not been a secret of their comings and goings with the doctor or of the movement of guardsmen throughout the kingdom but there was no doubt in her mind that she had been watched the past week. The farther she went, the faster she nervously walked until she came to the clinic. When she stepped inside, she found it bustling as usual and she fell right into her normal duties. About midday, Dr. Stehle called for lunch and taking the lady to the side asked if she was well for she was rather pale. Josephine dismissed it as having a restless night and they continued with their duties. That evening when the doctor called it a day and they were walking back to the inn together he again addressed the lady's quietness. This time she gave the excuse of having a lot on her mind. Dr. Stehle teased, asking if she was missing a certain young man and she admitted that although she was, other distractions were plaguing her thoughts. At supper, she picked at her food and finally excused herself for the night. She was halfway down the corridor leading to her room when she came to a sudden stop. Could someone be waiting there for her? And, even if she found the room empty, would she be able to rest that night wondering if someone was spying on her? She was staring at the far end of the hall when the door to her left opened, startling her.

"Good evening," Wilhelm said as he folded down his collar. He had just changed clothes, and in a hurry to eat supper, his shirt was not buttoned nor tucked in yet. Josephine's first impulse was to reach for him, to lay her head against his shoulder in relief, but she didn't as she managed to keep her emotions under control.

"We were not expecting you," the lady mumbled. Seemingly caught off guard, she stood motionless before him as he began buttoning his shirt. On the third button, he stopped and reached for the lady's arm only to feel her trembling.

"I didn't scare you that much. What is wrong?" he asked. The words of the kidnapper echoed through her mind and Josephine battled what she should do.

"It's nothing. I take it things went better than you expected," she said, faking a smile, hoping to change the subject. A guardsman walked past, and greetings were exchanged. Before he was out of sight, Wilhelm took the lady gently by the shoulders.

"Look at me," he said softly. "I know you better than that." Josephine could only look at him a moment before she closed her eyes.

"I need to speak with you," she whispered. Wilhelm let go of her long enough to address someone standing behind her.

"Have my supper brought to my room and send Vaughn as well." The prince's gaze returned to the lady and she opened her eyes. "Come. Tell me all that is troubling you." He led Josephine back inside his room leaving the door wide open for honor's sake. He took a seat, but she walked to the fireplace and stared at the flames. After a few minutes had passed, Wilhelm came beside Josephine.

"I have done something that may have been very wrong," she began as she turned to face him. Her countenance was now terribly pale and her eyes were full of tears. Vaughn stepped into the room carrying a tray. Wilhelm motioned for him to shut the door, and when it was closed, Josephine began her tale. She had only made it to the part of being blindfolded before Wilhelm exploded about how she had not heeded his warning and was trapesing about the kingdom without an escort. Vaughn was standing near enough that he touched the prince's arm and spoke keeping his voice low enough that the lady could not hear, but it caused Wilhelm to stop in the middle of his ranting. Josephine defended her actions stating she had just parted from Dr. Stehle and who would have known anyone was brave enough to abduct her from the main street? As the lady began to cry, she asked how was she to know her every move was being watched to the point that her enemy could do with her as they pleased. The statement shocked both men, and they asked her to explain what she meant by it. This time Wilhelm's reaction was entirely different as Josephine described what had happened. The prince realized how foolish he was for rebuking the lady for even if an escort had been present he would have been overcome and killed. Josephine had played her part in the situation wisely and by keeping her focus had made it back safely. By the time she came to the end of her tale, Wilhelm had made his way to the trembling lady and had taken her in his arms. As he looked across the room where Vaughn was seated, it was agreed the time had come to be more careful with who knew their personal agendas as all doubt had been removed about spies being in their midst. As far as the threat for the lady to remain silent, the men were not sure whether the "lives" meant the abductors or the people working near Josephine. Searching the village at that hour would put the guardsmen at a disadvantage that might cost them dearly. The matter would have to wait till morning, and by then, the men would more than likely be gone. Josephine was commended for daring to press the men for information and although she did not feel like she learned anything of value she was assured it would help in discovering their enemy's plot. The lady would be discreetly placed in another room for the night with not even the innkeeper knowing of the switch. Josephine's color had returned and she wasn't trembling anymore, and Wilhelm knew she was feeling better when the lady insisted that he stop fussing over her and eat his now cold supper. He obliged the request as Vaughn left the room to do what was needed for the night and Josephine took a seat across from the prince and told of news that had filtered into the clinic while Wilhelm ate. The prince couldn't help but wonder how close he had come to losing the lady forever.

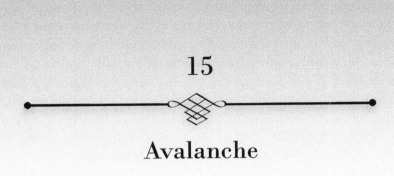

15

Avalanche

"Have you gotten your fill of snow yet?" Wilhelm asked with a laugh as large snowflakes began to fall from the sky. Josephine returned an exaggerated smile that faded quickly for she was already cold from riding that morning. Over three feet of snow was still blanketing the ground from the last week's storm, and by the look of the clouds, another several inches was on the way. The lady had traveled with the prince and the guard to Delsan two days earlier to check on troops and speak with Duke Mendelson. His couriers had brought word that several caravans were seen moving through the passes which alarmed Wilhelm enough that he thought a visit was needed. Mendelson's loyalties were with the king, and the older ally was not ashamed to beg for reinforcements doubting that his defenses would hold if attacked. A company of soldiers had been brought to secure the area. The lady had been asked to accompany the troop hoping to calm nerves, in an effort to keep life as normal as possible under the threat of invasion and was to make a list of basic necessities that were in short supply since most of the people were afraid to venture very far. With the first half of their mission accomplished, the prince and lady had started back to Guttenhamm with only a dozen of the Elite Guard as their escorts. Despite Wilhelm's teasing, Josephine had enjoyed the trip for the snow was much deeper in the mountainous range and looked quite picturesque. Twice already the riders had been caught in the weather but had taken shelter in a nearby home until it was safe to take to the road again. The snow made for a long, slow trip, and all the fur lining the queen could have added to boots and clothing couldn't keep Josephine warm but a few hours and then, she just had to endure until she reached her destination. Of course the lady dare not mention this to the prince for he was always asking if she was warm enough and she had taken to answering that she would always be colder than he was. It wasn't that Wilhelm was trying to coddle the lady, for he didn't consider her physically weak by any means, and the day when she fought against the recruits at the garrison had proven it, but he respected that God made her in a delicate frame that although strong, should not have to endure extremes for extended periods of time. Wilhelm admitted to pestering the lady by asking if she was warm enough or uncomfortable or tired, but as she rarely complained, he was at a loss but to have to ask. For the longest time, it had annoyed Josephine, but things had changed between them and she understood his intentions and was no longer offended.

"I still think the snow is beautiful," she replied to the prince but not loud enough to hear added, "except when you are caught out in it so far from shelter and frozen to the bone." The group kept riding with the snow falling harder until the front of the procession could no longer be seen from the rear of the procession. Josephine was directly behind Wilhelm and saw him raise his arm for them to halt. Turning his horse, he rode back toward the middle, calling for the men to gather in. The wind had picked up enough that the prince had to raise his voice to be heard.

"How far would you guess we are from Jansville?" he asked. Vaughn answered with Niethel agreeing. "And the last home we passed is more than a league away."

"Are you thinking we should turn back?" Niethel asked.

"It's coming down too fast to keep toward Jansville," Wilhelm answered.

"What about Maylor's cave?" Vaughn suggested. "Isn't it somewhere around here?"

"Yes, but it's been a long time. Can we find it in less time than it would take to ride elsewhere?" Wilhelm asked, looking in the direction of the mountain.

"If I remember correctly, there were smaller caves dotting the hillside. All we have to do is find one big enough for all of us," the captain replied. Wilhelm shifted in his saddle as he contemplated a decision.

"All right then, everyone ride toward the hill." Within ten minutes, they were facing a bluff rising more than a hundred feet straight up. Josephine was to stay put as the center marker with half the men going left and the other half going right along the rock with the group meeting back in the middle if needed. Time was precious as the weather got worse by the minute. Josephine had dismounted and was pacing to and fro to keep warm while she waited. Finally she heard someone yell, and she returned a call in time to see a figure emerging from her right. Vaughn's group had found a cave large enough to shelter even the horses. As he traded places with the lady, he explained that it was hundreds of feet away but for her to stay against the bluff and she would find it. After what seemed like forever and having to feel her way along the rock in the blinding snow, Josephine came to the entrance. The cave was about eighty feet deep with a slight curve to it. At the opening, it was about twelve feet high, and then at the rear, it suddenly sloped down to almost nothing. As the lady warmed herself by the fire that had been built, Lt. Drake explained that this was definitely a smaller one of Maylor's caves as the biggest one went back into the mountain hundreds of feet with a huge cavern in its belly. The others came leading the horses about a half an hour later and none too soon for the snow was piling up. When the animals were inside, they were unsaddled and then the men set to making a makeshift wall of branches to block off the cave entrance. Not only would the wall keep the horses in but the wind and snow out. Pine and cedar branches were also cut and brought in to lay blankets on for sleeping later that night. When the shelter was finished, the men removed boots and coats to let their bodies soak up the warmth, and Josephine passed out jerky and bread. Every so often, the makeshift outer wall would creak and sway in the wind, but as the snow grew deeper, less of a breeze made it to the back of the cave. After two hours had passed, it was agreed that more wood had to be gathered before it was completely dark. Shortly the men returned pulling what they had found inside the cave and then took turns chopping the wood with the two axes that had been brought with the supplies. Feeling set for the night, the men seemed more at ease and settled around the fire, leaning back against their saddles. As she was falling asleep, Josephine wondered what they would do if the blizzard lasted more than a day but then decided if the men were not concerned, then she wouldn't be either. After all, they had managed quite well before.

The prince slid his sword from under the edge of the lady's blanket, startling her. "What is it?" Josephine whispered as Wilhelm rose up on one elbow.

"Don't know," he said as he watched the cave entrance. Two of the guards were already to their feet and cautiously moving past the horses, whose neighing had woke everyone. Carefully the men peered through the snow clad wall of branches and then gave a laugh. In the light of day, they could see rabbits bounding outside the entrance in the fresh snow. It was humorous not only that all had slept later than usual in the tomblike silence, but that for a moment, they thought they had been surrounded by their enemy. There was just enough jerky and bread left for breakfast, and it took only a few minutes for the horses to be saddled and repacked.

The snow clouds had given way to a brilliant blue sky, but the air remained bitterly cold. The company had ridden for more than an hour passing Capresan and was at the last rise of bluffs leading into the foothills. Suddenly, something was spotted up ahead and two guardsmen went to scout. While they were waiting, Wilhelm called Josephine's attention down the hillside to a clearing where more than a dozen deer were pawing the snow for food. The animals noticed the humans long enough to lift their heads but not feeling threatened, returned to their foraging. A whistle was heard from up ahead and the group began to move, except for Josephine who stayed behind to watch the deer. She was just about to leave when she heard voices in the distance. She stopped to listen, thinking the men were calling to her, but as she looked, she could see no one turned in her direction. In fact, it seemed as if they were moving around something on the ground. Suddenly, she heard voices again and turned to look at the road behind her but then realized the sound was coming from the bluff above.

"Almost there," a man said. Josephine could clearly make out each word, but his voice seemed so unusual, being very deep and almost growly like a bear as he spoke.

"No, wait. He's already too far past us for it to do any good," another man replied.

"It'll take him out, I guarantee that. He won't know what hit him. Just watch me." Josephine heard a shuffling sound. The lady rose up in her saddle, straining to see around the ledge above. Suddenly there was the cracking sound of rocks shifting and then a rumble.

"No, wait. Stop! The lady is down there. No!" Josephine looked up in time to see the movement of large shadows above and a fear gripped her heart. Frantically she dug her heels into the sides of her horse and screamed. The horse reared and lunged but did not make it a full two strides before a wall of snow hit, washing the pair down the hillside.

When Josephine awoke, she was lying in a bed in a dimly lit room. She did not recognize the surroundings, but glancing around, she saw the top of Wilhelm's head. He had pulled a chair beside the bed and had fallen asleep with his head coming to rest on the blanket beside her hand. The lady began to flex her extremities and the only pain was coming from the right side of her body where she had hit the ground. Wilhelm was truly exhausted for with all her movement he had not stirred the slightest bit. She debated whether to let him sleep till morning or wake him but then reached for his head and began to stroke his hair. The third pass her fingers made with no response the lady almost stopped, but as she thought how worried he was about her, she continued. Finally he let out a sigh and lifted his head from the bed. As soon as he saw Josephine's face, he began to weep and took her hand to kiss it. He asked how she felt and then she asked where they were and how they got there. The men were just far enough away not to be washed down the hill in the avalanche as she had. When the river of snow stopped, they climbed down the hillside just able to see the top of the horse's head where the pair had lodged against an outcropping of rock. Frantically the men dug her out. The lady had remained unconscious until she was lifted into Wilhelm's arms when he was mounted to ride. At that point, she mumbled something then slipped away again. Fifteen minutes later, they came to the house they were now in. The lady of the home undressed Josephine and looked her over for injuries, finding none but warned that it didn't necessarily mean everything was fine on the inside. Not knowing whether it was safe to move her by horseback, some of the men had went on to the next village in search of a sleigh and brought one back just after dark. Wilhelm had not left the lady's side, deciding not to chance the sleigh ride until she either woke up or they could bring Dr. Stehle to examine her. While Wilhelm and Josephine spoke, the lady stretched her arms and legs and then asked Wilhelm to steady her for she wanted to try to walk. He was not privy to the idea but reluctantly agreed because she was aching from lying for hours. Josephine had pulled the blanket back and started to turn to put her legs down to the floor, when suddenly she cried out in pain and then grew very still.

"It's my ribs, on the right side of my back," she stated. The prince moved his chair to where he was directly in front of the lady.

"Has the doctor shown you how to check if they are broken?" Wilhelm asked, and Josephine said he had. "Well then, you know what I need to do. Let me help you to the edge of the bed." The lady leaned forward with her arms coming to rest on his shoulders. For discretion's sake, he had her cover her chest with her left arm since she was only wearing a gown and the pain was on her right side. Starting at the lowest point, he began to carefully trace the bone to feel anything out of the ordinary. On the third rib when he was almost to her side, he grazed the sore spot and she gasped. "Let me go over that place again." She nodded. Before his fingers touched her side, she suddenly gave him a serious look and grabbed his arm.

"You have not mentioned my horse. Did she make it out all right?" she asked. Wilhelm did not answer and kept his attention upon the task. Nothing more had to be said for the lady knew the horse had perished. It only took a second for the prince to touch the sore spot again, and she flinched.

"I am not feeling a break but that doesn't mean it isn't cracked," Wilhelm said.

"I know," the lady replied in an agitated tone because he hadn't answered her question about the horse. Turning toward the door of the room, the prince asked in a louder voice if something could be found to wrap the lady's ribs. Vaughn had heard the two talking and had come to the door to see how she was.

He took a step into the room and asked, "Broken?"

"Thinking they are cracked . . . but I am not willing to chance it." When they were alone once more, the prince looked very somberly into Josephine's eyes. "I am sorry that your horse didn't make it. She was truly suited for you in every way, but we will get you another one. Right now the focus is on you. After a few days rest here, then we will see about going home."

"We can't wait that long," Josephine said, interrupting him. "What about the men on the bluff, did you find them?"

"What men?" Wilhelm asked as Vaughn came back into the room and handed him a small roll of cloth.

"The two that were on top of the bluff that started the avalanche," Josephine replied as she reached for the bandages but the prince moved his hand where she couldn't take them from him. When he did, he gave Vaughn a questioning look which Josephine saw. "I may have hit my head, but not hard enough to dream it up." Wilhelm had the lady rest her arms back on his shoulders as he began to wind the cloth around her torso. "Wilhelm, please. At first I thought it was one of you calling to me, and then I realized the voices were from above me and I tried to get a better look. The first man was talking about how he was going to take you out. The second man tried to stop him, saying the avalanche wouldn't reach you, but the first man didn't listen. And about that time is when the second man saw that I was below the bluff. He begged the first man to stop what he was doing, but it was too late. That is when I understood what they were talking about and tried to get away but . . ." Her voice broke with emotion and she looked down at the floor. Wilhelm stopped where he was and dropped his hands to her waist.

"You are safe now and that is all that matters," he whispered. The lady looked up at him.

"They were trying to kill you," Josephine said with tears in her eyes. "I have delayed you too long already. Leave me and you go on to safety. The more distance between you and them . . ."

"I am not leaving you, now or ever," he said firmly. She shook her head to protest. "No one will go anywhere until light, and then we will only leave if there is no risk of injuring you further."

"Fine then. Finish and help me to my feet," she said. The lady made it across the room but had to stop for her head was spinning. While she stood clinging to the wall, Wilhelm and Vaughn agreed the story seemed feasible since the road had been blocked by several trees which was why they had to stop to begin with. Josephine added that she was certain she could identify the first man by his voice. In the middle of her statement she paused and Wilhelm caught her as the strength left her body. She did not completely lose consciousness and when she was tucked back under the blanket she begged for them to leave at dawn. She continued whispering that her head hurt more than her ribs so she could travel. Wilhelm hushed the lady, demanding that she rest and reminded her that he would be making the decision best for all. As soon as she closed her eyes, she was fast asleep.

As the lady had hoped, the company left at dawn. Josephine was not nearly as dizzy while she walked to the sleigh where she was to ride with Lt. Drake at the reins as the sleigh was not large enough to comfortably hold three people. When they came to Kensithe, they stopped long enough to water the horses and stretch legs. Very discretely Drake told the prince that Josephine was struggling to stay awake and had complained how it was terribly cold outside. This time when they got ready to leave, Wilhelm climbed into the sleigh with Drake and made the lady sit crossways on his lap. Josephine was not happy about the new arrangement, considering it an insult, but didn't argue very long as she didn't possess the strength to do so. They had not driven very far when she rested her head against the prince's shoulder and fell asleep. When they arrived in Guttenhamm, the lady was taken straight to the clinic. A small bruise was now visible upon Josephine's ribs, but Dr. Stehle said nothing was broken. He did suggest a day or two of rest followed by a week of light duty. The doctor knew the lady well enough to know she wouldn't remain still much longer than that. Back at the castle, Josephine was not in a hurry to stir much and followed the instructions and rested.

The next morning as Wilhelm and Josephine were going from the chapel to breakfast, the prince's curiosity got the better of him.

"So how are you really feeling?" he asked.

"Better every day," the lady replied as they approached the top of the staircase. The prince turned and stopped her before she could take the first step down, but he stepped down two steps which made them look eye to eye. He didn't believe her. "You think I am lying?"

"I wouldn't go that far. I just find it strange that the lady who scared me half to death jumping out a barn loft window for fun has willingly stayed in her room for a whole day. Either you are hurt and don't want us to know, or you are up to something." At the latter comment, Josephine's gaze left the prince's for a moment, and when it returned, he had raised an eyebrow and tilted his head.

"My body is fine, but my mind had been consumed with other things," she answered, but still not satisfied Wilhelm took hold of her hands.

"And what other things would that be?" he asked. The lady knew he would not be happy with the truth, but she decided to say it regardless.

"I have been trying to figure out where to start looking for those other men."

"You are not doing anything of the sort," he scolded.

"Not alone, but if we . . ."

"There is no *we* in the matter because you are not to be out and about yet. Besides how do you know where to look? They may not still be in the kingdom," the prince reasoned.

"I believe they are," she said, and Wilhelm shook his head in disapproval but the lady continued anyways. "They had to have been seen in one of northern villages at least." She began to explain that she believed they were not part of a larger group because if so, they all would have been killed long before they reached the bluff area. Being loners meant that they would have been in a village for supplies, since it would be too hard to live off the land being winter. She was convinced by their accent that they were not locals which meant that *someone* would have noticed the strangers. All she would have to do is ask around, describing the unusual voice of the first man, and they would have a lead on where they were now, or at least the last place they had been. She might feel up to riding by the next morning and the quicker they began searching, the quicker the men would be found. Wilhelm had begun to pull the lady toward him as he listened and now his hands were resting gently around her back. When she was done, he gave a smile.

"Perhaps we should have given you a different government position."

"What do you mean by that?" she quipped as she thought he was mocking her.

"Because," He leaned close until his forehead touched hers— "that is the same conclusion Father and I reached the day we returned." Josephine leaned back far enough to see Wilhelm's eyes as he continued, "Now we are just waiting for word that they have been caught." The way the prince smiled let her know he was proud that her thoughts were in line with his. "Let's go eat. I am starved."

Breakfast was halfway over when a messenger stepped to the doorway. The king motioned for him to approach, and after only a few words, Hubert rose to his feet and nodded for his sons to join him. They were in the hallway but a few minutes when Wilhelm came back to ask Josephine if she felt up to a briefing. She agreed, he took her arm, and they walked out together. Hubert explained that the lady's theory had been proven correct as the two criminals were last seen in Lithel. The description Josephine had given matched perfectly with what the villagers had said concerning the men's voices. The lady was relieved the men had been found for there was no longer an added threat to Wilhelm's life and justice would be served for her accident. A strange look crossed the king's face as he began to explain that justice had already been served for one of the men. The man with the growly voice had been discovered hanging from a tree the next morning *after* the avalanche. He was dead long before inquiries had begun concerning the incident, and it could only be assumed that someone else knew of the deed and had taken it into their own hands. Josephine grew pale and asked to return to the dining room to sit down. Leopold took her and left her with his mother but quickly came back to the hallway. He found his father unrolling a parchment that the messenger had given him. It was pinned to the chest of the dead man.

> Woe be to anyone who
> harms my beloved.

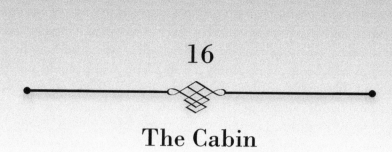

16

The Cabin

"My liege, there is a courier up ahead," Niethel called out, and brought his horse alongside the carriage. Slowly they came to a stop to receive the message. A few minutes passed and while Wilhelm read the parchment, Josephine took the opportunity and stepped out to stretch her legs.

After she was back in the carriage, the lady asked, "Is everything all right?" Wilhelm's countenance was not troubled, but she was curious what had been important enough to warrant a courier being sent out.

"Everything is well. We've been invited to supper," the prince said with a smile. "But it will put our schedule behind by a day."

"I thought we agreed not to be frustrated by delays," Josephine reminded him. It had been just over a month since she had been buried under the snow and had not ventured beyond Guttenhamm, content to wait for signs of spring while she recuperated. Winter had tapered to an end with the snow beginning to melt in the lower elevations of Gutten. Knowing how much she enjoyed travelling, Wilhelm had asked the lady to accompany him as he checked outposts in the western quadrant. The particular region they would visit had been blessed with peace throughout the winter, and although the outing would last the better part of two weeks, it would be a welcome relief.

Despite Josephine's profession of being carefree, Wilhelm knew she didn't tolerate unnecessary delays.

"We did agree not to fuss about things that are out of our control," the prince said, still smiling as he watched for the lady's reaction. Suddenly the carriage slowed and made a turn to the left. Josephine glanced toward the window and then back at Wilhelm.

"Are you going to tell me where we are headed or are you making me wait until we arrive?" she asked, causing the prince to give a hearty laugh.

"After the scare you gave me on our last outing, I think you should have to wait to find out," he replied and turned his head away, pretending to ignore the lady seated across from him. Josephine couldn't help but smile. The prince seemed amused to keep her in suspense, so she knew she would be pleased when the secret unfolded. The road wound through the foothills and upward into the mountains. Finally the carriage came to a stop and the door was opened to reveal a massive log cabin more than two stories high with a covered porch that stretched across the front.

"My lady," Wilhelm said, stepping from the carriage and turning to reach for Josephine's hand. "Welcome to our mountain hideaway." The lady found herself smiling from ear to ear having heard the cabin mentioned but never imagining it to be so grand. The pair had barely made it inside when they were called to by the king and queen. Hubert and Agatha had slipped away from Guttenhamm for a few days of peace and quiet. They had not been in the mountains very long when it was mentioned that the young lady had yet to see the royal retreat. The prince and lady should be passing through the area and a courier was sent out to find them. Josephine teased that word must have reached the king's ears that the accommodations at Sarna the evening before were lacking and she needed a good night's sleep. Agatha quickly whisked Josephine away to give a tour of the cabin before showing the young lady to her room to freshen up.

The ladies had only been in Josephine's room a few minutes when Wilhelm came to the door asking if his travelling companion felt up to a brisk walk into the woods. Without hesitation, Josephine agreed, overjoyed to resume activities that she had missed the past few weeks. Some snow was still upon the ground, but not enough to hinder the pair as they quickly moved through the forest. Finally, Wilhelm paused as they came to a cluster of fir trees where two walls of rock seemed to overlap. He took the lady by the hand and they ducked under the tree branches, then carefully squeezed through the jagged outcropping. When they emerged on the other side, they were standing on a ledge of rock about twelve feet wide that was suspended hundreds of feet in the air above the valley below. Wilhelm felt the lady's fingers tighten between his as she leaned back toward the wall behind them. Being accustomed to the height, he would have stepped forward, but not wanting to frighten her, the prince leaned back as well and rested against the mountain.

"I was afraid we wouldn't make it," he said as Josephine glanced toward him. "I thought you might enjoy seeing the sunset from here. You have to admit it's a rather unique viewpoint."

"How did you ever find it?" Josephine asked, bravely taking a step away from the wall.

"I can't take the credit, for it was my grandfather who stumbled upon it," the prince said, moving away from the wall but still holding on to the lady's hand. "And he brought my father up here and then when Leopold and I were old enough—"

As she took another step and glanced over the edge, she interrupted him, "And your mother?" Wilhelm stepped closer and steadied the lady as she swayed a bit at the dizzying height.

"Father said that he brought her but never mentioned that she returned with him after the first time." The prince glanced at Josephine and with a smile added, "She's not as eager to explore nature as some that I know." Both laughed for it was true that the queen did not enjoy the outdoors with all its inconveniences.

The pair quietly watched the sun sinking behind the distant mountains, and then Wilhelm whispered, "There is a catch to this splendid view." Josephine turned to look him square in the face, eyebrows serious. "When the sun sets, we will have to be in a dead run to make it to the cabin before it's completely dark." The lady shook her head and looked off in the distance one more time.

"And just when I thought I had made it a full week without being in trouble."

They made it to the cabin as dusk was falling and the only comment from the king as they rushed into the great hall was that baths awaited them upstairs before the queen would let them come to the supper table. When the last plate was empty, the family made their way to the great room and settled into comfortable chairs in front of the rock fireplace. Only a few minutes had passed before Hubert asked Agatha to join him on the front porch, and as they began to leave the room, Josephine noticed the older couple reaching for each other's hands. They had just made it to the doorway when soft laughing was heard as Hubert put his arm around his wife's shoulders. Josephine lowered her head and smiled at the sweet scene. It brought back memories of her parents slipping away in the evening to walk along the lane together. So many times she and Arlene watched as their parents stopped at the last gate and embraced. The girls would giggle to each other, teasing about how foolish it was, but they never doubted the love their parents had for each other. Josephine was smiling to herself when suddenly she remembered how Wilhelm had taken her in his arms upon the staircase when she was pressing him to look for the men that caused the avalanche. The lady rose to her feet and strode across the room trying not to look in his direction.

"I think I'll turn in," she announced, and before Wilhelm could get to his feet, she hurried to the staircase. She had almost reached the second floor when she heard the prince bid her good night. She looked over her shoulder, replied and then left him standing alone. Quickly he stepped backward until he could see the doors along the upstairs hallway, and watched Josephine go into her room and shut the door. With a long sigh, he walked to the fireplace and leaned against the mantle as he stared into the flames. He was lost in thought when the king and queen returned.

"Wilhelm . . ." Hubert said as he surveyed the room. "We expected to find you and Josephine together." His son turned to look at him.

"Yes, this is not how I thought the evening would end," Wilhelm said, not hiding his disappointment. Hubert and Agatha exchanged looks and then his mother asked if something had happened. "Not a word was said after the two of you left the room and I didn't have the chance to even suggest sitting together." Wilhelm took a few steps and then looked up to the balcony. "She just hurried away so quickly that I couldn't even ask if she was all right." He shook his head seemingly perplexed and then added. "The one time we were finally alone without a catastrophe bursting through the door or a castle full of eyes and ears and . . ." Hubert and Agatha smiled at their son's statement and was glad he didn't notice their reaction.

"Where is she now?" the queen asked softly, walking to her son.

"She's in her room," Wilhelm replied as his mother reached for his arm.

"Don't worry. I will look in on her."

A few minutes later, Agatha knocked on the young lady's door and let herself into the room. Josephine was standing near the fireplace with her back to the door.

"You are just as I left Wilhelm downstairs," the queen said as she went to the bed and turned down the blankets. Josephine didn't move or reply, so Agatha went to her and gave her a hug. "He is worried that you are upset with him." The words caused the young lady to look at the older woman.

"He has only been good to me," she stated. "Always treating me better than I have ever deserved, taking me to hidden places that should only be reserved for royalty . . ." Her voice trailed off and she looked away.

"Is that what is bothering you? Why should he not share something so beautiful with his closest friend?" Agatha took hold of Josephine's shoulders and gently turned her to see her face as she continued, "Oh my dear, he has ached for months to spend time with you unhindered by the affairs of state. You, who understands him better than anyone else, who cherishes all the things that he holds dear to him, why wouldn't he take you to the ledge to see such a sight?" Josephine's heart raced as a fear grew in her mind. Agatha let loose of the lady's shoulders and motioned her to follow as she began to help her undress.

"It's just that sometimes . . . well, sometimes . . . I can't describe the look I see in his eyes," Josephine mumbled as she slid her nightgown over her head. Agatha had taken the young lady's dress to lay it over a chair and was thankful her back was to Josephine for she could not hide the smile upon her face. The situation was as she had guessed. Returning from across the room, she fluffed the pillows as the young lady climbed into bed. When the blankets were pulled up, Agatha took Josephine's hand.

"Has Wilhelm ever done anything that you cannot be alone with him?" Suddenly the queen noticed tears welling up in Josephine's eyes.

"I will not risk our friendship over one foolish moment," she whispered with determination. Agatha smiled and patted the young lady's hand.

"It will not be lost, but you must trust him. I heard him asking his father about taking you sightseeing again tomorrow. Go with him and enjoy the time together, alone," she said, drawing out the last word. "It may be a while before either of you can escape your duties." Kissing Josephine, the queen said good night, blew out the lamps and left the room.

The next morning just after dawn, Josephine awoke, dressed and went downstairs to the kitchen. Only a few minutes passed before the prince came into the room wanting to know if the lady had left any coffee for him. With everything in him, he wanted to ask about the hasty departure the evening before, but he bit his tongue and instead began to discuss the outing he had planned. Josephine fell right into the conversation, which set his mind at ease. They would leave after breakfast and return by midmorning. Only one horse would be needed, as part of the trail was extremely steep, and the prince felt better being at the reins with his arms secured around the lady. Josephine did not protest riding double for the last time they had ventured up a mountain side the prince ended up moving her to his horse, as she was not stern enough with her mare to keep her climbing up the steep grade.

An hour later, the pair dismounted at a small but steady stream, and taking the lady's hand in his, Wilhelm led Josephine along its banks. As they rounded a large fir tree, a waterfall could be seen in the distance. The prince explained that they would go no further because of the remaining snow but promised that at the first opportunity, he would bring her back to the place. Even at a distance, the falls were beautiful and it made the lady anxious to return. At first, Wilhelm was not going to tell the secret of the falls, but almost exploding with excitement, he began to explain. If their footing was steady, they could pass through the water to find themselves in a small cave that ran a short distance into the mountain. Josephine was impressed, squeezing the prince's hand as he assured her she would enjoy the experience although she would be soaked through and through by the frigid water. The lady would have been content to stay longer, but the prince reminded her that he still had one more place to take her before they headed back to the cabin.

This time when they mounted, Josephine was helped into the saddle first, and she knew it meant the ride was about to get rough. Wilhelm retraced the trail they had come but then turned the horse down a little path that led north. As the way grew steeper, Josephine became anxious as it was harder for her to keep from leaning back against Wilhelm. The horse scurried up a little outcropping, and Josephine slammed backward into Wilhelm's chest. Suddenly the prince pulled the reins tight bringing the horse to a halt.

"Have I the plague that you cannot touch me?" he asked bluntly, as he shifted in the saddle to see the lady's face better. Josephine did not answer as thoughts from the night before raced through her mind. Wilhelm's irritation was replaced by concern as the lady's silence was not normal. "Do you still want to go on up the mountain with me?"

"Yes, of course," she said quickly and managed a smile. "Please forgive me, I . . ." Her voice wavered, and the prince couldn't help but tighten his grip around the lady reassuringly.

"All right," he said, wishing he was bold enough to ask her to finish what she was about to say. "It only gets steeper from here on. It won't do to bang our heads against each other, so we need to move as one." He shifted in the saddle again and moved closer to the lady. "Lean back against me and keep there. I need my hands on the saddle horn to steady us, and you will have to hold on to my arms where you can. Are you ready?" he said, leaning to one side as she turned to answer him. He was about to nudge the horse when he paused.

"Wait," he said, passing the reins into his left hand. With his right hand, he reached for the lady's hair. "Do me a favor and tuck these lovely locks into your collar so they won't be tickling my nose. You would hate to have me sneeze on your neck," he said with a smile.

"Or spook the horse," Josephine teased.

It was more of a climb than the lady had imagined, and several times she had to close her eyes to calm her nerves. Both Wilhelm and the horse knew what they were doing, and the prince was not alarmed one moment. Finally he turned the horse and they slowly made their way eastward along a bluff.

Suddenly he raised an arm and pointed. "My lady, behold the western plains of Gutten." Josephine's mouth fell open in awe as she could see nearly seventy miles to the east and south. The next half hour passed with Wilhelm pointing out landmarks and villages among the winter forest. He was quick to remind the lady the view was lacking in color with the sparse foliage, but the leaves would hinder her view come spring. They could see as far as Kensithe on the east and Madna to the south and even northward where the river marked the border with Aikerlan.

"So now you have shown me the western and eastern face of this mountain, what of the northern side?"

"You have seen that already," he answered, smiling widely at her. They had remained seated upon the horse, and Josephine had forgotten her fear of being held in the prince's arms. The lady's eyebrow rose with curiosity.

"Jansville?" she asked and he gave a nod. She looked away and he gave her a gentle squeeze.

"Tomorrow you will see the southern face of the mountain from the road," he concluded. "Are you ready to head for the cabin?"

"I could stay here for hours and not be ready," the lady said, looking in the distance.

"I think a cold rain might change your mind," the prince said, pointing to dark clouds that were creeping across the western sky. Josephine gave a reluctant sigh.

"All right," she said with disappointment.

Wilhelm leaned to whisper in her ear. "I promise I will bring you back, and with no limit on how long we stay here gazing."

"I will hold you to that," she said, turning her head just enough when she answered that it caused his nose to unexpectedly brush against her face. To her surprise, he did not pull away nor apologize but kept his face touching hers. Slowly the lady lowered her head not sure as what to do, and the prince was in no hurry to move and spoil the moment. Finally he nudged the horse to go down the mountain. He had no doubt the lady was aware something had transpired between them for he felt her hand grip his arm as his face touched hers. It could not be brushed away as the lady needing comfort and him being a faithful friend as in the past. No, both had clearly felt something that had brought them to a halt and to Wilhelm's relief the lady had not pulled away from him nor rebuked him for it.

The ride downward proved scary enough that Josephine resolved to keep her eyes closed, and rested heavily against the prince. After what seemed like forever to the lady, the ground began to level out and she opened her eyes. Just before they reached the cabin, light rain began to fall. Their bad luck had returned and they were grateful that dry clothes and a warm fire awaited them. The rain continued throughout the afternoon with several episodes of heavy downpours, and the king declared the pair would have to wait till the next morning to continue their journey. By evening, he and the prince had committed to a game of chess and Agatha had resolved to finish a forgotten needlework. After several trips outside to the covered porch to listen to the rain, Josephine finally gave up and returned to the great room to sit with the others. Shortly after eight, the lady excused herself for the evening. This time Wilhelm was quick on his feet and walked the lady to her room. He teased that they had arrived at her door far too soon and suggested they continue on around the balcony and go down the other set of stairs only to cross the room and go up again which made Josephine laugh and she agreed to do so. The second time they arrived at the lady's door, she bid the prince good night and went inside her room. Wilhelm was disappointed yet he had peace knowing the lady was not upset with him as he had assumed she was the evening before.

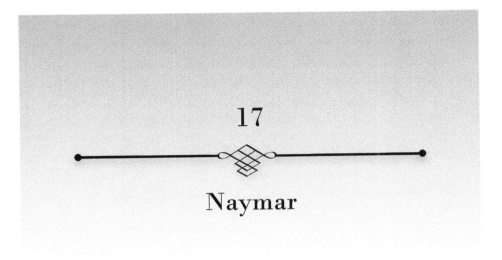

17

Naymar

Thankfully the rain stopped before daylight, and the travelers took to the road after breakfast. Before midday, they had crossed the Pinard road and were making excellent time headed toward Madna. Clouds could be seen along the western horizon and they hoped to reach their destination before rain descended again. Suddenly shouting was heard as the driver brought the carriage to a stop. Niethel let the prince know there was an issue that needed his attention. Wilhelm stepped out and walked on ahead with the guardsmen. Only six men had continued on as escorts once they reached the main highway through Gutten, with the others returning to the outpost at Hermonn. After a few minutes had passed with no sign of the men, Josephine climbed out of the carriage to stretch her legs. The farther she walked along the road, the louder the sound of rushing water became. Hearing familiar voices, she hurried on ahead and then stopped at the crest of a hill. Her mouth fell open as she saw the once small stream had overflowed its banks. The men were standing at the water's edge, and the lady could see they were not pleased with the situation. The small ferry could be seen tied to trees on the opposite bank, and it was explained that trying to cross was too dangerous with the water moving so swiftly. Even if the ferry came across, there was no guarantee it could be safely guided back with its cargo. When she asked about going a different route Josephine was told the only other way to Madna was to go all the way back to the Pinard road, to travel west another hour and then go on the road south. They were still staring at the waters when thunder was heard. The men turned to look at Josephine who could only shrug her shoulders as she turned red with embarrassment at the silent incrimination which made everyone burst into laughter.

As they began walking toward the carriage, the prince spoke, "Isn't there a large estate not very far from here?" Josephine held her breath as her eyebrows rose in anticipation.

"Yes, sire. The road is not a mile back on the right," Niethel replied as he caught Josephine glancing toward him. She made a face and shook her head ever so slightly hinting to the guardsman. The captain returned a questioning glance as Wilhelm turned to help Josephine step up into the carriage. The prince saw the look and tilted his head, letting the man know he had noticed the behavior.

"Josephine, do you know who it is we are thinking of?" Wilhelm asked. With one foot now on the step, the young lady paused long enough to answer.

"That would be one Gregori Naymar." She glanced toward Niethel again and then stepped on into the carriage. The first glance would have been excused, but upon the second, Wilhelm knew something was up.

It did not take very long to arrive at the estate, and it was as Josephine remembered. The three-story mansion was crowned by marble columns with a courtyard that flowed into a covered breeze-way eventually leading to the foyer. Naymar's Hanoverian horses were of renown and his five stables were the glory of his holdings. His business was quite prosperous, and Josephine had enjoyed her tour of the property the previous fall until she was introduced to the Lord himself. Although he was the prime example of success, the lady was not impressed with the man. As the visitors made their way through the breezeway, Josephine couldn't help but wonder how her presence would be received this time by the host. As the door opened, thunder was again heard and the butler invited the prince's party inside, leading them to a parlor to wait while he went to find his master. Josephine began to look at books lying on a table while the prince and Niethel went to a window to watch the light rain that had begun to fall.

Noticing the lady nervously fidgeting, the prince whispered, "What is it about Naymar that has her ladyship so worked up?" Turning their backs to Josephine and pretending to gaze outside, Niethel quietly began to tell of the lady's trip to the estate months earlier. He was part of the escort that day, and he would have never suspected anything out of the ordinary until halfway through the visit. Naymar had offered to give Josephine a tour of the stables and she of course could not resist the invitation. When they returned to the residence an hour later, she wore an unusual look and asked her escorts to remain close by while she was shown the offices. Both the prince and Niethel glanced over their shoulders at the lady across the room before the captain continued. He knew Josephine did not like anyone hovering over her while she worked and she seemed extremely nervous. It took only a few minutes for him to see why as the lord of the manor was watching the lady's every movement with great care.

The prince gave a smile as yet again Josephine's beauty had inadvertently drawn attention, but Niethel shook his head in disapproval as he whispered, "No, sire, it was not harmless admiration." He hesitated. "Let's just say that if a man looked at my Marie in that manner, I would black his eyes for it." Wilhelm's smile faded. He had just started across the room to question her about the trip when Manuel came back with his master.

"Prince Wilhelm, it is such an honor," Naymar said, bowing. Wilhelm approached the man and took his hand, and shook it politely.

"Lord Naymar, it is good to see you. The weather seems to have gotten the best of us, but I am sure your butler has explained that already."

"Yes, my liege. Unfortunately your company is not the only one to seek refuge under my roof," he said, apologizing. "There are only two rooms that are not spoken for."

"What you have available will be fine my lord. We are grateful to not be out in the cold rain," the prince said with a laugh. Feeling

Josephine's hand rest against the back of his arm, he turned slightly. When Naymar saw the lady, he cried out in surprise.

"Lady Josephine." He gave a smile and bowed. "It is truly a pleasure." The lady nodded reverently.

"Lord Naymar." Josephine slid her arm through Wilhelm's as she came beside him. "I do hope to meet your wife during *our* stay." As she said "our," Wilhelm noticed an emphasis on the word but the manner in which the lady turned and looked at him caught his attention even more.

"Yes, my lady, she is home and you will see her at the supper table." Quickly he turned and addressed his servant. "Manuel, have refreshments brought while rooms are made ready for our honored guests." The man looked at the prince again and added, "I have already instructed that your luggage be brought inside. Please forgive me, but I was in a meeting and need to return to my colleagues."

"Yes, of course. Your hospitality is appreciated, my lord," the prince said as respectful nods were exchanged and Naymar and Manuel left the room. The moment they were gone Josephine turned loose of the prince's arm and went to the window. Wilhelm and Niethel exchanged glances, and then the prince went and stood behind the lady.

"Is there something that you need to tell me?" he asked quietly.

"Nothing to speak of," Josephine said as she leaned to the left looking through the rain-streaked glass. "Hmmm . . ." she mumbled. Suddenly the lady turned and added. "If you will excuse me, I need to freshen up." She had only taken a step before Wilhelm caught hold of her arm.

"Is it wise to wander off alone?" he asked but the lady only gave a mischievous smile and went on her way. As she left the room, Niethel shrugged his shoulders.

"What was that about?"

"I don't know, but something has her curious enough to venture off." The two men went to the window and began to look outside. "What would catch her eye that didn't catch ours?" Wilhelm mumbled as they stared into the pouring rain.

A few minutes passed and then Niethel spoke, "There are more than a dozen Friesians in the field by the second barn. But why would a man known for his chestnut bays have so many horses of another breed in his lot?"

"Most horses in our kingdom are descendants of Naymar's pedigrees. So . . . my lord's business colleagues are from the north?" the prince commented.

"Or coincidence has it that all the weather plagued travelers just happen to own blacks?" The men looked at each other. "Has Naymar ever made trade agreements with Aikerlan before now?"

"Not to my knowledge, but the one person who would know just left the room." The men were still looking out the window when refreshments were brought in. They took a seat as they waited for the lady to return.

Finally Niethel asked, "So what do you think?" The prince let out a sigh.

"Time will tell. We will keep our eyes and ears open and be very careful." He paused thinking hard about the situation. "And if Josephine doesn't return shortly, we will go looking for her." A few minutes passed and the young lady came in with Manuel who announced that two rooms were ready. The older man was apologetic that it had taken so long, but guests had been shuffled to give the prince and his men a larger room. The disappointing news however was that Lady Josephine's suitcase had been misplaced. Efforts were being made to recover it, and she was assured it would be in her room before she retired for the evening. Josephine was shown to her chambers but did not stay as she had no need and followed the men on down the hall to see where they would be spending the night. The room was much larger than the lady's with two double beds and a couch. Several of the men would still be sleeping on the floor and straws would be drawn. Supper would be at five thirty, which was fast approaching. The prince had hoped to ask the lady about Naymar and why she had been gone so long, but privacy had not yet been afforded. They were ushered to a formal dining room where they were introduced to the lady of the manor and various guests. The prince and the lady were placed near the head of the table and to Josephine's relief she was next to Wilhelm not Naymar. The room was quite full with extra tables being brought in and not an empty chair in sight. Almost immediately, the prince noticed Josephine was surveying the room, leaning this way and that and finally he whispered to ask if she was looking for someone in particular. She didn't answer him until Naymar excused himself from the table to politely check on guests that had been forced to dine in another room.

"I happened upon a gentleman earlier," the lady excitedly whispered.

"While you were spying?" the prince asked at which Josephine gave such a strange look that both snickered. "And?"

"He confirmed what I already had suspected," she replied.

"About Naymar's colleagues from the north." The remark drew another look from the lady but this time she teased.

"You catch on quick young man. Yes, the gentleman addressed me by name which is not entirely unlikely but when I asked where I knew him from he warned me not to trifle in his affairs. His accent told on him and the fact that just before I came across him in the hallway I passed a room that held no less than a dozen men seated at a table. Thankfully their backs were to the door."

"Hmmm . . ." the prince mumbled. He glanced around the room and then leaned toward the lady to the point his arm was completely around her with his hand coming to rest on the table's edge. Josephine felt herself blushing as Wilhelm began to whisper in her ear. "We need to discuss this further, but not here." She started to lean away but he only let her move a few inches until she felt his hand upon the small of her back. Startled she drew a quick breath, but as their eyes met, he gave a mischievous smile to which she gently shook her head. "Play along." He leaned toward her again, and she turned her head back where she looked across the table. This time the prince's nose rested against her ear and the lady was sure everyone at their end of the table had noticed. Suddenly Wilhelm stood to his feet and looking to Lady Naymar complimented the meal and then excused himself and Josephine. She tried not to look shocked as he moved her chair and took hold of her hand and wound it around his arm as they started to leave the room. Lord Naymar was just coming back through the doorway and when the prince saw him he bowed and explained that he and Josephine needed a few minutes alone, which drew a curious look, but Wilhelm did not remain and led the lady on into the hallway. As they passed other people, the prince said not a word but kept Josephine tucked closely until they reached the front parlor. The room was empty and to the lady's surprise Wilhelm did not close the door behind them but led her across the room to a buffet table against the wall. He turned and leaned back against it and drew the lady into his arms.

Josephine smiled and shook her head as she whispered, "What your brother would give to trade places with you this time." Wilhelm gave a laugh and leaned closer.

"Plenty no doubt, but matters are serious to warrant such a pretense. Now tell me all that you know of Naymar." Josephine gave an uneasy look causing Wilhelm to add. "And you can't slip away from me this time." Josephine gave a quiet sigh and began to speak in a low voice. Her back was toward the door, but she knew Wilhelm was keeping a watchful eye on the hallway. Naymar had been generous with complimenting the lady, but when they were alone in the last stable not only had the words been more suggestive in nature but he was making a point of looking at her eye to eye. She admitted she was not comfortable being alone with the man and had asked Niethel to stay close the rest of the visit. Wilhelm told the lady it was not merely her imagination for the guardsman had picked up on the same signals she had. The prince then asked what Josephine knew of Naymar's business dealings outside Gutten, but the lady confessed that although she saw his books she was too shaken and only glanced at them. It was agreed that the black horses in the pasture were not breeding stock which meant their company was outnumbered if it came to a fight. It put both the prince and the lady in mind of her encounter in Seim and the riddle of who was a friend and who was an enemy. Wilhelm wondered if the gentleman in the hall was one of her abductors, but Josephine was sure he was not. Whether Naymar was willing to betray the crown or was just a greedy businessman, they did not know, but the next few hours would reveal how much danger the travelers might be in. Wilhelm had just declared they would keep to themselves when footsteps could be heard.

"Someone's coming," Josephine whispered. Wilhelm looked past the lady to see a shadow almost at the door, and before Josephine could turn to look, the prince had pulled her to him and began to kiss her. Suddenly a familiar voice was heard.

"My liege, I . . . beg your pardon for interrupting . . . I," Niethel stuttered. "I was beginning to worry when I couldn't find you," he said as Wilhelm motioned to him, loosening his hold around the lady.

"We were posing as a couple to discuss new developments," the prince stated as he looked toward Josephine. Too embarrassed, the lady had turned her gaze toward his shirt. "I will fill you in on the details when we are inside our room." The three began to walk, but before they had reached the door, Wilhelm slid his arm around Josephine, holding her at the waist.

"My liege," she said, blushing again. "If you hold me any closer, I will have to demand vows be taken." She teased. The statement did not deter the prince.

"Would you rather it be my arm around you dearest or Naymar's?" he said, stopping long enough to kiss the lady's forehead.

"I am not your mother to have my forehead kissed," Josephine whispered, giving him a push at which Niethel gave a muffled laugh.

"Perhaps I should leave the two of you alone to work out this little spat?" he said in a low voice.

When they came to Josephine's room, the men stepped in and looked around and then left her for the evening. The lady felt at a loss for her suitcase was not present, and she could only wash her face and turn down the blanket to get ready for bed. She had only been seated for a moment when her mind wandered to Wilhelm's kiss, and she rose to her feet and began to pace the room. She wanted to be irritated with him for taking his liberty with her yet the manner in which he had handled her made her smile. Even in the awkwardness he had been gentle with her and she was not afraid of him. Josephine was staring at the fireplace lost in thought when a knock was heard at the door. "They've found my luggage," she said to herself as she walked across the room. She opened the door to find Lord Naymar, who bowed politely.

"Good evening, my lady. I am sorry if I have disturbed you." Josephine gave a nod in acknowledgment. "I must apologize but your belongings have yet to be located," the man said stepping into the room. "I am sure they will be found by morning." He moved past the lady. Josephine felt her temper flare up. How could this man keep track of every mare that roamed his vast fields yet lose one piece of luggage in his own home? Suddenly Josephine realized she had made a great error, freely allowing the lord into her room and he was now standing near the fireplace looking her over from head to toe. The lady took a few steps toward the opposite wall but stopped as she noticed something draped over the man's arm. "Please let me know of anything that you need to make your stay more comfortable." A chill ran down Josephine's spine as the tone of his voice changed. Boldly he took a step in her direction. "My wife has sent a gown for you tonight." He paused and lifted the garment from his arm and held it up for her to view. Through the lace the flames of the fireplace could be seen flickering. Comments he had made to her during the evening suddenly made sense. She now understood the looks given were in hopes to appeal to a lady's need for the companionship of a man. Resisting the urge to run for the door screaming, Josephine drew a deep breath and answered boldly but tried to sound indifferent to his gift.

"Your hospitality is appreciated. Your wife is so lovely and kind." As the lady spoke, she walked to the door and took hold of the knob.

"*Anything* we can do to make your stay . . . more comfortable," the man replied in a sultry tone. Disgusted, Josephine caught herself reaching to place a hand on her stomach. How could a married man make advances toward a lady half his age? "If there is anything I can personally do . . ." Naymar said, laying the gown over the end of the bed and walking to Josephine. In shock, she stood not able to move as he reached for her arm. "If you need anything during the night," he whispered. "My door is at the end of the hall." Coming to her senses, the lady shook free of his grasp and took a step backward.

"Thank you again, sir. If you don't mind, I would like to retire for the evening." Not waiting for his response, she reached for the door and swung it wide open and gave a curtsy. She dared not look up, too afraid he might offer his companionship again, but to her relief, he gave a bow and left the room without another word. As she closed the door, she leaned hard against it, being sure it latched securely. She had no sooner rested her head upon the wood when she realized she had yet to hear the sound of footsteps. Straining her ear, she waited, and finally she heard the man's boots upon the floor, a pause as he hesitated and then walked away. A soft thud could be heard as his chamber door closed. Quickly she opened her door, looking left and right and raced the other direction to Wilhelm's room, and knocked softly on the door. Even as gentle as she had tapped, the sound seemed to echo through the hallway and she held her breath hoping it had not been heard by Naymar. What if he should catch her out alone? The few torturous seconds that passed seemed like minutes, but her agony was quickly relieved when Niethel opened the door. The look on the lady's face told enough that without a word being spoken, he motioned her inside the room. He leaned into the hallway to glance around before he quietly shut the door. There was a scramble as the men rose to their feet at the lady's presence. Josephine put a finger to her lips, motioning with her other hand for them to remain as they were but the prince was already to her side before she could utter a word. Patiently he waited for her to begin as she looked as if she would burst into tears at any moment. She swallowed hard to compose herself.

"My liege, will you and Niethel please join me in my room. There is . . ." Her voice faltered at which she turned toward the door. The three quietly returned to the lady's chambers where Josephine walked toward the fireplace as she began to explain that Naymar had come to call on her. She purposely kept her back to the men as she continued, "He apologized for my suitcase not being found and brought a token of his hospitality and offered the use of . . . his services." She pointed toward the bed. The men turned to see what Josephine meant with the prince walking over and picking up the garment that lay across the blanket. The moment his hand felt the soft lace and satin he knew exactly what the gesture was implying. Niethel stepped closer to see what the prince held in his hand and cleared his throat as he looked at Wilhelm.

"Ahem . . . Well, that removes any doubt of his interests in her ladyship." Too angry to speak, Wilhelm let the gown fall back onto the bed as thoughts of beating Naymar flooded his mind. Josephine knew the prince's intolerance of such things and came to his side, taking hold of his arm.

"Please, we are not in any position to do anything rash," she pleaded.

"I would have thought with the lady upon my arm the man would have taken the hint that she was not available," Wilhelm said, sliding a reassuring arm around Josephine as he made the comment to his captain.

"So would I, sire, but maybe he thought she would take a higher bid."

"Gentlemen please!" Josephine interrupted. "The thought of such things makes me ill." She looked up at the prince. "I am sure he will come back to me again tonight."

"Undoubtedly," Niethel replied as he strode over to the fireplace. Wilhelm stood silently for a moment, looking at the young lady hanging upon his arm.

"Finding out his business with the men from the north will have to wait." A look of mischief crossed his face and then he added, "Let him come." The comment drew looks, but the prince merely leaned toward Josephine and kissed her temple and then letting go of her joined the guardsman at the fireplace.

"Sire, we cannot adequately defend should you confront him," Niethel warned.

"Confronting him is not my plan. Removing any doubt that the lady is available though *is* my plan." He glanced across the room toward Josephine who drew closer with a curious look upon her face. "I'm going to end up owing you a month at the cabin to make up for what we are about to do," he concluded.

Just after midnight, the door of the lady's chambers opened, and Lord Naymar quietly stole inside the room. He had only taken a few steps when he came to a stop and drew a stifled breath. He could clearly see the lady asleep in the bed facing in his direction but draped over her torso was a man's bare arm.

The next second, Wilhelm sat up in the bed and spoke, "Lord Naymar, is something wrong that you would come at this hour?"

Startled by the prince's presence, the man stuttered with his reply, "All is well, my liege. I . . . just . . ." Josephine stirred and mumbled as she began to roll over to face Wilhelm. Naymar squinted in the dim light of the fireplace to see her arm, clad in an oversized white sleeve, stretch out and her small hand slide up the prince's chest until it reached his shoulder.

Wilhelm took her hand in his and leaned down to kiss the lady's neck and said, "There is nothing to worry about, my darling. Go on back to sleep." Rising up again, he addressed Naymar who was now wide-eyed. "What were you saying, my lord?"

"I was just checking on her ladyship. A few of our guests are . . . shall we say . . . lacking in honor." Wilhelm looked down at the lady and gave an exaggerated smile before looking back to the man.

"She is safe and seems quite comfortable. My lord, if there is nothing else, the hour is late and I hope to leave early tomorrow morning."

"Of course, sire, good night," the man said with a nod. As he pulled the door behind himself, Wilhelm saw him take one last look toward the bed. The prince let out a sigh as soon as he was sure the man was gone. As he looked down, the lady pressed her face against him. It took only a few seconds for him to feel tears on his skin as Josephine began to cry.

"Sire, did he fall for it?" Niethel asked, stepping from behind the dressing screen in the far corner of the room.

"Yes, but I think it would be safer for us to remain here the rest of the night." Niethel and the other guardsman agreed and laid back down where they had been hiding.

As he draped his arm over the lady once more, Wilhelm leaned closer and whispered, "Be at peace, the worst is behind us. Hopefully we just bought safe passage through the night." Josephine looked up at him.

"And what of Naymar's colleagues?" she said.

"My men and I will return on another day. He won't get away with any of this," Wilhelm said, giving her a faint smile. Gently he reached to wipe a tear from her face and then crawled out of the bed, taking with him the blanket and cape that had been rolled up in between their bodies. Making a pallet on the floor beside the bed, he laid down to sleep.

18

Regrets

"Over here, please!" A soldier begged, helping the comrade that was leaning heavily against him to sit down. Josephine hurried across the tent and began to assess the wounds. Shouts were heard as more guardsmen rode through the midst of the makeshift medical camp on their way to the nearby village of Lithel. Of late the enemy had taken to raiding larger villages and were able to retreat virtually unscathed across the river before reinforcements could engage them in battle. This time the raid was far enough south that Prince Leopold's forces from Dahn had blocked the escape route and the men of Aikerlan had hunkered down in the nearby foothills, surrounded but not willing to surrender. The guardsmen were carefully searching every crook and crag not willing that their foe go undetected and had slowly closed in the circle around them. Unfortunately, the soldiers stationed at Lithel had not fared well during the initial battle. The medical unit had been called for, arriving the next morning and for easier access had set up camp along the road south of the perimeter being searched. With the situation under control and the battle drawing to an end, Josephine had been allowed to accompany Dr. Stehle as her services were greatly needed. The morning had proven busy, but by late afternoon, most of the wounded had been tended to with only a few stragglers trickling in. Most of Lithel's townspeople had sought shelter in the rock church in the center of the village and Leopold and his officers were helping them return to their homes. The only excitement since that morning had involved some contrary goats that were enjoying a taste of freedom. Suddenly a trumpet was heard, causing all to look to the road where about two dozen guardsmen were seen approaching fast. They were directed to where Prince Leopold and his officers were headquartered.

"Brother, what are you doing here? Didn't my message reach you?" Leopold exclaimed as Wilhelm rode closer. The younger prince reached for the horse's bridle as his brother dismounted.

"Yes, it did. We were on the way to Whatise and were almost to Jantak when we happened to catch a glimpse of a host making their way across the plain of Sithen."

"What on earth? So they are attacking from the south?"

"You wouldn't be expecting them from that direction now would you?" Wilhelm commented as a page took the horse's reins from his brother's hand. The two princes began to walk discussing the events of the last two days when suddenly they were interrupted by shouting as a soldier frantically rode into the village. Wilhelm turned to his brother. "I beat your scout by a good three minutes!" he said, causing all who were standing near to burst into laughter.

"My lords, a company from Aikerlan is coming up from the south! If they stay their present course they will overtake the medical tent in less than ten minutes!" Suddenly as if time stood still, Wilhelm and Leopold's minds fixed upon the realization that Josephine was in the path of the enemy.

"Page, bring my horse quickly!" Wilhelm screamed as he took off running toward the corral. Leopold and the officers were not far behind, with the younger prince trying to reason to let him go after the lady instead.

"We cannot risk you falling into their hands. Let me go."

"We don't have time to argue about this. My horse is saddled and I am still wearing armor."

"Wilhelm!" Leopold pleaded as his brother took the reins from the lad. As he mounted and turned the horse, he saw his men had quickly followed his lead and were reaching for their weapons. "If you won't trade places with me, at least listen to what I have to say. Send the wounded on the road straight to the village but lead those who are able on horses back down the valley that lies to the west. I will have an ambush set with bowmen. When you hear my whistle, have the men ride up the hillside to hide among the rocks and my soldiers will take care of the rest. May God be with you brother and bring her back safe." Wilhelm gave a nod, and with a shout, the men spurred their horses and rode away. The riders had just made it to the edge of the village when the horn of retreat echoed through the hills. The few minutes warning would give the medics just enough time to have the wounded in wagons or on horses before the prince and the Elite arrived.

As the call of retreat rang out, all movement in the medical tent stopped. The next few seconds that followed were filled with fear and confusion until Dr. Stehle called for everyone to listen to him. Only one wagon had a team hitched to it and the severely injured would be loaded into it. The others would be helped onto horses, doubling up if needed, and sent on toward Lithel as fast as they could go. Not a word was mentioned concerning the staff, and they knew there was a good chance their escape would be on foot. Tension mounted as men were loaded with eyes watching the woods to the south and west for the enemy. Josephine's mind had already began to wonder where Leopold's troops were as she knew that unless they had been cut off reinforcements should have been there by now. The village was more than a mile away but surely it was secure as they should have been able to hear if a battle of that magnitude had broken out. The last two horses were being loaded when the sound of hooves could be heard in the distance. The lady stepped into the tent to retrieve her sword and returned to where Dr. Stehle was standing. The sound was growing nearer and the older man had just instructed the lady where to hide among the trees when the whinnying of horses could be heard from the opposite direction. To their relief, they saw guardsmen approaching but then disappointment too at how few there were. A familiar voice called out.

"Dr. Stehle!" Wilhelm said as the soldiers drew near.

"My liege, are we ever glad to see you. Our enemy is not far by the sound of it."

"Yes, I know, quickly now. We have extra work still yet to be done," the prince said as his eyes fixed upon the lady who was running toward him. As he motioned to Josephine, he slid from his saddle and explained to the men to double up on the horses as they were to lead their enemy into a trap in the valley. Shocked looks crossed the medics' faces, but the prince did not waver stating that they had to get moving or they would be caught at the wrong end of the camp with no reinforcements to rescue them. Wilhelm hoisted Josephine into his saddle and climbed up behind her and not waiting even a second spurred his horse onward. They had just passed the last tent when men on black steeds could be seen on the road behind them. The company rode hard followed closely by their enemy but managed to put a little distance between them. As they approached the place Leopold had spoken of, Wilhelm had the lady pass him a whistle that was hanging from his saddle and he gave a short blow on it.

A few seconds later, a reply was heard and the prince leaned toward the lady and said, "Hold on, we're going up." He turned the horse abruptly with the others following suit. Josephine wasn't sure which was worse, the ascent itself or the brush that tore at the riders not willing for them to pass. They made it to a clearing and just when she might catch her breath the sound of arrows flying past filled the air. Wilhelm stopped his horse for a moment to look down the hill at the approaching enemy. Shouts could be heard as the prince and the lady were seen with the command being given to go after them. "Brother, don't fail me now." Josephine heard Wilhelm whisper and then he called out to his men to keep climbing and into the brush they rode again. Josephine was beginning to worry as she was not sure if this was part of the plan when she saw a clearing up ahead. This time she could see its upper edge was flanked by large rocks, and then suddenly she could see dozens of bows with arrows aimed at them.

"Wilhelm!" she screamed. The prince spurred his horse harder and yelled to drive it on faster. Then he turned his attention to the lady.

"It's *our* men." Josephine was not convinced and gripped his arm as he held on to the saddle's horn to keep the pair steady. Suddenly a shout was heard as the bowmen made ready, and then the call for aim and the lady could not help but close her eyes as she knew the word *fire* was about to be heard. Josephine flinched hard as a rushing sound filled her ears. The next thing she knew their horse was landing hard as Wilhelm brought it to a halt among the large rocks. She had barely opened her eyes when the prince slid from the saddle and scooped her in his arms. After he had taken several steps he lowered her feet to the ground. The horse was shooed away and shouts could be heard coming not only from the hill above them but from the valley below. The prince led her by the hand among the rocks, climbing upward to safety as Leopold's men, who were scattered throughout the hillside, provided shelter for the retreat. Wilhelm and Josephine were nearing the crest of the ridge when they were forced to take shelter as the enemy had unleashed another round of arrows toward them. As they ducked behind a large boulder, they heard Leopold's voice ring out.

"Has anyone seen the eagle?" Josephine looked over in time to see Wilhelm smile.

"I am alive and well," he yelled back. "And our little songbird is with me." He gave the lady's hand a reassuring squeeze.

"Shall I help you out?" Leopold called.

"No, don't risk it. We have found a nice cozy nest and are not in a hurry to be shot full of holes. Just repay our enemy for the inconvenience her ladyship had suffered *please*," Wilhelm said, reaching to move a strand of hair that had been tore loose from the lady's braid by the branches they had ridden through going up the hill.

"Yes, sir, we will gladly do that. If you need anything, just let us know," Leopold answered and then called for the bowmen to prepare to fire again.

"So that's it?" Josephine asked, looking at Wilhelm.

"Yes, we can wait. I am not chancing it when we are safe. It has been a close enough call already wouldn't you agree." The lady nodded as she turned loose of the prince's hand and started to shift to move away from him. Suddenly arrows rained down above them ricocheting among the rocks causing Wilhelm to pull her close shielding her in his shadow. As they waited for the volley to end, Josephine's mind went back to when they had returned from Naymar's estate. King Hubert had sent troops to investigate the gentleman with him pleading ignorance to his colleagues being connected with Aikerlan. The foreigners and their black steeds were long gone, but a detail of soldiers was placed at the estate to monitor further activity. Neither Josephine nor Wilhelm were pleased that the Lord seemingly had got away without punishment for his deeds but then again certain details had been omitted from their account concerning Naymar's visit to the lady's room that night. The greater problem began to surface as the prince and the lady found themselves struggling as a longing for companionship had been stirred that they had not expected. After the third day with the lady having done everything she could to avoid the prince, Wilhelm confronted her.

"What is going on?" he said as he stopped her in the upstairs hallway after supper.

"What do you mean?" she said, glancing around to see if anyone else was nearby.

"I mean, it's been days since you have looked me in the eye and you act as if you are afraid of me." Wilhelm answered as the lady brought her gaze to meet his.

"That is not true," she said but then glanced down at the floor. "I am not afraid of you and the other . . ."

"What have I done that you cannot look at me?" Wilhelm pleaded and took her hand and tried to look into the lady's eyes as he moved closer. "What has happened? You have been acting strange since we returned from . . ." His voice trailed off. "We done what we had to, Naymar did not have his way with you and we all made it safely home. I don't understand what is going on."

"Did you honestly think we could walk away from this and our feelings for each other not be affected?" Josephine pleaded as she pulled her arm free from the prince's grasp. "No woman, married or not, could be held in your arms without wanting the moment to be real or not dream of being embraced like that again." Wilhelm was reaching to take hold of Josephine when her words brought him to a standstill. Was he hearing correctly that she found herself longing for him? He took a slow deep breath.

"I see," he answered quietly. As much as he wanted to take her in his arms, he could not afford to make an error and offend her further. "I will do whatever you ask of me. Whatever it takes to make things right between us again." Josephine's gaze returned to his and she swallowed hard fighting back tears.

"Perhaps we should put some distance between us, at least until . . ." She looked down at the floor. "I cannot think clearly anymore. Please understand I . . . I am still praying about what to do."

"I will respect your wishes." Wilhelm took a few steps. "And I will be praying as well." And he left her standing in the hallway. Even when she was distraught with her family, she couldn't remember feeling so alone. The next few days she only saw Wilhelm in passing for he was not present at meals and kept himself busy at the garrison. She had expected the queen to ask her if they were in a spat, but she didn't, which let Josephine know that Wilhelm had forbid his mother from bringing up the subject. She wasn't sure she was comfortable discussing the matter with Agatha anyways, as it was too personal and she dare not admit to the incident at Naymar's. Every day the time spent in the chapel grew longer and finally the king approached the lady suggesting that she make a trip into town to speak with the minister. By that point, she did not protest and allowed him to call for a carriage. Just before dark word was sent not to be alarmed but that she was still praying at the church. It was late into the night when a guardsman escorted her back to the castle. She arose the next morning with her burden lifted and was her cheerful self again, only acting more reserved when the eldest prince was present. She did not avoid him, but as they walked, she did not reach for his arm nor did he offer it to her but Wilhelm held onto the glimmer of hope in the lady's confession. He knew she was afraid to give her heart to any man if there was a chance of it being broken and he would be patient with her now as he had in times past. Try as she had, Josephine could not free her thoughts of Wilhelm, and it seemed that everywhere she turned something reminded her of him and with him being at the garrison so much she began to miss his companionship even more than she knew she could. But she had agreed not to be together as much as they had and she would have to keep her word concerning the matter, and she was at a loss at what else to do. When the call went out that the enemy was on the move it was a relief to the lady and the prince as both hoped that the deployment would provide them much-needed focus on more important matters.

Josephine's mind came back to the present as Wilhelm asked the lady to move to the right a few feet, so they could sit and rest while they waited in their hiding place. It was a tight fit between the large rocks, and it took only a moment for them to have to move again for an arrow fell piercing Josephine's cape. Wilhelm shifted, pulling the lady much closer toward him with her face only inches from his, explaining that at this distance even if he was struck an arrow couldn't penetrate through his chain mail. For the first time that day, Josephine began to relax, and for a moment, she closed her eyes and leaned her head against the prince. Suddenly she thought of the last time they had been that close standing in the hallway at the castle, and she started to pull away but Wilhelm was quick not to let her as he looked her in the eye.

"This is not working," he said quietly.

"Where will we move to?" the lady asked not understanding.

"No, we are safe here. I mean putting distance between us *is not* working," he said, looking deeply into her eyes. Slowly she closed her eyes hoping to resist him in some small measure, but she knew it was true. He leaned until their foreheads touched. "I have done as you have asked but this isn't working and I would venture it has made us both miserable. In fact, it has taken me to the verge of madness." The comment caused the lady to lean back giving the prince a concerned look. "My mind is not about me. Why . . . last week I misjudged mounting my horse and fell hard enough that I was out cold. Dr. Stehle kept me at the clinic overnight to watch me." Josephine gave a questioning look.

"No one told me, I thought you were just out late on rounds and then left early as well to avoid seeing me." The prince shook his head, amused by his clumsiness.

"I forbid father from letting you or mother know about it. It was pretty humbling but not nearly as much as the repenting that I have done for what happened at Naymar's."

"That was all we could do under the circumstances. It was not just your decision. I agreed to do it," the lady replied.

"Maybe so, but I should have been honest with you going into it."

"What do you mean?" Josephine asked as shouts were heard from the valley only to be responded to by the clamor of swords clashing as the two forces engaged each other. The prince rose to his feet, looked out, and then sat back down again saying the battle was halfway down the hill from them.

"I wasn't pretending when I kissed you so passionately," he said, face turning red as he sheepishly looked toward the lady. "I don't know where either of us came to the conclusion that we would never be attracted to anyone—it's a foolish notion and was just proven otherwise." Josephine had to look away for the statement made her blush for Wilhelm was right on both accounts. "If I would have known what we did that night would have worked against us it never would have played out the way it did. If I've repented once, I've repented a hundred times over it already and all I can do if ask you to forgive me and then let the past be the past." Josephine looked back toward the prince. "Something would be wrong with us if we didn't feel convicted. I know nothing inappropriate happened, but we sure gave the appearance that is had which shouldn't have been. We will not put ourselves in that place again for we know better than to be tempted. Josephine that night cannot be undone, but we can move forward . . . together," Wilhelm suggested. A shout was heard as arrows flew overhead yet again but this time they were fewer in number.

"I have already forgiven you, but I will not remain close only to be a foolish distraction that could cost your life in a battle," Josephine pleaded as the prince leaned to shield her again. When they parted this time, he gently took both of her hands in his.

"And which had been the greater distraction? For days my thoughts have been tormented by the chance of losing you." He looked deeply into the lady's eyes. "You were upon my arm long before we went to Naymar's estate and you have sat with me in the library talking late into the night before then as well."

"I only want it to be as it was before that night," Josephine whispered.

"It will *never* be that way again," Wilhelm replied. "Our relationship will be stronger because we know what it is like not to be together and I for one have missed my closest friend." He gave a smile. Josephine started to smile but was still concerned.

"There is a lot that is not settled," she said, but Wilhelm only leaned closer and whispered toward her ear.

"And if everything felt between us was pretend, then it wouldn't have bothered us afterward, would it? We have worked through things before, and I believe we can again. All I know is that I need you beside me. We will take better care of what we have." Josephine nodded and then leaned back and gave him a hard look.

"Speaking of taking care, what did you think you were doing riding straight toward the enemy? You heard them call for your head to be removed," Josephine scolded. "You shouldn't have come for me."

"You are worth it to me," the prince added, smiling as the lady was starting to act more like herself.

"Do not value my life above your responsibilities to the kingdom. One life does not equal thousands," Josephine said as the prince reached for the loose strand of hair once again and shook his head.

"I will do as I must. Which reminds me." He smiled at the lady, and she could see mischief in his eyes. "I will not promise that I won't ever kiss you like I did in Naymar's parlor." Josephine felt her face turning red as she leaned back away from him. "There are times a man can find no words to express himself and well . . . as my brother would say the kiss was worth a slap to the face."

"Wilhelm Von Strauss!" the lady said, trying hard not to smile from ear to ear.

"Josephine Eloise Armand," the prince whispered, leaning toward the lady. She was sure he was going to try his luck when suddenly a sound could be heard and Leopold called out from above.

"Sound off if your section is clear." More than a dozen lieutenants answered, and then Leopold spoke again, "It's safe to move brother, come on out."

19

Return to Frive

"Good afternoon your majesty, my lady," Karl said, bowing as the two came into the foyer. "It turned out to be a fine day." Wilhelm began to help Josephine take off her cloak. As the prince handed his cloak and the lady's to another servant standing nearby, Karl spoke again, "My lady, a letter came for you."

"Thank you, Karl," Josephine replied as she took the envelope from his hand. She recognized her father's handwriting and smiled. When she first arrived in Gutten, the king had stayed in touch with Renard but she chose not to correspond with her family. Wilhelm had encouraged her to do so but the pain and resentment she bore in her heart only resulted in a handful of letters full of shallow words. But the day at the old mill changed her forever and the next letter from Picardell was read through different eyes and the words seemed to leap off the page and touch her heart. Within an hour, she had penned a response with her burden being lifted and she no longer dreaded when Karl announced news had come from Frive. It seemed that her father was writing more frequently. Josephine tucked the letter into her ledger, and she and Wilhelm walked on to their separate offices.

The lady had been sitting for a few minutes when the queen came to the door. It had been left partially open, and Agatha knocked softly as she stepped into the room. Josephine greeted her with a smile but could tell by her countenance that something was wrong. Quickly she rose to her feet and came around the desk, taking hold of Agatha's hands.

"What is it?" she asked.

"You haven't read your letter yet, have you?" Josephine glanced toward the desk.

"No . . . Why?" The queen told her to sit and asked where it was, retrieved it from the ledger and handed it to the young lady. With her hands now shaking, Josephine broke the seal. She sat emotionless while she read and then reread the letter again. The queen pulled a chair close to watch and wait for the young lady's reaction, but it was not as she expected. Finally Josephine folded the parchment and rose to her feet. "If you will excuse me, I would like to be alone for a little while. I need to think and . . ." She could not finish her sentence but looked away and closed her eyes. She opened them again and looked at Agatha. "I need some time to think and pray." And then before the queen could take hold of her hand, Josephine dashed out of the room. She ran toward the foyer intending to go outside, but then as she came into the entryway, she changed her mind and went up the stairs. She hoped no one was in the hallway for she was not able to speak. Tears began to blind her eyes, and when she stopped to wipe them, she found herself standing at the chapel doors. Quickly she went inside and made her way to the front of the room, falling to her knees in front of the altar. Leaning heavily upon it, she began to sob as she let the letter drop from her hand onto the floor.

My dearest Josephine,

It grieves me to write you with such news, but I cannot afford to come in person due to the circumstances. Your grandmother's health has taken a turn for the worse. The doctor says her heart is failing, and he is not hopeful that she will last more than a few days. Thank God she was visiting us when she collapsed and has remained here in our home as she is too weak to travel.

Your mother is at her side, and Arlene arrived last night to help as well. Phillipe cannot leave Natalee as she is now seven months along. We are praying that you can make it before Camille passes, for she is asking for you and sends her love. If it is not safe enough to travel, then please do not risk it as we cannot bear losing both of you. There is nothing more I can say except that I am sorry for such news.

God speed and all our love,
Renard Armand

While she laid there upon the altar, Wilhelm quietly slipped into the room and made his way to the first pew. Josephine was not sure how long she cried and prayed but finally she felt like God would give her strength for what lay ahead. She had just tried to stand but faltered some as her feet had fallen asleep beneath her when Wilhelm caught her in his arms. As he steadied her, she found herself afraid to look at him as she might burst into tears again. She looked toward the floor, and he moved closer, keeping his head above hers as he had done that day at the cabin when he had spoken to her of his past.

Quietly he said, "I started to look for you in the library, but my heart told me you I would find you here instead." The lady tried to ask what he knew but couldn't as her voice cracked with emotion, but Wilhelm understood her enough to reply. "Father has made preparations for us to leave in the morning."

"Us?" Josephine asked, leaning back to look into the prince's eyes.

"Yes, us," he answered with a faint smile. "We are to leave by eight o'clock."

"I cannot ask you to do such a thing." She began, but Wilhelm interrupted her and pulled her closer.

"It is not your decision, but mine." She shook her head in protest. "I will not allow you to travel without adequate protection, and as your friend, I will not allow you to bear this loss alone." She could not muster enough will power to overcome the desire to fall into Wilhelm's arms and let him hold her. As her head rested upon his chest, he began comforting her, reminding her that her grandmother was not yet gone. After a few moments, he leaned back to look at her and gently wiped her tears. "Let's go find Mother so she will know you are all right." He took her arm in his. As they guessed, the queen was pacing in the hallway just outside the library. When she saw the young lady, she hurried to embrace her. They walked on into the library where Hubert was waiting for them. As they took seats, he began to explain that word had already been sent to Armand to let him know Josephine would be leaving the next morning. The king of Frive would be notified that the prince would be accompanying her ladyship to visit her dying grandmother. A smaller, plain-looking but well-equipped carriage would be used to not arouse suspicions and only six of the Elite Guard would be escorting them. The utmost precautions would be taken as travelling with so few soldiers put them at a greater risk. No one must know that the pair had left the castle, least of all the kingdom, and a meeting had already been held with the servants concerning the secret. At this point, Josephine tried to persuade Wilhelm not to go with her, but he refused to change his mind at which the king continued explaining his plans. Because of the lack of space, Katrina would not be able to accompany the lady, and as he glanced toward his wife, he said luggage would be limited as well. Leopold had already offered to fulfill his brother's responsibilities, and they agreed Wilhelm had a two-week window to comfortably be absent. After that time span, Wilhelm may need to return, but the king assured Josephine that she would not be rushed to leave, even after her grandmother had passed. She could stay as long as she liked, and if she chose to remain in Picardell, they would arrange for her things to be brought to her and with their blessings. As the words of staying fell upon the lady's ears, it was as if everything came to a sudden stop. *Her, stay in Picardell?* The news of her grandmother's illness caused her to feel like the breath was knocked from her lungs, but the feeling that came over her now was worse. She rose to her feet and walked to the fireplace placing her hand across her stomach as it grew uneasy at the thought of facing her father. Lately she had longed to see him and her mother, but had things between them changed? Was the relationship repaired enough that she would want to return to her home? So many thoughts raced through her mind that her head was swimmy. Suddenly she heard Hubert's voice behind her as he came to where she was. It took but one look from the insecure young lady for him to take her in his arms with her head coming to rest against him in despair.

"My dear, what is it?"

"How can I face my father? What if things are not better?" she whispered.

"You must have faith that God has moved upon their hearts as He has yours. Have your father's letters not been different than when you first arrived?" The king lifted her chin to see her eyes, and she smiled and gave a nod.

"But what if they try to make me stay?" she asked, swallowing hard. He gave a wide grin and glanced across the room at Wilhelm.

"I know a certain young man who would never let anyone force you to do anything you didn't want to."

The next morning dawned in a dreary looking fog. The family came downstairs to find several servants waiting in the foyer for Josephine. Karl spoke for them all wishing her a safe trip and sympathy for her family. He reiterated that not a word would be spoken of her leaving but for her to know that she would be missed and they would look to her quick return. Katrina and the queen were the worst as both clung to the lady, longing to be with her, but knowing they could not. Finally the king took Josephine in his arms, hugging her close and then said with a squeeze.

"Do not fret. All will be well. Enjoy the time with your family. Rejoice knowing that your grandmother has reached the end of her journey and her reward is nigh at hand." His words gave Josephine a sweet peace and she smiled. When she turned to look at Wilhelm, he nodded.

"It is time," he said.

Not much was said as the travelers rode along, partly because of having two guardsmen inside the carriage but mostly because

Wilhelm and Josephine's thoughts were elsewhere. Wilhelm's mind wandered back to conversations with his father. Before Hubert had finished sharing the bad news, Wilhelm had pleaded to accompany the lady home. With the tension just having eased up between her and Renard, the prince wanted to be sure Josephine made it safely and he could not trust her to just anyone's care. It had also brought back memories of losing his grandfather twenty years earlier, making him want to be by the lady's side all the more in her time of sorrow. The king agreed to let his son go with her but with one condition: Wilhelm was forbidden to say or do anything that would influence Josephine to stay in Frive or return to Gutten and the choice had to be the lady's alone. Reluctantly the prince gave his word that he would do as his father had requested with his only consolation being that Hubert had reminded him to trust Josephine. She now understood that she would never be truly happy unless she continually sought God's will for her life, but Wilhelm wondered if she felt a pull toward Gutten or Frive. Finally, the prince resolved not to think about the lady's decision but rather to focus on helping her spend precious time with her grandmother.

The first day of the trip seemed to Josephine like she was caught in a dream with time passing quickly and the travelers only stopping to tend the animals and stretch legs. Josephine found herself thinking about her childhood memories of visiting her grandparents' large estate. The second day, her mind was on the morning they had left Guttenhamm. She and the queen were headed down the hallway going toward the foyer when Leopold came asking for a word alone with Josephine. The queen excused herself and went on as the young man reached for the lady's hand.

"You know, I will always love you," he said, looking deeply into Josephine's eyes. She smiled and shook her head as she often did when he was flirting with her. The hours they had spent together at the blacksmith's shop had cured her of being frightened by the young man's advances.

"Yes, and I will always love you . . . but as my brother," she added. He did not return his usual smile but instead looked down at the floor.

"I realize that now, and I will learn to accept it." The comment was not typical and unexpected. "And things will never be the same after this trip."

"What do you mean by that?" Josephine asked, gently squeezing his hand, hoping it would cause him to look up at her. "You are acting strange, as if I were the one dying—never to be seen again." Leopold turned his gaze to the lady, studying the details of her face and began to slowly smile.

"There *is* something that I must tell you," he said, almost whispering. Suddenly the familiar twinkle of mischief was in his eyes, and she leaned closer to hear what he was about to say. "Although the carriage looks plain, it is in fact very special. There are secret compartments made to hold weapons." Josephine's eyebrows raised in curiosity as he went on. "Wilhelm keeps his sword in the right compartment, and I have taken the liberty of placing yours in the left one." Josephine could not help but laugh aloud at the thought of him sneaking her sword into the carriage. "Just in case you need it." Leopold was very pleased with his secret. "But," he pulled her very close, "do not reveal that you have it unless the need is dire. You may receive mercy for being a lady but not a lady wielding a sword. Do you understand?"

"Yes, and thank you for doing so," she answered, smiling at him. Leopold leaned toward her, and she knew he wanted to kiss her. He paused for a moment as if to ask permission, and to her surprise, she closed her eyes and let him. When she opened them, she expected to see him beaming, but instead he looked sad. She was about to ask what was wrong when he suddenly stood upright and looked down the hallway. He looked at her once more, bowed, and left. Turning, she saw the king, queen, and Wilhelm in the distance. She had thought long and hard about Leopold's strange words and hadn't come up with an explanation but could only assume he thought she would be returning to Frive for good.

About one o'clock the third day, they stopped in Sprineton to buy provisions and water the horses. Wilhelm could tell Josephine was getting anxious for she walked faster while she stretched her legs. When he asked if she was all right, she said she was, but the scenery was familiar even though they were still a few hours away. The closer they rode, the more Josephine fidgeted and Wilhelm was amused as it had been a long time since he had seen his companion that nervous. Finally he took her hand, asking her to tell of the countryside they were passing through. Word was given to the driver of which road to take within Picardell and then which turn to take that led to the Armand estate. When at last the carriage came to a stop, the guards exited and Wilhelm turned to face the lady. He had expected to see her on the edge of her seat, but instead she had settled back against the cushion with a solemn look upon her face.

"Where is the bold young lady who commands the attention of all who fall prey to her presence?" he asked, hoping to provoke a response. "Come, let us go inside." He reached for her hand. They stepped out from the carriage with the lady following at first a step behind the prince. As they continued down the sidewalk, she came beside him as was their custom, linking her arm in his. Suddenly the front door opened, and a man stepped onto the porch, the sight of which made Josephine stop in midstep. Wilhelm paused but then took another step, forcing her to start walking again. The closer they came to the man, the more Josephine began to smile, and when they were upon the porch, she let loose of the prince's arm and hurried to embrace her father. Not a word was spoken for several minutes as none were needed, and the two just stood clinging to each other. When Josephine finally lifted her head from her father's shoulder, she asked about her grandmother and was told she was weak but still alive. The young lady left her father's arms and stepped back toward Wilhelm, who was waiting patiently. Renard started to bow respectfully to him, but both Wilhelm and Josephine spoke.

"Please don't," they said in unison and then turned to each other and laughed.

Wilhelm spoke first, "My lord, due to the delicate circumstances, I must ask that you keep my identity a secret while I am here. Please, just call me by my first name." To Renard's astonishment, he bowed to him instead. "I am at the disposal of your daughter." Renard was taken aback and started to protest such a notion, but Josephine stopped him.

"Please, Father, this is the way it must be. Not only for the sake of diplomacy between nations but for the safety of his life, it must *not* be known that he is abroad." Renard reluctantly agreed and then invited them inside. The housekeeper had just taken their cloaks when a squeal was heard from the hallway, and as Josephine turned, she saw her sister running toward her. It was another heart-felt scene of embracing but with so much more talking and laughter mingled in. Renard motioned Wilhelm to the parlor, leaving his daughters but also asked the housekeeper to let his wife know they had guests. Josephine and Arlene followed the men, hardly taking a breath between words. Arlene told that her husband had business matters that would not allow him the liberty to join her except for the day of the funeral. Shortly Laurie came into the parlor, but when she saw Josephine, she let out a gasp, covered her mouth, and reached for the doorway with her other hand. Fearing the lady was about to faint Wilhelm quickly came to her side, offering her his arm to lean on and helped her to a chair. As soon as she was seated, Josephine fell down at her mother's knees and began to rub her hands as she spoke softly to her. Finally, Josephine rose to her feet and was almost through the doorway when she stopped, remembering her companion and turned to look at him, and without saying a word, he gave her a nod as he knew she was going to her grandmother.

Camille was sleeping peacefully when Josephine peeked in. The young lady quietly went to the chair beside the bed and started to wake her grandmother but just couldn't disturb her. She sat and looked at the frail body lying before her and then closed her eyes to pray. When she opened them, she found Camille was watching her, a smile upon her face.

"I knew you would come," she said in a feeble voice. Without hesitation, Josephine climbed into the bed and laid her head against her grandmother's shoulder and wept. "Do not cry for me, I have lived a good, long life and am ready to go to heaven my child." Josephine did not answer but lifted her head to see Camille's face as she continued to talk. "I have been told about your life in Gutten, but I want to hear it from your own lips, my darling." With a feeble hand, she reached to wipe her granddaughter's face, causing Josephine to smile. Quickly she composed herself and began to tell about being the commerce director, serving on the High Council and then of life with the royal family. Camille listened intently only asking questions here and there. After an hour, a knock was heard at the door with Arlene announcing that supper was ready. Josephine begged to remain but both the ladies insisted that she refresh herself after such a long journey.

Finally Josephine gave in when her grandmother said, "Go now and let me rest. It has been enough excitement seeing you wearing a frilly dress. Come back in a few hours and when you do bring the young man with you." The ladies had just made it to the foyer when Josephine excused herself feigning that she needed some fresh air and was out the door before Arlene could stop her. Quickly she retreated to the far end of the porch and took hold of the railing. The excitement of the afternoon had affected her nerves, and she was shaking badly. She did not hear footsteps until Wilhelm was directly behind her, but as soon as he said her name, she turned to face him and he took hold of her hands.

"Are you all right?" he asked, looking into her eyes. She nodded and smiled.

"It's a lot to take in," she replied. Thoughts began to cross the prince's mind of things he wanted to say, but remembering the promise to his father, he gave a sigh. "Let's go back inside so they won't worry about you."

Supper lasted more than an hour as the family done more in the way of visiting than eating. Despite all the joyful reminiscing, Josephine found herself watching the clock, anxiously waiting to rejoin her grandmother. Everyone moved to the parlor and another hour passed in conversation and finally Laurie went to see if Camille was ready for company. The older lady was and the ladies left the men alone. Only a little while had passed before Josephine came back to the parlor to retrieve her companion. As the prince stepped into the bedchamber, Arlene and Laurie excused themselves, and Josephine brought Wilhelm closer to the head of the bed. Camille gave a wide grin and then looked over at her granddaughter.

"Introduce me to this handsome fellow." Josephine was not sure who blushed more, her or Wilhelm. Kneeling beside the bed, the prince took hold of the old woman's hand and kissed it gently.

In her own language, he replied, "It is an honor to finally meet you, my lady. However Josephine did not tell me that she had your blue eyes." Carefully he lowered her hand, but to his surprise, she held on to his and replied.

"But . . . she also has my frankness and love for mischief, which I am sure you have already discovered."

Wilhelm remained kneeling by the bed as Camille asked both of them questions about their life in Gutten. She watched them smile at each other as they took turns answering and laughing, so eager to share stories with her. A half hour passed quickly and Arlene slipped back in to listen, bringing a chair for Wilhelm. Someone looking on from the outside would not have known that Wilhelm was not part of the family for how comfortable he seemed. When an hour had passed, Laurie came in bearing the bad news that the patient needed her rest. Josephine quickly volunteered to sit with Camille during the night, but her mother refused, insisting that she rest as well. Wilhelm took the young lady's hand, as his way of hinting that her mother was right. Both rose to their feet with Wilhelm stepping to the head of the bed to kiss Camille on the forehead and wish her a peaceful night's rest. Josephine took her turn and they left the room.

When they came into the parlor, Renard informed them one of Wilhelm's men was outside wishing to speak with him. The prince felt the lady's grip on his arm tighten, but he assured her it was probably nothing more than the evening briefing before all turned in for the night. Renard seemed curious, and Wilhelm took the opportunity asking him to join them on the porch as he wanted to discuss another matter without the others being present. Josephine had let go of Wilhelm's arm thinking that she was to remain inside, but when he had taken a few steps with her not following, he stopped to address her.

"My lady, your presence is welcome," the prince said, and without letting a second pass, Josephine came to his side and wound her arm back around his. "There will never be anything that I discuss that your ears cannot hear." They smiled at each other and then with a laugh he added, "Unless my father forbids me."

Niethel was waiting upon the porch and greeted them.

"My lieg . . . my lord," he said, stumbling not to call the prince by the wrong title. "Your ladyship." He nodded respectfully toward Josephine. "Reporting that all is well and the area is secured. Our night watch is in place and your luggage has been taken to your rooms. Concerning your swords, sire, we would rather they be with you should the need arise for arms." Wilhelm started to say something but then paused and gave Niethel a questioning look.

"Swords did you say?" he asked.

"Yes, sire. Yours and the lady's." Josephine felt her face turning red as she realized Leopold had not told his brother that her sword was in the carriage. Before she could offer an explanation however her father spoke up with a loud voice.

"Is the situation in Gutten so grave that my daughter carries a sword?" All was quiet for a moment, and then Wilhelm gave Niethel a nod dismissing him to leave the three alone. Wilhelm still had Josephine's arm in his, and he reassuringly gave it a pat with his other hand as he began to address Renard's frustration.

"The situation has indeed escalated but not to the point that your daughter has ever used a sword for anything but sport. As you noticed, I was not aware that it had been brought along, but if I had given it any consideration, I would have consented as she is quite capable. But, yes, as our correspondence has indicated the need for protection by arms is at hand." Renard did not hold back his opinion of the matter, not happy that his daughter was in harm's way. Wilhelm explained that he understood completely and began to elaborate on the precautions being taken for her safety. Renard paced on the porch as he listened closely, agitated by the matter. Finally Josephine let go of Wilhelm's arm and interrupted.

"Father," she said, stepping closer to him. "We are being very careful. But I am not a child. I know the risk and am willing to take chances for the exchange."

"I would rather be hearing you say there is *no way* for you to be in harm's way because you are staying *away* from danger," he said firmly. Josephine felt her temper rising up, but she chose to suppress the impulse. Instead she reached for her father's arm.

"When I am riding near Guttenhamm, I have an escort, but I do not travel north unless I am with Wilhelm and the Elite Guard goes with us. Father, I have seen the aftermath our enemy has left behind. Our people need medical attention, food, and shelter. My conscience will not allow me to cower behind stone walls. I cannot look the other way and leave them to suffer and die when I am able to help meet the needs of our people. Make no mistake, I am not out and about for mere commerce figures, but I go to assist Wilhelm with his work." Renard looked hard at his daughter. Night had fallen but there was enough light from the moon that he could see the determination upon her face. This was not the same young lady that had left six months ago. His daughter was known for her reckless boldness and intelligence beyond her years but could never harness it into the poised diplomat standing before him touching his heart with her words. He thought for a moment and then gave a sigh.

In a calmer voice, he spoke, "All this time I have read the letters of where you were and what you were doing, but it only seemed as a dream or story until now." He leaned forward and kissed her cheek. "Wilhelm, you have my permission to bring the swords inside," he said, turning to face the young man. "And carry out any measures that you feel necessary concerning your safety and that of my family." Relieved Wilhelm walked closer to the pair.

"Thank you, my lord," he said. Renard looked at him and smiled.

"I suppose it is foolishness to ask you to bring her inside by curfew." He gave a soft laugh, and with a bow, he added, "I will leave you two alone."

As soon as Josephine's father stepped away, Niethel reappeared with the swords and then excused himself for the night. Josephine felt the need to apologize for the awkward moment and explained what Leopold had told her the morning they left Guttenhamm. She began to tell how strangely the younger prince had spoken to her and suddenly Wilhelm grew extremely interested. He gave a laugh and stepped to where the lady was standing. Not that he wanted her to know, but he understood perfectly well what his brother meant and was relieved that he had abandoned the quest to win her heart. Now Wilhelm reached for the lady and teasingly pulled her close to him.

"So the kiss was his way to say goodbye?" Josephine was not sure why he was so amused with the account, but she was just glad the prince was not disappointed with her not mentioning the sword had been stashed in the carriage.

"Yes, I suppose it was," she answered as she let him pull her closer still. She moved her hands to rest upon the front of his shirt and then leaned toward him until her forehead was against his chin. Josephine sighed and closed her eyes. "What a day it has been," she commented softly.

"Uhh hmmm," he agreed. He was not sure whether the lady was too tired to realize what was happening or that she did and was comfortable with it. Either way, he was not going to miss the opportunity to hold her with chaos not breaking out around them as in times past.

20

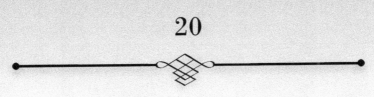

Inheritance

"I had hoped you would have slept a bit later," Wilhelm said as Josephine stepped onto the porch and closed the front door quietly behind her.

"Habits are hard to break," she replied as she walked off the porch and joined the men on the sidewalk. "Morning briefing?" Niethel nodded and then he repeated his report for her sake. He excused himself, and the prince invited the lady to walk with him down the lane and back before they went inside to breakfast. When the meal was over, Renard asked Wilhelm to join him on business errands which he was happy to do, and Arlene headed into town for a bit. When all had left, Josephine convinced her mother to take a nap while she took a turn sitting with her grandmother. When Arlene returned a few hours later, she was bubbling with the latest gossip having seen Josephine's newly married best friend at the mercantile. Gabrielle was hosting a dinner party that evening and begged for the sisters to come to the event. Josephine was quick to turn down the notion, not wanting to leave her grandmother under any circumstances. To everyone's surprise, when Camille learned of the invite she insisted that Josephine should go. The young lady tried in vain to argue but Camille persisted.

"It has been a long time since you have seen your friend and it may be even longer before you have the opportunity to do so again," the old woman stated and then paused to catch her breath. It seemed that since the night before she had grown much weaker. "The business of the crown takes precedence over social matters." This time when Camille paused she closed her eyes and gave a deep sigh. Josephine was watching closely and had just risen to her feet and made it to the edge of the bed when her grandmother spoke again. "Go tonight and show off your handsome fellow." She opened her eyes and gave a smile. "Ah, I think some more rest is in order for me." And with that, the younger ladies left the room.

The men had returned and were seated in the parlor, but Wilhelm could tell when the sisters came into the room that Josephine was agitated and asked if anything was wrong.

"Grandmother is insisting that I go to a party tonight at Gabrielle and Stuart's." Wilhelm shifted to the left and motioned for her to join him on the divan.

"Isn't Gabrielle a dear friend?" he asked.

"Yes . . ." Josephine answered, drawing out the word. "But I came to see Grandmama, not to go gallivanting around the province." As she sat down, she turned to look at him.

"Do you want to go?" he asked.

"Under different circumstances, yes, of course," she said and gave him a questioning look.

"Then you should go," he concluded as he leaned back and put his hands behind his head, relaxing into the divan.

"But on the condition that I was to take you with me," Josephine added curtly. She figured the last comment would cause him to agree that going was not a feasible option. He sat there for a moment, and then he rose to his feet and strode across the room.

He turned to face the lady and said, "It would make it easier on our men, if I went along."

"And what do you mean by that?" Josephine demanded as she stood up and started toward the prince. Renard and Arlene watched to see how Wilhelm would react, knowing that Josephine was about to argue her point.

"It means that if I stay behind, they would have to split up to protect the two of us which is not wise," he said, stepping closer to the lady.

"No . . . Because I won't need anyone coming to protect me. I am not the one who wears a crown, remember," she replied. They were not an arm's length apart, and accordingly, Wilhelm continued in a quieter voice.

"But you would be a greater prize than I."

"And how is that?" she asked, glaring at him.

"I would only be caught to be tortured and killed, but you . . ." He looked deeply into the lady's eyes. "If they snatched you, they know we would do almost anything for your release." He paused and then smiled as he added, "And then they would torture and kill you." She did not like his joke, especially about such a serious subject.

"I don't find that amusing."

The prince leaned closer and whispered toward her ear, "Nor do I. I have wrestled with the knowledge of this for weeks now. You know it's true. But never mind all of that, we will be going together tonight." For a moment, it was as if they were the only ones in the room, and then they were interrupted as the housekeeper stepped to the door and announced that lunch was served.

The afternoon seemed to fly by. It was no surprise to Josephine that Agatha had packed a ball worthy dress. The young lady's mother and sister were quite impressed not only with the gown but with the fact that Josephine was not protesting having to wear it. They found it an amusing penance that Josephine now had to don such things on a regular basis and they reminded her of all the times she had thrown a fit begging to be clad as a page in britches. Wilhelm spent the afternoon with Renard and the two came back about an hour before it was time to leave for the party. When the carriage was called for, Josephine was found begging to stay with her grandmother. The young lady had climbed up in the bed to ask if she was being sent away so her grandmother could die.

"Oh my dear, I have no intention of leaving just yet," she said, reaching to touch Josephine's dress. "You know I love you." Wilhelm had slipped into the room and came up behind the young lady. Camille looked up at him and smiled.

"Josephine, your grandmother is in God's hands whether she is here on earth or in heaven, and there is no better place to rest. Come, we don't want to be late." He said as he gently laid a hand upon her shoulder. Without another word, Josephine climbed out of the bed and turned toward Wilhelm. As she stood there, a single tear slid down her cheek and the prince quickly reached to wipe it away. Camille noticed her granddaughter did not pull away from the man but let him put his arm around her and lead her from the room.

As he was closing the door, Camille spoke, "Look in on me when you get back. I want to hear all about your evening together."

It had been decided that Wilhelm would be introduced as Josephine's German-speaking escort from Gutten in order to limit conversation and questions. Renard and Wilhelm had carefully discussed the possible guests and if the duke could recall any of the men being present at the ball in Competta that the prince had attended a few years prior. Stuart was the only one that may have been, but even then, the likelihood of him recognizing Wilhelm was slim, especially considering that the prince now sported a beard. It had also been decided that one of the guardsmen would remain at the estate to rest before he took his turn at watch later than night. Two guardsmen would serve as coachmen, and the other three would ride on horseback keeping distance between them and the carriage so as not to be noticed. They arrived at the party and were announced with no reaction from the guests. Josephine was relieved as she had fretted as if Maximillian himself was lurking in the shadows. Arlene did not hesitate to head off on her own, and Josephine with Wilhelm on her arm began to search the crowd for familiar faces. It was not long before she found Gabrielle and Stuart, and Josephine introduced Wilhelm pretending to translate as they in turn greeted him. It was hard however for Stuart to say too much as the women talked excitedly to each other, and finally he just began to laugh with Wilhelm joining him with a smile.

Several times, Wilhelm and Josephine commented to each other in whispers of how odd it seemed to not be the ones in charge of the evening. It was stranger still as the party moved from the dining hall to the ballroom, and the pair found they could enter the floor at their own convenience, not having to start the dancing nor stay in the center of the room. Just after the second dance had begun, Wilhelm felt the customary tap upon his shoulder of another man wanting to dance with his partner.

"May I?" a gentleman asked. Wilhelm nodded, but as he stepped away, he saw Josephine's countenance change. He took a step back toward the lady, but seeing his reaction, she assured him in his native tongue that she was all right. He hesitated but then bowed, leaving the two upon the floor. Wilhelm looked about the room, hoping to find Arlene to ask who the man was as something did not sit well between Josephine and the gentleman. When Josephine's sister was found, the prince took her upon the dance floor, and when no one else could overhear them, he began to inquire of the gentleman.

Arlene was not happy when she saw Stephan. He had claimed for years that he would make Josephine his wife and had proposed to her upon two occasions. The first proposal was done quietly with the lady telling him that it was just a childish notion that she refused to take seriously. Stephan was not discouraged but said he would finish his schooling and return in a year to make an even better offer of marriage. Sure enough, he showed up the following summer rather unexpected to a dinner party only to propose in front of a room full of people. Josephine managed to convince him to speak with her in private where she tried to explain that she was not interested. She said he tried to persuade her, stating they were meant to be together, but finally she outright refused him, saying she would only marry for love and despised the very appearance of him. That night, Josephine suddenly reappeared by her sister begging for them to leave at once. Arlene was not sure what exactly happened or how Josephine had slipped away from Stephan for her sister would only say so much and then stop talking. By the time Arlene finished the tale, Wilhelm wore a concerned scowl and tried to spot the young lady in the crowd but with no luck. When the music stopped, they began to search the room more diligently. Now alarmed by the lady's absence, the pair went to the host with Arlene explaining a word in private was requested. When the two men were alone in a hallway, Wilhelm quickly began speaking in French, apologizing first for the false pretense but then asked if there was somewhere Stephan could have ushered the lady. Stuart did not stumble at the misrepresentation but sensing the urgency led the prince toward other chambers. Suddenly voices were heard in the distance, and they recognized one of them as Josephine's. Both men began to run down the hall and found the missing guests in the last room arguing. Coming through the door, they saw Stephan had taken hold of Josephine and had forced her against the far wall. Stuart looked toward Wilhelm, and there was no mistake about the rage in his eyes, and quickly he took hold of the prince's arm to slow him down.

"I will not do anything of the sort. Let go of me, I say. Let go," Josephine cried out.

"You will see things my way, my darling," Stephan replied as he leaned toward the lady.

"I suggest you do as the lady says," Wilhelm interrupted with his voice so loud that it startled all that were present. Stephan turned to see who it was and took a step back but did not loosen his grip upon the lady.

"This is none of your business," he snarled.

"She *is* my business," the prince said as he slowly began to walk across the room.

"Please, Wilhelm, don't do anything to him," Josephine pleaded as she tried in vain to wiggle free. "He's not worth—" she stopped, fearing that she had said too much already.

"I will not ask again," Wilhelm said, coming to a halt a few feet away. He drew his breaths very slowly, trying to remain calm and not think about ripping Stephan into pieces. He knew Josephine was right that they could not afford an incident, but he continued to glare at the man and finally, the grip on the lady's arm began to loosen. As soon as she was free Wilhelm let out a sigh, but not taking his eyes off Stephan, he addressed the lady. "Josephine, leave us please." The tone in his voice made her cringe, but she obeyed without hesitating for the tension in the room was frightening. Equally frightening was the thought of what would transpire between the men when she was not present. Josephine hurried down the hallway not wanting to hear what was said. Arlene and Gabrielle were anxiously waiting, but the lady was quick to caution them not to cause a scene. No matter how many times they asked her if she was alright, Josephine replied that she would be fine as long as Wilhelm was fine. She did however tell her friend that a hasty exit may be needed and apologized for spoiling the otherwise pleasant evening.

The fifteen minutes that passed seemed like hours as the ladies waited for the men to reappear, but they kept smiling, pretending to visit among themselves. Finally Stuart and Wilhelm returned with Stuart quietly stating that Stephan had been asked to leave and had done so thankfully without force. He assured Josephine that no complications from the altercation would arise and changed the subject by asking his wife to dance with him. Wilhelm followed suit with Josephine, but as he laid his hand upon her waist, he could feel the lady trembling. Pulling her closer than usual, he leaned toward her ear and began to whisper.

"I will say no more of this until we are at your parent's home if you but tell me that he did not hurt you." Afraid that her emotions would overtake her, Josephine did not reply but shook her head. Wilhelm kissed her temple and replied, "What I would give to take you anywhere without our luck following us." Satisfied with not discussing the matter, they turned their attention to salvaging the remainder of the evening.

About nine o'clock Josephine caught up to Arlene and asked if they could leave as she felt they had been away too long already. The sisters talked some on the ride home, but Josephine was not her usual self. Wilhelm guessed that the lady's first instinct would be to go to her grandmother's side, but he desperately wanted to speak with her about Stephan. As expected, Josephine darted from the carriage before he could say a word and remained in Camille's room until most of the household had retired for the night. By that point, the prince knew the lady was far more upset than she had let on in front of her friends. He hoped her faith in him had not been crushed by his failure to keep her safe.

About midnight, Wilhelm could bear it no longer and decided to go to Camille's room. If Josephine was still sitting with her grandmother, then he would ask her to step out for a moment, but if some-one else was there, he would offer to take a turn as he was not able to rest with his mind in torment. Opening the door, he found Renard who to his surprise, motioned for him to come inside. Wilhelm sat down, and for the first time he could remember, he felt overwhelm-ingly inadequate. Nothing was said for a few minutes as Wilhelm stared at the floor and fidgeted with the signet ring upon his finger.

Finally Renard spoke. "Arlene said something happened at Gabrielle's," he whispered.

"Yes, my lord, and I am ashamed to say that I did not protect your daughter as I should have." Admitting the failure to Josephine's father was humbling for the prince.

"Tell me what happened," Wilhelm nodded and began to whis-per. He concluded that he had yet to speak with Josephine about what had transpired when she was alone with Stephan, but he knew it could not have been good. He also believed that she had avoided him when they returned, and he could only assume that she was upset with him. Renard had listened carefully and was about to give his opinion when another ever so feeble voice was heard.

"She is not upset with you, young man." They turned to look at Camille. "She was frightened for your safety, not hers."

"My lady," Wilhelm replied.

"When you returned, I could tell things were not well. When we were alone, I asked what had happened and she burst into tears." The old woman paused, struggling to breath. "She did not elaborate as you have done now, but she kept mumbling how she had put you in danger." Wilhelm rose to his feet and walked over to the window to look out into the darkness.

"What on earth?" he said and then sighed loudly. "I don't know what to do with her at times. She is always thinking of someone else, with no regard for herself."

"There is only *one* someone her mind wanders to." Camille said, causing the prince to look in her direction. He couldn't help but smile, hoping that she was referring to him. "Come, sit down. There are things I need to say with the two of you present." Wilhelm done as he was told, and the older lady began to explain her will. Years before, her husband, Nicholas had implemented measures to reward their most faithful servants with small parcels of land upon his death. Most of that had been carried out already but a plan to keep the estate and its holdings prosperous had also been devised. Rosadane was virtually self-sufficient with it workings operating under the care of their regent Cyril. Although this was all well and good, upon Camille's death, the estate would have to pass on to someone. Even as a small child Josephine had reminded Nicholas of his wife and they discussed bequeathing everything to her. She was no doubt a favorite grandchild, coming often to visit her grandmother and Camille admitted she had a heavy hand in spoiling Josephine not to conform to society's vision of the perfect lady but had encouraged her to pursue what interested her most.

"You know how she loved to come to visit. She loved the countryside and the house more than all my children and grandchildren. She would follow the servants about, learning what duties each of them had. She would help whenever they would let her, never looking down on them but always thanking them for doing their part to make everything run smoothly. Yes, the decision to bequeath it to her Nicholas and I made before he died. He knew she would cherish the inheritance. Of course, I never told anyone, not even her." Camille paused to put her hand upon her chest and pressed it for a moment. When the spell had passed, she began again. "I was afraid that if it was known that she was to inherit, that a gentleman might take advantage of her. I could not let it become a hindrance to her. No matter how many times I wanted to tell her, I knew it would be best . . . for her happiness." Although Josephine receiving such a gift was good news, Wilhelm rose to his feet again and began to walk the floor. "She must not know until I have passed." The old woman glanced at Renard and then to Wilhelm. She knew the prince's mind had already raced to the effect it may have on her granddaughter.

"Josephine will be very pleased to learn of this. Not only because it is a part of you and happy memories but it will give her the chance to fulfill her aspirations," Renard commented as he looked at Wilhelm, who had come to a stop in his pacing, but purposely did not face the two.

"Yes, she will be happy about the inheritance," he said in a solemn voice. "To oversee Rosadane, with society forced to acknowledge her positon because your law demands it. Yes, this is what her heart has desired most."

"I have to disagree, young man," Camille said, causing Wilhelm to turn around. "She will enjoy her inheritance, but it is not what her heart desires most. Come and sit down, you have nothing to worry about." The three talked for a while, and then Camille sent Wilhelm on to his room. The old woman struggled throughout the night, having more discomfort from her heart but she would not allow Renard to awaken the others. She knew they would need the extra strength before the following day was over. Laurie came at dawn to trade places with her husband, but not a word was spoken of anything that happened during the night. A few hours after breakfast, a carriage rumbled up and out stepped Phillipe. It was a bittersweet reunion, with him not being seen since November as his employer could not spare him extra time to be away. He was still greeting his sisters when he saw Wilhelm standing at the far end of the porch. He gave the prince a hearty handshake, and although nothing was spoken, looks were exchanged between the two. Josephine noticed and when the opportunity arose, she questioned her brother about it. After making her promise not to tell, he explained that Wilhelm had contacted his employer, making an offer the man could not refuse to allow Phillipe to have the week off with pay and had arranged for two servants to be at Natalee's disposal while he was away. He would have no worries while he paid his last respects to his grandmother. Josephine was amazed but not surprised by Wilhelm's generosity. Before midday, Laurie's three other sisters and their husbands came as Renard explained that he had sent for them in the night as Camille had instructed. A few hours later, the old woman passed away and word was sent to her estate. The regent came with the will which was to be read after the evening meal to allow time for the required two officials to be present. After supper was over, everyone congregated in the parlor with extra chairs being brought from the dining room and placed in rows facing the doorway. Knowing the gravity of the news about to be broken, Renard asked Josephine to sit next to her mother, but the next thing he saw was Laurie's older sister sit down in the chair, clinging to her sister's hand. Josephine didn't seem to mind and headed to the back of room to stand behind the last row of chairs, near the windows. Wilhelm had helped carry in the chairs and was turning to leave when Renard politely asked him to remain, motioning toward his daughter. Glances were exchanged with Wilhelm nodding in agreement. Although she was across the room, Josephine had noticed, and when Wilhelm was beside her, she felt compelled to ask why he was staying as she knew it wasn't like him to listen in on other people's affairs. He gave a sheepish grin, wondering how he would explain without telling too much but didn't get the chance to speak as Cyril called the meeting to order. Carefully, the regent distributed a copy of the will to each of the officiating men and the third he kept in his hand. The family watched as the seals were broken, and several sheets of paper were unrolled. Clearing his throat, Cyril began to read. It took only a few moments for Josephine's mind to wander as sums of money were called out along with names of cousins, aunts, uncles, and particular servants.

She whispered to Wilhelm, "Did I ever tell you that there is another copy of the will?" Wilhelm couldn't help but turn and look straight at the lady at which she nodded. She motioned for him to lean closer and began to whisper again. "It is hidden in a secret compartment made into the end of the mantle in the parlor at Rosadane."

This time, Wilhelm leaned and whispered into Josephine's ear, "Did you read it?"

She smiled and looked up at him. "I was on the third page when Grandmother caught me."

"How many pages are there?" he asked, wondering if she knew more than everyone guessed.

"Five," she whispered but not quiet enough for her words drew her sister's attention from the row in front of her, and she turned and placed a finger to her lips for silence. Josephine rolled her eyes and ignoring Arlene leaned toward Wilhelm to finish her story. "Grandmother took it from me, lit a candle, and sealed it in front of me, forbidding me from opening it until she was dead." Wilhelm leaned close enough that his chin touched the lady's hair.

He slid an arm behind her and asked, "So, did you look at it again?" She shook her head that she hadn't. It was about that time that Cyril began to mention the estate itself and the holdings that accompanied it. Wilhelm watched the lady's reaction. At first it was as if she was going down a checklist in her mind as the regent read and she thought of each property, business, and assets that he named. Suddenly he called out her full name slowly, and as she heard it, her face went blank. Wilhelm watched as she stood motionless as Cyril finished the last sentences and announced the reading was completed. The sounds of mumbling and chairs creaking could be heard as the family shifted to see where the heiress was. Josephine's mind was overwhelmed. Could it be that the estate was now hers? What did the family think for they had been bypassed for it to fall to her, the youngest of them all? And what of the servants at Rosadane, would they be happy with the thought of her as their new mistress? She was so lost in thought that she almost didn't reply when an official called her name.

"Lady Josephine, we are ready for the papers to be signed."

"Yes," she answered and began to walk across the room but in a daze. Suddenly she came to herself. "Gentlemen, if I may have a few minutes to speak with my council." The extended family exchanged curious glances at her words, but it didn't hinder the lady from motioning to her father. When he was at his daughter's side, she began to whisper, "What should I do?" Renard looked at the young lady standing before him. Suddenly she seemed insecure and afraid, but he wondered if it was the thought of the inheritance that had shaken her or another matter.

"You should sign the papers," he said as he reached for her arm. She did not answer but waited as if hoping that he would say more. By the hesitation, he knew it was not Rosadane that was weighing upon her mind. "You will sign the papers and then let Cyril know that you will correspond with him often." It was as if Josephine had come out of shock, and she took a deep breath.

"I do not know which way—" she began to say.

But her father interrupted her and leaned closer to whisper, "There is no choice to be made here. You will go home and come to visit as often as you can be spared." Josephine leaned back to see her father's face. His eyes were full of tears but he was smiling. "Whether you are there another six months, six years, or the rest of your life, you must go. The estate will always be here for you." Josephine smiled and patted his arm.

Clearing her throat, she announced that she was ready, but before she made it to the table, she turned and said, "Wilhelm, my lord, will you be so kind as to assist me?" Quickly he strode across the room.

"Yes, your ladyship," he answered. She asked him to read the document while she spoke with Cyril. She turned to the regent who reverently bowed to her.

"Dear Cyril, I am pleased beyond words that the estate has come to me." She paused as she choked back tears of joy.

"We could have never wished for a kinder soul to call our mistress," he replied as he took hold of the lady's hand. "You are so dear to us."

"As you all are to me," she added. "It grieves me that I cannot go to Rosadane on this trip, but I must return to my home in Guttenhamm." As the last words were spoken, Wilhelm almost dropped the parchment he was holding. He kept his eyes upon Josephine as she continued, "I do not want you to think that I have abandoned you or that I don't appreciate this gift, but I have affairs that I have committed to and treasure dearly and must return home. As soon as I can, I will return to visit. Until then, I will write often and please don't hesitate to send word to me of anything." She gave a little laugh. "And everything that happens. I have always enjoy being at Rosadane and will be anxious for news." She assured Cyril that the estate would never be neglected, but all Wilhelm could hear was his heart pounding since she said the word *home*. She finished and turned to the prince. "Is the will in order, my lord?"

"Yes, my lady," he said with a smile. The two officials showed Josephine where to sign and affix her seal. She began to explain that she could only sign as she had no seal.

But Wilhelm stepped closer and whispered, "My lady, a word please." He asked for the necklace that she wore which belonged to her grandmother. "If I may try something?" She watched as he slipped the pendant from the chain. He took a plain piece of paper and dripped wax upon it and then removed the signet ring from his finger. He placed a small scrap of paper over part of his ring and then carefully made an imprint in the wax. Before it could harden, he quickly pressed the back of the pendant below his insignia. A few seconds passed and then he lifted the paper for the lady to inspect.

"How did you . . . it reminds me of the view near the falls. How did you know the pendant would make an impression like that?" the lady asked.

"One of those times we were caught in the pouring rain you tucked my ledger along with yours inside your cloak. It took me more than a month to figure out what made the markings. The indentation is still in the leather. But do you like it?"

"Yes, I love it, but can it be replicated small enough for my finger?" she asked smiling.

"When we get home, I will have it made whatever size you so desire," he answered, wishing that they were not standing in a room full of people. Carefully Wilhelm applied the makeshift seal with the others watching, and then he turned and bowed to the lady.

"It is done," Josephine said with a smile.

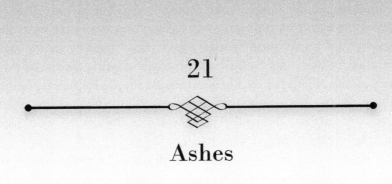

21

Ashes

"My lord, please have pity." The desperate cry echoed through the foyer. Wilhelm and Josephine had just left the chapel to go downstairs to breakfast when the pair came to a halt as the man cried out and then muffled voices were heard. Just out of sight from those below they waited for the visitor to leave but instead they heard a commotion erupt. Cautiously Wilhelm walked closer, not wanting to get involved if the matter did not pertain to him, but the moment the visitor saw the prince, he cried out, "Your majesty." And he knelt down to the floor. Wilhelm looked toward Karl who motioned for him to join them and slowly the prince came down the staircase. When he was closer, the man began to plead for an audience with the king. He claimed to have ridden all night from the river town of Alsat to bring news the village had been attacked, and Klairan was now in danger. Still kneeling before the prince he described the scene, but broke down several times as he could not control his weeping. When the man had finished speaking Wilhelm extended a hand, helping the man to his feet and led him to the parlor to rest. Josephine had slipped beside Wilhelm and was quick to bring the man something to drink. A few minutes later, the butler returned with the king, and again, the visitor fell to his knees in respect. At Hubert's request, the man began to tell the full tale of what had happened during the past two days. Alsat had been pillaged and burned. He had been knocked unconscious and thought as dead for the raiders left no one alive. He had walked south to seek refuge at Klairan but yesterday morning, three men on horses were spotted on the far ridge toward the river. Several times these men were seen coming and going along the ridge watching the village below. He volunteered to ride for help as he had nothing to lose but might prevent others from meeting the fate of his beloved family. Their only hope was that the enemy would not invade before he returned with soldiers.

News of this sort would have frightened Josephine when she first came to Gutten, but unfortunately, it was now a familiar sound to her ears. Several times she had found herself in the midst of a battle as her and Wilhelm had stumbled upon homes being raided while on their rounds with the guardsmen. She would hunker down in the safest place she could find while the men fought until the enemy was defeated or had retreated beyond their reach. The king was not pleased to say the least about the lady being in the midst of these incidents, but both the prince and the lady argued in their defense that they had done everything in their power to prevent such situations. In the end, more caution was advised and the lady was allowed to go out again as her skills were needed for Dr. Stehle was with Leopold's forces in the northwest quarter. All parties did agree to shield such occurrences from the queen's knowledge. Agatha however, was not ignorant of the matter and suspected as much since most of Josephine's petticoats were missing layers of fabric that she guessed had been used as bandages. The young lady tried to pack plenty of supplies, but when the need arose, she did not hesitate to use the resources she had available. Although riding into the midst of an attack was harrowing for her, she found it even more troubling to come upon a home destroyed and the owners murdered with their bodies lying where they fell. Her heart grieved with every bad report that came in and she had visited enough throughout the kingdom to know some of the victims personally.

When he was finished, the man was taken to the dining hall to be fed and then rest. Hubert was very quiet, and Josephine and Wilhelm remained still as they knew he was deep in thought. After a few minutes had passed, he asked for them to accompany him to his office. As they began to walk, Karl joined them, and when the door was shut behind the four, the king began to speak. Wilhelm was to take a regiment of the guard to Klairan. Hubert spread a map upon a table and pointed out positions. They had no choice but to assume a full-blown battle was at the end of their destination, and they must be prepared for nothing less. Word would be sent to Leopold to group his forces in Dahn and there await orders. All villages in the northeast quadrant were to be put on alert with those closest to Klairan evacuating south toward the capital. The medical unit would be mobilized with Josephine accompanying them. Wilhelm dreaded to hear his father mention the lady taking part in the mission, but he knew she would be needed. Time was of the utmost importance, so departure would be in the next few hours. Karl stepped out to assign duties to his assistants and messengers and when the three were alone in the room, Wilhelm turned to Josephine.

"Did the supplies get moved as we discussed?"

"Yes," she replied with a nod. "Shall I fetch my ledger?"

"No, that won't be necessary. Dr. Stehle assured me he has three wagons ready to leave at a moment's notice, and he came back to Guttenhamm earlier this week," Wilhelm added. The king glanced at his son and then back at the lady.

"There is something that I must say," Hubert began as he turned toward the lady. "You do not *have* to go on this trip." Josephine was looking at the map but stopped and looked up at him shocked.

"You would rather I not go?" she asked bluntly.

"That is not what I said. This time I have to know it is by your choice not because you think it is expected of you." He moved closer and placed his hands upon the lady's shoulders. "The risk is greater than before, and I have to know that you fully understand that your life will be in danger." The king could see his son stepping closer out of the corner of his eye as he too was waiting to hear the response. "There is nothing that says you are bound to this cause to give even your life."

"Nothing, except my heart," Josephine answered. "I choose to go to help our people."

"You were not born to Gutten so you are not bound to . . ."

"These are my people. They captured my heart months ago, and I never intend to ask for it back," she pleaded. "They are counting on me now more than ever. If I have to beg to go, I will. I understand what may await us and am willing pay the cost as it is." As she said "us," she looked toward Wilhelm whose countenance was solemn. The king removed his hands from the lady's shoulders.

"I love you very much, and as bad as I want to forbid you from going, I cannot. And the only way you would stay behind was if I locked you in the garrison." He turned where he could see both his son and the lady. "You know it grieves me that I cannot go with you."

"Father, there is no need to apologize."

"Yet now more than ever I hate that I am not the one at the fore front, leading our men into battle. It should be my life on the line not my two sons'." Josephine saw the remorse upon the king's face as he spoke. She remembered Wilhelm telling how his father had been injured a few years earlier. His limp was not noticeable unless he had sat for a long time, but the injury made it very difficult to ride a horse and he certainly could not bear arms on one. The extent of the disability had been realized when he could not go into the field as he wanted to defend his people.

"You have done your part, and you are still so vital to everything Leopold and I do. We both know that you would be with us if you were able. It takes the two of us to compensate for you," he said, hoping to lighten his father's mood. The king managed a meager smile and patted his son on the back.

"You both are ten times the warrior I ever was."

"But that's not always how the battle is won, is it?" Wilhelm replied. "That is why you are needed now more than ever." He glanced toward Josephine who smiled in support of what the prince had said.

The king gave a sigh and said, "I will leave the two of you to discuss other matters." After he had left the room, Wilhelm outlined a few more details to the lady, and then they left to finish what was needed in order to leave.

They left Guttenhamm shortly before ten o'clock with the peasant man joining the caravan for he refused to remain behind. Dr. Stehle rode with the prince and captains as well as Lady Josephine, but the rest of the medical team followed at a slower pace in wagons. It was not a straight course to Klairan so at nine o'clock that evening the group finally came to a stop having rode several hours in the darkness. As urgent as it was to arrive at the village, Wilhelm knew rest would be needed if a battle lay ahead. At three the next morning, they broke camp and were riding as the sun rose. When they came to the old fortress of Bartlestoff, they stopped. From that point forward, the men were in battle gear, donning chain mail and armor. Dr. Stehle and Josephine remained at Bartlestoff to wait for the rest of the company but they were not alone as families had fled to the fort.

Before they had left Guttenhamm, Wilhelm had a serious conversation with Josephine.

"Anything we need to say to each other needs to be said now before we leave," the prince declared. Josephine had just stepped inside his room and asked if he needed help with anything as her preparations were completed. He finished strapping on his arm guards and strode over to where she stood beside the door. She drew a deep breath and leaned back against the wall while she thought. "When we step outside, I will be *captain* of the king's guard and *you* the Lady Josephine," Wilhelm added and stepped closer.

"I know," she said and stood up straight as she reached to trace the edge of his shirt's collar. She kept her gaze from meeting his, but he gently took hold of her arms. The moment he did, she whispered, "I hate all of this."

"As do I, yet every day, we move closer to this being over." She looked up at him. "Your sword will need to be brought," he said, and they exchanged grins thinking of the trip to Frive. "And the dagger in your boot." This time she blushed as she remembered back to the night long ago when he found her sleeping in his room. "And the other dagger."

"And how do you know about that one?" she demanded.

"Well, uhh . . ." he stuttered as his face turned deep red. "I had noticed something when I helped you on your horse and then when you were unconscious and I carried you after the avalanche." Neither could bring themselves to say more about the second knife for both knew it was strapped to the lady's upper leg.

"I told you I was being extra cautious," Josephine replied. Suddenly the prince's countenance fell.

"It tears at me to think I will not be able to come to your aid should the need arise." The agony in his voice tugged at the lady's heart.

"I will be fine," she said to reassure him. "Besides, you are in greater danger than I." She returned her gaze to his shirt.

"I will need you to be brave for our people," Wilhelm said and slipped his arm around the lady's waist. "They will look to you in my absence and above all you have to be calm and strong for them . . ." He paused. "And for me." His words caused Josephine to look at him. "I can't count the times I have come to you perplexed and upset, and your presence alone has restored my perception of the situation and given peace to my mind." Josephine had never given thought to it but what the prince described was true, but not only for him but her as well. "And you know, it will take all my wits about me to stay ahead of our enemy." The lady nodded but could not muster a smile as a wave of dread washed over her again. Wilhelm leaned his head against hers. "Tell me."

"I am afraid for you," she replied.

"We cannot let our minds wander in that direction or it will drive us mad. Now is the time to put our feelings aside and do what we must. As you said, our people are depending on us. Look at me." She raised her head and looked into his brown eyes. "I will protect and defend them while you will give them hope and healing. This will all be over soon, and for every day of sorrow I will make it up to you." He smiled so big that Josephine couldn't help but return one to him.

"I will hold you to that," she said.

Now, she found herself pacing to and fro in the broken-down fort waiting for news from the prince. Before he left, he had reminded her not to look for news until late in the evening. She of all people, understood about delays and that scouting took time for he was not willing to lead his men into a trap. Any stragglers found along the way would be directed to the fort until the area had been secured. A few more families had wandered in from south of Klairan and were thankful to see the guardsmen. Just after lunch, Josephine was upon the north wall tower when she noticed the sky toward the border with Aikerlan looked rather hazy. She called for the doctor to join her, and as she began to ask about it and point, he motioned for her to stop. Quietly he explained that he saw the haze just after the soldiers had left early that morning but dismissed it as fog in the distance from the river. As the day progressed, it had remained and he could only assume it was smoke. Josephine's heart fell as she envisioned the village burning, but Dr. Stehle advised her not to think the worst just yet for it could still be a wildfire but the best thing to do was to not mention it to the others to avoid needless panic. When word came from the prince, they would know what it was.

A few hours passed before the next family came to seek refuge at the fortress. After they were fed, they told how they had fled from Klairan the evening before. For two days the enemy's scouts were seen moving back and forth upon the ridges that surrounded the low flat plain. No army was seen, but the people thought themselves to be surrounded and with no adequate defense they barricaded the town as best they could. Just before dark, several families took a chance and fled hoping not to be ambushed on the road to Revall. The prince's scouts had intersected the travelers and directed them to go to Bartlestoff first before continuing their journey.

On through the afternoon, the smoky haze could be seen from the north tower and Josephine began to brace herself for bad news. An hour before dusk, guardsmen were spotted riding slowly toward the fort with the prince and captains leading. A sadness was seen upon their faces even before they came near. Not much was said as the soldiers dismounted, save Wilhelm calling out a few orders. Josephine waited patiently to be addressed, but not knowing where to begin, Wilhelm said nothing. After he had removed his outer armor, he turned in the lady's direction and asked her to walk with him and not wanting her arm against his rough chain mail he took her by the hand. They hadn't taken more than a dozen steps into the courtyard when he began to speak in a hushed voice, so only the lady could hear him.

"We were too late," he said. The regret in his voice made Josephine cringe, and she could see pain in his eyes.

"By midafternoon, we knew the haze in the distance was not fog from the river," she said quietly.

"It's gone. And when I say gone—all of it, only ashes remain." The prince stopped walking. Josephine turned toward him, but he didn't move as if in a daze. He hesitated and then added, "Bodies lay everywhere. Men, women, children." The news was horrible, but Wilhelm's countenance as he spoke was almost more than the lady could bear.

"The last family that came said they had fled yesterday evening," she stated.

"Yes, it looks like the village was attacked after dark. The fires had burned down before we arrived." Finally he turned to look at the lady. "We have spent most of the day digging graves while the scouts kept watch on the perimeter."

"And Maximillian's army?" Josephine asked.

"Tracks led in from the east and go out to the west. I wouldn't let the men scout farther than two ridges, and even then, I had them signaling us. I was too afraid for their lives to let them pursue, and if the enemy was spotted, we were all to retreat. It was all I felt we could do not knowing more. I have never seen such . . ." He stared out across the courtyard as if reliving the gruesome scene in his mind's eye. A few moments passed, and then he looked to Josephine again. "Will you join me in prayer?" She nodded, and to her surprise, he took only a few steps before he dropped to his knees. The lady followed suit beside him and closed her eyes to cry out to God as she could hear the prince doing likewise. A good while had passed before either opened their eyes, but when they did, they found they were not alone but had been joined by most of the guardsmen. It was a solemn time, but all felt encouraged for they knew their true strength came from their faith and they were not ashamed to bow their knee.

22

Fortress

"My liege, you called for me?" Josephine asked as she came to the prince's side. Wilhelm held up a solitary finger for the lady to wait as he turned to Bernhardt.

"Go now, I will join you shortly." Nods were exchanged and the prince and the lady were left alone. "I have a favor to ask."

"I am at your bidding," Josephine replied, but noticed his countenance change.

"You may not like what I am about to say," he stated. She couldn't help but wonder if she was about to be sent back to Guttenhamm alone. "I feel we must go on toward Revall to see if any survivors fled in that direction, or . . ." He hesitated as if the next words were difficult to say aloud. "If Maximillian's army is awaiting us." Josephine's heart fell as his eyes met hers. "My captains have agreed that is what we should do at this point." Josephine felt as if her body had grown numb and she found herself staring blindly at the crest on Wilhelm's breastplate. The dread of an all-out battle seemed to hold her mind captive to fear, and she didn't realize Wilhelm had spoken until he reached for her arm as he called her name a second time. "Josephine, he has to be stopped, and if this is the opportunity, then I must take it." She shook loose of his grip and took a few steps back.

"I know," she said solemnly. She mustered her courage and gave a faint smile. "It is what you should do." Wilhelm could tell she was not pleased with the announcement despite her words of support, but before he could say anything, a soldier interrupted them with an update. Josephine would have slipped away, but the prince caught her hand as she tried to brush past him. When they were alone once more, he continued their conversation.

"Now I must ask the favor," he said as he raised his left eyebrow anxiously. "I will need you to help here at Bartlestoff." Josephine felt a wave of relief as he had not demanded that she return to Guttenhamm.

"What is it that I need to do?" she asked curiously. It took only a few minutes for the prince to explain that he could not afford to leave any soldiers behind if a battle lay on the road ahead, so she would be in charge with Dr. Stehle assisting her with any decisions she was unsure of. Josephine could not hide her nervousness, but Wilhelm persuaded her that the task was not as daunting as she thought it to be. The fort was far enough away from danger yet close enough to send the wounded to. Finally the lady agreed to the arrangement and then asked the dreaded question of when he would be leaving. With a sigh, he answered that it would be within the hour. Neither spoke for several minutes as they were deep in thought. Finally Wilhelm broke the silence as he offered the lady his hand.

"Come with me as I walk among the men." The troops were almost ready and were checking saddle straps a second time. Suddenly Josephine felt a wave of fear grip her heart as the order to mount was called out. Wilhelm had released her hand as he looked toward the others but then he turned toward her and drew close enough to whisper. "Do not take any chances. If there is anything suspicious, send for us." Josephine wanted to look up at him, but as reality set in she could only stare in his direction. The prince hoped her gaze would meet his as he wanted to be sure she understood the graveness of what may lie ahead, yet her reluctance to look him in the eye affirmed that she knew. He wanted to reach for the lady but instead reached for the reins of his horse. He mounted, gave the call and the troop rode away.

Josephine watched as they disappeared down the road. She felt horribly alone and was afraid. When trouble had called before, Wilhelm had always seemed to be there or at least close by, but now . . .

"My lady." She jumped as Dr. Stehle called to her. "We have much to do while we are waiting for their return," he said as he patted her arm reassuringly as they began to walk. They needed to set up a better facility for their patients and temporary repairs could be made to the fortress. Several sections of the southern wall were missing but could be secured in case of an attack. Josephine admitted that she felt at a loss to be placed in command, but Dr. Stehle disagreed, stating that he had confidence in her as did the prince.

So the first day passed with every person that had stayed behind working to secure the old fort. Trees that had fallen close by were drug to the wall and used to block the breaches. Firewood was brought in and water gathered in every available vessel. Although the fort had not been actively used in years, the furnishings had not been removed but were locked in the towers. It was decided that the two northern facing towers alone would be used to conserve resources since both roofs were intact, had working fireplaces and afforded a view of anyone approaching from the road. By nightfall, Josephine was feeling better about things in general, and watchmen were appointed and placed upon the walls. They had cots for most of the people, and others were able to sleep on pallets close to the fireplaces.

The next morning the work resumed. It was still early in the day when a rider was spotted coming from the east. A signal was given to assume posts, and when he was closer, he was told to halt and state his business. He claimed to have a message for Lady Josephine. Very cautiously, he was allowed to enter the gate and brought to the lady who was joined by the doctor. Gasping as if utterly exhausted from his errand, the man began to tell his tale. The doctor and his team were to leave for Vingaar immediately as the prince would lead his men into battle by the following afternoon. The man was very convincing, and for her part, the lady looked concerned, as she nodded and listened intently. Dr. Stehle paced as the man spoke, and when it seemed the message had been delivered, he ordered refreshment to be brought for the messenger. Subtly he motioned for the lady to step away with him. When they were out of earshot, the doctor ordered the man to be watched and subdued if necessary. The older man was pleased when Josephine spoke up.

"He has not ridden the distance he claims, the horses' lather tells otherwise."

"I agree, my dear," the doctor said. "And that is by no means a direction our men would have gone without passing our gates in doing so."

"I suspect a trap," the lady commented as she looked back across the courtyard where the man was seated at a table. "But what should we do? Surely this means our enemy is to our east."

"And much closer than we realized," Dr. Stehle added. Josephine turned to face him again. "And they know we are vulnerable."

"What should we do then?" the lady asked with a quiver in her voice.

"I think we have a better chance defending ourselves within the fort than if we took to the road. But we cannot do so for very long. Someone needs to ride for help. If the message said to be there by tomorrow, then our enemy would be waiting at Vingaar tomorrow. One person might make it out without being seen whereas they would notice if all of us left."

"And no doubt they have spies close by to know our defenses are weak," the lady added.

"Yes, my dear, I am afraid so."

Both were silent for several minutes as they thought, and then Josephine spoke up. "I should be the one to ride for help." The doctor looked surprised, but she continued, "If the fort is attacked, I will be of little use and every man will be needed. I have ridden between here and Dahn several times on horseback, and once Wilhelm used a short cut on a logging trail. It would save me valuable time." The doctor had reached up to stroke his beard in thought as she finished, and with a sigh, he agreed to her plan. She would walk her horse due south for a distance and then ride west parallel to the road for a mile before she took to it. The messenger would be held prisoner until the prince returned and would decide his fate.

Josephine donned her cape and took her sword and quietly led her horse through the last remaining gap in the wall. She wanted to look back over her shoulder, but she was afraid that she would not have the courage to go on by herself. She did as the doctor suggested and within an hour had intersected the road. She was thankful no one was watching for as she mounted her horse she was shaking badly from nerves. She rode hard and made good time. When she was close to Loftein she slowed her pace to be sure not to miss the shortcut. She found it without trouble, and after another hour of riding through narrow places with clawing branches, she reemerged onto the main road. She had just resumed a faster pace when she thought she heard someone. Carefully she glanced over her shoulder but saw nothing except the empty road behind her. Only a few minutes passed before she heard a sound again, but this time when she turned, she saw a rider about ten lengths behind her. She tucked herself low and spurred her horse on faster. Suddenly, another rider came out of the woods in front of her and with a scream she jerked her reins back. A commotion followed as her horse whinnied and reared violently as Josephine clung to her back with her knees and reached for the mane to get a better hold. To her horror, the riders reached for her, and quickly she turned her horse to and fro to avoid their grasp. She demanded to be left alone, but their only replies were of laughter as they told her to settle down. Although she kept free from their grasp, her horse was trapped between the two men and she could go no further.

"Let me pass!" she screamed.

"What is your hurry, my lady?"

"I have urgent business. Let me pass!" she yelled again as she frantically tried to turn her horse.

"I think your business is with us today, my lady," one man said as he reached for the lady. Josephine managed to avoid him. "We won't harm you. We are just following orders not to let anyone pass."

"Whose orders?" Josephine demanded.

"The prince, of course," the other man replied.

"And where did you see the prince?" Josephine asked. She wondered if these ruffians were telling the truth.

"The royal guard is just over the hill watering their horses." As the man spoke, he turned to point and Josephine saw her opportunity. With a shout she spurred her horse and lunged past the pair before they realized what had happened. Josephine dared not look back as she heard cries. She desperately hoped the troops were close by as her horse could not seem to run fast enough to put a reasonable distance between her and the would-be captors. She had just crested the hill and started the downward slope toward the stream in the distance when the shouts behind her stopped. Not a moment later, she saw two soldiers emerge from the woods ahead and a wave of relief came over her. Regardless, the lady maintained her speed until she was right upon the men at which they motioned her to their left. As she turned her horse, she could see the guardsmen sprawled out along the stream bank just as the ruffians said. Suddenly she heard the familiar voice of the prince and saw him running toward her. He looked alarmed, and before her horse stopped moving, she began to convey to him the events of the morning. Carefully the prince helped her from her saddle and steadied her on her feet. She continued to explain while she clung to Wilhelm out of breath partially from excitement and the hard ride. Wilhelm knew as soon as the watchman announced that she had been spotted that something was terribly wrong. If he had not been almost entirely supporting the lady as she stood there, he would have paced but when she had finished, he gave orders for the men to prepare to ride. He apologized for the quick turn-around, but as time was of the essence, he hoisted the lady back into her saddle and motioned for his horse. They rode hard, and by using the shortcut, they made it to the fort just after dusk had fallen.

Under Dr. Stehle's guidance, preparations to solidify the breaches had continued throughout the day, and the prince was extremely pleased with the progress. A meeting was called to discuss strategy should the fort be attacked and positions were assigned. Several more families had heeded the warnings and made their way to the fort, and now the courtyard was half full of wagons and livestock. The next few hours went by too quickly, yet not quick enough, for most feared what lay in the darkness, feeling better to see the enemy approaching than be blind to their whereabouts. Josephine had finished preparations in her tower and then went to check in with Dr. Stehle who was stationed in the other one. She was coming back across the northern wall when she saw Wilhelm approaching.

"I thought you would be resting by now," he said and lowered his eyebrows with concern.

"I had things to do first. Besides, I doubt I could fall asleep yet anyways," she answered as she came up close by him.

"You need to try . . ." His voice trailed off as he looked around and surveyed the fort. Josephine found herself watching his every action. He seemed so tall and strong there upon the wall beside her, but the worry upon his forehead made him look much older than he was.

"And when will you stop to rest?" she asked. He turned his gaze to the lady and gave her a smile.

He reached for her arm and replied, "What say we take a rest here?" He glanced around again. "This should afford me a good view. Go, fetch a blanket to wrap up in and we'll sit here together." Josephine nodded and walked toward the tower. She was a bit surprised by his offer to rest, but she sensed he wanted to talk to her more than sleep. When she returned he had already sat down with his back to the outer wall. "No need to be an easy target for arrows." She knelt beside him. She got settled with her blanket over her legs as the prince laid his sword near his right side and propped his shield against the wall. There was no moon that night, but the torches burned brightly upon the walls and in the courtyard below. Josephine listened intently as she could not see over the inner edges of the wall, but it seemed to her that the occupants were quieting down and perhaps some sleep would be afforded after all. She had just rested her head gently back against the cold stone wall when she felt Wilhelm's hand slide over hers. She turned to look at him, and as she did, he gave a gentle squeeze. "You never cease to amaze me." Josephine felt herself blush at the statement and was thankful her reaction was hidden by the darkness. "You were very brave to ride out alone." He said as he took a better hold of her hand and seemed to look toward the courtyard. "And then to remember the shortcut."

Josephine's heart beat faster as she thought about the ride. She had yet to tell the prince about the ruffians and probably would not for some time. The way Wilhelm held on to her hand was comforting, and she welcomed it but she wondered if he was preparing her for something. Several minutes passed and the noises within the fort fell to the occasional sound of quiet conversation. Wilhelm was glad that everyone seemed to be taking advantage of the calm, but he found he was struggling on the inside. Where should he begin to let Josephine know how rough things were about to become? He had promised to keep her safe, yet here she was stranded with no way to send her away. Her medical skills would be needed but at risk to her life. Every time he thought he found the words, he opened his mouth but nothing came out. He placed her hand in his left palm and began to trace her fingers with his right hand. Very seldom had Wilhelm shown any expression one would consider weak, being the prince and future leader of the kingdom, his every action was scrutinized and he could not afford to be seen as anything less than honorable and courageous. Even now with an attack inevitable, he had to guard his reactions and not until that moment had Josephine realized that he was afraid. Under all the stately composure and military skill was a man who respected his limitations and had doubts like any other mortal man. The longer they sat there in silence with her hand in his, the more Wilhelm's behavior worried her.

Gently she leaned her head against his shoulder and whispered, "What is it that you are wanting to say?" the bluntness caused the prince to stop for a moment.

"I need to apologize." Wilhelm began and swallowed hard.

"What for?" Josephine asked as she raised her head. To her surprise, Wilhelm turned to look at her.

"There is no guarantee that we will leave here alive," he whispered in such a grave tone that Josephine felt herself shudder. "I have no idea if fifty men are waiting to attack us or five hundred." There was a desperation in his voice that she had never heard before. He continued in a whisper. "I would wager there was more than fifty that wiped out Klairan but who knows how many are coming. We can defend for a day, maybe two, but depending, I . . ." His voice trailed off as he turned his gaze back toward the courtyard. He drew a deep breath and squeezed her hand then looked at her again. For a moment, he leaned toward her and stopped a few inches away. His moment of insecurity faded and with renewed courage he whispered, "We can hold our own, can't we?" Josephine agreed as he repeated himself. "Yes, we can hold our own." He moved back to where he had been and rested his head against the stone wall. He let out a sigh as Josephine leaned her head against his shoulder once again. A few minutes later they were both sound asleep.

Suddenly, Josephine found herself headlong in a dream. She was playing in the hayfield with Phillipe and Arlene. They had just trodden down a place for a blanket to be spread out where they could lay in the bright sunshine when all of a sudden she heard a rustling sound in the distance. She asked Phillipe if he heard it and he just laughed, mocking that her imagination was running wild. The noise was getting closer and frightened she pleaded with him to stand up to look. He just laughed again and covered his ears with his hands. Frustrated to the point of tears, she yelled at him, vowing to get to the bottom of it and stood to her feet. A covey of quail flew up from before her causing her to scream which woke her up. It took only a split second for Josephine to realize that although her dream was not real, she had heard something.

"Wilhelm," she whispered as she shook his arm.

"Hmmm?" he answered.

"I hear something."

"Something like . . ." He opened his eyes but pressed his arm across the lady to keep her quiet as they listened. A sliding noise could be heard and then it was as if the wind blew gently through the trees. Josephine knew when Wilhelm identified the source of the noise as almost simultaneously he and the watchman cried out.

"We're under attack!" The next moment, Wilhelm reached for his sword, and a clamor could be heard as others scrambled into positions. Wilhelm had just made it to his feet when a rushing sound was heard and arrows filled the air. Josephine struggled to get free of her blanket and had only made it to her knees when she threw herself back against the wall, narrowly escaping the first assault. Suddenly she saw something else come over the wall and land about halfway across the walkway. As the metal hooks began to slide toward her, a horrible screeching sound was heard and then she could see other hooks sailing through the air with the sound resonating to her left and right. Before she could even react, Wilhelm had turned and with one swing of his arm cut through the rope closest to her with his sword. Several minutes passed with intermittent showers of arrows and grappling hooks raining down. Very few of the enemy were successful enough to make it over the wall. The prince and his men would move about as they could and then hunker down under shields as the next round came. Josephine had stayed flat against the wall where she was, not able to move very far for the barrage of arrows flying through the air. To her relief, Wilhelm realized her predicament and came back in her direction. He turned his head away from her and yelled for his bowmen to prepare to fire.

He turned to the lady and quickly spoke, "On my word, head for the tower. Lock the door and only open it if one of ours is bringing in wounded like we discussed. Under no circumstance are you to come out. Do you understand?" Josephine answered and had barely managed to get her feet under her when he gave the signal and shoved her in the direction of the door as he shielded her the best he could. They were within ten feet of the door when a man came climbing over the wall before them. Knowing that the appearance of the enemy scaling the wall would mean that the shower of arrows would temporarily cease, Wilhelm lowered the shield to his side and turned his attention from Josephine. The young lady did not have to be told what to do next and carefully maneuvered away from the fight and safely into the tower. As she locked the door, she felt helpless as she waited, safe but alone. The thick walls dulled the sound of the battle some but not enough, and anxiously she began to pace and wished she could see what was happening but then again maybe she wouldn't want to know. What if a great host had mounted the wall already? Her fears were running wild when she heard a familiar voice at the door. "Josephine, he needs help!" Carefully she opened the door to find Wilhelm and a soldier who was bleeding and leaning heavily upon the prince. Without a second thought, Josephine traded places with

Wilhelm, and as he pulled the door, his only words were, "Lock the door but stay ready."

Josephine helped the man to a chair and sighed with relief. Her brief view of the walkway had not been filled with a host of the enemy but merely a few bodies lying upon the stone. As she began to mend the man's wound, she drew him into conversation to learn that the enemy was not faring well thus far and had not penetrated into the fort.

Just as she finished, she heard voices draw near and Wilhelm call out her name. Within an hour, she had six patients join her, thankfully only having minor wounds, and she allowed two men to rejoin the battle. The door had just been relocked when she heard her name again, but this time, the voice was not Wilhelm's. She stooped to peer through the key hole and saw Duke Graham propped against the wall about thirty steps away. She watched as he fell forward to his knees. Quickly she unlocked the door and darted to him. As she came near, Wilhelm came from behind the duke and helped him to his feet. She was not scolded for being on the walkway, but in fact, Wilhelm draped the duke's arm over the lady's shoulder for her to support the man's body. Screams could be heard behind them and the sound of armor clashing against stone. A rushing noise could be heard, and to the lady's dismay, arrows began to rain down upon them. Several ricocheted off the duke's helmet and shoulder armor, and she heard her own voice as if calling in the distance for the man to move faster. The duke mumbled, but she could not understand as the screech of grappling hooks digging into stone filled her ears. She did not want to be outside when someone came over the wall.

"Move, now!" she screamed and tried to quicken her pace as she pulled on the duke. It was a futile effort on her part for the wound in his left thigh only allowed him to slide his leg along. Finally the threshold was cleared and Josephine glanced over her shoulder to see that the door had swung fully open out of her reach. She helped the duke take a few steps farther inside the room and then explained that she had to turn loose of him to close the door. He motioned toward the wall, and the lady helped him rest his weight against it. Quickly she slid from under his arm and headed toward the massive oak door.

She was merely two feet away from completing her mission when she paused and took one more look outside. A man clad in armor had just scaled the wall and planted his feet on the walkway. She watched as he drew his sword from his belt and then to her relief began to move in the opposite direction. The man took a step to the right which afforded a view of what lay beyond him and Josephine gasped as she saw the silhouette of the prince. Wilhelm was engaged in hand to hand combat with his back to the tower and was not aware that the other man was coming up behind him. Without a second thought the lady grabbed her sword from beside the door and ran toward the man. She was still a few lengths away when she saw him raise his sword and grunt loudly as he came at the prince, but she lunged forward and shoved her sword toward the man with all her might. He cried out and then his sword came downward, but now it seemed misguided and did not hit its intended mark. Suddenly Josephine felt her sword move, but not of her doing, and she realized it had penetrated deep enough into the man's body that she could not pull it free. As he turned, she let go of the hilt and he began to yell and swing wildly at her like an angry bull. Blood oozed from his mouth, and she stumbled back to avoid his reach but was not quick enough as his thick arm knocked her back against the wall. She could not help but scream as she felt the rough blocks scrape her back. The man fell back and pinned her against the wall and gave a final groan as life left his body. Josephine screamed and Wilhelm turned in time to see the pair fall but could do nothing to help as he still struggled in his own confrontation. He did however see the tip of the lady's sword protruding from the dead man and knew she was still alive. Shaking badly, Josephine shoved the body away and tried to stand up. Nervously she half-crawled, half-stumbled back to the tower and closed the door tightly. The duke had managed to keep his feet under him but was near fainting as the lady came to his side again. She helped him to a cot and tried to calm down as she assessed his wounds. Carefully she began to remove his armor and cut away his clothes where necessary. His thigh had a deep gash which needed stitched, his shoulder was cut and a deep bruise was upon his forehead. Thankfully the longer she worked, the less her hands shook and the quiver in her voice went away. She was interrupted to let two guardsmen with minor wounds inside and was told that things were quieting down outside as the first round was over.

A few hours had passed since Duke Graham was injured, but he was feeling revived enough to insist the lady open the door to allow fresh air inside the tower. Josephine was not surprised that he was so demanding of her as he had given her grief ever since she had been appointed to the council. He didn't seem to like her no matter what she said or done or didn't do for that matter. She had to admit that his attitude was less harsh toward her since she had sewn up his wounds. Finally, she conceded to his request but found herself almost ill as she reached for the door handle. The terror of her last venture outside flooded back, and she was not sure she would keep her composure if the man she had slain still lay upon the walkway. Tactfully she turned her gaze toward the room as she threw open the door and then retreated to a chair to roll bandages. A short while later, Dr. Stehle came to check on her patients. He was thoroughly pleased with Josephine's handiwork and to her surprise the duke bragged that she had no doubt saved him from bleeding to death. All in all, they had been fortunate and had only lost two men in the attack. Four more were severely wounded but considering they did not know the number of their enemy's host, Dr. Stehle counted them blessed. Josephine was relieved to learn that the enemy's wounded and dead had been carried to the old stockade cells which meant she would not have to look upon them. When she inquired of the prince, she was told he was well but already preparing for the next attack. No longer afraid to go near the door, Josephine strode with the doctor out onto the walkway. It was nearly dawn and all was eerily still save the sounds from the courtyard below. Her curiosity got the better of her and she stepped toward the outer wall to look about.

"Did we gather their dead from outside the fort as well?" she asked. The doctor explained that the prince would not permit any-one to leave the fort until daylight so they had to assume the bodies had been retrieved as all knew for certain many had died attempt-ing the wall. The doctor advised her to rest until she was needed again and then stepped away. As she turned, she caught sight of the prince in the courtyard below. She watched him long enough to see that he seemed to be moving fine, which let her know he was not injured. She had just sat down again when Henri called to her from the walkway to ask for her help. She had to laugh to herself as at the mention of food it seemed that her stomach growled. To the best of her knowledge, she had not eaten since breakfast the day before. She put Duke Graham in charge of her patients and stepped away. As they headed toward the makeshift kitchen, Henri apologized and explained that his helpers needed a sword in their hand instead of a ladle. The lady laughed as she understood and was not offended.

Dawn came and went with no disturbances. Now more confident, the prince sent out the scouts. A staging area for the battle was found, but no soldiers from Aikerlan were seen. Josephine made rounds with Dr. Stehle and then helped Henri serve breakfast. Lunchtime came and still no sign of the enemy but word was brought that more of the king's guard would arrive within the hour. The news encouraged spirits throughout the fort but it was not a total surprise to the lady. She vaguely remembered a rider leaving the troops when they were at the stream and guessed that was what had settled Wilhelm's nerves when they sat together upon the wall. When Leopold arrived at the fort he had but a fourth of his men with him, as he had positioned the others along the road to secure their retreat back to Dahn. The enemy had not been seen but he advised abandoning the fort and moving the people closer to the capitol. Wilhelm agreed and the wagons were loaded for departure. They hoped to camp at the stream that evening before the ride to Dahn and then on south to Guttenhamm.

Josephine was beside her horse preparing to mount, when Dr. Stehle called out that she was needed in the wagons to help tend the wounded. She obliged his request, but as they approached the wagon, she felt her heart drop as she could see the soldiers inside. Dablin had drifted in and out of consciousness and was not expected to make it to Dahn. Robart's leg had been shattered from the knee down and he had lost a lot of blood. The look in the doctor's eye let her know the man may make it as far as Dahn before they had to remove his leg. Josephine felt a wave of panic welling up inside, but as she heard the orders to move out, the jostling of the wagon helped her to shake it off. It did not take very long for blood to show through Robart's bandages and the young lady found it difficult to apply enough pressure to keep it under control without the man crying out in pain. To make matters worse, Dablin began mumbling nonsense and she answered to ease his mind. She had just gotten Robart's bleeding under control when to her surprise Dr. Stehle rode up beside her wagon.

"My lady, I need you urgently with another patient."

"Doctor, the bleeding has just now slowed down. I cannot possibly . . ."

"It will only require a few minutes my lady, please," he interrupted. The desperation in his voice caused Josephine to rise up and move toward the edge of the wagon. He extended his arm to steady her, and she managed to put out her leg just far enough to hop in the direction of the horse's back. It was a rough landing, but she made it and before her other arm was around the older man's waist, he spurred his horse onward. She had imagined an emergency involving a surgery of some sort, but the scene the lady was brought to caught her off guard. In the wagon lay Jean Rienhold, a nobleman and soldier who lived south of Guttenhamm. Josephine had visited his business during her rounds through the countryside, and his family was one of the first to embrace her efforts and had been influential in persuading others to trust her. Now he lay mortally wounded. As Dr. Stehle helped her climb into the wagon, she felt as if her heart would burst with sadness and she looked back toward the doctor for instruction, but the agony upon his face only tore at her again. "He wants to give you words . . . for his wife." Josephine shook her head as if to argue that it could not be true but the doctor continued, "He knows his time is drawing near."

"Doctor, I can't . . ." Her voice broke up as tears fell.

"You can and you must. He has asked for you to come and you must not abandon him now." Before she could respond, the doctor turned his horse and rode away. Such turmoil raged in her mind and for a moment thoughts of running away came flooding in.

"God, please help me. I know you are with me in my time of need. Help me with this man," she whispered and closed her eyes for a moment. Suddenly she felt warmth upon her and opened her eyes to see a ray of sunshine peeking down through the trees upon her face. With a deep breath, she knelt beside the man, took his bloody hand, and called out his name until he came to. A faint smile crossed his mangled face, and he began to speak the best he could. His efforts were labored but Josephine managed to understand enough of the messages to be given to his wife and children. She assured him not to worry about his family as they would be kept under her watchful eyes. The lady could not however control her weeping as he turned his gaze to the sky and recited the Lord's Prayer and ended with a faint smile. He looked toward Josephine once again and whispered that he was ready. "Go on and be at peace," she answered him, and with those words, he closed his eyes and was gone. The lady had just laid her head upon his hand when Dr. Stehle called her name. She wiped her face with her sleeve and raised her head to see him motion to her.

"I need to get you back to Robart. He is trying to sit up and is bleeding heavily again." She glanced toward the dead man at which the doctor added, "Come, for he can be helped no further." Reluctantly, Josephine rose to her feet. With a resentful attitude, she climbed onto the doctor's horse again which caused him to say, "There will be a time to mourn for him, but right now we must work to save the others." She knew the doctor was right. He understood how powerless they were against the grip of death, disease, and war and yet he maintained his focus in order to save the next patient.

Josephine climbed back into the first wagon to find Robart now delusional with fever and talking out of his head. Another soldier had climbed into the wagon to hold him down but with no avail. Very tactfully, Josephine joined herself to Robart's conversation and in a matter of minutes convinced him that it was nine o'clock in the evening, and he needed to rest for the night. The sound of her voice calmed him and she told him she was straightening his bedclothes when in fact she was addressing his bandages. Twice she nearly had to sit upon him when he stirred, but finally his wounds were repacked.

She did not have five minutes of peace when to her amazement the other patient sat straight up in the wagon. She managed to reposition herself to face in his direction and then he suddenly moaned and began to heave. She screamed for the doctor as dark blood oozed from his lips, and she tried to keep the man still. Dr. Stehle rode up but took one glance, shook his head, and turned his horse away. Before Josephine could call out to him, the soldier gave a gasp and fell back lifeless in her arms. So unprepared was the lady that she almost fell onto the man, but as she pushed herself back, she saw her apron was covered in his blood. In a panic she fumbled to untie it and cover the man's face with the cloth. She could not bear to look at him any longer and again felt the desire to run away when a hand closed around her wrist. She turned to see Robart looking at her, his eyes bloodshot from the fever.

"My lady, am I going to lose my leg?" he asked as he gripped her wrist tight enough that it hurt. She reached to pry her hand free of his grasp as she spoke.

"Robart, I am not a doctor." She reached to stroke his forehead as she added, "I am doing everything that I can." She spoke in a calm voice and held on to his hand. Thankfully the man drifted into unconsciousness for the young lady was at a loss as what to say. She knew that when they reached the stream Dr. Stehle would be forced to amputate the leg and her heart weighed heavy at the thought. She had been with the doctor only one time when amputation was necessary.

Finally, Josephine recognized the landscape as the terrain began to slope toward the stream. In a daze, the lady remained seated in the wagon long after it had stopped. The sound of orders being given, the whinnying of horses, and the sounds of hammering as tents were erected were but dull to her ears as she tried to distance herself from her surroundings. She heard the doctor call her name, and took a deep breath and rejoined the world. She was told a wagon had been prepared to use as a surgery table, and she was to administer ether to keep the patient unconscious. Later, she vaguely recalled pleading with the doctor that she couldn't go through with her part, but the older man took hold of her and insisted since she was the only one with them who knew how to use the ether. She had to be strong to spare Robart the only relief they could afford. Somehow she pulled herself together, and thirty minutes later, the deed was done. Almost in shock, Josephine remained with Robart until after dark and only left his side as he was moved into the medical tent.

About eight o'clock, a soldier came to say the prince requested Josephine's presence in the officer's tent. Dr. Stehle gave her leave, and reluctantly she followed the messenger across the field and snaked their way around tents and small campfires. A larger fire burned outside the last tent, and through the canvas, she could see the glow of lanterns. The messenger held open the door flap and motioned the young lady inside. A makeshift table had been placed in the center of the tent and was surrounded by more than a dozen of the officers, but her arrival was not noticed as attention was fixed solely upon a map spread upon the table and the briefing being given. For a moment, the lady thought of slipping back to the medical tent, but then she heard the prince remark to a captain and quickly she came behind him and spoke up.

"My liege . . . you sent for me?" she asked. The prince turned slightly to acknowledge her but kept one hand upon the map and did not look up from it.

"Yes, my lady. Supper is almost ready and we are about to call it a day." As he spoke, the officer who stood to his left turned to look at the young lady. As she began to speak again, he couldn't help but take hold of the prince's arm.

"If there is nothing more, my liege, I will return to my patients." Wilhelm's first reaction when Vaughn touched his arm was to look at the man with a questioning glance which was met with a concerned frown as Vaughn pointed to the lady. Now alarmed, Wilhelm quickly turned to face Josephine and was horrified by what he saw.

"Please tell me none of this belongs to you," he said and stepped closer as he reached to take hold of both of her hands. She stood in shock with her response to his question delayed. "Josephine." He looked her over. Almost every part of her dress had bloodstains especially her torso and forearms. Something dark was smeared across one cheek and the part of her forehead that was not covered by her now disheveled hair. She stood still as her face shone ghostly white. Wilhelm said her name again, but this time, she blinked and looked at him. "Are you hurt?" he asked and she shook her head no.

"It is the blood of your men . . ."She paused and then began to plead. "My liege, I have wounded waiting. If I am needed no further here . . ."

"No. You will not be returning to them tonight," he said, firmly interrupting her.

"My liege . . ."

But before she could say another word, the prince added, "You will remain here." He hoped she would not try to argue with him as she looked terribly exhausted and did not need a battle of stubbornness. Quickly he asked, "Have you another dress with you, my lady?"

"Yes, yes, I do. If I knew where my saddlebag was," she answered, surprised at his question.

"Very well then. Our saddles and gear have been brought into the tent. Gentlemen, shall we allow the lady a few minutes?" The officers began to leave the tent with the prince being the last one to the doorway. "When you are finished, please give your dress to Niethel so he can see that it is burned."

"Burned?" Josephine asked wide-eyed.

"Yes, burned." Wilhelm took a few steps back toward the lady, pleased to have a more normal reaction from her. He smiled with relief and added, "I would rather not lose my hide should my mother stumble upon your blood stained dress. Would you?" Josephine smiled in return at the thought of the commotion that would result from such a discovery. "I am already due a whipping for having you in harm's way let alone having something so . . ."

"I understand," Josephine interrupted. "Go." And with a curt bow, he left her alone in the tent. It took only a few moments for Josephine to change and step out of the tent to signal the men to resume their meeting. Supper was brought, and before the hour was up, most of the men had laid out pallets to sleep upon. Although a few cots had been brought along, none of the officers would use them but sent them to the wounded. As it was not the first time to sleep overnight in the officer's tent, Josephine crawled into her fur-lined blanket and fell asleep while she listened to the men talk quietly but wasn't asleep more than fifteen minutes when she began to dream. Men were dying everywhere she looked. She gasped and sat up to look around, not sure whether she had cried out loud. Some of the men were still talking with a few having fallen asleep, but no one seemed disturbed. When her heart stopped racing, the lady laid back down and in a few minutes was asleep again. The nightmares returned, but this time, Josephine could not wake herself.

About an hour passed before Vaughn quietly spoke up. "My liege, will you not have pity?"

"How so?" answered the prince who was lying but a few feet from the captain.

"The lady is tormented so, can you not comfort her?" The sound of blankets shifting was heard as Wilhelm sat up, pulled his knees toward his chest, and draped his arms over them.

"It is not my place to do so," he said regretfully, but to his surprise, another voice was heard.

"If not your place, then whose?" Bernhardt asked. "There is no other man who has a worthy claim save you, my liege." To the prince's astonishment, several men mumbled that they agreed.

"It's not that simple," Wilhelm replied.

"Then you would rather another man comfort her?" Vaughn asked.

"No, I wouldn't!" Wilhelm answered so quickly that a few laughs were heard. He let out a sigh as his feelings toward the lady had not been masked well enough.

"As if she would let just anyone," Bernhardt added.

"My liege." Vaughn began again. "We are not suggesting anything indecent but merely that you move beside her and let her know you are close by." The tent grew silent again, but an argument was taking place in the prince's thoughts. How could he go to the lady and comfort her? He would not jeopardize the trust he had worked so hard to rebuild since that night at Naymar's, yet deep down, he knew the day would come when the line of friendship would have to be crossed. Would Josephine think him too forward for moving beside her in the night or would her mind go to the times she had fallen asleep against his shoulder with arms intertwined on long carriage rides? Despite the precautions he had taken over the past few months, enough had transpired between him and the lady that the officers felt he held her affections and welfare in his hands. But should he comfort the lady or keep his distance? He had just laid his chin upon his knees and was wondering what his father would suggest if he were here when Josephine sat straight up and cried out.

"No! Stop him, no!" Everyone in the tent stirred at the sound, and without further hesitation, Wilhelm went to her side. Gently he placed his hands upon Josephine's shoulders and said her name several times until she was awake and could answer him. He leaned near, and though only one of the lanterns remained lit, he could see tears streaming down her face. He began to wipe the tears as he explained he would move his things to where she was at. The lady began to apologize as he retrieved his blankets but he bid her to lie back down. To her surprise the prince lay down close enough that he stretched his arm over her body until his palm rested on the ground behind her.

"Now," he said as he laid his other arm above her head. "All you need to know is that I am here and you can rest peacefully." Part of Josephine wanted to protest, but the moment she felt the weight of Wilhelm's arm across her body a wave of relief came over her. Without another word, she rolled to her side and turned her back to the prince as she took hold of his hand and closed her eyes. She was listening to the sound of his steady breathing when she fell asleep.

23

The Man at the River

As soon as Josephine was asleep, Wilhelm removed his arm from over the lady and laid his sword between them. Twice during the night, the prince heard a whimper from the lady and opening an eye he reminded her that he was beside her and laid his hand upon her shoulder for a moment. All was quiet until just before dawn when the men began to stir. There was just enough light for the others to see that the prince and the lady were still asleep and the officers did their best not to disturb the pair. A noise outside the tent caused Wilhelm to draw a deep breath and almost instantly he thought of Josephine and opened his eyes to see if she still lay beside him. The noise hadn't awakened her and she was resting soundly. As he watched the lady, his mind wandered to a conversation from the evening before when Dr. Stehle had requested to speak with him in private. He gave the prince a stern warning.

"Take care," he said, taking hold of Wilhelm's arm. "I am not sure how much more her ladyship can deal with." He shook his head regretfully. "I have asked too much of her already." He faced the prince and looked hard at him. "She is a strong woman and one of our greatest assets." He paused. "We could not have made it without her. But . . ." he said, emphasizing the word. "I am sure she is at her breaking point. She won't admit to it or ask for help but don't let her be alone and keep her close." Wilhelm could hear the last words over and over. Had he prevented the lady from falling apart or had his pride only let him catch the pieces? He guessed he would know when she awoke. Although the prince lay toward the rear of the tent, he faced toward the door and could see the men as they moved about. Vaughn came near and whispered that all was quiet, and that they hoped to afford the lady some well-deserved rest. Another half hour passed before the noise outside the tent grew loud enough to wake Josephine. She had forgotten where she was until she heard Wilhelm greet her and quickly she sat up. The events of the night flooded back to her and she looked at Wilhelm's blanket draped over his body and then to her own that was tightly wrapped around her body. She blushed as she glanced around the tent and saw only two officers who were busy packing their gear. Wilhelm could guess the thoughts that raced through her mind as Josephine turned her back to him embarrassed, and the prince could not let the uncomfortable moment go unexplained.

He reached for her arm as he gently spoke, "Forgive me if I have offended you." He paused as she turned her head slightly toward him. "My conscious would not allow my friend to face the nightmares alone." The hint of a smile crossed her face as his words were sincere and appropriate to what had taken place. She managed a quiet thank you and began to crawl out of her blanket. Josephine scolded herself for letting other thoughts enter her mind for she knew she could trust Wilhelm's honor and honestly with the special blanket the queen had made, no one else could take advantage of the lady with the sides and end being sewn together. With the awkwardness only slightly abated, Josephine needed some distance between her and the prince and rose to her feet and started for the door. "Don't go very far," Wilhelm warned. "At least not alone." Josephine nodded as the prince's eyes were still upon her.

As she emerged from the tent and looked in the direction of the stream, dim rays of sunlight could be seen breaking through the trees. Wilhelm might balk at her for going alone, but it was in the opposite direction of any trouble that might arise. As she passed through the midst of the camp she was respectfully waved to. She walked through a grove of trees along the stream bank and then spotted a place near the water's edge that wasn't too steep with a nice gravel bar that would serve her purpose well. After she had knelt down Josephine began to splash water upon her face. As she watched the ripples move upon the glassy surface she drifted off in thought. It was a relief not to hear her name being called out or be jostled in the bed of a wagon. She had leaned down to take a drink when she realized it was strangely quiet. Dread swept over her as she knew something was not right. Slowly she stood to her feet and tried not to panic as she returned to the shore and glanced around while she pretended to straighten her clothes. Slowly Josephine began to walk toward the grove of trees, but suddenly she heard the sound of rock against rock and quickened her pace. Was it a person or just an animal? She tried to listen, but it was difficult over the sound of her heart beating loudly in her ears. She was a few yards into the grove when she heard the noise again, and not able to bear the suspense any longer, she turned back toward the stream. Before she could get a good look she felt an arm close around her and a hand was tightly placed over her mouth. Her toes brushed the ground as she was lifted up and then pulled behind a large oak tree. Nothing could describe the horrible numbness that overtook her body as she felt powerless against her captor, and in the next instant, she felt lips press against her ear and heard a faint but tender whisper.

"Shhhh." She closed her eyes in relief as she felt the blood rush to her head. Wilhelm held onto her firmly, and she wondered if he knew how closely she had come to fainting. She felt the prince shift suddenly and opened her eyes in time to see the silhouette of a man as he crept toward the grove. Stealthily Wilhelm moved his hand from her face to his sword's hilt. The man came closer yet the prince remained quiet. Josephine closed her eyes to keep from making a noise as she realized Wilhelm was going to let the man pass them by before he confronted him. Seconds seemed like minutes as the man walked on unaware of their location and was several lengths beyond before the prince shouted. "State your business!" At the words, the intruder turned quickly and started to reach for a weapon, but two of the guardsmen appeared from behind trees and took hold of his arms. He ranted as he struggled against his captors. Wilhelm nudged Josephine. "Let's go on back to the camp. They will take care of him." As the two approached, the intruder turned his attention to Josephine.

"My lady, my lady," he cried out as he let the guardsmen hold his arms behind his body. "Lady Josephine, it is such an honor to meet you. You, the favored one of his majesty, my lady." The man attempted to bow but the guardsmen stopped him as they told him to be quiet. He mumbled something to them under his breath but quickly returned his attention to Josephine. He staggered a few steps toward her but Wilhelm put himself in the way and demanded silence. The man paid no mind to the prince and leaned this way and that to see the lady better as he continued rambling. "Lady Josephine, he will be pleased to know you are well. Beautiful too, I might add." The last words caused the soldiers to give the man a hard jerk and he was again commanded to be quiet. Wilhelm and Josephine had already moved past the man but the statement caused them to turn and look at him again. Wilhelm tugged on the lady's arm, and shook his head in disbelief. They were halfway through the grove but could still hear the man as he called. "Lady Josephine, please don't let these barbarians hurt me. Your servant has done nothing wrong. Have mercy my lady. I am here to serve you. My lady . . . my . . ." The last words were muffled and although it seemed cruel Josephine hoped that the guardsmen had gagged the intruder's mouth. When they came into the camp, Wilhelm motioned to Vaughn to come to him and then turned to Josephine.

"Please go on to the tent and wait for me there. I will be but a moment." The scowl upon his face told enough that Josephine did not hesitate but nodded and left without a word. When Vaughn was at the prince's side, Wilhelm spoke solemnly as he looked toward the grove. "Find out *why* that man is here within our borders." He paused as he could see the guardsmen drag the intruder closer. "And what he wanted with her ladyship. There are more to his words than just preying upon her for mercy." Vaughn agreed and left the prince.

When Josephine entered the tent, she found that she was alone. She shook terribly and her mind was scattered. Her eyes fell upon her saddlebags, and quickly she went to them, removed her brush, and began undoing the braid in her hair. Maybe if her hands were in motion Wilhelm wouldn't notice that she was trembling. She wondered if she would be scolded for venturing alone to the stream when he had given her warning not to. Hearing the tent flap shift, she turned her back to the door, to keep Wilhelm from seeing her face and began to brush her hair. The prince could tell she was upset and he was as well. Several moments passed as he considered what to say and then finally just blurted out.

"I would like to leave for home within the hour. Will you be ready?" Wilhelm was not prepared for the reaction that he got.

"I will not be able to check on my patients in such a short amount of time. No, that will not do." She concluded as she turned to face him as he strode across the tent toward her.

"I think," he said in a stern voice. "You should not see any patients this morning. The doctor will manage without you." The words struck Josephine wrong, and all she could hear was how incapable she was. Had her weakness in the night brought on the prince's decision? He saw the fire flash in her eyes at his words. Josephine took a step in his direction, but the moment she began to move her legs felt weak and she was reminded how shaken her nerves were. Hoping to disguise her shortcoming, she gripped her brush and turned her back to the prince again. No matter how badly she wanted to persuade him otherwise, she did not have the strength to do so.

"I would have liked to follow up, but as you wish, my lord. I will be ready to leave shortly." Although the words would have sounded sincere to anyone else, the prince knew she was not pleased. Before he could ask about the sudden change, Leopold stepped into the tent and greeted them. The younger prince had returned from his watch during the night and was happy to report no sign of the enemy.

Leopold stayed behind to command the retreat and ensure outposts along the way were emptied as they retraced their steps along the road to Dahn. As he had said, Wilhelm and Josephine left within the hour with a few dozen soldiers. Hardly a word was spoken between Wilhelm and his men as they rode hard toward Guttenhamm. At first, such quietness bothered Josephine, but as time went on, she understood as she too needed time without conversation to sort through things that happened before coming back into the realm of friends and family and the questions of the council members. As the riders mounted from a quick rest and they prepared for the last stretch to the capitol, Josephine's mind was upon two things: Robart's injuries and the man at the stream. She could not be free of the sound of the intruder's pleas and that he called her by name.

They came to Guttenhamm late in the afternoon and arrived at the castle and managed not to be heralded by trumpets. Wilhelm thanked the guardsmen for their service and bid them a good evening as he dismissed them. He helped Josephine from her saddle, and the weary pair went inside and made their way upstairs.

As they passed the library, Wilhelm commented, "We are almost there. I keep imagining falling back onto the soft blankets."

"Take a bath first," Josephine teased as she pinched her nose and pretended to be in disgust.

"No. Let me sleep and then I will think about a bath." They gave a laugh as they slowly walked along. Whether their hands were sore from holding the horses' reins all day or whether they were just too tired to think about it, Josephine was not upon Wilhelm's arm as usual. Suddenly Wilhelm had a thought and reached for Josephine, but when his hand touched her back, she cried out in pain and flinched. The reaction startled both of them, but Wilhelm carefully reached for Josephine's arm and turned her to face him. "You are hurt, aren't you?" he questioned.

She looked away and mumbled, "It's only where I fell against the wall." She wouldn't look him in the eye which only made him angry.

He demanded, "Did you have Dr. Stehle take a look at it?"

What is he doing? she thought. *Who does he think he is, restraining me and questioning me as if I am a wayward child?* Defiantly she pulled free and stepped backward as she replied, "Do you think I would trouble him with a scrape when men were falling about us?"

"Did you at least clean it?" the prince asked, but Josephine turned and began to walk toward her room, not wanting to admit she hadn't and could only hope it was a simple scrape, for it felt worse than that. She didn't make it very far when Wilhelm stepped in front of her and took hold of her by the arms again.

"Let go of me. Let me be, Wilhelm," she said as she struggled against him.

"You will have your back looked at or I will take care of it myself!" By the look he gave, the lady could envision him bending her over his knee like a child and ripping the back of her dress open to survey the wounds. The realization that he was strong enough to move her about however he wanted made her cringe, but the prince didn't get the chance to do anything as another voice boomed.

"You will do nothing of the sort!" Both froze as the king stepped beside them. "What is this? Have you been hurt, Josephine?" The lady felt the grip upon her arms slacken but remain as she glanced at the floor. "Tell me, now." Wilhelm looked hard at the lady who stood before him as she took hold of his shirt sleeves. His gaze was met by hers, and they knew for sure they were in trouble. Wanting to protect her, the prince started to answer but was promptly interrupted by the king. "I asked Josephine and I believe she is quite capable of speaking on her own behalf."

The guilty pair exchanged glances once again as Josephine began, "I scraped my back against the wall at the fort, my liege. There were others that needed tending to far worse than I and . . ."

"I thought we agreed that you were to stay behind the battle lines, a safe distance away," Hubert stated.

"She was father," Wilhelm answered. The king stomped a few steps away.

"Was?" he said as he turned back to look at the pair. By their actions, he knew much more had transpired than what had been said thus far. "Was, as was at one time, or she remained away from the battle the whole time. Which is it?"

Here it comes, Josephine thought. Everything she did not want to ever be mentioned was about to be told. Wilhelm stepped close enough to the lady that she could have rested her head against him.

"Father, may I speak to you alone. She needs to rest. Please."

"Not until I have some answers," the king demanded. The anger he had heard in his son's voice at the lady's stubbornness only a minute before had been replaced by concern.

With the truth being the only answer that would be accepted, Josephine spoke up, "I will own up to my part in this matter." She glanced again at Wilhelm who offered an excuse for her behavior.

"You had no choice."

"As if you did?" she asked but then continued as she looked toward the king. "I was a safe distance from harm until we were deceived." She looked to Wilhelm. "How could you have ever known what would happen?" She gripped his arms through the fabric of his sleeves and let her gaze fall to his chest.

"Our enemy doubled back to where she and Dr. Stehle were stationed," Wilhelm explained.

"At Bartlestoff?" the king asked, and both Wilhelm and Josephine nodded. "So why didn't you send her away?"

"It was too late. I couldn't send her alone, and even if I sent a handful of guardsmen with her, it would not guarantee her safety."

"He had no choice my liege," she finished for him. "I knew the risk." Hubert could see the agony upon the faces of both.

Much calmer, he asked, "How is it that you were hurt?" Josephine stepped back as she attempted to get free of Wilhelm's grasp, but he managed to keep hold of her right hand. She let her gaze fall to the floor as the memory of seeing him almost perish upon the wall flooded back to her mind. Wilhelm began to explain before she could speak.

"She had been safe inside the tower caring for the wounded. She was letting Duke Graham inside when a man made it over the wall and came for me. I was fighting for my life and not even aware the man was behind me."

At that point, Josephine cried out, "My liege, I could not stand there and do nothing!" Her voice broke up as she fought back tears.

"I would not be alive father if she hadn't killed the man."

"As he was going down, he knocked me back into the wall," Josephine mumbled. Wilhelm tried to pull the lady close again, but this time, she would not let him. Suddenly she looked up, stepped toward the king and took hold of his arm. "I do not regret what has happened, but I ask one thing, please." Hubert surprised by her actions, moved closer, and nodded for her to continue. "Please don't let the queen know what happened. I do not want her upset over things that cannot be undone. Please my liege," she begged.

"Oh, my dear girl," the king said and tilted his head with compassion. Although he still only had a shallow knowledge of the outing, he knew it had been difficult enough on all involved. He wanted to scold the young lady for landing herself in trouble yet again, but when he saw the anguish on her face, he couldn't do so, at least not right then. "Have Katrina examine your injuries and don't think that I won't question her to be sure it was done. Swear her to secrecy concerning the matter, and I will not mention the details to my wife. In fact . . ." He gave a stern look to Wilhelm who had finally let go of Josephine's hand. "From the sound of it, no details of this outing should be discussed." Wilhelm nodded his head in agreement, and the king looked back to the lady. "Go on to your room and call for Katrina. I will arrange for supper to be a little later to let you both rest longer." He kissed Josephine's forehead and motioned for her to leave them. As she stepped away, he said, "As for you my son, there is much to discuss before I let you go."

"Yes, Father," the prince replied, but he reached for Josephine's hand as she moved past him. "May I check on you?" She didn't look at him but was quick to slip free from his grasp.

"No. I just want to be alone." She tried to take another step but he blocked her from going further.

"You don't need to be alone after all of this." He stepped close and laid his hand upon her shoulder. As he leaned to look at her she closed her eyes and took a deep breath.

"Let me be, Wilhelm." Quickly she stepped to the side away from him and opened her eyes. He would have stopped her except he felt his father's hand come to rest heavily upon his shoulder in disapproval.

Just before six thirty that evening, Katrina woke Josephine and helped her fix her hair before she went down to supper. The lady in waiting had examined the lady's back and found it scraped along with her shoulder but nothing significant enough to warrant further concern. Josephine had managed to rest very little for when she began to drift off she would start to dream and see the enemy raise his sword above Wilhelm, and as he brought it down, she would scream his name and wake up. She had tried to sleep in a chair but as soon as she closed her eyes she could hear the man from the stream call to her and would abruptly jerk out of fear. Thankfully, no one heard Josephine call out. When the queen saw the younger lady in the dining hall she embraced her and whispered in her ear, "I was told not to ask questions about your trip but to let you rest. Something happened and there is tension between you and Wilhelm?"

"Something like that," Josephine whispered in return. "But I am feeling better already just being home." As the ladies parted, Wilhelm came to Josephine's side and helped her be seated at the table. Twice during supper they were interrupted by messengers. At the sight of the men, the lady's heart raced terribly and time seemed to stand still as she watched the king's response as words were whispered back and forth. Wilhelm's reaction was no better, for he was as alert as if still on the battlefield. The queen noticed that when the first messenger came, Josephine took Wilhelm by the hand and when the second one arrived the prince found the lady's hand. Agatha couldn't help but wonder if the spat between them had been reconciled. Both interruptions were of minor importance and the evening continued. After supper, the family went upstairs to the library and settled into what had become routine during the winter months. The king and queen resumed their readings, and Wilhelm and Josephine found themselves beside each other on the divan once again. It was Wilhelm's turn to read aloud, but after one page, he turned to the lady.

"Forgive me but I cannot continue." He looked toward Josephine who stared toward the fireplace. Her face showed no emotion as if in a trance. He wondered if she had heard him speak at all. "I am too tired to see straight let alone translate this passage in French," he said but she did not move or even blink. He laid the book upon his knee and he reached for her arm. "Josephine." Startled, she looked over at him.

"Hmmm?" She could tell by the look on his face that she had missed something. "I'm sorry, what was that again?"

He laughed softly and said, "I was just saying how we are too tired for reading and should turn in for the night." He rose to his feet and pulled her up with him by the hand as he did. She gave a hearty laugh and then said good night to the king and queen. As they often did they linked arms but Josephine began to cling tighter to the prince with each step they took closer to their chambers as she dreaded the nightmares that haunted her sleep. She was so lost in thought that she did not realize they had stopped in front of her chamber door. "Josephine," Wilhelm said her name quietly to catch her attention. When she finally looked toward him, he chose his words carefully to not upset her as he had earlier that afternoon. "I am worried about you."

"I am all right," she answered as she reached for the doorknob.

"I don't think you are," he said and reached for the knob as well to prevent her from opening the door. "I don't think you should be alone just yet." His comment caused her to look at him.

"I cannot come running to you when I am having a bad day or get my knee scraped, Wilhelm," she said curtly. The conversation was not headed in the direction the prince wanted it to go. The lady turned the knob and gave the door a push.

"This has been more than that and . . ." he said and stepped to block her from going through the doorway. With little to lose he slid his arms around the lady. Wilhelm did not make eye contact with her at the moment but kept his head above hers. "Let me help you."

"I don't need your help," she replied.

"And when the nightmares return, what then?" As he spoke, he leaned back to see her reaction.

"Then I will face them," she answered bravely, but the fear in her eyes said otherwise.

"Like last night?" The words cut deep by the look upon the lady's face, and Wilhelm wished he could have taken them back.

After waiting a few seconds she said, "I appreciate what you did, but that was last night."

"And what about tonight? If you cannot find sleep, what then? You cannot go days on end without rest," he said but she looked hard into his eyes.

"And if I give in tonight, what about tomorrow night and the next? You cannot hold me every night," she replied defiantly and shook her head as she finished.

"If that is what it takes, then I will do it," Wilhelm answered. Very tenderly, he reached to stroke her hair, and as he did to his surprise she closed her eyes and leaned against him. Perhaps he had persuaded her to listen to reason, he thought to himself. Josephine gave a deep sigh and then stood up straight again and opened her eyes.

"No," she said. "I will not let it come to that. This is *my* struggle and *I* have to face it." The determination in her voice resonated as she gently pushed the prince away. He could not believe himself, but he let her go. The lady said good night, but as the door was closing between them, he reminded her that he was still just across the hall.

Wilhelm stood outside the door for several minutes before he stepped away and only made it to his door before he headed back down the hallway. He marched past the library and had almost reached the staircase when the king called his name.

"Wilhelm, where are you headed at this hour?"

Too upset to face his father, the prince stopped long enough to say, "I need to get some air."

At first, the prince just walked the grounds but then he went to the stables and brushed down the horses. He was angry with Josephine for being so stubborn, but then he realized he was angrier with himself. How could he have let her slip through his arms yet again? He could never find the words he needed when they were alone together. As badly as he wanted to make her see things from his point of view, he knew he couldn't make her do anything she didn't want to. He wouldn't like the outcome if he tried, so the lady would have to come to the conclusion that she needed help on her own. Several hours passed before he came back inside. Finally he went back to his chambers but began to nervously pace the floor. What if he heard her cry out in her sleep? Would he be able to refrain from going to her? Not wanting to find out and hoping it was far enough away he retreated to the library. He sat down in a chair, leaned forward, and buried his face in his hands. After a little while he sank back into the chair and began to doze. He did not know how long he was out when suddenly he was startled by a noise and looked across the room to see Josephine standing in front of the map wall. He watched as she extended an arm to touch a location, but to his surprise, her hand did not go left toward Frive but right to Bartlestoff. Again, he heard the sound which had first awakened him and realized it was her softly crying. She leaned her head forward until it touched the wall, and quietly he rose to his feet, and when he was almost to her, he could remain silent no longer.

"Josephine," he whispered as he hoped not to startle her but his efforts were in vain.

Quickly she began to wipe her face as she spoke, "I'm sorry, I thought I was alone."

"I am the one who needs to apologize. I am sorry for not being a better friend." The words caused the lady to turn and face him, but then she wished she hadn't. The expression the prince wore made it hard to resist his words and she wasn't ready to admit that he was right about the nightmares.

"I am going back to my room. I am sorry if I disturbed you. Excuse me," Josephine said as she moved quickly to avoid him taking hold of her as he had earlier. She was not fast enough for he caught her just outside the door.

"Wait, please," he pleaded. This time he had a gentle but firm grip upon both of her shoulders but remained behind her. "I will not let you go upset." He drew closer, and she could feel his chin just graze her hair. Neither spoke for a moment as Josephine closed her eyes as if to shut out everything he was about to say.

The longer they stood there, the weaker her will became and finally she blurted out. "I am doing everything I can to keep myself together. Don't make matters worse." Her voice wavered with hesitation as she added, "Let me go on."

"I can't do that," he whispered. Like an animal that had been cornered, she turned to face him, eyes wide and on the defense.

"I will not be the weak one. I have to remain strong and keep myself together. What would the council say if I faltered now?" She did not realize that she was yelling, and the prince found himself doing likewise as he confronted her.

"Is that what this is about? What someone would say? Josephine, I thought you were past the foolish opinions of others long ago." Wilhelm took a few steps back as he continued, "So you should suffer for the sake of looking infallible? I think not! Enough of this!" He began to move toward the lady who was shocked by his reaction. It was as if she came to her senses from a dream-like state as he took hold of her again. "And don't you think," he pulled her closer and looked hard in her eyes, "for one minute," he let his voice return to normal. "That anyone could *ever* call you weak. Not after all you have been through and done this week." As the last words were spoken, he reached to stroke her hair.

She closed her eyes and whispered, "I cannot do this any longer." A tear ran down her cheek, but the prince was quick to catch it.

"Let's do this together," he whispered as he rested his head against hers.

The argument had brought the king and queen to the door of their chambers just in time to see Wilhelm half-drag, half-lead a sobbing Josephine back to the library. Agatha did not know what had transpired and was headed to their aide but the king restrained her and explained that Wilhelm was the only one who could give the comfort that the lady needed. Hubert stationed the night guard at the door close enough to be sure nothing inappropriate happened but far enough away that their conversation could not be heard. Wilhelm persuaded Josephine to pour out her heart to him and in hysteria she relived the scene upon the wall and the haunting voice of the man at the stream. For a while, Wilhelm struggled to convince Josephine that it was in the past, but finally he just pulled her close and squeezed her gently to demonstrate his point.

"Do you feel my arms around you?" She nodded as tears streamed down her face. "I am alive and here with you now. Hear me, I am safe with you," he repeated. "You saved me, remember?" He leaned back to see her face again. "Hear the sound of my voice not that crazy man's." For a moment, the lady closed her eyes and concentrated as he spoke. "Hear my voice, Josephine." He leaned his head against hers. "My arms are around you, not that man's. He cannot touch you nor can anyone else and you are safe in my arms. You will never see that man again." The words seemed to melt away Josephine's fears. Wilhelm tucked her beside him on the divan and with her head against his arm, peaceful sleep fell upon them both.

Close to dawn, they were awakened by the king who advised them to return to their rooms. They were about to part at their chamber doors when Josephine remembered her promise to Jean Rienhold, and explained to Wilhelm how she needed to pay the family a visit that morning. He leaned to kiss the lady's forehead and announced he would see to things so they could leave together within the hour. The visit was gut-wrenching, and although Josephine held her emotions while they were with the family, she could not keep from crying when they were back inside the carriage. She had just composed herself and leaned away from Wilhelm's shoulder when they rolled back into Guttenhamm. As they looked out the window, she couldn't help but smile as so many familiar faces waved to them as they passed by. She was reminded that all the torment of the last few days was worth it to keep the people safe. By the time they reached the castle, both were in much better spirits and had begun to discuss business that needed to be taken care of due to their absence. They went inside, and Josephine excused herself upstairs to trade her cloak for a shawl before she joined Wilhelm again.

Wilhelm had stepped to his father's office door to let him know they had returned only to find the king solemnly staring out the window. He asked his son to be seated and explained word had been received from the garrison that the intruder from the stream was not cooperating, having chosen to remain silent with his only words being that he would talk to the lady and her alone. The very thought of the man asking for Josephine made Wilhelm angry yet his father had entertained the idea or he would not have mentioned it. The prince was quick to argue the folly of such a notion, but the king reminded his son they needed information, for the chance to know their enemy's plan far outweighed the risk of the lady speaking to the stranger. Wilhelm rose to his feet and strode to the window as his father reminded him that they desperately needed answers. Finally Wilhelm could not stand it any longer.

"She cannot see the man, Father. Part of why she was so upset last night had to do with what he said to her at the stream. We cannot allow that again. This is such a fragile time for her." Wilhelm's voice rose with excitement as he spoke.

"I understand but we cannot let this opportunity pass us by. What if he knows something that will prevent lives being lost? What then?"

"I promised her father!" Wilhelm yelled as he walked to his father's desk and slammed his hand down upon it. "I promised that she would never have to look at that man again!" Frustrated he turned and went back to the window. Hubert rubbed his forehead and let out a sigh.

"I am making the decision, not you," he said sternly. "And we can only go through with it if she agrees to the meeting. I will not force her." Wilhelm did not turn around but stared out the window. Neither of them spoke, but suddenly a voice was heard from the hall.

"Is everything all right, my liege? I thought I heard shouting." Wilhelm had not expected to remain with his father and had left the door open when he came into the room.

"Yes, Josephine, please come in. I need to speak with you." The lady had not made it to a chair when Wilhelm came to her side. He looked upset but before he could speak, Hubert said, "Wilhelm, please leave us." The prince acted as if he was going to say something but didn't and then abruptly left the room. Growing numb with fear, Josephine sat down, and to her surprise, the king left his seat from behind his desk and moved to a chair closer to the lady and took her hand in his. "You know that I would never put you in harm's way." She nodded as he continued. Briefly he explained about the prisoner, his demands and then gave the possibilities of information that could be gained if he talked. The drawback would be having to face the man again, but it would involve more than that. She had to be wise enough to lead the conversation so that he told more than what he wanted to reveal. She would have to control her emotions and fears and turn her words into a weapon that would cut the very devices of their enemy. He himself would go with her to the meeting, but the prisoner may refuse to talk with him being present so she would have to be prepared to face him alone. The king stopped and looked hard at the young lady who sat before him. "I know this is a lot to ask and I am certain that it will be difficult but . . ." He was not able to finish as she interrupted him.

"I will do it." She agreed so fast that it surprised the king.

"Are you sure?" he asked which caused Josephine to look away for a moment, but when her gaze met his again, there were tears in her eyes.

"There are questions that I need answered. I have to know why he said certain things. I saw the look in Wilhelm's eyes, and he knows there is more as well." Hubert patted the young lady's arm.

"I am sure there is."

They sat for almost an hour and formed a list of questions and then the king began to coach Josephine how to dig for more information. He warned the lady to prepare herself for foul manners and vile words from the intruder's mouth. He braced her for the worst, but most of all he reminded her not to lose focus of the goal. Finally, the king declared that she was ready, and together they walked to the foyer. Josephine expected to find Wilhelm waiting, but his father broke the news that his son would not be allowed to go with them for when it came to the lady being abused, the prince's temper could not to be trusted. When they arrived at the garrison, it was announced that a lady was present and the inmates were warned to be on their best behavior. The king and Josephine were escorted into a room where a long table stood flanked by six chairs. They sat down on one side, and a few minutes later, the intruder, in chains, was brought into the room and directed to a chair opposite them. Josephine felt her heart beat faster as the man was much closer than she wanted him to be. She was comforted when she felt the king's hand upon her arm.

"What is your name?" Hubert asked. The man looked Josephine over and then smiled ridiculously from ear to ear. "Did you hear me?"

Rudely the man replied, "I did, but I am not here to speak to you . . . but to the Lady Josephine." Josephine could not help but shudder.

Focus, focus, focus, she told herself. *Lead him into conversation.* "If I may ask then, what is your name?"

"Ivan, my lady." Josephine detested the sound of the man's voice and the way he addressed her.

"Ivan, how came it that you were within our borders?" Hungry for the lady's attention, the man was more than willing to tell his story. He was just an honest, hardworking man who hoped to improve his situation, if she understood his meaning. At first he spoke with no vulgarities, but then on occasion, a foul word was used at which he would apologize for not being used to sitting before such a noble lady. Josephine played along as he explained that he was employed by the king of Aikerlan and all had been well until that fateful night at Briasburg. Upon the king's death, he had been displaced for a time until word came that the castle was to be rebuilt. The new king had quickly rallied his people to avenge his father and brothers' deaths and all who could fight had been recruited. Suddenly the prisoner began to rant against the injustice of Gutten and began to hiss and snarl toward King Hubert until finally the guards threatened him. He calmed down and gave a smile as he apologized to the lady. Josephine loathed the man and somewhere during the conversation she began to dig her fingernails into the underside of the tabletop as thoughts of scratching his ugly face flooded her mind. She spoke up and tried to steer the man back on course.

"So you were building his castle?" she asked.

"Was, ma'am." He corrected. "You will be pleased when it is finished, I am sure you will like it." For a moment, Josephine's curiosity almost got the better of her as she wondered why her opinion of the castle would matter.

"Was? You are no longer there?"

"My lady, opportunity came knocking." He gave a smile and leaned back in his chair very pleased. Rewards were being given to people who could provide the king with "certain information." Josephine's eyebrow rose as he described spying in such a manner, and she wondered where all he had traveled in the kingdom. Had he made it as far as Guttenhamm? He must have, she thought as pleased as he seemed. Carefully she asked him how he had faired with his rewards and had it been worth his time. He gave a snarl and conveyed that he had brought back information about how many guards were stationed in the villages, but that wasn't good enough he was told and received a disappointing wage but was given another opportunity.

"Why wasn't it good enough?" Josephine questioned. Ivan leaned forward as he had sparked her interest.

"Old news, the king said. Others had already told him those things." The moment he said "others," Josephine had to muffle a gasp and it felt as if the blood had drained from her head. She felt Hubert's reassuring hand upon her arm again. She was so engrossed in Ivan's tale that she had forgotten he was still beside her. She glanced toward the king who suddenly nodded in the direction of the prisoner to encourage her to ask another question.

"So what did you do?" The lady was curious, but not nearly as much as she pretended to be. The man bought it and was so eager to answer that he leaned forward again.

"That is when I found you." He smiled devilishly at her.

"Me?" she exclaimed at which he began to laugh.

"Yes, he promised great wealth and land to anyone who would bring word of your whereabouts. I arrived in Dahn last week and was told you were in Guttenhamm. I planned to start south, but then rumors came of soldiers on the move so I stayed put until I was sure they were gone. Not as many travelers upon the road as there used to be and I didn't want any special attention coming my way. I wasn't too happy when I heard you were headed east toward Bartlestoff with the doctor. Then more soldiers came to Dahn, I had to get out . . . too stuffy for me. Then word came of a retreat so I had a notion to venture out."

"Is that when you saw me by the stream?" Josephine asked.

"Yes, my lady. Such good fortune it was. I saw you there and I knew."

"Knew what?" she asked.

"I knew it was you," he answered with a grin.

"But I don't understand, Ivan, how did you know it was me?" The lady was not prepared for the explanation that followed.

"He described you perfectly, my lady. Your dark hair, graceful figure, eyes that captivate your very soul. You are just as he said. Her majesty's beautiful." The words uttered from the man's lips made Josephine ill, but she managed another meager question.

"He who?"

"Why the young king, of course," he replied. A wave of fear washed over the lady, and it felt as if she was sinking down into her chair. Ivan did not seem to notice her reaction and rambled on. "He only wanted word of where to find you." He laughed again. "But I was going to bring you to him." Josephine could not help but close her eyes and then she opened them again as anger overtook her. She refused to be moved by fear and leaned forward as she snarled.

"You honestly think I would go with the likes of you anywhere?" She detested the very sight of him, the shaggy beard, the unkempt hair, the missing teeth; he reeked of filth of many days without bathing.

"Well, I was prepared to persuade you, if you catch my meaning, my lady." He leaned toward her and grinned. "I know you would have seen things my way and cooperated." At the suggestion, the king could take no more and rose to his feet and reached for Josephine's shoulder as he did.

"That will be enough, Lady Josephine." For a moment, the lady thought of slapping the prisoner's face, but before she could, he began to curse again and she followed the king out the door instead. Not a word was spoken during the carriage ride back to the castle, and she was halfway up the stairs in the great hall when the king called out to her.

"Wait." She stopped, and when he had joined her, he continued, "I commend you for the fine job of interrogating him. Josephine, you were very brave and he played into our hands very well."

In a shaky voice, the lady replied, "I hope so." She hesitated. "I need to be alone for a little while." She turned to face the king. "But I will have Katrina with me, I promise." The king winked at her.

"So I need to keep Wilhelm away?"

"Please," she said and he nodded.

He started back down the steps, but as she began to move, she heard him say, "Thank you, Josephine."

It was at supper time that Josephine ventured out of her room. She had managed to fall asleep for over an hour, and although her nerves had calmed, Katrina refused to leave her side. Wilhelm was quieter than usual, and she was sure the details of the meeting had been disclosed to him by his father because of the scowl he wore upon his brow. Despite his somber mood, the others went about the evening as if nothing had happened. They had made it upstairs and were about to enter the library when Wilhelm let his mother and father go on ahead of him but asked Josephine if he could speak with her privately. She consented and took his arm but to her amazement, he led her across the room to the map wall.

"Father and I agree." He looked toward the lady. "We are spread too thin to play Maximillian's game. It's time we go for help." As he finished, he rested his hand upon the far right side of the map.

24

Andervan

"Josephine, I believe we are coming into Merhausen," Wilhelm said softly as he gently shook the young lady. It had taken five days by carriage to reach the kingdom of Andervan in the mountain ranges of the east. Andervan did not border Gutten but possessed great wealth and military might, and twenty years prior during the Ten Weeks war, they had been proud to help defend the smaller kingdoms to their west. With war eminent, Gutten's High Council had met, and it was decided that alliances from times past must be secured. A message had been sent ahead to announce a party would arrive to seek the wisdom of Andervan's council and king. The circumstances within Gutten were dire, and as armed men may be needed at home, Josephine would be sent to represent the council along with Prince Wilhelm. Katrina had been brought for Josephine's sake but only a dozen soldiers which included the carriage attendants could be spared. Blessed with no mishaps and good weather, the travelers were almost halfway through their journey as the road wound through the mountains and toward the capital city of Andervan. Josephine had fallen asleep leaning heavily against Wilhelm's arm, but as he shook her, she opened her eyes to see the carriage turn between a massive outcropping of rock. There ahead lay a town more than twice the size of Guttenhamm and the spires of a castle could be seen upon a distant hill. Katrina who was across from Josephine, began to point at other sights out the window and talk about the mountain peaks rising above them. It took almost an hour for the carriage to travel over the river and through the winding streets to ascend the hill and turn toward the castle. As they came up the final approach, the sounding of trumpets could be heard. Nervously the ladies fidgeted as the carriage came to a halt in front of a line of people who welcomed the visitors in formal fashion. They carefully stepped out and began to make their way to the entrance where they could see the king waiting with a crown upon his head.

To their surprise, as the visitors drew near he called out, "Prince Wilhelm, it has been far too long. What, three years since the hunt in Pietra?"

"Yes, honorable king," Wilhelm replied, bowing deeply in reverence.

"Welcome! Please, let us go inside," King Sven said as he motioned toward the entryway behind him. Josephine, Katrina, and two of the escorts were a few steps behind Wilhelm and had just made it to where Wilhelm was when he bowed. The king's attention had been fully upon the prince and he did not see the ladies until Wilhelm turned to find his counterpart and reached for her arm. When the king saw Josephine, he gave the prince a questioning look.

The prince replied, "My king, let me introduce her ladyship, Josephine Armand." Then, to everyone's surprise, the king bowed toward the lady and smiled.

"I welcome you to Andervan, my lady." Josephine felt herself blush and managed a feeble nod as she curtsied in return. Inside the castle, the escorts and Katrina were directed to where they would be staying, but the prince and Josephine followed the king on to the great hall where they stood and talked. Shortly a servant came through to announce that supper would be at six o'clock in the dining hall which was about two hours away.

"That will be enough time to settle in and freshen up," the king stated as he glanced toward Josephine. As the men continued on in conversation, the lady stepped away to admire the artwork of the cathedral-like room. So many beautiful tapestries hung upon the wall telling scenes from a story and scattered here and there were tables upon which stood sculptures of marble. Stealing another glance of the lady, the king added, "I had no idea that your party of two would include a female." It almost seemed as if a question had been posed, and Wilhelm felt compelled to give an answer.

"She has come to us from Frive. She has worked in our commerce department since she arrived and has been well received by our people."

"Studying abroad?" he asked as the pair both turned to look at the lady and the king couldn't help himself, "She is very lovely." The two looked at each other, and Wilhelm shook his head and gave a laugh.

"Those are fighting words with her," he replied but quickly tried to compose himself as he noticed Josephine coming closer to rejoin them.

"By the look on your face, I have missed something amusing," the lady stated. Neither man answered but only continued to smile.

A few moments passed until the king said, "My lady, your chambers are ready. If anything is not to your satisfaction, please let me know. It has been a long time since we accommodated such a lovely guest and from so far away. I would hate for your stay with us to be unpleasant in any way." As he finished, he took her hand and bowed again to her.

"Your majesty, I am sure everything will be splendid. Your hospitality is appreciated."

She had expected at her words that the king would have released her hand, but instead he placed his other hand over hers as he smiled again and added, "I will be asking if everything is in order." Josephine blushed and quickly withdrew her hand, smiling politely. Sensing the uncomfortableness he had caused, the king called for servants to take his guests on upstairs.

They came to Wilhelm's chambers first and then Josephine was led on a few doors down to her room. She found Katrina anxiously waiting her arrival, and the ladies began to chatter about the lavish furnishings and the overwhelming size of the castle itself. They were not certain they could find their way back to the great hall and had seen so many corridors along the way that they imagined themselves easily getting lost. The two relaxed across the large bed and were staring at a painting on the ceiling above them when they dozed off. Suddenly Josephine heard a noise and rose up off the bed to see an older lady standing a few feet away.

"Oh my, oh my!" the maid said, her eyes large in amazement.

"What is it?" Josephine asked, alarmed.

"Supper will be served in fifteen minutes and you are not ready," she answered.

Josephine reached for Katrina and cried out, "We fell asleep!" At which both ladies scrambled from the bed and began a frenzy to get Josephine looking presentable. Another dress was pulled from their luggage and slipped into; hair was brushed and simply pinned to the side. There was no need to pinch Josephine's cheeks in place of rouge as she was quite flustered already. Katrina begged to remain in the chambers, and reluctantly Josephine obliged as the older lady pushed her toward the door and promised a meal would be brought to Katrina.

As they approached the great hall, Josephine could see a good number of people waiting to file through the doorway and she was relieved as no one should notice that she was late. The chambermaid excused herself and left Josephine amid the people. As she listened to the conversation she discovered the dinner that night was only preliminary in lieu of a ball that would be held the following evening in honor of Prince Wilhelm. Everyone seemed so dressed up with fancy gowns and jackets that Josephine wondered if she looked decent enough. Thoughts of slipping back to her chambers tempted her, and she knew she would not be missed by anyone save Wilhelm; well, maybe the king would notice. If inquiries were made of her whereabouts, she could always feign that she was exhausted. As she stood and waited among the noisy throng, her mind wandered to the king. He was not at all what she had pictured from Wilhelm's account during the carriage ride. He was a widower with three sons but having seen him in person, he seemed much younger than three children would have afforded. Wilhelm had spoken of the man's wisdom and how vibrant he had been before his wife's passing, but since had been more reserved with a sorrowful look in his eyes. While in the great hall, Josephine had not seen anything to make her think the king was sad. In fact, his countenance said otherwise as he and Wilhelm had grinned and laughed like school boys plotting mischief. She recalled his eyes; they seemed to look at her so intently. Her thoughts were interrupted.

"Lady Josephine." As she turned, she saw the older man who had walked her to her room. "If you please, my lady, come with me. The king is waiting for your arrival at his side." The servant took her arm and led her back and down a hallway, then through several smaller connecting passageways until they emerged at the far end of the great hall near the throne platform. Josephine found Wilhelm beside the king and as the servant disappeared behind her, Sven offered her his arm. She found herself glancing first to Wilhelm who nodded his approval, and then very timidly, she took hold of the king's arm.

"We missed you," he said quietly as he resumed his position in front of his throne.

"My apologies, I was detained," she replied sheepishly, not wanting to admit what had happened.

"I thought as much," he said, smiling at her.

"I was not expecting this many people, your majesty," she added.

"My apologies for not mentioning that earlier," he answered as he began to walk toward the center of the room with her arm still in his with Wilhelm following close behind. The king freed himself and made a short speech to his guests, inviting them to the dining hall where supper was ready. He added that a few dances would follow to allow the musicians some practice for the next evening. While he spoke, Josephine retreated to Wilhelm's side and had started to reach for his arm when the king turned and extended his hand as he begged for his guest to concede her ladyship to his companionship for the evening. Josephine blushed from the way he spoke on her behalf, but the flattery was replaced by resentment when Wilhelm agreed to the king's terms. She quickly had to redirect her efforts from irritation to formality when she found herself seated at the king's left hand with Wilhelm to his right. Throughout the meal, she imagined Sven stealing glances of her to the point she was self-conscious of her every action. Were her table manners lacking, or was he admiring his female guest? The lady remained quiet, listening to the conversation surrounding her, but her silence was broken when the king turned to Wilhelm and asked, "Are the ladies of your court permitted to speak, noble prince?"

There was an awkward pause among the guests, but to the king's delight, it was not the prince who answered the question.

"Forgive me, my liege, but the conversation has been quite intriguing to me." The smile that crossed his face as he pushed his chair back from the table and extended a hand in friendship toward the lady put everyone at ease.

"My lady, all will be forgiven if you will do me the honors of a dance?" Instantly Josephine returned a smile and reached for his hand, and to her surprise, he rose to his feet and led her to the great hall where a small orchestra has assembled near the throne platform and were tuning up. Sven motioned for them to play, and then with a bow, he gracefully took Josephine into his arms and began moving to the music. There was no mistake that Andervan's king knew how to properly hold a lady. The placement of his hand upon Josephine's lower back allowed him to guide her perfectly with his every step to the music and the way he elegantly brought her near as they seemingly hovered over the floor, was proof enough. The closeness with which he held the lady would have been uncomfortable save the uncanny grace with which they moved. Although she concentrated on the dance itself, the king was focused on the lady he held in his arms. The moment he saw her, something had stirred in his heart that he had not felt in years. His wife's death devastated him to the point that he became quite ill. For the sake of his children, he had continued on and slowly recovered but in many ways did not feel alive. But when he saw Josephine that afternoon, it was as if he drew a long-awaited breath once more. It was not entirely for physical beauty that the king found himself drawn to the lady but because of the humbleness he sensed and the way she carried herself. The qualities he saw in Josephine brought back bittersweet memories of his Ava. The dance ended only too soon for Sven but he did not hide his favor for the lady as he promised to dance with her the following night. The attention was duly noted for almost all present were aware that the king had refused to dance with any lady since the queen had passed. Wilhelm on the other hand did not seem the least bit concerned with the dance, as his telltale eyebrows had not raised in disapproval nor was any sign of concern upon his face. Josephine trusted his judgment even more than her own, and if he was fine with her being beside the king most of the evening, then she was fine with it as well. She did wonder if the prince's passive attitude had to do with the dire need of supplies and reinforcements for the war. Was he using her as leverage to secure a better arrangement with the old ally? The thoughts of mistrust bothered the lady, but she quickly rebuked herself for thinking ill of Wilhelm.

The evening continued on as usual evenings do at court—socializing among guests, refreshments being served, and an occasional interruption by a court jester to entertain. As Josephine expected, King Sven remained close by, and she found his conversation interesting enough that she was disappointed when she heard a clock ring out eleven times. The change in her countenance at the sound did not go unnoticed by the king who commented to the lady that he would announce his retirement for the evening which would immediately cause his court to depart. His plan worked well and as the room emptied, the royal entourage made their way upstairs and through the castle toward the bedchambers. The prince, Josephine, and the king were at Wilhelm's chamber doors when Sven spoke up.

"I have taken the liberty of moving her ladyship to a different room." The statement was unexpected, and Josephine, being used to speaking freely when alone with the royal family, spoke before she checked her tongue.

"Whatever for?" she asked. "My room was perfectly adequate." And then she quickly became quiet, realizing she had forgotten her manners. The statement didn't set well with Wilhelm, and his remarks were direct.

"Your hospitality is appreciated, good king, but I must request being made aware of any change concerning my ward, including where she will be sleeping." The tone he used made Josephine cringe as she could tell he was angry. Quickly the king offered his apology, stating he had no intention of deceit or not providing proper security but merely wanted to treat the lady to a more splendid view of the mountain from her chambers. Josephine closely watched the reactions of both men as Sven plead his cause and was relieved to see the wrinkle across Wilhelm's forehead begin to fade as he accepted the reasoning behind the change. When Sven had finished, the prince turned to Josephine.

"Will this be fine, my lady?" he asked. Josephine was not sure what to do but agree with the arrangements. "My liege, how do I reach her new chambers from here?" Wilhelm returned his attention to the king.

"At the end of this hall, go right and her room will be the last one on the left." Both royals nodded to each other, and without another word, Wilhelm stepped into his room.

"Shall we?" the king asked as he motioned to continue down the hallway. With every step Josephine took farther away from Wilhelm, the more she felt uneasy. The tension between the men over her being relocated was not her imagination, and she wondered if more was going on than she was aware of. "I hope my actions have not troubled you," the king said, interrupting her thoughts.

"Somewhat," she admitted.

"My intentions are pure, I can assure you." Despite the hallway being dimly lit, the king was watching every expression upon Josephine's face. She was still looking rather solemn when they reached the last door on the left. "I was told your lady in waiting is already settled in and," he said as he reached for the door knob before she could, "another maid is at your disposal."

"Thank you for your kindness, but there is no need," she said as she discovered he still held her hand. The look on his face was as if he did not even hear her protest.

"I enjoyed your company this evening, my lady, and am very pleased to have you as my guest." The sincere tone in his voice and the way he tilted his head as he looked at her caused Josephine not to argue over having a second maid assigned to her. Before she realized what was happening, he brought her hand upward and leaned over to kiss it.

Quickly she pulled it from him and said, "Thank you again, my liege." He opened the door for her and with a nod left her presence.

Not to her surprise, Josephine found Katrina anxiously awaiting her lady's return. The new chambers were three times larger than the first and included several rooms within. The décor was more elaborate, resembling the downstairs rooms and the young ladies decided they could have stared for hours. Katrina tucked Josephine into bed and retired to her servant's quarters which adjoined the bed room, but both agreed the door would remain open as neither was comfortable being alone. Since it was nearly midnight when they turned in, sleep came easily.

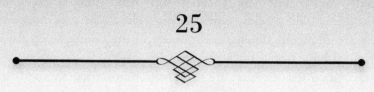

25

Kings and Princes

About three o'clock in the morning, Josephine stirred to a sound reminding her of light rain falling. She had just closed her eyes again when she heard the noise, but this time, it sounded like the swishing of a lady's petticoat dragging across the floor. She held her breath for a moment to listen and would have dozed off except that suddenly she felt as if she was being watched. Cautiously she opened her eyes at which she heard a giggle. There on tiptoes was a little boy in his nightgown leaning against the edge of her bed. He was peering through blond hair that partially covered his eyes and couldn't have been but five years old.

"Hello." Josephine uttered as she rolled over to see the boy better. Boldly, he asked, "What's your name?"

"Josephine," she answered with a smile. "What is yours?"

"Fin," he said proudly. He was teetering up and down on his toes trying to keep in her sight.

"Little Fin, what brings you to my room at this hour?" Josephine asked, sitting up and pushing the blankets away to afford a better view.

Immediately the child's countenance changed as with a stutter, he began to speak, "Dr . . . dream. I had a bad dr . . . dr . . . dream." She thought he was going to burst into tears at any moment.

"Come up here with me," she said, invitingly throwing the blanket to one side. For a moment, the boy hesitated until the woman spoke again. "Let's get rid of those bad dreams for good, eh?" And with that, she held out her hand to help him climb into the bed. Instead of reaching for her hand, Fin quickly reached for the footpost of the bed and with an exaggerated leap climbed up beside her. She couldn't help but laugh as she remembered how much energy little children had, even when sleepy. She ran her fingers through his hair as she began to talk quietly about chasing the nightmares away. He listened so closely, soaking up her words and didn't seem to mind that she had continued running her fingers through his hair. Suddenly she saw a yawn and her opportunity. "What do you say we close our eyes and get some rest?"

"Do I have to go back to my room?" he whined pitifully.

"Not yet. Not if you settle in and lie very still."

"Yes, I will," he answered, happy with the bargain and wiggled down until his head was against the pillow and his back was against the lady. She put her arm over him. "Good night, Josephine."

"Good night, little one," she answered. For a moment, she lay there smiling, thinking about the little boy in her arms. Suddenly she wondered who he was. Perhaps she should let someone know he was there with her. She contemplated what to do and how she should go about it to not awaken him. She was listening to the soft sound of his breathing when she drifted off to sleep.

She remembered hearing voices in the distance, but ever so sleepy, Josephine did not pay attention to them. She felt a hand graze over her arm, and again she heard a distant voice but this time she opened her eyes slowly. The room was still dark save the light coming from the fireplace. Suddenly she realized that the king was crouched beside her bed.

When he saw that she was awake, he smiled and shook his head as he whispered, "You seem to have found what I have lost." Both looked at the boy who was sound asleep and snuggled beside Josephine.

"Forgive me for not sending word," she whispered. "I could not bear to disturb him." Over the king's shoulder, she could see a servant coming into the room.

"Let me carry him to his room my liege," the man spoke quietly. The thought of the boy leaving her was saddening.

"He can stay here till morning," she offered as the king began reaching for his son.

"We'll not trouble you," he said as the boy opened his eyes and mumbled as Sven lifted him from the bed.

"One so precious is no trouble," Josephine replied as she repositioned the blankets to cover her body again. The king transferred his son to the servant's arms who promptly left the room. To her surprise, Sven knelt beside the bed again to look face to face with the lady.

"And if I leave him here tonight, what will happen when he dreams again and you are not here to console him?" Josephine knew he spoke truth from a father's point of view, yet she found herself wanting to hold the child.

"He is very darling," she said with a sigh. She had grown fond of several children in Guttenhamm and took treats to them when visiting the town. She also discovered that playing with them was a weakness that caused her to lose hours from her schedule.

"You know . . . I have two more sons," the king stated as he remained beside the bed, watching closely to see if the lady's reaction was unfavorable.

"Do they all have their father's eyes?" she asked and then wished she had chosen another way to compliment the resemblance she had seen. The king was pleased with her remark and smiled.

"Yes, they do. I am sure you will meet them during your stay," he added.

"That will be nice," she replied. Curiosity got the best of her judgment. "What brought the little one to *this* room?" She watched the king's face carefully to see if it told a different story than his words did.

"When his grandmother comes to visit, she uses these chambers," he replied. The look upon his face was as if he was remembering a distant story from the past.

"Is that the reason you moved me to this room?" Josephine asked but heard a soft laugh at her question.

"No, it isn't," he said, pausing to emphasize each word clearly. "When it is daylight, you will see my reasoning." He shook his head as if to shame her for the suspicions of another motive. Without warning, Josephine burst into a yawn. "But maybe a little more sleep first?" He rose to his feet. "Rest well, my lady." And with a nod the king left the room.

This time Josephine awoke to Katrina and another maid bustling about with a bath having been prepared. Breakfast would be served in one hour. The room was well lit with sunlight and suddenly Josephine remembered the king's words about the eastern windows of her chambers and hurried out of bed. As she pulled back the curtains, she could not help but gasp when she saw the mountains before her. The sky shone a glorious blue, trimmed by white caps upon the mountain peaks and down in the shadows lay the town. If the king was hoping to impress her, he had done a fine job. Her thoughts were interrupted by the maids hurrying her along.

Breakfast was not at all what Josephine expected with hardly a dozen guests in attendance, and the king was not among them. She wanted to inquire where he was, but it was none of her business and she was sure he was a very busy man. She had been seated across from Wilhelm, who despite many interruptions from the other guests finally managed to break the news that his affairs that day would not need her presence at his side. Josephine was getting flustered with the conversation, the people's questions, Wilhelm not needing her, when suddenly a messenger appeared beside her bearing an envelope. She felt a lump in her throat as she guessed it had to be bad news to have found her on such a trip outside of the kingdom. She glanced across the table to Wilhelm, who was also imagining the worst. Carefully she opened the envelope and to her surprise found a note written in beginner's script. She looked at Wilhelm and gave a wide smile hoping to ease his fears.

Lady Josephine,

You are invited to play a game in the courtyard immediately following breakfast.

Please come, Fin

319

The signature was from a different hand than the writer. The messenger waited until she folded the paper and then said, "I am to escort you there, ma'am, if you are willing."

"Yes, it would be my pleasure," Josephine said, rising to her feet.

Wilhelm met the lady at the far end of the table. "What is it?" he asked with concern.

"I had a visitor last night," she replied as they moved toward the doorway. Wilhelm's heart fell. Had the king been the visitor? Was that the motive for moving her, putting her farther from his protective watch? Surely he wouldn't be so bold, he thought to himself. "The youngest of the princes had a nightmare and stumbled into my room." Josephine was so tickled about her invitation that she did not notice Wilhelm sigh aloud with relief. "Now he has asked me to come and play with him this morning." Wilhelm could see how overjoyed the lady was about the request.

"I heard there had been a scare in the night, something to do with the family, but . . ." The look in Josephine's eyes made Wilhelm smile in return. "It is well that the lad has asked you seeing I have abandoned you today." Becoming more serious, Josephine reassured her companion.

"You do as you must and don't worry about me. The little boy is absolutely adorable, and I am sure he will be quite entertaining." It had been a while since Wilhelm had seen the lady this happy as her thoughts had been upon the grim things concerning war.

"I will see you tonight then, at the ball," he replied and the two parted ways.

Much to Josephine's delight, all three sons were waiting for her in the courtyard. Fineas, she discovered was in fact five years old, Kristoff was eight and Raiflan had just turned twelve. The older two sons were not friendly at first and understandably so, but the awkwardness was compounded as Fin acted as if the lady was his lifelong friend. She wanted to win their trust but knew they were at the age that it may take several meetings to accomplish it. They were in the middle of a game of shuttlecock when to their dismay the birdie became lodged in a tree limb along the edge of the courtyard. Before Josephine could warn them otherwise, Kristoff had tossed his racket up at the birdie but only succeeded in entangling the racket as well. None of the nearby guards or servants had taken notice and not wanting the boys to be scolded for the mishap, Josephine carefully relocated a chair to help in the dilemma. She positioned it under the tree limb, stepped up onto it and had just taken hold of the racket handle when suddenly she felt fingers poking her ribs and heard a shout.

"I caught you!" She was so startled that she lost her balance and let out a scream as she began to fall backward. She only fell as far as the king's arms, which were waiting to catch her as he was the culprit playing the prank. All Josephine could hear was laughter from him and the boys who were now gathered around them. Hearing the lady shout the guards came in her direction but were quickly shooed away at the king's command.

After she realized that she was safe, she was not the least bit upset as the king had taken advantage of the perfect opportunity she had given. "You scoundrel!" Josephine yelled trying to sound angry. Sven saw that she was playing along and scooped her into his arms and swung her around in a circle. The boys, loving the excitement, were screaming, and laughing wildly at her supposed misfortune. "Put me down this instant!" she barked, trying not to let down her façade.

"Only, if you say please," the king replied as he swung her around yet again.

"Please?" she begged as she caught herself letting a smile slip out.

"Please, and I will behave, your majesty," Sven added as he nodded toward his sons to move back to give him room to sit her down.

"Yes, yes," she said, pretending to gasp. "Please, and I will behave, kind sir. Please sit me down gently." The boys began to move away as their folly seemed to come to an end. Quickly they retrieved the racket and birdie which were now upon the ground and returned to batting it about. "Careful, please my liege. I am a bit dizzy. Thank you." Josephine added with a laugh while clinging tightly to the king's arm.

"I have no intention of letting you fall," he said, continuing to hold the lady securely. He was so close that she felt his breath upon her neck. She started to step away, but her head seemed to spin and caused her to lean into his shoulder. "Steady now," he said with a little laugh. "But forgive me for the joke is over and having you this dizzy was not part of the plan."

"It was fun though," she said, glancing in the direction of the children. "The boys loved it." When she looked back at the king, she found his eyes fixed upon her hair. He seemed to be studying it, and then he moved his gaze along her face until his eyes met her own. She noticed that his brown eyes were framed by wrinkles that one could only see when he smiled. He almost seemed lost in thought as he stood there. "Did business keep you from breakfast this morning?" the lady asked. She noticed that he watched her lips as she spoke.

"Yes, I had business," he whispered.

"And now?" she asked as his gaze met her eyes again.

"I was on my way to the throne room," he answered with a smile. Josephine leaned away.

"We have detained you?" She was shaking her head in disbelief. "It is not good for you to be late, not because of me. My crisis is over, go on now." To her surprise, the king pulled her close, at first playfully, but then she realized how serious he was when their noses touched.

He whispered, "My crisis is not over." Josephine closed her eyes as her heart began to race, and she felt warm all over. "I am king and I can afford to be a few minutes late for a worthy cause." Josephine felt a tingle run down her spine as the last words fell upon her ears, and to her surprise, she found herself not wanting the moment to end. She opened her eyes and moved her head to see Sven's face better.

"Please . . . for my sake, go now." The statement seemed odd to the king, but she continued on. "You are the king . . . kings are always prompt and honorable and . . ." Her voice trailed off as she felt his lips brush against her cheek but manage to refrain from a kiss.

"Yes, my lady," he said, and as quickly as he had come into the courtyard, he left.

As Josephine turned her attention back to the shuttlecock game, it seemed that the boys had not noticed their father's deed but were glad for her to rejoin them. Overcome with emotion, Josephine was useless to score points and was relieved when the governor appeared and called for lessons to resume. The harmless prank seemed to have mellowed the older sons' attitudes, and she was asked to play again another time. As she had guessed, Fin was not happy about their parting, and she had to promise him upon her honor that they would spend time together again. They had no sooner left the courtyard when Josephine's appointed maid appeared and ushered her on to a meeting of the ladies of court. Josephine was not looking forward to the gathering at all. Very seldom had she felt truly welcome at such assemblies and in this instance as the outsider she was sure she would be the subject matter being discussed. It always seemed disastrous when she attended, for her opinions did not conform to that of most ladies at court. She was outright dreading each step closer to the parlor. Per instruction of the king, Josephine was taken to Duchess Aidenvonn who was overseeing the meeting. The older woman introduced her to approximately twenty ladies seated in the room but they showed little interest in the visitor from Gutten. It didn't bother Josephine that noses were turned up at her insignificance, but she found it a relief not to be hounded by questions as she had at the breakfast table. The duchess began to speak promptly at the top of the hour but the topics discussed were not nearly as interesting as Josephine had hoped. It was mentioned that more ladies would be arriving for the afternoon session and that a buffet lunch would be served in the adjoining room. Finally, the duchess adjourned the meeting but reminded everyone that they were to retreat to the gardens after lunch to await the gentlemen. Josephine was delighted at the idea for she preferred to be outdoors for if conversation failed she would have the beautiful scenery to keep her attention. The gardens indeed were no disappointment with their elaborate terraces adorning the hillside and splendid view of the mountains towering in the distance. Josephine could not overcome her desire to walk the well-worn stone paths and left the other ladies. She could imagine frequenting the garden daily just to think amidst the beauty and the crisp mountain air. An hour had passed without her speaking to anyone when to her surprise, she saw Katrina coming toward her. A chambermaid had rescued the lady in waiting from her solitude and brought her to the gardens to be at her ladyship's side. They walked arm in arm while Josephine shared the events of the morning with her companion and finally they decided to rejoin the other ladies on the terrace. Shortly they heard men's voices and noticed a group coming from the castle toward them. Josephine and Katrina would have been content to remain unnoticed but seeing the two ladies off to the side four brave men came in their direction. Katrina attempted to dismiss herself, but Josephine caught hold of her arm.

"You, Lady Katrina, will not leave me here alone to these vultures," she demanded. Reluctantly Katrina gave into her wishes, and turning to face the men, gave a fake smile. She did not mind accompanying Josephine as her hand maid, but she was not comfortable in the new role she had been given as her lady in waiting when she had to be in the public's eye. As expected, the men proceeded to flirt which Josephine was not the least bit interested in. Her mind had wandered to her many complaints about royal courts when suddenly she heard her name being called out from the direction of the castle steps.

"Lady Josephine Armand." The herald paused for a moment to look the crowd over for a response. Josephine raised her hand as she began moving toward the man, and as everyone else had stood still, she was quickly seen. He motioned for her to join him upon the steps. "My lady, a gift for you," he said in his loud tone of voice and motioned to a lad who stood at the castle door. "From his majesty." The boy presented a bouquet of flowers and bowing reverently the herald held out an envelope. Josephine accepted both, and before she could ask any questions, the pair left her standing there upon the steps. She was not alone however, for the crowd had gathered in to hear the herald's words, and Josephine could feel their eyes heavily upon her as she struggled to break the seal upon the envelope and remove the paper inside. Although only she read the script, she blushed all over and even lowered her head, fighting back a smile.

Carefully she slid the paper back into the envelope, and taking a deep breath, she turned to her lady in waiting and loud enough for the people close by to hear her words. She said, "Lady Katrina, shall we go inside and find water for these lovely flowers?"

"Yes, I should think so," Katrina replied and took hold of her arm.

No sooner had the chamber door shut behind them, than Josephine laid her gifts upon a nearby table and headed for the windows. She opened one slightly and began taking in several long deep breaths while struggling to undo the top buttons of her collar.

Katrina found a vase for the flowers. "Are you alright Josephine? You seem rather flustered." She placed the flowers upon the dressing table and went to her lady's side.

"I feel all stuffy," she said "Like I was just smothered in a well meant hug, but smothered none the less."

"Anything to do with the flowers?" Katrina smiled, as if she didn't already know the answer. "Or was it the note?" she teased as she had never seen this response from the lady before.

"Of course, from both," Josephine replied, now leaning her head against the glass of the window pane and closing her eyes. "Read it for yourself." She didn't have to say it again as Katrina was dying to know what the paper said.

Dearest Josephine,

A gift, to cheer your lonely heart. You may have stood alone in the gardens this afternoon, but tonight I will be beside you.

Sincerely, Sven.

It's no wonder, Katrina thought. Although she was not with her ladyship for every moment of the visit thus far, Katrina had noticed the king's unwavering attention to Josephine the night before and what Josephine told of that morning was even more convincing. The king definitely favored the lady, but did she favor him? She seemed flattered by his actions, but was the attention wanted or was she merely being polite? Had a chord truly been struck between the two? Yes, Andervan was a much larger kingdom with more power, and Sven was charming and undeniably handsome but he was almost twice her age and had children already. Did Josephine realize the differences in age and stages of their lives might prove to be difficult to overcome? Would she fit into his world, and what would his citizens think of the stranger than he was showering his affection upon? Katrina laid the note on a nearby table and glanced toward her friend.

"What are you going to do now?" she asked, watching for a response.

After taking another slow deep breath, Josephine replied, "Go to the ball, I suppose." Katrina thought she caught a glimpse of a smile at the corner of the lady's mouth but then words were formed. "What else *can* I do?"

26

Mountains and Dungeons

Six o'clock came all too quickly for Josephine. She had attempted to take a nap to calm her nerves but never managed to fall asleep. Then she was hustled and bustled as not only Katrina, but two more maids came to help her get ready for the evening. A knock upon the door sent her on the way as Wilhelm came to escort her downstairs. She was relieved to see the prince and found herself clinging more tightly to his arm than ever before. They joined nearly a hundred guests in the entry hall, with each couple waiting to be introduced into the grand affair. Wilhelm could see the lady's anxiousness and made a futile effort to keep a conversation going but he couldn't help but wonder if she was uncomfortable with the large number of people or if she was anticipating the king's behavior toward her. It was not the first time he had seen men stumble over themselves because of his lovely companion and Sven had proven no different. When they were announced, a few heads turned but nothing significant, and Wilhelm heard Josephine sigh when it was over and they began to mingle in the crowd.

"You, my lady, are acting rather strange this evening," he said discreetly and then nodded his head toward a gentleman a few feet away. "He is the director of Andervan's foreign affairs," he commented and then referred back to what he had been saying. "You are acting like you are afraid something is about to happen or . . ." He did not finish the sentence, but Josephine could feel herself tensing up as he spoke as she recalled the king's note. Was Sven referring to dancing with her again? Surely his time with her would be limited with so many other ladies present. Josephine only had a few seconds to think about Wilhelm's remark when a herald emerged from the crowd in front of them.

"My lady," he said with a bow. "His majesty is requesting your presence at his side." Josephine felt the blood drain from her face, but she found herself reaching for the herald's extended arm as she threw Wilhelm a look and replied.

"Something . . . like this?" And they disappeared into the crowd of people. Wilhelm stood there stupefied for a moment and then decided to follow them. He wondered what had happened for the lady to be so nervous and then turn pale when she was summoned. She may have never liked the formality at court, but this was not the typical reaction of the woman he thought he knew so well. He caught up to the pair in time to see Josephine graciously bow to the king as her hand was given to him by the herald. When the king saw the prince he greeted him. With Wilhelm close by, Josephine felt more comfortable and although it seemed awkward to be holding onto another man's arm the two men did not seem bothered by it and were talking freely to each other. After what seemed like forever, dinner was announced with the seating as it was the night before. Several courses of the meal were served, and then shortly after dessert, a few notes of music could be heard as the orchestra warmed up. A herald announced the ballroom was ready, and without hesitation, the guests left their seats and proceeded to the room. The king offered his arm, and without a second thought, Josephine accepted it but suddenly became aware of her surroundings as the king walked her to the center of the ballroom and came to a stop. The other guests retreated from the floor leaving the solitary couple, hand in hand.

Oh no! Josephine thought as she raised her eyebrows. The king bowed, she curtsied and when the music started they began to dance. *How do I get myself into such predicaments?* she thought, scolding herself. She was not sure if she had mumbled out loud or whether the king spoke because she was being so quiet.

"Say that again." She looked toward the man but the moment their eyes met she felt riddled with guilt over her behavior. It was not his fault that she despised court or being in the center of attention.

"I am so sorry," she said with remorse. "I am not comfortable . . . in front of so many people." She glanced away at the spectators who stood along the edges of the room watching them.

"Do the people make you uncomfortable? Or is it me?" She couldn't help but give him a sharp look for the comment. He seemed to be rather direct and to the point, whether the question cut like a knife or soothed like honey going down.

"It is the people that make me nervous," she replied after waiting for a few seconds. "Ask the prince. I have never claimed to like social gatherings."

"And yet are you not a part of them every day in Guttenhamm?" the king asked as the music came to an end. Reverently they bowed to one another as other couples joined them upon the floor and the next song began. "Shall we dance again to finish our conversation?" Sven asked but not waiting for the lady's reply reached for her and began moving to the music. This time he seemed to hold Josephine closer to his body.

"Yes, I am at court in Guttenhamm. My apologies, I should not have let their staring bother me."

With his voice much quieter, he replied, "I just don't want anything to spoil our evening." He seemed to lean his head toward her, and as the style of her dress exposed her neck, Josephine could feel his breath upon it as he spoke.

Resisting the urge to close her eyes, she replied, "Yes, my liege." The night drew on, and to Josephine's surprise, the king was not the only man she danced with. Contrary to her experience in the gardens that afternoon she was not alone for a moment with many interruptions of gentlemen cutting in to change partners. She was ever so relieved to hear a familiar voice.

"Do you need to be rescued, my dear?" By the way Wilhelm added the last word, Josephine knew he was teasing over the predicament she was in but she gladly accepted his offer. The prince took her onto the floor, and as they began to move, she felt a tingle run down her spine. The way he held her was the same as always, yet this time it seemed different. As he asked about her evening, Josephine found herself suddenly realizing how close their bodies were together with the prince holding her tighter than Sven had. She could feel Wilhelm's breath upon her ear as he spoke and she recalled how it had tickled the first few times it had happened. As the song played on, a gentleman tried to cut in, but to her surprise, Wilhelm bluntly refused to give the lady up and continued to dance. Finally, the prince asked about her gift that afternoon. With a surprised look, Josephine leaned back for a moment at which he quickly explained that the gossip concerning the flowers had circulated throughout the castle. With a sigh, the lady stumbled for an excuse and finally mumbled that the king was making her stay rather complicated. She caught a chuckle from the prince as he repeated her words.

"Complicated? Hmmm." If she had not been so confused with her own feelings about the matter, she may have joined him in the amusement, but as it was, she remained alarmingly quiet. Sensing her uneasiness, Wilhelm leaned toward her more and whispered, "Don't worry about him. While we are here, just relax and enjoy yourself." She wondered if the prince knew all that had transpired, would he still be saying those things? She leaned until her forehead rested gently against Wilhelm's chin. Part of her wanted to do as he said, forgetting about the war and the hard times that lay ahead. Why not let this king lavish his attention on her? Why shouldn't she put on airs at court and enjoy life among the royal family, and take in the spectacular mountain scenery? Was Sven just enjoying her company for the moment or was there more involved? And could she play along pretending she had feelings toward him only to disappoint him when it was time to return to Gutten? Her heart fell yet again as she wondered if she would still be pretending at that point. Would *she* be the one whose heart would break at the thought of leaving Andervan? What if she fell for the king? Suddenly she realized the music had ended and heard Wilhelm whisper, "No worrying." Then he conceded her hand to an anxious gentleman who had approached them.

It was not long until the king sent for her, and she was brought to his side where she remained while visitors came and went. She had just managed to discreetly slip off one of her shoes while standing next to the king and was flexing her aching foot when she caught Sven smiling oddly at her. Then he began to shake his head and she returned a questioning look. So as not to draw attention he asked if she had suddenly grown shorter. She appreciated his humor and admitted to her deed because her feet were in pain. She feigned that she had danced too much and begged him not to give up her secret.

"I will make you a bargain," he whispered still very amused. "I will let you retire for the evening, if you will join me in my chambers just before sunrise." Josephine could not hide the surprise upon her face at the request.

"Whatever for? And so early?" she asked.

"You will find out then. Do we have a bargain?" He was pleased for it seemed that he had her cornered for her curiosity would not let her refuse him. Josephine wondered if it was wise to accept the offer. If they were to be alone in his chambers she would have to decline the invitation. She had not yet replied when he added, "My servant Vhret will come for you." And before she could offer up a protest the king reached for her hand, kissed it and said goodnight. With a slight wave of his hand a servant appeared from the shadows and politely took Josephine's arm and led her away. They passed through several corridors, going upstairs and in a matter of minutes were in front of her chamber doors.

A few short hours had passed when Katrina awoke Josephine to let her know the servant had come for her. Josephine had managed to tell her maid the highlights of the evening before she had fallen asleep and both had reservations about the early morning rendez-vous. Vhret explained that the lady could only afford a few minutes to get dressed and simplicity was best and assured her that she would not be in public areas and not to worry about her appearance. As Katrina helped her into a dress, Josephine found herself wanting to look nice, for the king's sake. She had to laugh as she had never been one to fuss about such things, and yet she knew nothing could hide how sleepy her eyes must look. Then her mind wondered to the king; how rough would he be looking with so little sleep? She knew he would have been awake at least two more hours than she but would he have rested at all in anticipation of her arrival? Oh well, she thought, they both would be quite a pair to see.

Vhret led her through the halls and finally she summoned the courage to ask if others would be present for she would not be alone with the king. Politely Vhret explained that there were always two to three servants attending the king in his chambers, not to mention the guards who were stationed about. His tone changed somewhat as he did mention that concerning character, that he would personally stake his life upon his majesty's honor in the presence of the lady. Josephine was quick to offer an apology if she had offended. They had just arrived at a set of doors as they spoke, and Vhret paused and turned to the lady. He admitted that he had been apprehensive about bringing her to the king's chambers at such an hour, yet her true integrity had been revealed by her questions, and he was very pleased by what she had said and thought no ill of her. Before she could reply, he reached to open the doors and motioned her to enter ahead of him. The chambers were dark save a well-lit room in the distance. Before her feet touched the floor a second time, she saw the silhouette of the king rising to his feet as he heard them come in.

"Josephine," he said as he began to walk toward her. He was not wearing anything regal, only a simple tunic, trousers, and shoes but most of all she noticed how widely he smiled at her. She passed through several outer chambers before she was close enough for him to take hold of her hands to welcome her. "I am relieved that you humored me enough to come at this hour." Although the room in which they stood was shadowed, she could still make out the features of his face from the glow of light coming from the far room. Gently he pulled her hands coaxing her to follow him.

"I must admit, my curiosity would not let me resist," she replied. They had entered what appeared to be his study with a large desk along one side of the room and a small side table with chairs for eating on the other. She noticed covered dishes and a pitcher of juice on a tray upon the table but to her surprise the king did not lead her to sit but took her toward a set of glass doors on the left side of the room. He had just reached for the doorknob when he abruptly stopped and turned quickly as if struck by a thought.

"Wait. It is much too cool for you to go outside at this hour. Let me find something for you to wear." His voice broke off as he left her and hurried into the last room. From where she stood she could see a massive bed with elaborately carved posts that were partially hidden by curtains that hung from a wooden canopy. A fireplace was on the right side of the room and she could see a bureau chest with a portrait on the wall above it. She heard mumbling as the king spoke with someone and then his shadow fell across the floor as he re-emerged with a crocheted shawl in his hands. "I offer my apologies for leaving you. If I had thought ahead, I would have told you to bring a jacket. Will this suffice, my lady?"

"Yes, of course," Josephine replied. She couldn't help but ask, "Did you get *any* sleep?"

"Never mind about me," he replied. "Showing you this is worth many sleepless nights." Josephine started to shake her head in protest of his gesture, but before she could, he had reached over her to drape the wrap over her shoulders. "Come with me." He opened the doors, and they stepped out onto a balcony. Immediately a biting chill met them, and Josephine found herself squinting as her eyes teared up. The balcony seemed so high up above the rest of the valley with the hillside falling away to the town below. In the distance, she could see a pale sky and the darkness of the mountain range rising up to meet it. Very carefully, she stepped forward toward the thick marble railing that skirted the balcony's edge. She peered downward to view the town, asleep in the darkness and the blackness of the river as it wound through the valley. Josephine was still gazing upon the town when Sven came up close behind her and leaning toward her, he began to speak quietly. "Start watching the mountain peaks. In a moment, it will look as if the very edges of them are lit with gold." He raised his right hand beside her and pointed. "Then it will seem as if they are trimmed with the red flames of a forge." He drew the outline with his finger as she watched the gold color begin to appear as he had described. In a matter of moments, hints of orange and red were seen. "But wait." He moved closer to the woman. The excitement in his voice made Josephine smile. "As the sun begins to creep above the peaks, the roofs in the village will seem to dance with the light." Again, he began to motion with his hand, pointing out little glimmers here and there in the valley below. Words were not enough to describe the view, standing so high above the town as if in the very heavens yet there were higher heights still as the mountains rose up towering before them. It was a breathtaking sight as the sunrise burned vivid upon the snow-capped stone and the rays shone playfully upon the cliffs and rooftops. The excitement of the moment had allowed the king to place his left hand upon the lady's left arm and nestle her close while pointing to the sights with his right hand. Her head had come to rest against him as he described more of what was to come as other sights became visible. The blackness of the river was replaced by a golden hue as it too came to life with the dawn. In the distance, she noticed a small lake and delicate waterfalls could be seen spilling over cliffs. The king reached to secure the shawl about Josephine's shoulders as it stirred in the breeze. As she folded her arms and clutched the shawl, his arms came to rest over hers. The awakening of the valley was such a splendid sight that they remained on the balcony for several more minutes. Every so often, Sven would point to something and whisper a comment. Whether it was her leaning against him or him against her, it did not matter as the two remained close until the sun could be seen reaching above the highest peak. Finally it was the king who broke the silence.

"Will you forgive me?" he whispered, and Josephine felt a tingle along her spine again. He spoke in a romantic tone that made her heart melt. Suddenly she realized she had allowed him to take her into his arms, but for how long, she could not tell. Closing her eyes, she gathered her wits, and taking a deep breath, she opened them as she turned to face him. It was a pitiful effort for when her gaze met his, she found herself weak once more.

"Forgive you?" she asked as she lowered her gaze to his shirt. "For what, may I ask?" Great was the tension between them, and she felt her heart racing. Sven recognized the signs and was quick to seize the opportunity.

"Forgive me," he said, reaching for the lady's hands, "for waking you at such an hour." He paused long enough to let go of one hand to motion toward the scenery before them. "I hope you found it worthy of the inconvenience." He allowed his gaze to stay upon the mountains, and Josephine was thankful as she caught herself staring at him. She had thought him handsome before but now found herself admiring him as a schoolgirl would with a crush. She was still gawking at him as she noticed him starting to turn to her again, and to avoid embarrassment, she pulled free from his grasp. She took a few steps away, keeping her back to him as she pretended to look toward the town. The king had seen enough of her face as he moved that he could tell she seemed pleased with him.

Slipping up behind her again, he placed his hands lightly upon her shoulders and leaning toward her ear he whispered again, "Will you forgive me then?" He was standing just right to see a smile cross her face. "Or will I have to make it up to you?"

She gave a laugh at which he playfully spun her around to face him.

"You are forgiven," she replied, and they stood smiling at each other. She noticed the king's eyes dart away for a split second, and then his gaze came back to her own, but there was a change in his countenance.

Josephine raised an eyebrow, questioning the reaction, but before she could say anything, he spoke first, "Alas, it is time for us to part." She could not hide the disappointment no more than he could by the tone of his voice. "But"—sliding his hands from her shoulders to her lower arms—"may I see you again?" He watched her face for the reaction, hoping for any telltale signs to draw a conclusion from. He wanted to persuade her to agree to his request, yet managed to refrain. He could not imagine loving someone as deeply as he had Ava, but Josephine dared him to hope again. So compelled was he, that he had acted hastily to let her know his attention was more than mere flattery. He was not resigned to taking a chance of her slipping from his reach without efforts being made. Now here they stood together, but he needed to know that she felt more than polite obligation to be in his presence. He waited for a sign that she was willing to see him again.

Thankfully Josephine managed to control her emotions and not blurt out an emphatic yes to the king. The morning had been utterly romantic, but Katrina had made her promise to guard herself with the stranger and to keep her senses about her. She was trying very hard not to be overwhelmed and was studying his expressions as she contemplated how to answer him. Finally, she lowered her head and looked down at her hands which were in his and slowly answered, "I would like that."

"But?" he asked, drawing out the word. Josephine couldn't help but look back up at him. His eyebrows seemed knit together in a questioning frown and he had tilted his head to the side.

"But . . ." She searched for words and sighed. "But I am at the beckon call of Prince Wilhelm and . . ." She hesitated but then decided to be bold. "And this is a diplomatic trip, not a personal one." *There,* she thought, *I said it, and now he will know my position and we can regain our true focus.* Josephine assumed because of her words, the king would release her hands and step away, but she was not prepared for his reaction as he instead drew her closer to him. Very suavely, he slid his hands upward until he had hold of the back of her arms and smiled as he spoke to her very quietly.

"Yes, I know." He paused as he let his gaze fall upon her hair, and then she watched as his eyes began to study the details of her face. "I was not expecting this either." Josephine heard her heart beating in her ears, and she dared not move as she let him look at her. At any moment, she expected him to kiss her and wondered if she would faint if he did. It seemed he began to lean closer when suddenly she heard a woman's voice behind them.

"My king, you were in need of my services?" Josephine watched as a look of aggravation crossed Sven's face and then was replaced by a smirk.

"Yes, Saraina, I called for you." As he answered he released his hold on the lady's arms and took a few steps back, and turned around to finish his thought. "Please escort Lady Josephine to her chambers." With a sigh, he waved his hand for Josephine to follow the woman who had stepped forward into the room. Without a word, the lady nodded to acknowledge the king's request and began walking toward the hallway. With a curtsy, Josephine left the king and followed the woman. In a matter of moments, she was falling behind as the woman seemed to be in a terrible hurry. Actually, the woman was angrily marching along. About midway to her chambers a procession of servants with carts prevented them from going further. The servants were very apologetic and the way in which the woman responded to the mishap let Josephine know she was not a mere servant herself but what title she held she did not know. After a few minutes, the way was passable and the ladies continued on. They had just come to the last hallway leading to Josephine's room when the young lady stopped abruptly and cleared her throat.

"Your grace, if I may have a word with you?" Whether the lady was more startled by Josephine addressing her by title or just being bold enough to speak to her at all, the woman came to a halt and turned to face her. "It is clear that you do not like me," Josephine said, but to her surprise, she was quickly interrupted.

"I do not know whether you are the likable sort," Saraina replied in a rude tone, taking a step closer to the younger lady. "Any woman that would be in the king's chambers at this hour of the morning would be questionable in the opinion of most." The fire in her eyes as she spoke was incredible and caused Josephine to nervously shift upon her feet. The woman's reaction could only mean one thing.

"I would agree." Without giving a chance for a rebuttal, Josephine added, "Tell me, does your brother entertain women in his chambers often?" The words knocked the wind from the woman for a moment but with a blink of her eyes she came back at Josephine.

"What are your intentions toward my brother?" The threatening tone rang out and Josephine was thankful that she was still a few arms lengths away. Mustering up her courage again, Josephine knew she would not only need to come out of this encounter alive, but with answers about the king.

"I have none." The response was not expected and the look on Saraina's face was of shock. "I am part of the diplomatic envoy from Gutten. I am with Prince Wilhelm Von Strauss and am at his bidding. However, I would like to discover the king's intentions toward me and I am asking you, as his sister, to enlighten me. You know him better than I, and I would rather not be involved in careless folly as my reputation is at stake as well as my feelings. Do tell me your opinion, your grace." Again, Josephine's words struck hard enough that Saraina turned away from the young lady for a moment to regain her composure as she thought about what had been said.

"And if I tell you not to come when he calls for you, what then would be your answer?"

"Your grace, I do not consider this a light matter. As king, he does not need rumors of entertaining a lady in his chambers circling about. But speaking for myself . . ." Her voice broke off as she discovered her emotions were running higher than she realized. "I do not want to be played as a mistress. I will admit that I have enjoyed his company immensely, but if I am but one of many ladies that he entertains, it would be better for me to keep my distance and affections not grow." Finishing her statement, she swallowed hard fighting back tears. Saraina had turned and could see the wretched look upon Josephine's face as her gaze fell to the floor. She had assumed the young lady was praying upon her brother's position as king for personal gain but the words spoken told another story.

The princess stood motionless watching Josephine, then as if she stepped back into her role as regent, she spoke, "Will it suffice if I am allowed to answer you when the ladies meet this morning?"

Feeling a small measure of accomplishment, Josephine replied, "Yes, your grace." And she nodded reverently. She knew that if her own brother's welfare were at stake she might be defensive as Saraina had been. "If it will not offend you, I can see myself to my room as well. I know you were summoned to the king's chambers for more important matters than to escort me about."

"My lady," Saraina replied and with a nod the two women parted ways.

As Josephine was dressing properly for the day she began to relate her incredible visit with the king to Katrina. The other maid, Anna, came and began working Josephine's hair into an elaborate up-do which did not afford for the conversation to continue. Several quiet minutes passed before Katrina spoke up.

"My lady, you are not falling asleep, are you?" with a laugh, Josephine replied.

"No, my dear. My feet hurt far too much for that." All three ladies burst into laughter.

"Is it true?" Anna asked as she moved to get a better view of Josephine's face. "Did the king dance with you last night?"

"Yes, he did," Josephine answered. Anna's eyes grew wide as her mouth dropped open.

"Oh my . . ." she said.

"Why is that shocking, Anna?" Josephine asked as the servant's hands stopped moving.

"The king has danced with no one since the queen's passing. No one!" she said and then repeated it again. "No one, until you." The last words were spoken hoping to taunt the lady to a reaction. Josephine found herself struggling not to smile from ear to ear with delight as she thought about the king that morning but managing to keep a solemn look she asked.

"And how am I any different than anyone else?" At her reply, the maid could contain herself no longer.

"My lady, please do not be upset with me for saying such things." She blurted out. "But you are different. All the talk is about how you have drawn the king's attention by your humbleness and beauty. How he looked at you while you seemed to float together upon the dance floor last night. Oh my lady, are you not pleased that you have caught his eye?" Suddenly the room seemed stuffy to Josephine, and she gasped several times mumbling about needing fresh air. Katrina opened the windows and then came to her side. She took hold of Josephine's hand and patted it while Anna resumed her handiwork. Josephine closed her eyes to keep from revealing her feelings about the subject. Very tactfully, she questioned Anna more about the king and his late wife and the servant was eager to provide any answers to aid the lady. Every so often, she would throw a hint toward Josephine wanting details of the ball, but Josephine would promptly redirect with another question.

Finally Katrina spoke up, "My lady." Josephine opened her eyes to look at her. "It will not matter how tightly you close your eyes to avoid answering Anna, if you are smiling from ear to ear instead!" All three ladies gave a laugh.

"Do you favor him?" Anna asked as she pinned the last strand of hair in place.

"Yes, I do," Josephine finally conceded. "But on your life do not utter this to anyone, understand me? I am quite overwhelmed with his attention and am not comfortable with such matters. And the court here in Andervan is much larger than we are accustomed to in Gutten."

"As you wish, my lady," Anna promised, very pleased with the answer. Josephine was not sure that the secret would be kept but as Katrina said her face told on her when the king's name was mentioned.

Still feeling uneasy from the excitement of the morning Josephine persuaded Katrina to accompany her to breakfast. Wilhelm was waiting in the hallway and at the sight of him, Josephine felt much better. Like always, it took but a moment for him to take her arm and they walked on. He could not resist the temptation however to tease Josephine about rumors of her dancing and then inquired about her feet. He assured her the latter story had not been circulated, and he would not have known except Sven had confided in him when the prince inquired of the lady's whereabouts. Josephine carefully watched Wilhelm's face to see if he knew of her early morning rendezvous with the king, but when the prince changed the subject, she sighed with relief as the secret was safe. Most of the people at breakfast were the same from the day before but the conversation was directed toward the visitors. It was very clear that Josephine was now the center of attention, no longer hidden behind Wilhelm's coattails and had become a visible presence beside their king. All three were relieved when the meal was over and the people dismissed themselves from the table. They had just reached the main hall where a throng had gathered when to Josephine's dismay she spotted Saraina coming in their direction.

"Not again," Josephine said to herself. It seemed like she had just relaxed from their earlier encounter and was not ready for a possible war of words so soon. *Too late.* The princess approached them, exchanged greetings and then Saraina directed her attention solely upon Josephine.

"My lady, it seems I have misjudged you," she said humbly. "If I may, I would like to start over." She tilted her head to the side as she made her plea. "And I heard that you have yet to tour our castle. May I have the honors?" For a moment, Josephine was not sure how to answer. Was this a true apology for her rudeness earlier or was she about to be guided ever so politely to be locked in the dungeons or the tower?

"I will gladly accept your offer, if I may bring my lady in waiting along," she said, reaching for Katrina's hand.

"Yes, of course. I am very pleased." Saraina smiled and added "We should be able to see several rooms before our meeting at ten thirty. If schedules permit, shall we eat lunch together as well?" Josephine was relieved to hear the sincerity in the princess's voice. She almost felt guilty for thinking of Saraina leading her into harm, but Wilhelm had always taught to err on the side of caution.

"If I may have a moment with the prince, then I will be ready," Josephine said.

"Yes, of course," Saraina said, and pointed to a doorway across the room. "I will wait for you there. Thank you, Prince Wilhelm, for letting me steal your companion for the morning," and with a curtsy, she left them.

When the princess was far enough away not to hear, Katrina pulled on Josephine's arm and asked, "Are we really going with her after what happened earlier?"

Wincing, Josephine hoped Wilhelm hadn't heard what was said, but she was mistaken.

"And what happened earlier?" he asked in a serious tone. She was terrible about keeping things from the prince especially when he asked directly for he had a way of reading her expressions like an open book. One look at Wilhelm's face and Katrina excused herself and headed into the crowd. Knowing any attempt to conceal the matter would be futile; Josephine decided to admit to the confrontation in the hallway but was vague as to the details of how they had come about.

"It seemed the princess was concerned about her brother's welfare and felt the need to make her feelings clear to me." Wilhelm turned to face the lady.

"You mean to say she threatened you?" he asked at which Josephine looked away to avoid his keen eyes and offered an excuse.

"I would do the same in her position."

"Maybe . . . but do you think it is wise to go with her on a tour?" the prince questioned as he glanced across the room at Saraina.

"I plan to be very cautious. Hence Katrina will remain with me, and, yes, I do think this will be the only way to address the matter. But . . ." she said as she turned to leave. "You will come looking for me if I don't show up at supper?" The lady had taken a step but could go no further as Wilhelm had taken a tight hold of her arm and pulled her back closer to him. He was not happy with what he had heard.

"You *will* be very careful." Very seldom had he scolded her in this tone and it stung. She started to turn toward him but instead he pressed his lips to her ear and whispered, "I worry about you." His voice faltered and Josephine wanted tell him how much hearing that meant to her, but the next second, she felt his grip release upon her arm as he pushed her away. They exchanged solemn glances, and then she turned and began to make her way through the crowd where she joined Saraina and Katrina.

Much to the ladies' relief, the princess's intentions were good and the tour was pleasant. Although time did not allow for much what was seen proved very beneficial. It always seemed that they went in one door and left by another, rarely using the same venues but now the ladies had their bearings on how the castle was laid out. Not to their surprise, the décor was lovely and only the beauty of the mountains could parallel the furnishings and exquisite taste. The three made it to the morning session as it began. Duchess Aidenvonn was again presiding, and while she spoke, Josephine could hear her own name being whispered among the ladies whom she guessed were single, titled, and eligible for an advantageous marriage at court. Her presence in the room had indeed upset the circle and to her surprise the princess was amused by this irritation. Through whispers, Saraina mumbled something about them wanting to sink their fingernails into her brother, and she relished the fact that they were in a tizzy.

And I thought I should fear her? Josephine thought. *No, it's the other ladies who think I am standing in their way of becoming queen.* The glares only worsened as the meeting went on, and she was relieved when lunch was announced.

They all had stood to their feet and were heading toward the door when Saraina spoke up, "Let's slip out here." She pointed to a doorway on the left. "Our lunch is ready upstairs." Gladly Josephine and Katrina followed her. They were about to enter a room when she heard her name being called and excused herself to join Wilhelm. He waited until they were close enough no one else could hear what was said before he began.

"I see you are still alive." He teased as he reached for the lady's hand.

"Yes, alive and well. Saraina has been wonderfully nice and it was not to lead me blindly to the gallows," Josephine replied, causing both to laugh.

"Good," Wilhelm replied. "I was worried." He drew a breath and sighed as he so often did when matters were serious and his left eyebrow rose anxiously.

"What is it?" she asked as she squeezed his hand.

"The council will hear last remarks and then take a vote this afternoon," he replied.

"So soon?" she asked as her mouth fell open with astonishment.

"Silly girl," Wilhelm replied, shaking his head, half in disbelief but still smiling at her. "While you ladies have been in your meetings, the council has met and discussed our cause for aide." Suddenly Josephine felt overwhelming guilt as what he said was true. She had been trapesing about court while he was pleading for support. When Wilhelm saw the lady's countenance fall, he quickly spoke up, "Forgive me, I was not accusing you. Your presence was not needed at the meetings and for once it did not hurt for you to be *among* the ladies." He had covered his words well, but Josephine still felt bad for her absence. "But I think you should be there to hear what is said this time and I will need you beside me, whether the outcome is good or bad." Suddenly the gravity of his words weighed heavy upon her. What if the trip was in vain? What if the council chose not to send supplies or worse yet, no military support?

"I will be there with you," she answered. For a moment, they stood there and the concern she saw in his eyes made her want to convince him that all would be well. Instead she found herself squeezing his hands. "I will be there and will do whatever you need me to."

"Thank you." Clearing his throat, he added, "I will come to your room at a quarter till three and we will walk down together." Josephine nodded and letting go of each other they went on about their business.

The room Josephine entered was solely for the royal family's personal use. Although the furnishings were regal, they seemed simpler with traces of frequent use upon the wood and fabric. The furniture was also placed closer together for a more intimate, casual setting for family and friends. On one side of the room stood a dining table surrounded by a dozen high back chairs where Saraina and the others were already seated, three of which were the king's sons and four, two daughters and two sons, belonged to the princess. The children talked throughout the meal of what they had been doing that morning and just as dessert was brought out a side door opened and a squeal of delight was heard. It was Victor, Saraina's husband who had managed to slip away for a short time in between meetings. He kissed his wife and daughters but only greeted the boys as they waved at him with one hand and kept hold of their spoon with the other. It was a touching scene to behold, but Josephine found herself wishing someone else would suddenly come through the door. When dessert was finished, the party moved to the couches where the children began to play while Saraina made proper introductions. Time was pleasantly passing along until Katrina nudged her mistress and called her attention to the clock. Thanking them for a lovely lunch, Josephine explained that she must leave them for the sake of business with the prince.

When they reached their chambers, Josephine found herself extremely nervous about the meeting. Her mind was flooded with regret for not being at the proceedings earlier in the week. She did not even know a lot about the council itself, how it convened, would she be called upon to speak, were there even ladies serving on the council? How had the atmosphere been concerning Wilhelm's request? She wished she had remained with Wilhelm as so much hinged upon the decision. She was stewing alone by the windows when Katrina showed Wilhelm in, and pointed him to where Josephine was standing. It took but one look for him to see the weight of worry she was carrying. Walking up behind her, he reached out till his hands touched the window panes and enclosed her in between his arms. Without a word, she sank back against him.

"I am out of sorts, Wilhelm. If I had not neglected my duties, I would be prepared." The despair in her voice told more than her words.

"Hush," he said gently as he leaned his head against hers. "If I had needed you, I would have called for you." He paused as he shifted slightly with his face brushing against her hair. "I wanted to spare you as much as I could, so you would not hear the horrible accounts told again." Josephine gave a sigh as she realized the length to which the prince had went to protect her. "Could I not do that for you?" he whispered toward her ear. Josephine closed her eyes and rested against him. Wilhelm had grown accustomed to relying on the lady's quiet strength at such proceedings, but he chose the sacrifice of being alone to spare her from what he said to the council. He was ashamed that she had seen firsthand the wounded, the battles, the deaths of young and old alike and hated the fact that she would never be fully released from the memories. Yet, even now, Wilhelm knew she would not fully escape all the torment of memory as she would hear his last petition of aid that afternoon. He drew a long, slow breath knowing he needed her beside him and that the time had come for them to leave their embrace and be on their way downstairs. Josephine recognized his sigh, and together they turned and solemnly left Katrina in the room.

Arm in arm, they went downstairs and stepped into the Council Chambers of Andervan. A soldier led them to the visitors' box to be seated and a few minutes later the session was called to order. Josephine's nervousness began to wane as she focused all her attention on the chief councilman who had begun to speak. He walked the main aisle in front of the members as he addressed them, and for a brief moment, Josephine's gaze fell upon the king who was seated on the far side of the room. She thought Sven had smiled at her but quickly dismissed it and brought her mind back to the task at hand. By the opening statements, one would have thought the council was fully in support of sending aid to Gutten but then as the floor was yielded for remarks Josephine's heart sank. The next gentleman who stood to his feet began a barrage of negativity and then another stood and gave a rally for support to be given. Josephine watched in amazement as the tone again turned as another gentleman stood and protested the number of soldiers proposed to be sent. Wilhelm seemed to handle the criticism far better than his counterpart who had begun to wring her hands. Finally the prince laid his hand upon the lady's hoping to settle her fidgeting. After an hour had passed, it was announced that a ten-minute recess would be taken. An older gentleman had just finished delivering a personal accusation against Wilhelm which made Josephine boil in anger. Frustrated, she commented to Wilhelm a bit louder than she realized.

"Youthful ambitions?" she questioned. To her surprise, the reply did not come from Wilhelm.

"We have to be cautious, my lady. Matters such as these cannot be taken lightly." Josephine looked up to see the first gentleman that opposed support for Gutten.

"Yes, sir, I agree. I know the gravity of the matter at hand."

"No offence meant my lady, but I do not think you could possibly understand." Even the way his words were formed by his lips irritated Josephine, not to mention the sarcastic tone in which he spoke them.

"If I may," she said rising to her feet. "I do understand perfectly well all aspects of this matter." The man began to shake his head and gave a laugh that was loud enough to be heard throughout the room as he mocked her. Josephine could not conceal the evil glare that she threw at him. She felt Wilhelm's hand touch her fingertips as he subtly reminded her that he was seated beside her. So many thoughts crossed Josephine's mind in a split second. What was she thinking to answer him in the manner she had? Would she be escorted from the room for her comments? Yet her conscience burned within her and she could not remain silent. But then again, would the council receive any remarks from her if she asked to address them? She was a stranger to the proceedings and a female at that with no other ladies present that day and she wondered if she had merely been allowed in the chambers as courtesy to the prince. Did the council have such an opinion as the duke had implied—that women were ignorant of the affairs of state. Did they think women served better at home than in the political arena? She despised the insinuation, that she could not possibly understand the suffering of war. The other council men had risen to their feet and had begun to mingle when they heard the laugh. The king too had left his seat and was coming to greet Josephine and saw the expressions on her face as she had stood to her feet. He stopped in the main aisle as the room suddenly grew silent. The next words heard were spoken by the king.

"Honorable Duke Heimel, would you care to make your comments know to the entire council?" Although her gaze was still fixed upon the duke, out of the corner of her eye, she could see the other men stepping to the side creating an aisle that led to where she stood facing him.

"No, my liege," he said and turned reverently toward the king but then back again to the lady. "I would not embarrass her ladyship with explanations of things she does not comprehend." He gave a sly grin and bowed his head still mocking her.

"My lady, have you any remarks?" the king asked politely but not expecting the lady to answer.

"Yes, my liege, I would like to clarify this matter to the duke before all." Her words were sharply spoken and did not sit well with the man.

"And who are you to address this council?" he snapped back at the lady. The resentment was very visible upon the duke's face and Sven was relieved when Wilhelm rose to his feet beside Josephine in her defense.

"King Sven, may I present Lady Josephine Armand, director of commerce and member of Gutten's High Council. She has journeyed this great distance to represent members who could not attend this meeting because of the pressing situation in our kingdom. She speaks now in full authority on behalf of our people." As she heard herself properly introduced, a wave of fear washed over Josephine. She drew a breath, regaining her composure as Wilhelm bowed to her and motioned for her to proceed. She began to speak.

"I had been told the men of Andervan were honorable, men of their word, men of compassion, men who in all their strength would assist those who are weak. Yet." She paused as she looked around the room making eye contact with as many as she could. "Here now accusations have been made against a fellow brother, a brother in need. Wilhelm Von Strauss came here not seeking fame or glory or power. He did not seek to enlarge his kingdom but to prevent the massacre of the innocent, to defend his people, to preserve their lives and homes. The duke has said that I could not possibly understand what is at stake here today. I beg to differ. I was at Bartlestoff when it was attacked. I have held the hands of men who were taking their last breaths, have heard final words to be repeated to their wives and children. I have held the flesh together while the surgeon tried to save arms and legs. My dress has been so soaked in the blood of our men that it had to be removed and burned before we could go on to the village, lest someone see it and fear overtake them. I know of bandaging the wounded found lying upon the roads with strips from my petticoats while watching over my shoulder to see if arrows were flying upon me. I know the blood, the death, and the fear when you find yourself trapped—hearing the sound of metal upon stone as the grappling hooks come over the wall and dig in with a screech. I have heard the sound of steel against steel as armor collided and I stood, without armor, without sword, waiting to see my enemy coming. I have went out knowing that I would receive no mercy being a woman, as no mercy had been given to the women at Larklan. I have held the lifeless bodies of children while their graves were being dug. I understand how it feels to be outnumbered and know that if you cannot muster enough strength to endure this battle that the next village down the road will burn. I feel no need to describe more. Andervan is not ignorant of these atrocities. The reports you have received or Prince Wilhelm's testimony should have been enough to warrant aid, but if it was not enough to prick your consciences and stir your honor then let my words bear witness of the dire circumstances before us. We made this journey with prices upon our very heads. Knowing our capture would end with torturous deaths we came none-the-less, hoping that pledges made in years past still stood as valid. Have we falsely placed our hope? My lords, is there still honor in Andervan?"

As she spoke the last sentences, she returned her gaze to the duke. No one had moved during her speech and all wore solemn expressions as they were deep in thought. Suddenly Josephine felt very self-conscious and turned in the direction of the king. "My liege, I apologize for the way in which I have addressed your council but I *will not* apologize for the words that I have spoken. If I may be excused, I will hinder this meeting no further." To her relief, the king nodded his approval and Josephine with legs shaking stepped from the visitors' box. She felt Wilhelm's hand touch hers but she did not linger, nor turn to look at him for fear of bursting into tears. As she made her way back to her room she found herself wiping her eyes. Josephine made her lady in waiting promise not to allow anyone to enter the chambers, mentioning two men in particular that she guessed would come for her. She retreated to Katrina's quarters to rest in seclusion with her lady in waiting promising to be firm with any visitors. When Katrina had shut the door, Josephine began sobbing uncontrollably until sleep overtook her.

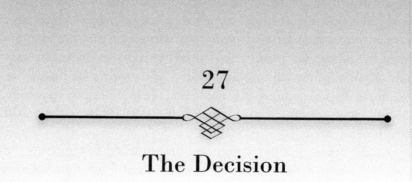

27

The Decision

Back in the council chambers, no sooner had the doors closed behind Josephine than the men were in an uproar. Never before had they heard a lady speak in such a manner, a manner that had cut to their hearts. The king was in shock himself and had returned to his chair, sinking back and stroking his beard as he thought about what had just happened. He had been given no hint by the prince or the lady that she was the other council member mentioned in King Hubert's correspondence. The way with which Josephine had spoken was nothing like his experiences with her thus far and the authority with which she addressed the room let him know that she had not stepped into the meeting as a novice. The villages and battles she had mentioned had correlated to information his men had brought word of during the last several months. But what moved him more than anything was the way she had described the fears of battle, the desperation of the moment and the summoning of courage from deep within when it felt as if courage and strength had been exhausted hours before. The king was not the only one who suddenly remembered how it felt for most of the men serving upon the council had once donned armor and weapons to fight beside the men of Gutten. Sven's father Andreas had died not two weeks before the Ten Weeks War began with alliances having already been made with troops marching in the defense of Gutten and Pietra, as the kingdoms of Aikerlan, Laetza, and Dentar had begun a military assault against them. The enemy's goal was to sweep through the region conquering all in their path and end their campaign by taking Andervan before the snow began to fall. King Andreas had made it clear to Sven how vital it was to defend their brothers who had endeavored to live in peace.

"God has blessed us bountifully and put us in this position as the stronger one to help those in need," he said. "Do not let them stand alone, my son." And Sven did as his father wished. What they assumed would be accomplished in a few weeks stretched to ten, thus the name the war was called. Despite the loss of lives, the mission had been fulfilled and peace had reigned in the region until now. For whatever reason, Airik Brias's outlook on peace had changed, the aggressive behavior had been noticed far and wide. Word of villages being raided had reached Andervan earlier in the year and informants were sent to keep news flowing and Sven knew King Hubert would make every attempt to maintain peace. Sadly correspondence came that a raid would be made on Briasburg Castle hoping to end the reign of terror and Sven remembered the bitterness with which he had made similar decisions. Yes, the consciences of many were pricked that afternoon as memories came flooding back. Could the men of Andervan turn their backs to allow innocent people to die without defense or just half-heartedly support their brothers?

King Sven let the men speak among themselves for several minutes and then called for the meeting to officially resume. Duke Heimel was quick to take the floor and made a motion for more aide than had been requested. A second motion was made for support and then a call for the vote to commence. It was unanimous that Andervan would aid Gutten and applause filled the room. The king rose to his feet, asking for any closing remarks, and when none were offered, the meeting was adjourned. Wilhelm sank back into his seat overcome with relief. Several men patted him on the back as they walked past while some shook his hand in congratulations. Seeing the king approaching, the prince left his chair to meet him in the aisle.

"Thank you, my liege," he said, reaching for his hand.

"Of course," Sven replied. "I gave my word and would have called for a second vote if the first had not gone well." They began walking toward the hallway.

"I am forever indebted to you," Wilhelm said, still overwhelmed that his petition was granted.

They had reached the main staircase when the king said, "It was quite a shock when Lady Josephine began to speak. I had no idea that *she* was the council member."

"I was hoping to keep her from the meetings altogether," Wilhelm admitted as they kept walking toward the hallway which led to the personal chambers.

"Why?" the king asked, fishing for information as he began to wonder if the lady's position had been withheld from him intentionally.

"You saw her face as she told of the villages, the battles, and the blood. We, as men of war, know the burden of the nightmares. She has seen too much already, and I hoped to spare her having to relive it yet one more time. I purposely encouraged her to stay with the ladies at court and to visit with the people, hoping to keep her from the meetings. It was a desperate attempt on my part to undo what had been done. As you saw today, she will never be free from the scars." They had made it to the final junction in the hallway—to go left would be toward Josephine's chambers, to go right would be toward Wilhelm's. The king, still suspicious, wanted to speak with the lady. He bid farewell to Wilhelm and had begun walking to the left when he was called to.

"King Sven, if you are hoping to see Josephine, you will be greatly disappointed," Wilhelm said in a matter-of-factly tone.

"And why is that, may I ask?"

"She wants to be alone." For a moment, Sven glared at the prince and started to make a rude comment in return but stopped himself. Wilhelm continued, "I have seen that look in her eye before and she will not see you. She will not see anyone until she is ready."

"She does not need to be alone," Sven replied as he envisioned himself holding the woman in his arms. "I will not let her be alone." The resolve in his voice got under Wilhelm's skin, and he found himself fighting his temper. Was the king suggesting he was the only one capable of comforting the lady?

"Yes, that is what I have thought so many times. There are times, like now, when what I want falls to what she wants. When she is ready, she will be found to be comforted accordingly. But . . ." he added as he made sure the king's eyes were upon him, "not now."

"Begging your pardon, young man," Sven replied sternly, "but I will do as I must."

"I understand," Wilhelm commented and with a bow, turned and walked toward his room. It was becoming more and more apparent to Wilhelm that the king was falling in love with Josephine. As one friend looking out for another, the thought would have been well received. The king was a good match for the lady and she would be treated well and be loved all of her days, but Wilhelm had felt jealously rise up in his heart, and the thought of Josephine being in the arms of any other man made him angry and sick at the same time. Thankfully, Wilhelm didn't get the chance to dwell upon his feelings as his men were waiting in his chambers for the news of how the vote had gone.

The king had indeed proceeded to Josephine's chambers where he was politely refused entry by Katrina. She was very adamant about his remaining outside the chambers while they spoke and mentioned that Josephine had warned her that he would come to call. She relayed the message for the lady's wishes to be respected to allow her to rest. The king was not happy but obliged the servant and returned to his chambers. He was not sure whether he was more irritated that he had been refused to see the lady or that Wilhelm had been right.

A half an hour before supper was to be served, Katrina woke Josephine. Word had been sent that the meal would be served in the family's private dining room. Josephine was relieved as her nerves were shaken, and she did not want to deal with the affairs of court. Wilhelm came to her door a few minutes early, and when she saw him, tears began to well up. Carefully he took her arm as if he hadn't noticed and began to talk of the mountains. He longed to hold her and assure her that things had gone well but he was afraid she would break down causing them to arrive late for supper. To no one's surprise, Josephine was quiet throughout the meal and most of the chit-chat that followed. They left the dining room and walked to the room in which Saraina had entertained the ladies at lunch. Everyone settled in with the children persuading Josephine to join them at a board game which had been placed upon a low table along one side of the room. Using the opportunity to avoid the other adults, Josephine took a seat on the floor beside the table with her back to the room. She still felt awkward over the speech she had given that afternoon and hoped not a word of politics would be mentioned. Thankfully Fin perched himself at her elbow and was determined not to share his partner with anyone else. Promptly at nine, the children's governor stepped to the doorway and called for bedtime. With complaints, the children rose to their feet but not before Fin had threw his arms around Josephine and begged for her to tuck him in.

"I will walk you to your room, if . . ." she said emphatically. "You will go on to bed, no whining." She pushed the boy away to see his face and he promised with a nod. "Let's go," she said, and he took her hand to help her to her feet. She half-expected to hear the king protest her offer, but all Sven did when she looked in his direction was shake his head and smile. The other children were pleased to have the lady with them and kept talking all at once, interrupting each other as they walked. Good nights were given at the cousins' chamber doors and it was but a few steps till the next round of good-byes came. Fin gave a hearty hug and left Josephine standing alone in the hallway. As she began to walk back, she thought of how much she had enjoyed the children that night. When she reached the junction of the hallways, she let out a sigh and turned toward her room instead of going in the direction of where the others were gathered. Staring at the floor she passed Wilhelm's door not paying attention as she walked on. Suddenly she looked up and saw the king leaning against the wall beside her door. At first she wanted to ask why he was waiting there, but she found herself blushing as she realized he had rightly guessed that she would not be returning to the others. She stopped a few feet short but then he came to her and with a smile reached for her arm.

"Will you walk with me?" he asked. Josephine smiled back, not able to refuse his request.

"Are we going to your chambers?" she asked as they turned to the right.

"Is there anything that gets past you?" he asked as he came to an abrupt stop, and turned to face the lady.

"Did you think I would not figure out where this hall led?" After Saraina's tour she had realized that she was taken the long way through the castle when she was brought to his chambers early that morning.

"I was afraid you might be alarmed at how close my chambers were." Ever so smoothly, he put both his hands upon her arms. If he had done something to warrant it, she would have been alarmed, but so far, he had remained honorable in his actions. She noticed his smile had faded into a frown. "I feel I must ask you about something," he said, looking hard into her eyes. "Why did you with hold from me that *you* were the council member?" The tone in which he spoke was laden with poisonous accusation. Josephine did not hide her resentment of his question and took a step back as she replied.

"You think I purposely kept it a secret to gain favor with you?" She felt her lips quiver and then realized it was not anger that possessed her as tears came to her eyes. Taking another step backward, she glared at the man in front of her. "What did my council position have to do with my feelings about you?" The words stung as she realized she had just admitted her weakness to him. "It was *your* child that stumbled into my room in the night, not I into his. Was it not you who requested I remain beside you the second day; and at the ball, it was not I who sought you out. I thought you were alone with me this morning as a man, not as king. We spoke of everyday things, not politics!" Josephine felt a tear escape and slide down her cheek. "You think I was seeking your favor for more troops?" Her voice broke up, and as it did, the king stepped forward and took hold of her arms again, this time looking tenderly into her face. She would have pulled away from his grasp, but he held her tight and began pulling her closer to him. He reached to wipe another tear as it fell and then tilted her chin upward.

"I believe you, my darling," he said as he kissed her forehead.

"I don't understand," she mumbled as he kissed her left temple.

"I had to be sure you were with me for the right reasons," he whispered in her ear. "I had to know for sure there were no other motives." Josephine rested her head against his shoulder as she tried to figure out what had just happened. She was infuriated with thoughts of slapping his handsome face entering her mind, yet she desperately wanted him to continue to hold her close. The longer they stood together, she could feel the tensions of the day fade away.

"Wilhelm confessed that he had prevented me from being at the meetings until today," Josephine said quietly as Sven began to stroke her hair.

"He mentioned something to me after you left the meeting." The king took a step back to catch Josephine's gaze and added, "You are an amazing speaker." The lady felt a twinge of pain at the statement which he was quick to notice. "I would have pressed for more troops and supplies, but your account secured double the amount. You moved the hearts of everyone in the room." Josephine managed a grin but dropped her head in sadness. Sven drew her close again. "Are you not pleased?" He sensed something more weighed upon her mind.

"I am pleased," she answered softly.

"What is it then?" he asked.

"I hate the thought of what lies ahead," she answered. "The families who will be destroyed by death, pain, and loss. You know as well as I what must happen to defeat Maximillian and his army."

"I remember well the scenes of war and the suffering," the king said, reaching to stroke her hair again. His voice lowered to a whisper. "I was upon the wall at Bartlestoff, when it was a fully intact stronghold of defense. I had taken a small troop north when we were forced to retreat to the fort. We were outnumbered and surrounded, and there was no way to send for help. Three harrowing days, we were besieged before reinforcements happened along, and by that time, part of the wall had been compromised. I did not think I would live to see Andervan again." As he ended speaking, he leaned back to see tears flowing down Josephine's face. "You should have never had to see what you described this afternoon." He reached to wipe her tears as she took hold of his shirt, steadying herself.

"It could not be helped," Josephine offered.

"Yes, it could have," he interrupted. "You have no place in battle. You should have been kept a safe distance away and protected."

"We done what was needed, being caught on the road returning from . . ." Her excuse was interrupted.

"The prince needs to make a better effort to keep you safe," the king replied as his hands returned to the back of the lady's arms. "Josephine . . ." His voice broke off as if his next words were difficult to say. "I want you to remain here in Andervan, at least until the war is over." It took but the first words for Josephine to gasp in shock. "Stay here where you will be safe. You said the journey itself is risky. So don't take the risk, travel when the war is over." Josephine began to shake her head, and her mouth had fallen open in disbelief. "Stay here and not be in the middle of the destruction, the bloodshed. Wait here in peace until it's all over. You have experienced enough turmoil. Let me rescue you from more." Sven was earnest as he pleaded.

"I cannot abandon the people at this hour. I will be needed," she replied.

"I am sending hundreds to take your place—let them fight the battle and tend the wounded. Please, Josephine. Wilhelm shielded you from the meetings. Let me shield you from the war."

"Sven, I . . ." Before she could utter another word, he had placed a finger to her lips, silencing her.

"Please," he begged. "Don't answer me tonight. Think about my offer." He removed his finger only to trace the outline of her face. "Promise me you will consider it." Josephine closed her eyes as she felt her will seemingly melt before him. "Do not think you will be forced to remain, as at any time you wish you can return to Gutten via armed escort. Josephine, I cannot bear the thought of you being killed or captured and turned over to Maximillian." The latter made Josephine cringe. King Hubert and Wilhelm had done their best to keep certain details from her, but she had pieced together enough to know Maximillian wanted her to be taken alive and in good condition. Suddenly another thought occurred to her.

"Would I be staying in Andervan for my protection or for your sake?" she asked, opening her eyes to see his reaction.

"I will not deny that I want you to remain." He tilted his head slightly. "I told you I would like to get to know you better, so, yes, staying would accomplish that." He swallowed hard and she saw his eyebrows rise. "But if nothing more than friendship developed between us, I would be glad to know you had been spared grief. That is my chief intention, but I will not deny that I desire time with you." The sincerity in his eyes spoke clearly causing her glare to soften. "I will speak to Wilhelm in the morning. Although your presence will be missed, I am certain he will agree for safety's sake." And at that, Josephine leaned forward until her forehead came to rest on the king's chest. The idea was tempting yet unsettling. She would be anxious for news if she remained but at least part of the time spent could be occupied with sightseeing and learning about Andervan. She believed Sven would keep his promise if she chose to leave before the war was over and the thought of bypassing the tragedies seemed to pull at her emotions, but could she pass to someone else what she thought was her part to do? But the greater temptation was concerning her relationship with the king. So far his attempts for her affection had been successful, and she had not been able to resist his bidding. Was she caught up in his charm or falling in love with him? If she remained, she was sure more was to come and leaving might prove harder and harder for her. She desperately needed Wilhelm's opinion on the offer.

"Sven, I will consider what you have said," she said quietly. "Will you see me to my room? The day has left me exhausted."

"Of course, my lady," he replied.

That night, Josephine tossed and turned as the king's offer was rehearsed over and over in her mind. Finally, she awoke to Katrina's voice with news that breakfast would be brought to the chambers as a trip into the town had been arranged for eight o'clock. Josephine knew it was the king's doing for she had hinted of wanting to see the town up close, and after the conversation the evening before, she guessed he was determined to impress her in every way possible. Just before it was time to leave, a messenger came to the door and offered an apology for the inconvenience, but there had been a delay and promised someone would come within the hour. Josephine was not alarmed as delays were expected when living among a royal family. Forty-five minutes later, the king himself came to the lady's door. The look on his face told her he was not his usual self, and although he sounded happy to be with her, she found him avoiding eye contact. As they were climbing into his carriage, Josephine asked if Wilhelm would be coming along, and the scowl Sven gave made her feel uncomfortable.

"The prince has declined to accompany us this morning."

Josephine took her seat. By his mood, the lady assumed it had not went well when the king had spoken to Wilhelm concerning his proposal. She wondered what argument was made against her remaining in Andervan. Although Sven had not said a word during the short trip to the town, the moment the king's feet touched the street, his cheerful demeanor returned. The town was lovely indeed with many of the buildings having intricate carvings of stone. The river wound through the center of town with several wooden bridges spanning its cold waters. Evergreen trees seemed to be the prominent foliage and although Josephine saw some flowers growing in gardens, she was told most cut arrangements were brought from the lower elevations. The king pointed out how the town had been designed to function amid the frequent snowfalls that covered the ground for at least four months straight. Josephine could not imagine such a thing as snowfall was not common in Frive, and when it had fallen in Guttenhamm, all business had come to a stand-still. The king found the struggle over the snow amusing and asked if they knew about sleighs or skis. When Sven mentioned the fun they would have playing in the snow an aching twinge reminded Josephine how badly she needed to speak with Wilhelm.

The morning went by quicker than they liked and before she knew it Josephine's stomach was growling with hunger. Much to her embarrassment, the king heard the noise and suggested that they dine at a nearby restaurant instead of waiting till they reached the castle. The proprietors were delighted to have the special guests and a tasty meal was served. Dessert had just been set upon the table when Josephine felt the hair on the back of her neck begin to tingle as she felt someone's eyes heavily upon her. Trying not to draw attention, she carefully turned and looked about the room. *There are so many people here, who would it be?* she thought. *How would I ever know friend from foe?* Not noticing anything out of the ordinary, she returned her gaze to the king, who had seen her face turn pale.

"May I ask what is wrong?" he whispered. Josephine started to tell him but then she changed her mind and mumbled.

"Nothing, I am sure." She dropped her gaze to her dessert and nervously shifted the cake upon her plate with her fork. She reached for her glass, but the king was quick and caught her hand.

"You are not telling me the truth, my dear." There was a scolding in his voice, but the concern spoke louder than the rebuke.

"I feel as if someone is watching us," she whispered. "And not out of curiosity." The king smiled at his suspicious guest and answered in a quiet voice.

"I am sure every eye is upon us. They have never seen their king taking a lady to lunch." Josephine returned a polite but fake smile as she was not amused. If he had been observant enough to see her countenance change, then why could he not believe her that trouble was brewing? "Don't let the staring bother you. My body guards are close by if there is a problem. Come, let us enjoy our dessert." Josephine started to argue that it was not her imagination, but she decided to drop it. Hopefully, he was right, especially when it came to his guards defending them for she would hate it if the matter proved otherwise. They finished eating and then resumed walking along the sidewalk together. The king pointed ahead and explained they were approaching the town's square which at this time of year was filled with the tents of vendors. He warned of how crowded it could be, and noisy, and how people would be rude as they bustled about. Laughing, she assured him this was not the first open-air market she had been to. Just before they were to the outskirts of the square, Josephine again felt as if someone was watching her. She tried to look around but had a poor view because of her height. The king took her hand as they began to make their way down the right side of the street. It wasn't long before Josephine let loose of his hand to examine the goods on display and for the most part, the king just stayed close by. As time went on however, more distance was allowed as different things caught their eye, but then shortly they would rejoin each other's company with Sven often taking her hand again.

Josephine had just stepped away to look at pottery when the hair on the back of her neck began to tingle. The vendor was showing her a finely painted pitcher, and she tried not to seem rude as she began to look over her shoulder, hoping to see the king nearby. The vendor kept talking and she tried to focus on what he was saying as she composed herself and waited for the king to reemerge. Surely being so tall, he would see where she was if she remained still. Stalling, she slowly admired other pieces in the tent, but when she reached the last table, she knew time had ran out. Where was Sven anyways, or his body guards for that matter, she wondered. With an anxious sigh, she stepped back into the street and continued on in the general direction they had been moving. Panic was setting in as she browsed alone among the next vendors when suddenly she looked across the street and with relief saw familiar faces. Josephine gathered up her skirt tail and quickly took off to cross the street where Wilhelm and four of his guardsmen were standing at the blacksmith's shop.

"My lord, Wilhelm," she said as the guards acknowledged her with a bow.

"My lady," Wilhelm answered, but seeing how pale her face was and the look of fear in her eyes he added, "What is wrong?" Stepping close enough to whisper, she told him what had happened. Josephine sensed Wilhelm acted different and she wondered if he thought she was overreacting. When she was finished, he called his men and spoke to them privately. The soldiers left the two, going in different directions as Wilhelm spoke to the lady. "Do you trust me?" He casually moved toward a display of metal works.

"Yes," Josephine replied but with a questioning tone. Wilhelm nodded his head, motioning for her to come closer and began speaking very quietly as they pretended to look at items hanging upon a rack. She was to go down the street as if continuing on with her sightseeing. There was an alley up ahead and she was to wander off into it. A peddler had set up his cart there and she was to look at his goods, keeping her back toward the street, as she was bait for the trap. Josephine felt light headed as he spoke, but she knew it was the only feasible alternative. The prince assured her he and his men would be close by, but not visible. Before the lady had time to agree to the matter, Wilhelm bid farewell and left her standing half in shock in front of the blacksmith. "No room to turn back now," she said to herself as she stepped back onto the street and done as she was instructed.

Twice before she came to the alley, the odd feeling of being watched swept over her and the last time she had to fight not to turn and look. Josephine rounded the corner into the alley and saw the lone peddler as Wilhelm had described. The weaver's tent was filled with tapestries and more fabric was draped over nearby poles with the smell of fresh dye filling the air. Suddenly, the overwhelming feeling of danger came again and the lady wanted to run, screaming for help but fought it off as her heart raced. From a distance the old peddler greeted Josephine and she returned a wave to him. The man had just stood to his feet in excitement of a customer when the lady saw a terrible look cross his face. As he gave a yell, she saw movement out the corner of her eye, and in the next moment, she was hit from the side hard enough to knock her to the ground. As she went down, she found she was more in a roll as someone had buffeted her fall. Josephine had closed her eyes at the moment of impact and kept them closed as she heard men yelling about her. With dread, she felt her assailant move, but when a familiar voice was heard, she opened her eyes.

"Are you hurt?" Wilhelm asked as he began to raise the two of them from the ground. "Josephine?" He pushed her back far enough to see her face. "Are you all right?" He was interrupted as the true assailant began to yell as the guardsmen secured his hands behind him. On the ground, a few feet away lay a large sack and rope. The peddler had cried out when he saw the man raising the sack to put it over the lady just as Wilhelm had taken her out of the way. The man continued ranting as one of the guardsmen left to find the king's soldiers and another threatened the man to mind his manners with the lady present. The mention of a gag quieted the criminal down as Wilhelm stood to his feet and helped Josephine to hers. Wilhelm motioned to move the man down the alley as he stood blocking Josephine's view of the kidnapper.

"Wilhelm," she feebly mumbled as the shock began to wear off and the reality of what almost happened sank in. Wilhelm instinctively stepped close and was reaching to take her in his arms when he checked himself and took a step backward instead.

"Are you hurt?" he asked.

"No, I don't think so," she said confused. She wished he would hold her as she felt her body beginning to shake. Suddenly she heard the voice of the king in the distance.

Before she could say anything, Wilhelm spoke, "I am sure Sven will see you safely back to the castle." Turning, he solemnly walked away only to bow toward the king as he left the alley. Josephine felt as if the very wind had been knocked out of her, and it was not from the fall. Never before had she felt such a coldness radiating toward her from Wilhelm. Yes, they had been at odds before with differences of opinion but never had he spoken to her in such a way that chilled her to the bone. It took only one glance at her pitiful state for the king to take her in his arms and apologize for his error in judgment. The kidnapper was led away and the carriage sent for as Josephine leaned hard against the king. Who was the attacker and what did he want with her? Was he a local rogue looking for an easy target or had he followed them from Gutten? On the ride back to the castle, Josephine's thoughts were troubled but Wilhelm's behavior cast the heaviest shadow of all. The king escorted Josephine to her chambers, and she tried to assure him she would be fine and that she had been through worse but the paleness of her face was not convincing. She faked a smile and teased that she was in need of a bath after rolling upon the street, but Sven was not amused, not willing to leave her. Finally, she pleaded that she desperately needed to lie down and thanked him for a lovely morning. The king promised a quiet evening during which he would make her forget all the woes of the afternoon. Reluctantly, he turned loose of her hand and bid the lady goodbye as Katrina shut the door of the chambers between them. For the second time in as many days, Josephine cried until she fell asleep.

Supper was again served in the family's private quarters but to Josephine's disappointment, she found that Saraina, her husband, and children had left, returning to their home that afternoon. The lady had hoped the princess would be staying not only for companionship at court but for any gatherings during the evenings. It would have been incredibly quiet except that Sven's sons quickly latched onto Josephine begging for more games after the meal was over. The lady was happy to oblige as again they provided the perfect retreat from adult conversation. The king and Wilhelm talked very little, and Josephine could feel tension between them but greater still she could feel an uneasiness from Wilhelm toward her. She thought of feigning illness and asking the prince to help her to her room so she could discover the root of his behavior, but she was afraid the moment she complained that the king instead would be at her side. She attempted to engage Wilhelm by challenging him to join in the board game. Although he agreed and took his turns he spoke only to the children and limited his comments to the lady. The king didn't seem to mind the quietness but rather found a perch seated behind Wilhelm on which to view Josephine's every expression without the younger man monitoring him. When the clock struck eight, Wilhelm politely excused himself and slipped away quickly. Josephine wanted to follow him but knew it would be too obvious. The king took the opportunity to move to the floor beside Josephine and selected his token to place upon the game board. Knowing that she was stuck, at least for a while, Josephine turned her attention to the game. It wasn't that the children were boring or unpleasantly rowdy, nor was the king irritating with his actions, but she would not have peace until the grievance was reconciled between her and Wilhelm. The king must have sensed her mood for he began to do little things to make her laugh, and in a matter of minutes, her mind was with the company before her. The longer the game went the more the two teased each other, much to the children's delight. The governor stepped to the door at nine, and Sven told him to return in fifteen minutes as the game was not quite finished and then bragged how he was about to win. He was promptly corrected by his sons with great protesting and laughter. Just as the gentleman came into the room the second time the last move was made and Kristoff began jumping up and down in victory as the adults applauded his efforts. The governor motioned to the children, and after good-nights and hugs were exchanged, they left the king and Josephine sitting upon the floor. The lady had begun picking up the game pieces and was reaching for the wooden box to place them inside when Sven took hold of her hands.

"Leave them," he said slowly. "Someone else can put this away. Come and sit with me?" The romantic tone in his voice made her smile. "Yes?" He rose to his feet and carefully pulled her up.

Ah, I should have known better, she thought as he did not let go of her hands but instead pulled her close to him, and then he wrapped his arms around her back.

Smiling, he began to speak again in a quiet voice. "You have not been yourself all evening," he said which caused her to lower her gaze. Suddenly she found herself reaching for the buttons on the front of his jacket, as she nervously waited for his next words. "What is troubling you, my darling?" Josephine felt a tingle at the last words, yet she did not answer him. What could she say, should she bring up the part about Wilhelm? It was all about Wilhelm's odd behavior, wasn't it? The king reached to stroke the lady's hair. "Are you upset with me for not believing you about being watched?" He tilted his head to the side and looked for a response upon her face.

"No," she replied, returning her gaze to his. "Mind you that all was rather frightening, but . . ." Her voice faltered as she searched for the right words. "But you do not know me well enough to have acted upon what I was saying." She watched as he blinked for a moment and she continued, "I would hope that if ever I mentioned . . ."

"I know better now," he interrupted "And I am sick over what happened." She could tell by the look in his eyes that it was not just words he spoke.

"But . . ." She hesitated for a moment. What if it upset Sven that her mind was upon Wilhelm while she was in fact being held in his own arms? But then how could they have any chance of developing a relationship if she were not able to come to him with every situation? "But why I have been quiet for the most part this evening . . ." Again her voice trailed off as she wanted to be held, to be assured that her relationship with Wilhelm was not in peril, assured better times were ahead with no fear of being kidnapped ever again. The king recognized that she needed comfort and took the hand that was upon her hair and gently guided her head toward his chest. The lady willingly took the suggestion and reached around his torso as she clung to him.

"Is this heaviness from a crime that I would not forgive, that you can't speak of it to me?" he whispered as he laid his chin upon the top of her head. "Tell me so I can comfort you accordingly." Josephine found herself melting into his arms. "Or is this over Wilhelm?" The last words made the lady lean back to see the king's face. "The tension between you two was thick enough to cut with a knife." Sven watched Josephine's reaction as he continued, "What has been said?"

"Nothing," she answered as she swallowed hard. "And that is the problem. Wilhelm and I have always talked freely, whether we agreed or not and the whole day he has said very little to me and acts as if I have the plague and won't come near me." Josephine's voice cracked as she felt a tear fall, but she was not prepared for the reaction that the king gave when he looked away. It was angry, yet solemn as if someone had just died. He drew a breath and then looked back into her eyes with a seriousness the lady had not seen before.

"It is my fault" he replied. Her eyebrows rose questioning. "I told you I would speak to him this morning, and I did." Again Josephine saw a flash of anger in Sven's eyes as he relived the moment in his mind. "It did not go well."

Josephine could not help but interrupt. "He did not want me to stay?" Sven shook his head and then twisted his mouth for a moment as he ran his tongue over his teeth before he composed himself.

"He, of course, questioned my motive for wanting you to stay." Again, he looked away and there was agony upon his face and something the lady guessed he chose not to describe. "He did however, fully agree that you would indeed be safer staying here until the war was over." Josephine felt almost light-headed at the thought. "But," Sven said loud and clear, "the final choice he said, would be yours to make." He had returned his gaze to the lady. "And I promised him that I would defend you with my life." He began to smile until it spread widely across his face and Josephine couldn't help but smile in return. "And that, my darling, is probably why he has acted differently toward you today." The matter of fact tone used made Josephine think the king was sure he had convinced her that his version of the meeting that morning was the truth, but the lady knew by his countenance that a great deal of the conflict that had taken place had been withheld. Although she thought most of what he said was genuine, she would feel better after she spoke to Wilhelm and heard his side of the matter. Nonetheless, it did explain the awkwardness between all parties. "Have you given any more thought to my offer?" Sven asked as he tilted his head to keep his eyes upon the lady in case she looked away. Josephine wrinkled her nose as she shrugged her shoulders and smiled.

"I am tempted." She hesitated. "I still have much to weigh in the balances."

"I would think this afternoon's events would weigh heavy on the side of remaining," the king replied.

"Yes, it does," Josephine answered slowly. "Reason's mind has been decided, but there are other matters that are still, well . . . undecided." She knew her words sounded strange but she could not say what she wanted to for she had not decided if her heart would let her leave or remain. The king reached for her hair again, but this time for a piece close to her face.

"Hmmm," he mumbled as he twirled the strand upon his finger. "Does this matter need advice?" Josephine looked at him and smiled as she knew he wanted to offer words of persuasion as to her staying. "What shall I say?" He leaned toward her until his head was gently against hers. "Stay because of me." They stood scarcely moving for a minute or so listening to the sound of each other breathing until Sven moved his hand from her hair to her chin and tilting it upward, kissed her softly upon the lips. For a moment, Josephine was overwhelmed with bliss but then as they parted and Sven rested his head against hers, she suddenly felt guilty. It was like a cold, cruel slap after such a tender moment, a moment that she had been anticipating for several days. Why should there be bitterness when she felt she was falling in love with the king? "I have not offended you, my darling?" Sven whispered.

"No," she replied quietly, her hands still clutching his jacket. Perhaps, she was just confused after the happenings of the day. Maybe her inexperience in matters of love was playing tricks upon her mind, thinking that a kiss was wrong. Why should she feel guilty to kiss him, especially after he had been so romantic and chivalrous and was doing a fine job of sweeping her off her feet? After all, she was not bound to any man and could see whom she pleased and travel anywhere including returning home to Frive of her own accord. She was still debating within herself when Sven began stroking her hair.

"What is it that you are thinking, dearest Josephine?" At his words, the lady looked up at him. "Your forehead is wrinkling up," he teased and began to run his fingers across her brow as if trying to wipe away her troubling thoughts. She had just drew a breath and sighed when he leaned toward her and embraced her again. This time as their lips parted he began to kiss her cheek and then her temple and finally her forehead before he stopped. Somewhere along the way, Josephine thought she was going to be ill as her heart began to anxiously race. They stood there again, this time with the king holding on to the lady more than she to him. She tried to calm herself and regain her composure. She certainly did not find the king revolting, yet she found herself very uncomfortable, and it was not that she was afraid of him or even the embrace itself, yet she felt like something was wrong. The king sensed her sudden change of demeanor. "Are we moving too quickly?" he whispered, still holding her close.

Josephine managed to shake her head. "This has nothing to do with you," she replied. She wanted to look at the man but could only manage to lean her head against his chest. "It is me, only me." She felt him squeeze her gently.

"Do you not want me to hold you, to kiss you?" he asked, nuzzling his face toward hers until he could feel her skin against his again.

"I thought I did," she said as she felt tears welling up. "I like you so very much, Sven." She searched for words. "Yet I feel such guilt right now that I can hardly bear it." Josephine's voice broke up as she swallowed hard and reached to wipe a falling tear. Suddenly the king drew a deep breath as what he had suspected that morning became very clear to him.

"I was told that you are not betrothed nor promised to another man, is that true?" he asked, and Josephine looked up at him.

"Yes," she answered. The agony upon her face was great, and Sven wanted to embrace her again to dismiss the apprehension yet he knew they both needed answers.

"But is your heart free to love me?" The question seemed simple yet suddenly very complicated. She was a free woman, free to her own bidding, making her own decisions, she was bound to no one, no man laid claim upon her future. Suddenly Wilhelm's words came to Josephine's mind. "I will not leave you nor will I forsake you." He had been encouraging her from the Holy Scriptures when he rescued her from the well, but had he not repeated that promise to her time and time again? Had he not risked his life so many times for her safety? Did he not go out of his way so many times for her to be comfortable, to do little things she liked even when it inconvenienced him? Had they not spent day and night together resolving matters of state, giving counsel to one another even when they did not agree? Did they not vow to reconcile before parting ways because their conscience could not bear it otherwise? How many times had they walked arm in arm through the castle discussing plans in future times as if they would always be together? Her conscience smote her as she recalled how many times they had fallen asleep against each other on long carriage rides and reading together on the couch in the library. Had he not been her closest friend, never leaving her in times of need? Even that afternoon in the town, he had believed her words and then rescued her. Her mind raced to the times he told her goodbye as he left for battle, had he not kissed her so tenderly upon her forehead or her cheek? Did not her heart ache terribly for his return and had he not promised her that things would not always be this way? Was the teasing about marriage for his mother's sake not a jest to him? Had she been blind to the fact that their friendship had grown into more? Suddenly Josephine had to know what Wilhelm thought about her staying and what his feelings were toward her. The look in the lady's eyes was not one the king had wanted to see.

"I have so many questions that need answers, Sven." She swallowed hard and continued, "My heart is . . ." She looked away for a moment and then summoning her courage looked him in the eye. "My heart is toward another man." She paused trying to compose herself. "And until I know for sure that his heart is not toward me . . ." Her voice broke up. "Please." She leaned her head against his chest again seeking comfort and strength. "Please don't woo me until I know for certain his intentions. My heart cannot bear unfaithfulness and I hope you will understand. Please."

The king led the lady to a couch to sit. Sven's heart ached and he wanted to convince Josephine that he was the man she needed and yet he knew if he did the lady would always wonder if she had made the right decision. He knew perfectly well who she spoke of as the confrontation that morning had given him the first half of the riddle. Wilhelm had made it clear that he was quite aware of the king's interests in Josephine's well-being and although he praised him as a worthy candidate for the lady, he had no intention of letting the woman he cared about so deeply not make the decision of her own accord. The king's reply was an outright threat that if the young man did not marry her within six months, he would personally come to Guttenhamm with his whole army and bring her back to Merhausen. Sven reminded Wilhelm that he knew the pain of losing someone you love so dearly, and he was not going to let Josephine slip through his fingers, nor would he allow her to suffer more pain as she had described. He agreed the decision would be the lady's and hers alone, but reiterated that if she returned the prince had six months and he was a man of his word. There was no doubt in Sven's mind that Josephine thought she loved Wilhelm, but yet she must have felt something for him more than just friendship or she would not have allowed herself to be in his arms. He wondered how strong his sway was with her? Could he convince Josephine to stay for safety's sake and hope her passion for Wilhelm waned? Would she despise him for trying to detain her? He would have to move her into an avenue of business affairs to satisfy her passion for she would never be content just being beside him as her sole duty. The evening definitely had not gone as he had hoped as far as making up for the lousy afternoon. One thing he knew for certain, she was still open to his presence, his words and his arms, even if the door to her heart was partially shut, and he was in no hurry to let go of her whether it be that evening or forever. They had sat for quite a while when the king finally spoke.

"I must tell you something." He stood to his feet and walked across the room, then returned and knelt in front of the lady. "Words were exchanged this morning between Wilhelm and I concerning you." He lowered his gaze to the floor. Josephine saw anger upon his face once more, but he closed his eyes for a moment, then opened them to look at her. "I have already fallen in love with you, Josephine, and I am not ashamed to say it." The lady's mouth fell open in wonder. "I threatened Wilhelm that if you are not wed within six months that I am coming for you." Josephine began to shake her head in disbelief as the king took her hands in his and continued, "I will bring you back here and marry you and not Wilhelm or any other man will take you from me. I am not just speaking idle words, my darling, for I am serious. I will not let another woman that I love slip from me without a fight. Wilhelm was not pleased with what I said, but I am not pleased with the thought of never holding you in my arms again." As he said the last words, Josephine saw that his anger had turned into tears.

"I am so sorry, Sven. I truly care for you, just . . ." she replied as she reached to touch his face. She began to stroke his beard.

"I know you care for me and I ache to persuade you, yet it would not be right, as Wilhelm said the choice has to be yours." Realizing he may not be able to control his feelings toward the lady if they remained together, the king stood to his feet and offered a hand for her to rise. Without a word, they made their way out of the room and walked arm in arm through the hallway till they were at the lady's chamber door. The king said good night and leaned to kiss Josephine upon her cheek. Tingles ran down her spine as feelings were kindled again while the king lingered only inches from Josephine's face. "Sleep well," he whispered. How could her heart be so cruel to her, Josephine wondered. Finally, after what seemed like minutes, the lady was able to speak.

"Good night, Sven, and thank you for your patience with me." Her voice cracked and realizing she was about to lose her composure yet one more time that night, she pulled herself away and quickly retreated into her chambers without looking back.

It took quite a while for Katrina to get more than sobbing from Josephine, but eventually words came with sadness. Did Wilhelm care for her as she did for him or was her hope amiss? Finally, Katrina convinced the lady that she was wasting her time worrying when the prince was down the hall and she could go to him and pour out her soul; Wilhelm had never turned her away before and would not now. Josephine even tried to reason with her maid saying the guardsmen may have already turned in for the night as it was about eleven, but Katrina kept after Josephine to go, even if it meant waking them as the matter could not wait till morning. Pulling herself together the best she could, Josephine washed her face and brushed her hair but left it down as it was much too late to fuss with such things. As the lady nervously knocked upon the chamber doors, it seemed the sound echoed loudly through the hallway. Alexander came to the door.

"My lady, something must be wrong to bring you out at this hour. Please," he said as he motioned. "Come inside and tell me what it is." The guardsman could see the lady was terribly pale save her nose being red from crying.

"I hope I have not awoken anyone," she mumbled. "I am sorry to bother . . . I . . ."

"Do not worry, my lady, we have not yet retired and were discussing our departure tomorrow morning. Please, tell me what brings you here."

"I need to speak with the prince," she answered, staring at the floor.

"Let me tell him you are here," he said as he quickly moved from the small sitting room and passed through a doorway into what Josephine assumed were bedchambers. As she looked around the room, she saw bedding upon the couches. Wilhelm had mentioned that although they had been given several rooms, the men refused to split up with part of them remaining with the prince at night for security purposes. As the minutes passed, Josephine began to wonder if Wilhelm was not willing to see her. She could faintly hear voices, and finally Alexander reemerged and bid her to follow him. The other men rose to their feet and nodded as they saw the lady. The right wall was flanked by several large windows and at the farthest one Wilhelm stood with his back to the room. He turned for a moment to greet Josephine but quickly turned again and began to move the curtain as if looking out into the night.

"What is it that you needed, my lady?" Josephine knew by the tone of his voice that he did not want to speak with her but was merely being civil. She had only taken a few steps before she stopped.

Taking a deep breath, she took a few more steps and answered, "I needed to speak with you, privately."

The prince did not move as he replied, "There is nothing that my men cannot hear." The words stung badly as she felt her heart seem to skip a beat. She could not bear Wilhelm being upset with her, and worse she had to have answers or she would be driven mad. As much as she wished they were alone, it would have to do that the others were present.

"If that is what you want, then I will continue." She hesitated, hoping for a reaction to her comment, but when there was none, she began walking closer until she was directly behind him. "Sven has said that you agree that I would be safer remaining in Merhausen than returning to Guttenhamm. Is this true?" she asked.

"Yes, you would be kept from seeing the suffering and wounded and hearing reports day by day of the battles. You would not run the risk of being captured on the journey back." He paused a moment as he let the curtain that he held in his hand fall back to its place. "I would not worry for your safety and he has sworn to protect you, whatever the cost, and I believe this to be true."

"He has said the decision would be mine to make," the lady said quietly.

"Yes, it is." Still the prince remained with his back to the woman. Josephine heard someone shift across the room but turned her attention back to her next question.

"The king has also told me that if I returned to Guttenhamm and was not wed within six months that he would come and bring me back here . . . to be his wife," Josephine said as a tear slid down her cheek. Her words had barely left her lips when Wilhelm abruptly turned to face her, his eyes full of anger.

"And I told him, only over my dead body would he take you from me!" he exclaimed. It took but one glance at the frail, shaking woman standing before him for Wilhelm to reach to steady her. The emotion with which he had spoken should have frightened the lady but instead the relief of his words gave her strength. Wilhelm wanted to embrace her yet he held back as nothing said had convinced him that the situation was any different than the king had spoken of that morning. If Josephine remained under the vice of safety, it would be a short time until she had fallen completely in love with Sven. If she returned to Guttenhamm and things drug on with the war and Wilhelm did not marry her in time, then the king would be waiting to snatch the lady at the first opportunity. The prince caught his hand reaching to wipe her tears but quickly pulled it back to his side clenching it into a fist as he did. He did not move fast enough as Josephine caught sight of his action and reached for the pleats of his shirt as she drew bolder and stepped closer.

"Will you not take me home?" she pleaded, looking into his eyes. For a moment, it was as if the world stopped and all grew quiet. Did he hear her correctly? Was she asking to go home?

He raised an eyebrow as he spoke, "Home to Frive?" Not being able to resist any longer, he reached for the tear that was still upon her cheek and Josephine closed her eyes as his hand touched her face and gently shook her head.

"No," she said, "to *our* home in Guttenhamm." She had opened her eyes to see his reaction as his eyebrows knit together in anticipation, and she thought she could see him almost smile.

But he set his chin and whispered, "Are you certain this is what you want?"

"Yes," she replied, and before she could say another word, Wilhelm pulled her close and kissed her ever so tenderly. They stood together several minutes with his head against hers, and occasionally he moved to gently kiss her temple as they clung to each other with relief. The decision had revealed that there was more to their relationship than either had realized before. Their solitude was interrupted when Alexander cleared his throat from across the room.

"I am sorry to interrupt my liege, but it is nearly midnight and since we are *all* going home tomorrow, I would think more of this might be in order . . . at a more convenient time." At which the other guardsmen broke into laughter and applause.

28

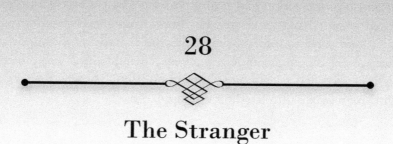

The Stranger

"Wilhelm, I wish to speak with you," Josephine said as she came through the doorway.

"Likewise," the prince replied, turning as he motioned the lady toward a chair. She started to sit down but hesitated and then bravely blurted out.

"You intend to leave for Danburout in the morning, don't you?" Sensing the tension, Wilhelm strode toward the window and without looking back in her direction quietly affirmed as he knew an argument was about to commence. "I want to accompany you," she said, following him across the room. He assumed the conversation would be about the battle, but was not expecting her to request to go along after the last few outings had resulted in bloodshed. "You know how much help I am to Dr. Stehle, but even if I am not with the medical unit, I can help in other ways."

"I cannot allow you to go with us this time." He kept his back to the lady hoping to avoid seeing her face as she pleaded, but persistent she took hold of his arm and began again.

"How many times have I helped weigh the balances toward life while waiting for the doctor and comforting those who were slipping into eternity and now you are telling me I cannot go with you?"

"No, Josephine," Wilhelm answered, raising his voice. "This is not open for discussion. Absolutely no!" The prince did not regard the harshness in his voice as thoughts flooded his mind of the messenger's words that afternoon.

"I do not understand you, Wilhelm!" Josephine cried out in dismay. "We finally have enough reinforcements that I will be safe this time and you are saying no." The prince turned and looked the lady square in the eye.

"No, you do not understand!" The seriousness of his countenance caused Josephine to take a step back. Wilhelm firmly took hold of her arms, pulling her closer to him. Swallowing hard, he searched for the right words. Hearing the loud voices, the king had hurried to the room but neither of them realized he was there, being caught up in the moment. The scene was concerning and he was about to part the quarrelers when Wilhelm began to talk in a quieter but stern voice. "For your safety, I cannot allow you to go to Danburout."

"I am not afraid of the . . ."

"Wait," Wilhelm said, giving the lady a gentle shake. "Let me finish." The painful look upon his face made the lady cringe. "Our spies returned this afternoon with a rumor. Maximillian is searching for a prize, one that he will pay dearly for." Wilhelm looked away, dreading to finish. He took a deep breath and looked back into Josephine's eyes. "He wants his future bride to be returned to him." As he uttered the words, his voice faltered and he tilted his head, raising his eyebrow to hint what was truly meant. It took a moment but suddenly the lady began to understand that she was the answer to so many questions over the past few months. A chill ran over her body as the woman turned ghostly pale. Her color quickly returned as the very thought of being any man's prize angered her. Before she could say anything, Wilhelm pulled her so close that she could feel his breath upon her face as he whispered. "I will *not* allow you to go." She started to move, but quickly he took hold of her chin and lifted it, letting him gaze into her eyes. "I will not give him an opportunity to steal you away. Please, Josephine . . ." His voice wavered. "Please do not argue with me and do as I ask this time." He leaned until his forehead touched hers and both closed their eyes. "I could not bear it if something happened to you . . . Surely you know that." Josephine leaned against him and whispered that she would do as he said. Across the room, the king sighed with relief. Hearing Karl call for him from the hallway, Hubert began to leave the room but as he did the floor creaked. Wilhelm looked toward him and was given an apologetic wave as his father left the two alone. Wilhelm released Josephine from the embrace but kept hold of the lady's hands. "Will you see me off in the morning?" Josephine's gaze fell to the floor as she struggled with the thought of him leaving for battle. "Josephine . . ." When she looked at him, her eyes were full of tears. "You cannot let your mind wander to the worst, we have discussed this before."

As a tear slid down her cheek, she answered him, "Yes, I know. What time are you leaving?"

Six days passed with the only word from the field being that the enemy had retreated to Aikerlan. It was agreed that Josephine would be allowed to go into Guttenhamm but with two escorts staying with her at all times. Word had been sent that the princes would be returning the next day permitting no new skirmishes erupted. The day of their expected return seemed to be the longest day ever to Josephine and about midafternoon the lady found herself anxiously pacing. Just before dusk, the trumpets were heard and Josephine thought her heart would explode with joy as she met the queen, and together they hurried down the hallway toward the grand staircase. The king had already arrived and was waiting in the foyer as the doors were opened and a dozen soldiers, clad in armor, came inside as well as several councilmen who had come from the town. Greetings were exchanged and laughter could be heard which set the ladies' hearts at ease.

The king motioned the men toward the great hall, but one soldier stopped and turning to the king said, "I will join you shortly father, but there is another matter . . ." and not waiting for a response, Wilhelm swiftly began to climb the stairs. Stopping just short of the top step, his eyes met Josephine's. She gave a wide smile and reached for his hands.

"Are you—"

But before she could finish, he interrupted her, "I am well." And before she knew what had happened, he leaned forward and kissed her on the lips. Voices mingled with laughter was heard from the men still standing below in the foyer. As the pair parted Josephine blushed, but Wilhelm did not let go of her hands just yet. Glancing toward his mother, he greeted her and asked for a hot bath to be ready for him and his brother and then asked Josephine for a favor.

"I have business to finish with Father, but then will you remain with me the rest of the evening? Can that be arranged?" he asked and smiling Josephine agreed. Once more he leaned and kissed the lady on the forehead and then excused himself.

Only two days passed before news arrived that Aikerlan's troops were seen crossing the river and moving south into Gutten. King Hubert sent word for the evacuation of villages in their path and orders were given for the guard to do what was needed to defend the people while trying not to engage the enemy. The sun arose through misty fog the next morning as the princes prepared to leave for battle. Agatha met her sons in the hallway upstairs to bid them farewell and after clinging to their necks she motioned them toward the staircase where their father was waiting for them. Together, they walked outside where a small band of soldiers was assembled awaiting the captains. As the king greeted his men, horses were brought forward. Wilhelm didn't hear the soft-spoken words of the page but he did instantly recognize the small delicate fingers that placed the horses' reins into his hand.

He leaned toward the page and whispered, "I thought we said our goodbyes last night."

"We did," Josephine answered, tilting her head upward to peer at Wilhelm from under her hood. "Forgive me, but I could not let you go without seeing you one more time." She half expected a rebuke for disobeying his request to remain upstairs to avoid her becoming emotional as she had the night before. Although her presence had gone virtually unnoticed by most, the hesitation of the prince to mount his steed had drawn the attention of his brother.

"I guess the page is getting a few words," Leopold commented to his father with amusement as he thought Wilhelm was not satisfied with something the young man had done. He motioned toward the pair who stood a few yards away. Wilhelm's actions had also caught the attention of the king but it had only taken him a split second to recognize Josephine's silhouette which was now overshadowed by Wilhelm. Leopold took the reins of his horse from the stable master, and as he was mounting, his father said with a hearty laugh.

"Well, this is the first time I have seen your brother *kiss* a page." Quickly Leopold turned his horse just in time to see his brother plant a kiss on a pale cheek that could barely be seen emerging from the dark hood and feeling everyone's eyes upon him his ears turned red from embarrassment. As if to answer the looming question hanging in the air, Wilhelm pulled back Josephine's hood to reveal her identity. Although his thoughts had strayed but a moment, his gaze had not left the lady's and he could feel a lump in his throat as his emotions now rose up. He desperately wanted to say more to her, but before he could speak, she did.

"I have delayed you long enough, captain. Godspeed." And with an unexpected lunge, Josephine tip-toed and kissed him on the cheek and then quickly stepped away. Wilhelm's next thought was to follow her, but his father stepped in between them blocking his path.

"Have a good journey, my son." Wilhelm gave the king a nod and mounted his horse. He called the soldiers into formation and turned to salute his father. As they began to ride, he could not help but steal one last glance at the porch where he saw his father standing with his arm around Josephine's shoulders.

The next week seemed to pass slowly and wore away at Josephine's morale. Wilhelm had made the lady promise to keep to her rounds within Guttenhamm hoping not only to keep the lady's mind occupied but to encourage the people by seeing her in their midst. The villagers seemed in fair spirits considering the kingdom was on the eve of war, but Josephine knew it weighed heavily upon their minds as well as hers. She had come to rely on conversation at suppertime at the castle as the high point of her day but that too had dwindled and the growing silence gnawed at her. She wondered if news had come that the king thought too disturbing to share with the womenfolk but she quickly dismissed the notion for council members would be called to the king if a battle had commenced. She knew in her heart that patience was the only salve for the restlessness.

The dawn of the twelfth morning came with no news from the field concerning contact with the enemy. Even before Josephine had finished eating breakfast, she was dreading starting her rounds, but she feared the idleness of remaining at the castle worse. She called for her horse and within a few minutes her and the two escorts were starting down the gentle slope to the village. As usual, greetings were exchanged as she passed the townspeople and she began to rehearse her appointments in her head. First visit was the smithy, but her heart sank as she remembered the eldest son had joined the guard and was stationed in Dahn for weaponry repairs. The thought of answering the people's questions bothered the lady for she had run out of things to say days ago. "Any word from the field, my lady? How goes the battle? Has there been a call for reinforcements? How long before the soldiers can come home, my lady?" echoed in Josephine's mind, and she almost wished she could remind them that she was as anxious as they were for news, after all, the princes were on the frontline and she too worried for their safety. Somehow, she had managed to stay calm and not spout out a rebuke but more often than not she was irritated, wishing to have normal conversation about anything but the war. Another point of frustration was the matter of having escorts with her at all times. She knew it was necessary but she still found it stifling and a great hindrance to her work. The soldiers done their best to give the lady as much space as they could while still keeping watch and often remained outside an establishment instead of following Josephine inside. They felt the capital was safe enough to warrant such liberty with the garrison being at the outskirts of the town and anything odd would be dealt with quickly.

Josephine had just finished her second visit that morning when she noticed two men lurking in an alleyway. It seemed that as she walked past they pointed as if speaking about her, and she almost went back to take another look at them but then she rebuked herself for being paranoid and went on down the street. After the fourth visit, she again noticed the same two men across the street staring at her. Although they were leaning against a hitching post, she could see they both were very tall with wide, strong shoulders. Their dark eyes stared at her from under heavy eyebrows and their wide chins seemed set on mischief. Quickly she glanced in the direction she had come from and saw her escorts waiting patiently with the horses and drew a breath of relief. The lady went on with her duties, but with every business she left, it seemed the two strangers were watching her from across the street. It was now midmorning, and wagons were going to and fro with enough noise that a mere conversation could not be heard, but having enough of being watched, she made her way across the street to confront the men.

"Why are you following me?" Josephine demanded as she approached the strangers. Now only a few arms lengths away, the men seemed more ominous, towering above her. The men were poised at the corner of a narrow street, and the lady realized her mistake when with a quickness that rendered her helpless they took hold of her and pulled her along with them. A large cart was being driven past and any attempt the lady made to scream was muffled in the commotion as help was obstructed from view.

"Yes, she's the one," the older man said in a low voice.

The two continued to drag the lady down the alley-like street as Josephine shrieked, "Let loose of me this instant. I am Lady—"

Before she could say her name the older man interrupted, "We know who you are and the price on your head is worth more than we could earn in a lifetime."

"Price, what price?" she asked, struggling against the men. They had stopped at the back of a house at the end of the street and were looking left and right as if trying to decide which direction to take their precious cargo.

"A treasure worth more than a kingdom," the younger man muttered as he took hold of both of the lady's arms as the older man motioned toward the shadows of the building to their right.

"I only have to scream and you both will be led to the gallows. Let me go *now* and I will ask for mercy on your behalf."

"Go ahead and scream if you think those guards of yours will hear you. As if they could raise a hair on our heads," the man chided causing Josephine to wonder where the guards were. Hadn't they noticed she had been abducted or did they think she had merely gone inside the next establishment? With her mind upon the absent guards, she hadn't noticed the younger man was looking at her in a strange way. Suddenly she was aware he was leaning toward her. He whispered about stealing a kiss to which Josephine warned him through gritted teeth not to do it. Ignoring her he moved toward her but she lunged back to prevent him. Angry with her reaction, he shoved the lady causing her head to violently hit the wall of the house. Suddenly she could feel the man's hands loosen upon her arms as he was pulled from the shadows and into the daylight. Weak with fear, Josephine watched as another man clad in a hooded cape assaulted her kidnapper, rendering him unconscious. The older man tried to draw a sword, but he too was struck several times and fell moaning to the ground face first.

"Come. Let's get out of here before they are able to stop us," her rescuer said in French as he reached for the lady's arm. They took the street going to the left and had gone a ways before the man hesitated. Footsteps could be heard, and after looking around, the stranger opened the door of a nearby shed and motioned Josephine inside, closing the door quietly behind them. After taking only a few steps Josephine bumped into what she thought was cured hams suspended from the ceiling. She turned around to face the door and had taken a step back in that direction when the hooded man took hold of her. "Stand still or we will be found out." With reluctance, she came to a halt and held her breath hoping to calm her nerves as she stared at the sliver of light coming from the edges of the doorway. Suddenly she heard the loud voices of her kidnappers which sent a shiver over her body causing her to close her eyes tightly. The man beside her must have felt her tremble for he softened the grip upon her arms and held her gently. Outside the shed movement was heard and then the men turned and went back the other direction. Josephine sighed with relief and opened her eyes. The hooded man released the lady's arms and cautiously opened the door of the shed and when he had looked in both directions stepped outside.

"Are you going to wait for them to return?" he whispered, offering the lady his hand. Without hesitation, she took it and he began to lead her down the street. At the sound of deep voices in the distance, the pair ducked into the shadows of a covered porch to hide. To the lady's surprise, her rescuer began to whisper, "What is her ladyship doing out alone upon the streets in such perilous times?" Josephine gave a hard look at the man who was now leaning to see past the corner post of the porch. She wished she could see his face better, but her efforts were in vain as he turned his head back toward her waiting for a response to his question.

"I am not alone. And honestly I do not care for hiding, let those men try their luck again and my guards will make quick work of them. And—"

She was interrupted by the man's agitated whisper. "You call those guards?" He motioned toward the main street. "Do they even know you were in harm's way? I think not!" Josephine had not realized that the man still had her hand in his until he pulled her closer to him. "They do not even know you are gone—stolen before their very eyes." The urgency in his voice sent another wave of fear over the lady, but in a totally different manner. Who was this man that had rescued her? His statement made her realize how easy kidnapping her would be, and easy for him still yet. She shook her hand free from his and took a step away.

"I thank you for your help, sir." For a moment, she hesitated. "I must rejoin my party as I know they will be wondering where I have been." Josephine turned and almost in a run went toward the street which was just a few buildings away. As she stepped into full view, the guards rushed to her side, and before much could be said, she declared it was time to return home and asked for her horse to be brought. A few nervous moments passed until the animal was at her side and then to her surprise, so was the hooded man. As he approached the lady, the guardsman started toward him in her defense, but Josephine spoke up assuring the man was a friend at which the soldier let him remain and stepped away to give the pair some privacy. The lady thanked the stranger again for assisting her that afternoon although an uneasiness of the man had fallen upon her thoughts. Josephine asked him for his name to repay him for his help, but he just shook his head and without a word, he moved beside the lady's horse, taking hold of the bridle and waited to help her up into the saddle. Even with his suspicious behavior, she allowed the man to come close hoping again to see his face. She reached for the saddle horn and had just placed her foot into the stirrup when he caught hold of her.

"The prince was unwise to leave you alone."

"You dare to criticize the crown."

"If it needs to be said."

"Then your allegiance does not lie with Gutten or you would mind your tongue," she snapped.

"I know where my loyalty lies," he replied.

"And where is that?" she asked.

"It is keeping you safe, and others apparently do not seem to share the same responsibility or you would not have been in harm's way."

"The guardsmen would give their lives to protect me."

"And yet here I am at your side instead of them. As I said, the prince should not have left you alone," he said boldly and then almost effortlessly hoisted her up into the saddle with a jolt. The suddenness of his actions following such a blunt statement caught the lady off guard and it took a few seconds for Josephine to settle in, but she turned in his direction to address his accusation.

"I told you, I am not . . . alone." Her voice drifted off as she looked around and saw the hooded man was making his way through the street. Something was definitely strange about him, and Wilhelm needed to be told immediately. Her heart fell as she remembered that her confidant would not be waiting for her that evening. With a disappointing sigh, she nudged her horse on toward the castle.

After supper, Josephine retreated to the library hoping to calm her nerves. Oddly, she was grateful the evening had been dull and uneventful for she was rattled over her morning and was still trying to think of a way to mention it to the king. She had just sat down when Hubert and Agatha came into the room and presented the young lady with a letter from Wilhelm.

Father,

We have arrived safely. Do not be alarmed at the infrequency of my correspondence, but I will only write when there is something worthy to report. We have seen a few skirmishes but nothing to speak of with only minor injuries and the enemy has been quick to surrender to our forces. Things are not how I thought they would be, better on our part but yet still strange as to how and if a battle is being planned. I am perplexed as it seems something more is underlying in this matter. Please send word if there have been any changes concerning our enemy as it may seem insignificant but may be the key to this mystery. Yours truly, Wilhelm

P. S. Neither I nor Leopold have a scratch upon us but are missing the comforts of home.

Josephine smiled as she let the parchment fall upon her knees. Although the letter brought comfort, her thoughts were overshadowed by the events earlier in the day with questions looming in her mind.

"Hubert, may I speak with you privately?" she asked as she stood to her feet. The solemn look upon the lady's face brought the king to her side and nodding he held out his arm for her to take. They walked together into the hall and to her surprise he led her to Wilhelm's chamber door. She hesitated, but then took the knob and opened the door going immediately to the fireplace where she had often stood when she and the prince had discussed serious matters together. Patiently Hubert waited at the door and when Josephine had found the courage she came back to his side and began to tell of her encounter in the village. "What do you think?" Josephine asked as she finished the tale.

"Very intriguing," the king said as he now strode to the fire-place, stroking his beard as he began to pace. "It does not comfort me to know the men were bold enough to take you in daylight in the very streets of Guttenhamm." He paused and then turned toward the lady who was now standing beside the divan. "But the other man concerns me equally as well."

"I fully agree," Josephine answered, fighting the tears that had been welling up. "And for him to remind me how alone I really was and openly criticizing Wilhelm."

"Yes," Hubert replied. "We need to know more about this man. But do you think the kidnapping was just a muse for him to get close to you—to deliver a message that our enemy knows more than we thought?" Josephine had wondered the same all afternoon, and she had rehearsed the man's words over and over again. When the lady did not reply, the king began to pace again and then asked another question. "You said you did not see his face?" He watched the young lady who was deep in thought.

"No, I didn't, but, well, this may sound strange, but I recognized him." She stuttered for a moment and then continued, "Well, there was something about him that was familiar. I have spent the whole afternoon trying to place what it was about him, it's as if we have met before." The statement brought the king to an abrupt halt.

"Something familiar would change everything. If we confided in him, he would know how to get close to you, and his motives may not even involve the war." Hubert began to pace again. A few minutes passed and then he stopped. "I have to ask you not to return to the village unless you have several guardsmen, at least half a dozen with you. No." He walked to the young lady and took her hands in his and earnestly pleaded. "I would rather that you stay here until I know for certain this sort of thing will not happen again." When Wilhelm had requested she remain in the castle, an argument had always followed, but under the current circumstances, Josephine nodded her head and then burst into tears. Hubert pulled the young lady to him and she laid her head upon his chest sobbing. He knew although the incident was troubling, her tears were more from missing Wilhelm.

Several minutes passed before Josephine raised her head and started to apologize, but the king wouldn't hear of it.

"You are no bother to me, my dear. I have considered you as my own child ever since you arrived and I would be upset if you hadn't come to me." With a father's manner, he ushered Josephine to her room and kissing her forehead the king bid her a restful night and assured her the matter would be looked into more the next morning. With her conscience released from worry, the young lady quickly fell asleep.

The first few hours, Josephine rested well, but then dreams began to trouble her slumber. Several times she awoke shaking with fright, recalling the events in Guttenhamm. When she next drifted off, she began to relive the near abduction in Andervan and the man at the river and awoke with a gasp. Giving over to exhaustion, she fell back asleep and seemed to settle down peacefully. Another hour passed before she began to dream, but this time, it was different. In the distance, she could hear a man's deep voice telling her not to be alarmed and that she was safe. She drew a long, deep breath at his words and would have stirred except that he bid her to rest, and she felt a reassuring hand rest upon her arm. A warm finger began to trace the outline of her jaw, and she felt him stroke her hair. Carefully he lifted a strand and let it fall to her shoulder as he spoke again.

"Our new home is ready and overlooks the orchards I showed you so long ago." Josephine welcomed the soothing sound of his voice, and it seemed to grow quieter yet it drew near. She could feel the man's breath upon her face as he whispered, "A few more days and I will rescue you from this wretched place. I will return for you, my darling." Josephine's mind latched onto his words becoming more alert but so tired was her body that she only managed to moan softly. Suddenly she felt warm lips press against her cheek in a long embrace and as if fighting against her own self, she screamed inside to wake up. Who was kissing her? Frantically she sat up in bed, pushing the blankets back away, gasping with her heart racing. She could see no one in the room, but was too afraid to lie back down. Without wasting any time, she dropped her legs over the edge of the bed and fumbled for her slippers. As she stood to her feet, she felt a bit dizzy and wondered if she had a fever as her head seemed warm. She slipped on her robe and decided not to call for Katrina for all she could think about was getting to Agatha, knowing the queen would hold her close and tell her the dreams would pass. By the time Josephine made it to the junction of the hallways, she had grown unsteady and knocked feebly on the chamber doors. The servant, who stayed at the king's door during the night, opened to the lady, and instantly knew something was not right. He helped the lady to a chair and then went to wake the king and queen. When they returned, Josephine rose to her feet and started to speak but suddenly stopped and reached for her head as she faltered and fell back into the chair. It took a few moments for the lady to recover, and Agatha tried to look for signs of illness but the lady was not with fever.

Josephine opened her eyes and smiling whispered, "I am so thankful I am with you both and not someone else." The strange words caused Agatha to look at her husband for an explanation, but Josephine spoke again, "I have had the most alarming dreams tonight." The king delicately asked if they had anything to do with what she mentioned to him earlier in the evening. "Yes, but the last dream was not the same at all." Feeling safe among her friends, Josephine began to admit it could not have been real and apologized if she gave them a fright, dismissing her near fainting to not sleeping well with the war weighing upon her mind. "I should not have bothered you. If I had just stayed in bed, I would have been fine. It's just my mind playing tricks on me, I am sure. I will go and leave you alone. "

"Nonsense," Agatha said, patting the young lady's hand. Knowing how strong the lady had been under pressure, the king was not convinced it was merely Josephine's imagination. Her account of the near abduction in Guttenhamm had plagued his thoughts the rest of the evening. He was convinced the enemy was using the supposed battle as a diversion while the real plot was unfolding elsewhere.

"Tell me what your dream was about," he asked. With Agatha clinging to her hand, the lady began to describe every detail she could remember. The queen was shocked by Josephine's vivid words, turning pale and shifting nervously as she could see how concerned her husband was. The look upon his face spoke a thousand words and its graveness was as if one of his sons were dying before him. "I need to step out for a moment. Stay here please." He was afraid to say more, hoping that his fears were unfounded. As he stepped into the hallway, he called for the guards to accompany him with swords drawn. When they came to the chamber door, they expected to find it wide open but instead it was shut. Carefully opening the door, they stepped inside and saw no one but began to look the room over. Hubert's heart skipped a beat as he drew near the bed and found upon the pillow a flower and a small piece of parchment. Before he even reached for the paper, he cried out, "Secure the castle!" The guards took off toward the door. "Someone is inside. Call for more men and be sure the ladies are well guarded. Quickly now!" It took only a few minutes for a half dozen more soldiers to make their way upstairs, and the commotion that followed could be heard even inside the royal chambers. Karl and several of the menservants joined the king in Josephine's chambers and asked what had happened. Still in shock, it took a moment for Hubert to explain what he knew but then added that the castle needed to be searched and the intruder found. Finally, he picked up the parchment and took it closer to the lamp to read it. His stomach turned with disgust, and he felt his temper rising.

I will return for you my love.

At the bottom of the parchment made from the wax of the very candle he was reading by was the imprint of Maximillian's signet ring.

Never before had the queen seen such a display as when the four soldiers burst into her chambers and began to position themselves to secure the windows and balcony. By that point, Josephine's thinking had cleared and she knew that it had not been a dream.

"What are you saying?" the queen asked immediately going to her husband's side when he returned. He took his wife in his arms but looked toward the young lady who was still seated.

"Someone *was* in her room and the castle will be turned inside out until he is found." Josephine lowered her head into her hands to cover her face.

"How do you know for sure?" Agatha asked, shaking her head in disbelief.

"He left something behind." Josephine felt the life leaving her body again as she mumbled and fainted back into the chair. This time when she came to, she was quite upset and began to sob. Hubert was not sure which lady was more upset as his wife became frantic over the whole incident. Finally, he persuaded the ladies to lie down to rest under the watchful eye of the guard. The search continued through the night but turned up no one and worse, no sign of entry or exit.

Morning came with more surprises as about ten o'clock trumpets were sounded to announce the princes were seen coming from the village. Whether from exhaustion or negligence, neither of the young men noticed extra soldiers stationed at the castle as they drug their weary bodies into the foyer. What did catch their attention was that no one came to meet them downstairs, and when they cleared the top of the staircase, they could see people gathered near the library doors. Leopold and Wilhelm exchanged glances and quickened their pace.

"Karl . . ." Wilhelm said and the butler turned and looked at him in surprise.

"My lords, we were not expecting your return." The hesitation in the older man's voice was not normal.

"May I ask what is going on?" And before Wilhelm could finish, Karl suggested that they speak with the king immediately and he went to find him. The princes had never seen everyone so strangely quiet as they waited. After what seemed like forever, they saw their father slowly ascending the grand staircase and coming toward them. Very seldom had he looked so weary, and they feared he was ill.

"I am pleased that you have returned. Let's step into the library." His voice faltered. "There is much to discuss." After Hubert had sunk into a chair, he conveyed the events of the past day and last few hours of the night. Several times the king stopped to answer questions as his sons paced to and fro in frustration. When Hubert began to tell of the intruder in the lady's room and the letter that was upon her pillow, Wilhelm could bear it no more.

"He walked into our very home and was in her private chambers! Where were the guards?" he screamed, his face red with anger. Leopold drew near his brother and stepped so as to block his view of the king.

"Can you not see Father's despair over this matter?" he said, turning slightly to look over his shoulder at the man who sat slumped in the chair, his face pale. Realizing the truth of his brother's words, Wilhelm gave a deep sigh knowing his father felt the weight of his error. Calmly he went to where Hubert was seated.

"Josephine and Mother, how are they?"

"Safe in my chambers, but . . ." Hubert muttered. "Your mother is on the verge of hysteria crying every little bit, and Josephine is not much better. She has tried to be strong but is shaking still and when she dozes off she has a nightmare and cries out. I have looked in on them as much as I could but needed to be out here . . ." His voice broke off as he clasped his hands together. Leopold looked at Wilhelm and then at his father.

"Let me take the reins for a few hours and you go to Mother and lie down. The rest will help you Father. And you dear brother," he said, putting a hand upon Wilhelm's shoulder. "Josephine needs your arms around her. Surely you can convince her to join you on the divan in Father's chambers." Leopold then offered Hubert a hand helping him to his feet and the three men began to walk. Allowing the king to go ahead of them, the brothers stopped in the hallway for a moment to talk.

"And what are your plans?" Wilhelm asked solemnly.

"After I let Karl know not to disturb you all unless it is dire, I plan to take a walk in the secret passages, just in case." He gave a wide grin as he thought of how many times as a child they had been scolded for disappearing within the castle for hours only to reappear unexpectedly frightening whoever was nearby. "It's been a while since I have gone exploring," he said and saw a faint smile cross his brother's face.

"You may find it's not as forsaken as you think," Wilhelm said, glancing toward the far end of the hallway knowing his brother would find the prints of a man's boots and that of a lady's.

"I will check in with you later this afternoon, until then rest well." And with that, the brothers parted.

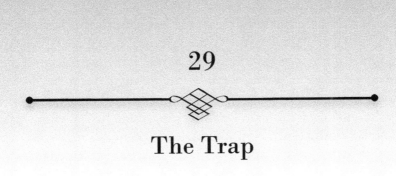

29

The Trap

"How could you ask me to return to Frive at a time like this?"

"It's not as you think, let me finish," Wilhelm pleaded as Josephine rose to her feet in disbelief and stepped away from where the others were seated. Earlier that morning, the king had called his closest advisors to the castle, and after an hour of discussion, the lady had been asked to join the meeting. She had prepared herself to answer questions concerning the intruder but was completely caught off guard by the prince's statement. After all that had happened in the past two days, travelling anywhere seemed absurd to the lady. Knowing Josephine's nerves were still rattled, he was only a few steps behind her as she walked across the room. Wilhelm took her by the hand as he explained, "We need only that it *looks* like you are returning to your family." As he spoke, he saw her telltale eyebrow rising in suspicion. "Please, I need you to sit down for the rest of what is to be said." Reluctantly she allowed him to lead her to a chair, but she knew by the look on his face that she would like the next part of the conversation even less. A knock was heard at the door and Leopold hurried in, stopped to greet Josephine and then took an empty chair near his father's desk. He had not seen the lady since returning from the field, having went to Guttenhamm hoping to find a lead concerning the intruder. With everyone settled in, the king began to explain the situation.

"It will be announced that due to dangerous times and the impending war, Lady Josephine will be returning to Frive." Giovanna and Cusall glanced toward Josephine to watch her reaction, and there was no mistake she was irritated by the thought. "And word of her departure must be spread far and wide to reach the right ears." The king hesitated for moment, knowing everything he was about to say would be in vain if the lady could not be convinced to play her part in the matter. "Even the details of what time and which day she is to depart." He looked at Josephine. "And you will need to make a fine display of emotions, so sad to leave our kingdom but being forced to for your own safety. Then you will be taken by carriage to Frive." Josephine's curiosity had been aroused and definitely was not satisfied with the lack of details.

"And the point of all of this would be?"

"That you would be captured along the way home," Heinds answered, as all eyes fell upon the lady. She wondered if she had heard the councilman correctly.

"Captured?" she asked. Suddenly her face grew pale, and fearing she was about to faint, Wilhelm left his chair and knelt beside the lady taking her hand in his. She looked hard into the prince's eyes and shook her head.

Giovanna spoke again, "You have always put the safety of our people as your priority, even at risk to your own life. Regretfully, we are asking that you think of them one more time."

"But do you know what you are asking of me?" she replied rudely.

"Yes, my lady, and if there was another option, we would take it. We cannot afford to lose more lives playing this game all summer, combing the countryside only to come up emptyhanded, him slipping through our fingers, yet wreaking havoc left and right. This venture could bring it all to an end within the week. If there was another, better plan that did not involve dragging you further into this, we would gladly take it." Josephine pushed Wilhelm away and rose to her feet to walk to the table across the room upon which a map was laid.

"And if I am caught, you think I will be taken to Maximillian?"

"Actually, we think he will be the one catching you. He has proven himself far superior than the rest of his company when it comes to moving about without being seen."

"You think he will fall for this."

"We will make it look good. I will be sent north to block any advancement against your route home, and Leopold would be doing similar." The lady threw a questioning glance toward Wilhelm, and catching it, he explained, "But it would only be a decoy as both of us will in fact be in other places. Word has already been sent out for all troops, regardless of location, to be on highest alert wearing chain mail, hoods, and helmets for safety."

"So it would not be apparent that we are elsewhere, as long as it is told where we are going to be stationed and our commanders are addressing our decoy as if it were us," Leopold added, beginning to understand the plan.

"I will remain with the lady and you will follow a sizeable distance behind the carriage. The idea is that she would be stopped, our soldiers flee and I will fall as if slain during the ambush and then track her through the woods."

"Don't you think they will suspect something if enough of a fight isn't put up?" Josephine asked.

"We'll fight, but only to give you time to run into the forest and lead them away. The carriage will not be heavily guarded as the idea was to send you on a swift journey back to Frive, and the lighter you travel, the better. You will be their focus, not a few guardsmen. And Maximillian cannot possibly have very many men with him or else we would have seen them by now, if it was even him that was in the castle the other night."

Josephine looked up from the map and interrupted, "I know without a doubt that it was him." The statement grabbed everyone's attention. "And it was him in town earlier that day. I was helping her majesty fix her hair this morning when I pricked my hand with a pin. When I looked down, I remembered what it was that I recognized about the man in the town." She walked closer, stopping beside Leopold and reached for his hand. She lifted it and pointed to the place in between the tendon of his first and second fingers. "There is a scar right here in the shape of an X."

"And how does that tie the man to Maximillian?" the king asked.

"That first night at Briasburg, Maximillian wore a bandage upon his hand. I asked about it while we were dancing and he brushed it off as being struck by an arrow." Sighs were heard at the confirmation of their enemy having been in their midst but the lady returned her thought to the more pressing issue as she continued, "I am not convinced that he would risk coming for me. Why would he not wait until I was back in Frive and then go to me there?"

"It would not give the same affect."

"Meaning what?"

"There are two things I am certain of concerning Maximillian. One, he wants revenge for his father and brothers, and two, he wants you. What better way to get even than to steal you within the borders of Gutten, so all will know that he did it. That is why he came to you the other night. He is trying to prove he can parade into our land, into our homes, and do as he pleases," Wilhelm said.

"I wish to God we had been here," Leopold added. "He would have thought twice about being so bold."

"We never should have let our guard down, assuming Guttenhamm was out of harm's way," the king said solemnly, as he still took personal responsibility for the incident.

"Yes, but we have learned our lesson and thank God Maximillian's pride worked to our favor," Heinds added. Josephine had begun to walk about the room, listening intently, contemplating whether the plan would work.

"And I am to run off into the woods," she said, interrupting the men.

"Yes. We think Maximillian himself may not be the one stopping the carriage, but would be waiting in the wings for you to be brought to him. Keeping some distance between him and danger, but not being too far away to retrieve his prize." The word sent a shiver down Josephine's spine. The fear of being handed over to the evil man as an object of great worth to him was worse to her than being slain in battle. "You must run as far as you can before being caught. Then, they will take you to him and all the while I will be following your tracks with Leopold and his men not far behind. When we find you, we find him."

"And then all this madness will be over," Hubert concluded.

"You are counting that he will value my life enough not to harm me." Josephine interrupted. "That is something that is not certain in my opinion."

"That is true," Wilhelm said, coming over to the lady. "I will not make false promises when we all know better. But he has had the chance to hurt you before and hasn't. His desire for you has held him back and we have to believe that it will again. But more than that, you have to keep in his good graces."

"Meaning what exactly?" Josephine asked, appalled at the suggestion of playing to their enemy.

"Meaning, it would not be wise to share your opinion of him unless you are prepared to receive his hand across your face. You would have to mind your temper and cooperate with him to some extent," Wilhelm replied bluntly. "The goal would be to stay alive and uninjured to buy time for me to find you."

"And for me to find him," Leopold said, looking toward his brother. "You may have to stall if he tries to pack you up and head out. And you would have to leave tracks no matter what."

"What if I wear that purple dress? You know the one I am thinking of, that annoyed me so."

"The one that shed those petals everywhere you went. Absolutely gorgeous dress, but what a mess it left behind." Josephine blushed with embarrassment remembering her last experience with the gown. "Yes, that would be perfect. Isn't there a matching hat too? It would look as if you were dressed up for the occasion. What a trail that would leave behind."

"Enough about my fashion blunders," the lady said, taking a swing and playfully hitting the prince's arm.

"Is there anything we have missed?" the king asked, looking about the room at the other men still seated before him.

"I would like more details of the area that I will be trapesing through. It would be better if I headed toward a fixed point wouldn't it?" Josephine asked.

"Done," Leopold said, standing to his feet again and going to retrieve map scrolls from a cabinet. A few more suggestions were made but all agreed the plan was well conceived and should work.

"My liege, if I may be excused," Josephine said to the king. Hubert nodded and the lady turned, gave a curtsy toward the other men, and left the room.

When the door was shut, Cusall asked, "Do you think she will go through with it?"

"I have no doubt for once she sets her mind to something it takes a great deal to change it, as you all well know," the king replied.

"I have only one thing to say," Giovanna said, standing to his feet and walking to where Wilhelm was. The prince's countenance was still somber, knowing how dangerous the venture was going to be for the lady. "I have never met such a remarkable young lady. You are making preparations to keep her with us, *permanently*?" he asked as the two exchanged smiles.

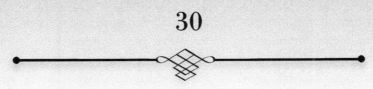

30

In the Enemy's Camp

"I would have thought we would have been ambushed by now," Josephine said, leaning her head back against the seat cushion in disappointment.

"I can only hope it will be soon or you will squeeze my fingers off," Wilhelm teased, making light of the lady's unrest. "Lay your head against my shoulder and rest while you still have the chance."

"I can't. My hair gets caught in the chainmail," she confessed. The prince apologized but encouraged Josephine to at least close her eyes and relax. He watched her for a few minutes and then turned his attention to looking out the carriage window again. He and Leopold had discussed the route for hours and came to agree on their best guess for the ambush to take place. The western stretch of the Pinard Road skirted the southern edge of the mountains except in one location. There it wound north into a small basin-like valley laden with thick forests and then returned to its course running westward. From a vantage point one could see a traveler enter the valley, disappear from view and then reappear roughly two hours later. The carriage had just started down the gentle slope, and Wilhelm guessed they would be attacked within a half hour, but he dare not tell the lady as things were about to be harrowing enough. When the enemy was spotted, he would push the lady from the carriage with him jumping too to draw attention from the driver and escorts. The two would run into the woods, the prince would feign a mortal wound, falling to the ground with blood oozing from his armor while the lady fled into the wilds. Not only did the brothers think the location was ideal but Leopold and his men had left the day before and were dispersed in the region, remaining hidden until the rendezvous time came. Wilhelm dreaded what was ahead for the lady and he could only hope that Maximillian cared for Josephine enough that he would not hurt her. But there was no guarantee that she would be spared as Maximillian's lust for power had only begun to be satisfied. The thought of the lady at his enemy's mercy had gnawed at him almost as bad as the chance of more innocent people dying, but Wilhelm knew he had to put his feelings for the lady aside as the plan had to be carried out successfully, no matter the cost.

Wilhelm had begun to trace the fingers of the lady's hand when out of the corner of his eye, he saw movement in the distance. Turning toward the window he saw two men on horseback riding in the forest, staying just to the rear of the line of sight of the footman but keeping pace with the carriage.

"Josephine, its time," the prince said. He slid the panel open and alerted the footmen but was careful to warn the men not to look about for they had to keep the carriage moving as long as possible. As he turned toward the lady, he saw fear in her eyes. "Remember what we discussed. Keep running as long as you can. The opportunity has to be there—I have to be sure I can take him down before I show myself and it may be several hours that you are with him so *don't* do anything to provoke him to hurt you. And no matter what, don't lose focus. Do you understand?"

"I am terribly afraid," Josephine whispered through teary eyes.

"I know, but you can do this. You *have* to do this." He looked out the window in time to see a few more men in the woods, with bows drawn. He began to pound the roof of the carriage, and with a sudden jolt, the pace of the horses quickened while the guardsmen began to yell to each other about being under attack. "Stay low until I tell you," Wilhelm said to the lady as he reached to the opposite seat and pulled his shield upward to block anything that might sail through the open windows. Several minutes passed with a frenzy of arrows flying at the carriage and a guardsman climbed down and around long enough to yell that the road was blocked up ahead. "Better than I hoped," Wilhelm replied. "You know what to do. Farewell." At which the soldier climbed back on top of the carriage. "This is where we get out." Wilhelm reached to open the door to his left.

"What?" Josephine asked in surprise.

"Don't think about it, just jump," Wilhelm said, pushing the lady in that direction. Fir trees lined the edge of the road and afforded a softer landing than Josephine had imagined. As soon as the prince hit the ground he rolled and was on his feet again, but Josephine had not fared as well struggling against her skirt. Quickly Wilhelm helped her up and began to speak so loud that the lady found herself begging him to lower his voice in fear they would be heard. In a normal voice, he reminded her that was the point and began to lead her away from the road. She glanced back in time to see two riders bringing their horses to a halt and then turn to come in their direction. "They've seen us," Wilhelm said. "Keep moving for I need a better place than this to take a fall." They ran a bit further before Wilhelm spoke again. "Whatever you do, don't use my name. Do you hear me?" He pleaded, coming to a stop. In the distance on foot, several men could be seen. "It is time we parted." In a loud voice, he yelled again, "Run, my lady, run!" Before Josephine could take a step, Wilhelm had turned and went back toward the first two men who were on horseback. She watched as the prince knocked them from their steeds, slaying one of them as he hit the ground. The second man however, was able to get an arrow off from his bow before Wilhelm could overtake him. In horror, she watched as the shaft settled into the prince's shoulder armor and stayed. The force with which it struck its target made Wilhelm lunge forward, causing the lady to scream. The next instant, she saw the prince swing his sword, and with a mighty blow, his opponent met his death. Wilhelm pulled the man's body to his and very tactfully fell to the ground to make it look as if he had perished in the struggle as well. The scene seemed so real that Josephine screamed again and ran to where Wilhelm lay.

"No, no, no!" Tears were streaming down her face as she tried to turn the prince over.

As her hand touched him, he spoke, "I am fine. You must run deeper into the woods."

"I can't leave you. You are hurt," she protested.

"It is not bad, but you have to go before the others get close enough to see that. Remember, my dying is part of the plan."

"Your being shot by an arrow was not the plan," she cried, reaching for his face. The prince caught hold of her hand and through gritted teeth he spoke again.

"You have to go or this all will be in vain. How many lives will be lost if he is not stopped?"

"I cannot leave you here to die," she pleaded. "Wilhelm, I am afraid."

"You will only lose me if you don't take off running right now for they will kill me for sure." Josephine clung to him, shaking hard. He had to convince her to leave him. "Listen to me. As long as I draw breath I will come for you. Remember that God will be with you even when I cannot. Scripture says that He will never leave you nor forsake you." Voices grew louder as the enemy moved closer, and Josephine stood to her feet for a moment to look in that direction. Summoning her courage, she knelt again beside Wilhelm.

"I will go, but first . . ." she said, looking toward his arm. Without warning, she grabbed the shaft of the arrow and gave a quick but steady pull upward. As his flesh tore, he gave a muffled groan. Even without the arrow sticking out, the prince's body looked ravaged for his outer garment had the blood of an animal upon it to give the illusion that he had been mortally wounded. Bending over him one more time Josephine kissed his temple and whispered, "I love you, Wilhelm Von Strauss." Before he could respond, shouts were heard again and the lady rose to her feet and took off running.

Wilhelm slowly but carefully moved his helmet and chainmail so that at a glance his eyes could not be easily seen. He watched as three men came closer, looked in his direction, but then their attention was drawn away. Not giving a thought to the two comrades that lay fallen, the men began to chase the lady. The prince remained motionless, anxiously watching them disappear into the forest. As badly as he wanted to get up, he had to stay put in case more of his enemy was lurking about. His mind started to wonder if they would be rough with Josephine when they caught her, but he chose to dismiss the tormenting thought. Surely Maximillian's orders would still stand concerning her welfare as the man who caused the avalanche had discovered. Wilhelm pushed himself off the ground allowing the other man's body to slide off into a heap. As he rose to his feet, he couldn't help but wince from the pain in his shoulder. Although it was the best thing the lady could have done under the circumstances, the removal of the arrow had left a ragged hole. With no time to spare, he ripped a piece of cloth from the dead man's shirt and shoved it under his armor to slow the bleeding. At first he walked at a decent pace as he knew the direction Josephine had ran, but after a short while, he began to study the ground much closer. It took several minutes before he found a petal from the lady's skirt, but when he did he had to smile for the idea had worked. On through the forest he walked slowly, not only watching for his enemy but being sure to mark a good trail for his brother to easily follow. Leopold and his men were to wait until three o'clock to gravitate from their hidden positions outside the basin and move inward until they found where the carriage had been stopped. The timeline had been kept from the lady to keep from frightening her at the thought of being a prisoner much longer than she was anticipating. The sad reality was that the brothers would not be close enough to execute the last phase of their plan until later in the evening and even then it may have to wait until morning. The situation would have to be assessed with the assassination of Maximillian being the priority over rescuing Josephine, a decision that both princes struggled with. But Wilhelm was determined not to think about that until they were faced with it. All he needed to do now was follow the lady back to Maximillian and so far with four people ahead of him, footprints and petals were in plenty. He was also relieved that the tracks gave no evidence that Josephine had been caught. More than an hour passed before the terrain changed with the forest now being younger and thick with underbrush. Suddenly the tracks split in different directions and there was no sign of Josephine's shoe print. Wilhelm knew she would do what was necessary to keep the men at bay, but the prince hoped she had not done too much. Finally he followed his gut, remembering how she had studied the map and kept pointing south. Minutes passed and still he saw no signs of the lady and was beginning to wonder if he needed to backtrack. He had just turned and retraced his last ten steps when he saw a small piece of purple fabric on a briar vine about a foot off the ground.

Josephine's heart was racing. The flight had been slowed considerably by thorny briar vines that covered the ground and ensnarled her skirt. The only good thing she could see about the situation was that she was more hidden from view but she had heard someone moving two different times. After what seemed like forever, she emerged from the brambles and found herself again in an older part of the forest with the trees several arm lengths apart and the ground carpeted with leaves of past seasons. Josephine had run a good ways when she thought she heard footsteps which caused her to dart behind a tree. She waited a few minutes, caught her breath and then peered out. Not seeing anyone, she took off again but had not made it very far when she saw the silhouette of a man in the distance. As she took cover behind a tree she was thankful his back had been toward her and perhaps he didn't know she was there. Trying to be brave, she leaned out slightly but to her dismay saw no one. As still as the grave, she crept to the next tree and waited, listening intently and looking cautiously about. Several more times she did the same, edging her way along. She had just passed an enormous oak tree when she heard a sound and turned to see a man coming around the other side of the tree.

"Why . . . hello," he said with a pleased smile upon his face. Josephine began to back away and had just turned to run when she felt his hands upon her shoulder. He did not get a good enough grip, but his hand slipped and caused her to lose her balance. With a grunt, she stumbled and fell to the ground. He gave a laugh as he stepped closer. "Did you fall down?" Josephine's back was to him so he did not see that a tree limb lay in front of her. The moment that her eyes fell upon the three-foot-long piece of wood, she knew what she must do. "Shall I help you to your feet my lady?" the man said snarling.

Carefully hovering so he could not see what she was doing, Josephine's hands gripped the limb, and as she started to her feet, as mean as she could sound, she replied, "Shall I help *you* to the ground?" As the last word was spoken, she turned and swung her weapon with all of her might. It landed against the side of the man's head as it caught him totally by surprise. The collision caused both to stumble, with the man reaching for his face as he cursed. Not waiting a second, Josephine took off running. Should he catch her again she knew he would have recompense upon his mind for her deed. She had just come to a place where the ground sloped down a grassy hillside dotted with trees, when she heard a yell and turned to see the man reaching for her. Again, his hands slipped as he tried to take hold of her, but instead he managed to tear part of the sleeve off her dress. Struggling to keep his balance, the man lost his footing, falling over the top of the lady and causing both to roll down the hill side. Josephine had just managed to get to her feet when the man grabbed her from behind. He spoke but she couldn't understand what he was saying for she was screaming at him as loud as she could. They continued to wrestle as he tried to restrain the lady but couldn't as the rocks were shifting under his feet. Suddenly she broke free and made it down the slope where the ground leveled out before he overcame her again and intentionally knocked her to the ground. She lay for a moment trying to breathe as her lungs ached for air. Her head was reeling, and when the man spoke, it was as if he was a long distance away.

"See how you like that!" he snarled, standing over the top of her. "Get up!" Josephine had landed face down and was able to lift her head but could go no further for how dizzy she was.

"The king will hear of this!" she replied.

"I am sure he will for it is he that sent me to find you." Josephine began to raise herself off the ground. Her left palm was skinned, and it felt like her arm too. She was almost to her knees when she realized her left leg felt strange. The man continued to hover over her, not willing to give her room to escape from him. Again, he demanded for her to get on her feet. Carefully she shifted and lifted the edge of her skirt to view the lower part of her leg. As she thought, she saw blood trickling over her knee coming from her thigh and her calf had several cuts on it as well.

"I am hurt," she said to the man, hoping to distract him.

"And you think that I am not? Taking a stick to my face . . . It serves you right, lady or no." While he spoke, Josephine slid her right hand into her boot and withdrew her dagger, keeping it hidden under the folds of her skirt. "All this fuss over a woman. I am losing patience with you. Get on your feet!" Slowly Josephine stood up with the man taking hold of her left arm. With a scream, she turned and stabbed her dagger deep into his forearm. In shock he took a step back, cried out in pain, and released her arm to grab hold of his own. As quickly as she had swung her arm, she withdrew it and took off running, not daring to look behind her. The man continued to rant, but the sound faded into the distance as the sound of her heart beating filled her ears. Should he catch her again it would not be good and she needed as much distance between them as she could, despite the fact that she was in severe pain both with her head and leg. She had just made it across a small clearing of tall grass and had entered woods again when she turned to look behind. She was still moving forward as she turned her head again only to see a silhouette a few feet away. She put her arms out trying to brace for the collision as she slammed into it. Looking up, she gasped.

"Maximillian," she whispered, as he steadied her and gave a smile.

"And where are you headed in such a hurry?" he asked. She watched as his eyes studied her face, and still smiling, he reached for her hair. Memories of her stay in Briasburg came flooding back to her mind. She had intended to only spend the first night at the castle and leave early the next morning, but Maximillian had persuaded her to stay another day to allow him to show her the orchards and vineyards located to the north of his home. The lady could not refuse the offer not only because of Montoise's reputable beauty but because the handsome prince had done more to win her affections in a few hours than Duke Alfred had in a week. The morning grew into afternoon before the pair returned to Briasburg Castle and by then King Airik insisted that the young lady remain another night before journeying on. Several more guests were at the supper table that evening and Maximillian's four older brothers had ladies upon their arms. Compliments were poured out toward the female guests making Josephine quite uncomfortable. Wine was served and the meal progressed into revelry. The dancing that followed was no better for the mood was too friendly to the point that Maximillian had words with one of his brothers over how he was handling Josephine. The king parted the hot-headed young men and a few minutes later Maximillian stole the lady away to walk with him upon the grounds, away from the others. As they strolled in the darkness he apologized for his brother's behavior. Although it was inexcusable he blamed the drunkenness upon the sorrow concerning the recent loss of their mother. Josephine had never been exposed to such things but having heard stories she believed the youngest prince and dismissed her alarm over the incident. A couple hours passed before the young man escorted her back to the guest room. Maximillian's defense of her honor that night was the chief reason she had doubted Wilhelm's accusations when she fled to Gutten. Even after being shown the devastation at Edgell, she found it hard to believe Maximillian was capable of such deeds and blamed the raids as his brother's doings. As time went on and reports continued to flow in, Josephine had to accept the truth that he had equally played his part in the massacres. But now as the man stood before her, she felt doubt rising up again. Tenderly Maximillian removed a leaf that had become entangled in Josephine's hair, and let it fall to the ground. From the way he looked at her, she knew Wilhelm had been right. He was very pleased to see the lady. Noticing the condition of her dress, the king leaned slightly to survey the left side of the lady's body. Suddenly the noise of someone running through the grass could be heard, and anxiously Josephine turned to look.

"I was fleeing from that man." She looked back to Maximillian who replied in quiet voice.

"He was sent to bring you to me." They both glanced away and then back at each other. Josephine leaned toward the king as if seeking what protection he would offer. The lady did not realize Maximillian had a hold of her wrist until he brought her arm up with his to view. "And what have you been doing with this?"

"Defending myself from that brute," she said with disgust.

"His blood, or yours?"

"His," she answered as Maximillian slid the dagger from her clasped hand without any resistance. To her relief he did not seem upset by her answer.

Then without warning, he called out, "Tolner!" He slid his hand around the lady's waist and together they turned to stand side by side. They watched as the other man backtracked through the woods and came to them. Josephine heard more movement and shifting, she could see a half-dozen men emerge from where they were hidden in the trees. She could feel their eyes heavy upon her with Tolner glaring worst of all. "How is it that your dress is torn?" Maximillian asked Josephine.

"Perhaps you should be asking him," the lady quipped, throwing an accusing look at the man who had chased her. She hoped to entice a response and he could not resist.

"She fell down, sire," he said.

"You knocked me to the ground, you filth!" the lady said, voice raised and fire in her eyes. She took a step in the man's direction and would have taken another but felt Maximillian's restraining hand upon her waist.

"Tolner . . ." the king said, waiting for an answer as he watched their reactions closely.

"Sire, she fought me the whole way. We both ended up on the ground. That is when she stabbed me," he said, offering an excuse as he raised his blood covered forearm.

"And the blood upon her dress, is that yours as well?" Maximillian asked as Josephine's eyes grew wide in astonishment that he had been so observant.

Tolner shrugged his shoulders, but the lady wanting to create more tension quickly added, "My leg was hurt during the scuffle, and my head." Maximillian's eyes did not leave Tolner, and a scowl was growing upon his face. His countenance made the hair on the back of Josephine's neck crawl.

"What were my orders this morning?" the king asked, making eye contact with each of his men for a moment. The tone in his voice made Josephine cringe even more.

"We were to bring the lady to you," Tolner replied, knowing he was the one expected to answer. Maximillian turned toward the lady and again leaned to view the left side of her body and then reached for her hair. He drew so close to the lady this time that she closed her eyes as she felt him gently remove a twig from her locks. Her senses fully awakened she was reminded how attracted she had been to Maximillian that fateful night at Briasburg. The lady did not disguise her feelings well enough, and the king took advantage of it lingering a moment longer before he stood upright again. As soon as he moved away, Josephine swallowed hard and opened her eyes.

"Did I say that she was not to be hurt?" he asked, not yet looking away from the lady's face. A dreadful feeling that something was horribly wrong began to sweep over Josephine as his eyes met hers and his countenance became grave. "Was that not my command?" This time Tolner did not reply but another man who wore a leather vest.

"Yes, my liege, those were your orders." Josephine felt Maximillian shift as he turned away from her to address his men who were now gathered a few arm lengths away. A look of concern was on their faces for they knew their king was angry. Releasing the lady from his grasp, Maximillian took a step forward and slid her small dagger in his belt and then turned to face Josephine.

"Where are your injuries?" he asked, but the lady knew his question held more weight than her answers alone. Afraid, she hesitated but then as his eye brows rose into a demanding look she was compelled to answer him.

"My head hit the ground, my arm was scraped, and my leg is bleeding."

"How bad is your leg injured?" he asked, glancing at the lady's skirt.

"I . . . I am not sure," she stuttered.

"Injured enough that you were limping when you crossed the field," he said, answering his own question. "Injured, when she was to be brought to me unscathed." The look in his eyes when Josephine's gaze met his was frightening. Suddenly without warning, Maximillian turned and with lightning speed drew his sword and thrust it deeply into Tolner's chest. Josephine screamed and started toward the man who was now falling to the ground. Maximillian caught the lady and pulled her back from the man who was groaning as his blood spilled out.

"How could you?" Josephine cried out, struggling as Maximillian sheathed his sword and put both hands upon the lady. "How could you?" The king turned her to face him and wrapped his arms around her to keep her from moving. "He has done nothing worthy of death!" Her hands came to rest upon the man's chest as she had no other place to put them.

"Disobedience is not tolerated," he replied. Josephine looked up into his eyes.

"And when I don't do what you want, will you kill me as well?" she said, taunting him.

"No, I won't," he replied, raising an eyebrow as he studied her tear streaked face.

"Then you will strike me to the ground instead?" Josephine asked, watching him closely. To her dismay, he leaned close enough that he put his head against hers.

He whispered toward her ear, "Do not force me to do such a thing, for your sake as well as mine." With his statement, Josephine leaned back to look him in the eye.

"And why should I be shown more mercy that the women of Klairan whose bodies were left in the ashes?" For a split second, the lady saw fearsome anger in the man's eyes—an anger that made her wish she had held her tongue for what he might do to her, but then he blinked and called to his men.

"Take care of the body. We are heading back to the camp." He looked at the lady. "Put your arms around my neck." Instantly Josephine shook her head to refuse, but he insisted. "Until I have looked at your leg, you will not be walking on it. Do as I say." He stooped slightly for the lady to reach, but as he touched her leg, she cried out in pain. As he lifted her, she gasped and laid her head against his shoulder to keep from crying out again. As he began to walk, she closed her eyes, and in a few minutes, the discomfort eased and became more bearable. She was sickened to the core that he, the man that she loathed for bringing pain and death to so many, now carried her in his arms. Finally, she was brave enough to open her eyes, and to her surprise, she realized it was not the first time she had been carried by him.

"Did the friend of a friend survive?" she asked. A smile crossed Maximillian's face. "It was you at Seim."

"Yes, it was me," he answered, pleased that she had been mindful of him. "And the man is alive and well. You will see him when we return to Aikerlan. I became involved when my sources relayed that the wound was mortal and that you and the surgeon fellow were in Seim. It was as my colleague said, Frederick was transported in hopes of receiving care. It was never my intention to be anywhere near Seim, but I decided to risk it in hopes that he could be saved and that I might see you again."

"Why didn't you reveal yourself to me then?" Josephine asked as she noticed a campsite in the distance.

"As was said, men would have died from both kingdoms if it were known who was truly in their midst."

"I *kept* my word as was asked of me in exchange for lives, no matter who's they were," the lady interjected, insulted that he thought she would have done otherwise. Maximillian carried her close to where a meager fire was burning. Saddles were placed round about the ring of stones. Kneeling, he lowered her to the ground. Quickly Josephine tucked her skirt and petticoat so the man would not be able to see more of her leg than was necessary. Maximillian retrieved a roll of bandages and a canteen of water. When the lady had drank her fill, he began to slowly pour water over her blood-stained calf. Josephine gasped as it stung and found herself reaching for his arm to cling to. The cuts upon her thigh ran along the back of her leg, and the more the wounds were cleaned, the more she squeezed his arm with tears in her eyes. To her relief, he declared no stitches were needed, and gently began to wind the bandage around her leg.

Trying to distract her mind from the unpleasantness of his hands being upon her she asked how the conflict between Aikerlan and Gutten had begun. Maximillian was happy to share his account, although it was nothing like King Hubert had described to Josephine months earlier. Sanctions had been imposed against Aikerlan as punishment for cruel treatment of their citizens. In Maximillian's words, the other kingdoms had interfered in personal business and then refused to allow goods in or out trying to force his father to bow to their wishes. When his people began to suffer, Airik was forced to "acquire" what was needed from the neighboring kingdoms out of desperation. The conversation was one sided, but it had served its purpose not only to keep her mind off her leg but to hear Maximillian's reasoning behind his actions.

When he was done mending her leg, Josephine asked to be helped to her feet. She had hoped she would seem less vulnerable standing, but her efforts were thwarted as she could not bear her own weight without extreme discomfort and instead had to lean against Maximillian. He didn't protest against the lady trying to stand for he knew her pride would only force her into his arms. Josephine was trying to figure a way out of her predicament when suddenly a commotion could be heard moving through the woods. By the sound, she guessed it was a large animal or maybe several of them. Again, she caught herself clinging to the chest of the last person she ever wanted to.

"Do not be alarmed," Maximillian said as the noise grew louder but nothing could yet be seen in the brush. "Do you remember my pets?" Josephine turned her gaze to him.

"Yes, I do. The hounds growled every time I moved."

"Actually, they were growling at my brothers, not you," he said, correcting the lady as two chocolate-colored vizslas came into view. "My brothers tormented them, and the dogs grew to hate them." As they came closer, Josephine could see rabbits hanging limply from each of their mouths. "Do not be afraid." Maximillian reassured the lady. "Come." The dogs obeyed him, and dropped their prey at his feet only to sit upright before him, still as statues. Proudly Maximillian introduced his beloved pets to the lady. "Otto and Fran." He pointed to each, and then he reached for the lady's hand that was gripping the front of his shirt. She knew what he was about to do.

"Please, no," she protested.

"My hand will be with yours. There is no need to be afraid," he replied, unfurling her arm and beginning to lower it. Josephine nervously buried her face into the man's chest and braced to feel teeth clamp down on her hand. Maximillian ignored her and a moment later, she felt soft fur against her palm. Trembling, she held her breath and then she felt the dog nudge its head toward her, wanting more attention. Surprisingly, whimpers could be heard as both animals eagerly scooted closer to the lady. Cautiously Josephine let loose of Maximillian's shirt and lowered her other hand which was met by a furry head. Leaning back to see them, she began to stroke the animals. The dogs continued to soak up the lady's attention and seemed to pay no mind to their master. Josephine said their names and watched as ears perked up and tails wagged in excitement. Pleased that the animals had taken to the lady so quickly, the king explained the commands his pets would respond to and then to demonstrate he told them to lie down. Neither moved, still nudging Josephine's hand for more, but when the lady gave the command, they laid down at her feet immediately. Maximillian threw his head back and gave a hearty laugh. "First my heart, now my pets. What next, my kingdom?" he said. Josephine had to bite her tongue to keep from replying. She'd like to take his kingdom from him all right.

"My king, a word please." A man called in the distance. Maximillian knelt and rubbed his pets, and after telling them to guard the lady, he stepped away. Still feeling weak with pain, Josephine retreated to a nearby tree and sat down to rest. Her leg and head were throbbing terribly, but those were the least of her worries as she watched the men stare at her from across the camp. Wilhelm had been correct to assume Maximillian's company was small in number and that she would be brought to where he was waiting. She wondered how far behind her the prince was. She hoped his wound had not slowed him down too much. Several minutes passed and then

Maximillian called all his men to him. From what she could hear, only half of the ones sent out had returned, but the present party was willing to wait for them. She heard "lookout point" mentioned several times, and then the meeting was adjourned as the men began to move away and went back to what they were doing.

A thin fellow came in the lady's direction and introduced himself as Netkar and then picking up the rabbits from the ground, said he would let her know when food was ready. Josephine was watching the man dress the meat when Maximillian knelt in front of the lady blocking her view.

"It seems we will be here a few more hours."

"So . . . you planned to rescue me, but you didn't have a plan to get me *out* of Gutten?" Josephine asked, giving him a sly grin. He returned a smile and teased back.

"If I remember correctly, my men and I have gotten in and out of Gutten plenty of times unaware so surely this time . . ." He gave a laugh and Josephine couldn't help but join him, having to admit it was true. She could not contain her curiosity.

"How did you get into the castle the other night?" Settling back on his haunches, Maximillian began to tell of a certain nearly blind woodcutter who often enlisted the aid of wanderers to help him in his deliveries. Josephine knew the one he spoke of, and it took everything in her not to voice her opinion of him taking advantage of the old man. So Maximillian had made arrangements to help the man on his rounds in Guttenhamm that day and then on to the castle that night. No details were held back as the king enjoyed bragging of his skills and answered any questions the lady had for him. When Josephine suggested the near kidnapping in the village was a ruse for him to rescue her, he was quick to deny the accusation.

"That was not of my doing and the bodies of those men lie in the woods of Andall for the wolves to feast upon. No . . . if you knew how many times lately that you have been in danger with no real protection from the crown of Gutten." As he spoke, his voice grew louder with irritation. "As I said before, the prince is a foolish man for leaving such a treasure unguarded." Trying to steer the conversation, Josephine asked another question hoping to gain more insight.

"Surely we are not crawling in the shadows of trees and rocks all the way back to Aikerlan?"

"By the time the guard realizes you are not on the way to Frive, we will be through the mountain pass." Josephine glanced at Maximillian as her thoughts went to a certain lodge that lay at the other end of the road of which he spoke.

"There is an establishment, a hunting lodge just before you come to Jansville," she said, watching him for a reaction. He gave a smile.

"Yes, I know. That is where I discovered you had not perished in the fire." Maximillian could see he had the lady's undivided attention as her mind went back to the last time she was at the place.

"You were among the men that day . . . the ones who made Johann and Rebekah so nervous."

"Roughians, isn't that what you called my men?" Maximillian said, causing Josephine to turn red in embarrassment as her exact words were repeated. Suddenly she became alarmed, wondering how the old couple had fared after she left.

"No harm has come to them?" she said, moving closer and taking hold of the king's arm.

A sly grin crossed Maximillian's face as he spoke, "They agreed to our requests in exchange . . ." Josephine gripped his arm nervously.

"In exchange for what?"

"That you would not be harmed and allowed to leave. Of course that was if you minded your own business." He seemed to relish the power he had over the elderly couple, and Josephine could only wonder how much they had sacrificed on her behalf.

Noticing movement behind the king, Josephine glanced away for a moment to see two men walking past. The scowl they gave made her eyebrow rise as she guessed what they thought of her. Maximillian turned to see what she was looking at, but by then, the men's backs were to him. Josephine took the opportunity to plant seeds of dissension.

"Your men are not happy that I am here," she said, purposely keeping her hand upon Maximillian's arm.

"What makes you say that?" the king asked as their eyes met again.

"The glares they keep throwing at me and Tolner said plenty against me."

"Tolner . . . is no longer a concern, and the men will do as they are told," he concluded, taking her hand in his. Josephine was not satisfied.

"And you are confident of that?" she asked, as he began to rub her hand.

"Completely," he said, moving uncomfortably close to her. With his other hand, he reached for a strand of Josephine's hair. "I have taken measures to insure no issues will arise."

"Measures?" Josephine said, as her pulse quickened as Maximillian continued with what he was doing.

"Like the ones taken in Jansville," he said, leaning closer. Not wanting to see his face, she closed her eyes. "They want to keep their families safe, as we all do." Josephine's head suddenly felt swimmy, and she leaned back toward the tree with a sigh and began to rub her forehead, her eyes still closed. Upon hearing a soft laugh, she opened them to see Maximillian looking amused at her reaction to him. She wanted to slap the grin from his face. How could he think she would be attracted to a man who had just admitted to holding his own men's families hostage to keep their loyalty? She did not know how much longer she could be civil toward this fiend.

"My king! My king!" was heard, causing Maximillian to rise to his feet and then as he saw who it was he took off in a run. Feeling the urgency of the situation, Josephine stood up as more shouting was heard as horses were led into the camp. Particular attention was being paid to a man's body draped across a saddle. Curious, Josephine limped to where the men were gathered to hear what was going on. She had just stopped behind Maximillian and put her hand upon his elbow when a rider spoke, half-panting for air.

"When we left the carriage . . . We found Barll and Jenk . . . slain . . . a far piece into the woods. Sorry, sire . . . but we never saw hide nor hair . . . of the lady." Josephine felt her ears grow warm as she was mentioned. As she guessed, Maximillian was quick to reply.

"No need to worry, for she has come to us." The king turned to let the riders view the lady, but before he could continue, another man cried out as the man draped over the horse was lowered to the ground.

"Sire, can the lady do anything for Larnell's wounds?" Carefully four men carried the body beside the fire and placed it on the ground again. Instantly Josephine felt a struggle within her. How could she save the life of this man? What if he had killed one of the guardsmen who was trying to protect her? Worse yet, how many innocent people had he slain in the name of Aikerlan? She could not save her enemy when he deserved death. Suddenly her conscience smote her. What if this man had been forced to obey Maximillian to save his loved ones? Did he have a wife and children waiting in Aikerlan for his return? As difficult as it may be, she could not stand by and let him die before her very eyes. Without waiting for permission or for the order to be given, she hobbled to the man and knelt down. She groaned as it felt like her leg wound split open, but she refused to give in to the pain. She had already peeled back the man's outer clothing when she realized Maximillian had joined her on the ground. He asked what she needed and as she lifted the bottom edge of the man's shirt, she answered him. Orders were given and then the king began to assist the lady as he had done in Seim. The wounds in his abdomen were sewn, but the situation was dire because of the amount of blood the man had lost. Several times Larnell raised himself off the ground fighting the efforts to mend him and the last time Josephine reached to pull him back down she made a startling discovery as her hand was full of dark blood. Carefully she rolled his body and saw what she had feared. Along his lower back was a deep gash that exposed more of his insides than she cared to look at. Maximillian leaned to see what had made the lady gasp and shaking his head said.

"There is nothing more that can be done." He began to rise from his knees. "Come."

"No, I will stay with him," Josephine protested, not able to look up from her patient. She could feel her emotions welling up for there was no hope the man would survive. Maximillian put a hand upon the lady's shoulder, but she brushed him away repeating that she needed to stay with the man. Now fully on his feet, the king took hold of Josephine and pulled her upward.

"I said its time to leave him. Come with me," Josephine tried to push Maximillian away, but the more she struggled against him, the closer he pulled her as tears blinded her eyes.

"It's my fault he is wounded, if he hadn't been looking for me . . ." She began to mumble as the king wrapped his arms around her until her head rested upon his chest. Slowly Maximillian began to inch back toward the shade of the trees while the lady clung to him. What was she doing, allowing the evil man that she loathed to console her? How was it even possible to find comfort in his arms when he seemed incapable of caring for anyone other than himself? Was he upset that his comrade lay dying as consequence to choices he had made as king? Maximillian's gentleness was surprising, and the lady couldn't help but wonder if he wasn't taking advantage of her distress. Despite all that she had known prior, was there another side to the king that he had reserved for her alone? Suddenly she raised her head to look at him and sincerely began to plead, "No one else has to die. You wanted me returned and now you have me. Take me back to Aikerlan, stop this bloodshed. Please . . . Promise me there will be no more killing, please." Josephine watched as Maximillian began to smile as he studied her tear stained face with his dark eyes. He leaned and kissed her cheek, and puzzled by his reaction, the lady did not stop him. Josephine felt her pulse quicken as he lingered. She remembered how it felt with Sven and his honor had held him back, but she doubted Maximillian would do the same. He kissed her temple, and then as he was leaning to kiss her ear, he paused.

"I cannot let the deaths of my father and brothers go without punishment. Justice has to be served." Josephine leaned away from him so he could see her face.

"Justice does not involve the innocent dying to carry it out!" she said, rebuking him. She knew hundreds had died already, and the crown guessed there were more bodies yet to be discovered left in the wilds. "Hasn't enough blood been shed already? Stop this madness, please."

"It is not that simple," Maximillian said, as he ran his fingers over the rip in the shoulder of Josephine's dress and touched the bare skin that was exposed.

"It should be," she replied. "Are you not king?" He gave a smile, but the lady knew it was not because he agreed with her suggestion. Not willing to give up her plea just yet, she gave him a serious look. "I will not share your heart with revenge as your mistress!" The words that came out of Josephine's mouth were unexpected, and she was as shocked as he was by her statement. It took but a moment for him to respond, smiling again and leaning close enough to touch her nose with his.

"It pleases me to hear you say that," he whispered and then he passionately kissed her. As the embrace ended, Josephine found that she was lightheaded and clinging to him with weakness flooding over her. "You will not have to share my heart for long, my love." Overwhelmed, Josephine could only rest in his arms. Wilhelm had been right to assume the two things that motivated their enemy. The lady knew that for the moment she was definitely in the good graces of the king, as sickening as that was to her.

"Sire," Secry said as he approached the pair with a reverent bow. "Forgive me for interrupting but what are the orders now that all the men are accounted for?" Maximillian gave a look toward the other men who had now gathered. He looked as if he was deep in thought and Josephine hoped that he was considering what she had said. This time when he began to speak the authority in his voice made the lady cringe with fear.

"When night falls, we ride hard for Whetla. I suggest you take some rest for there will be none until your future queen is safe within our borders." The men gave a nod and stepped away. Josephine let loose of Maximillian and slowly sat down under the tree where she had been earlier. The king was about to join her when Larnell began to moan. He returned to the man's side, and a few minutes later, he came back to the lady and said the man was gone. They watched as the body was taken to where the horses were tied up, and then to Josephine's dismay, Maximillian stretched out on the ground beside her. He folded his hands behind his head and closed his eyes and within minutes was asleep. The lady found her temper flaring at his lack of grief for Larnell and thoughts of murdering him entered her mind. But she knew there was no real way for her to overpower him and would only succeed in making her situation worse, and right now she wasn't feeling well enough to fight him off. Josephine had just resolved to close her eyes and save her strength for the ride ahead when out of habit she reached to take hold of her necklace, but it wasn't there. She glanced around where she was sitting, even checking her dress to be sure it hadn't become entangled in the fabric, but saw no signs of it. She had just risen to her feet when she felt a tug on her skirt.

"Where are you going?" Maximillian asked, his eyes still closed.

"I have lost my necklace." The lady answered, taking another step. "I was going to see if it fell off where Larnell's body was."

"I will get you another one. Rest while you have the chance."

"It belonged to my grandmother and cannot be replaced," she answered, pulling her skirt from his hand. For several minutes, Josephine retraced her steps around the campfire, but with no luck, she returned and sat down under the tree. In disappointment, she closed her eyes and fell fast asleep. When she was awakened, it was pitch-black and the moon had not yet risen. Maximillian helped her to her feet and then removed his jacket, placing it around her shoulders. The horses had been saddled, and the company was beginning to mount when someone rode up.

"Sire, we have a problem," the man called out anxiously.

"Let's hear it," Maximillian demanded, letting go of the lady who he was about to lift onto his horse. The scout began to tell how fires could be seen along the road which meant the path north was blocked. The only way to avoid the considerable looking host was to go farther east or west before attempting to cross the plain. Maximillian called for two of the men, and as they stepped away, cursing could be heard as the conversation became heated. Clearly the king was not happy with the development, and Josephine understood that they were in disagreement about what to do next. Suddenly she was addressed. "Councilwoman, why is there a company of soldiers in this part of Gutten?" The three men came back to where Josephine was standing, and trying not to be intimidated, she answered quickly with boldness.

"I know nothing of troops moving about, save the ones who were rotating on furlough and the ones the princes took north toward the river to secure my route from being hindered." The sound of laughter was heard for the irony in the latter part of the lady's statement.

"How successful those endeavors have proven," Maximillian said, mocking the princes efforts since the lady had been captured. Josephine almost slipped with a smile as she knew the plan was in fact working but instead gave a grunt, pretending to be offended.

"If you are so smart, then what is your plan with the road now blocked?" she quipped. All the men laughed except for Maximillian, who was not amused. He walked to the lady and roughly pulled her close to him.

Through gritted teeth, he said, "That will be enough. Do not disrespect me in front of my men."

"Or what? Will you knock their future queen to the ground before their very eyes?" she asked defiantly, her temper raging. She saw movement in the darkness and expected to feel his hand against her face, but instead, he kissed her hard upon the mouth.

As he drew back, he said, "There are other ways you will learn submission." Josephine started to lift her hand to hit him, but he quickly took hold of both of her arms and held her firmly. "Do not hope that those poor excuses of men will rescue you. No one will steal you from me again." He turned toward his men as he let the lady's arms drop. "We will stay here till dawn and then see what the day has for us." The men began to disperse leaving Maximillian and the lady alone. "Come, let's lie down." The king held out his hand.

"I will not lie down beside you," Josephine said, not moving. She listened in the darkness, and when he didn't say anything or move himself, she added, "It would not be right for us to be together . . . at night . . ." She paused but still nothing was heard and nervously she held her breath not knowing what else to say.

Maximillian took a step closer and in a low voice replied, "Do not try my patience." He laid his hand upon her arm and Josephine just knew he was going to force her to go with him. The thought of being beside him sickened her, and she needed a more convincing argument to protect her virtue.

"There will be no illegitimate heirs upon the throne of Aikerlan," she whispered.

"Nothing will happen until vows are taken," he replied, giving a gentle pull. She moved one step and then planted her feet again.

"You cannot promise me that, so I must insist for honor's sake that there is distance between us tonight," Josephine said in desperation.

"Do, as I say!" he demanded, still managing to whisper. He reached for the lady's shoulder, but she shifted to keep him from taking hold of it. "You are stubborn." He let go of her altogether. It seemed she was making some headway.

"As much as you have watched me, I am sure you must have known that before now," the lady replied. "And you know in your heart that something could happen that should not." A long deep sigh was heard as if he was considering what she said and then he spoke again.

"If that's the way you want it." Reaching for her, he removed his jacket from her body. "We'll see how you like it when you are cold with no way to stay warm tonight for we cannot afford our fire to be seen." And then he walked away leaving the lady standing alone in the darkness. Josephine gave a sigh of relief as she had no doubt what was on his mind, despite what was said. She would only hope that he was as stubborn as she and would not come to her during the night. Quietly she went toward another large tree and sat down at its base, drawing her knees up under her chin. Even if part of her dress hadn't been ripped off, the delicate fabric it was made from was too thin to keep her comfortable. For a moment as she sat there, she gave into self-pity. Wilhelm had said it would be a while before she would be rescued but more time had passed than she thought should have. She worried that the arrow had hindered him more than what he had let on or that . . . No, she couldn't let her mind go to worse thoughts. Perhaps he and Leopold had other, better ideas for a rescue that took time to carry out. She remembered Duke Cusall stating that the moment Maximillian took her by force across the border it would give the council full legal grounds to invade Aikerlan to retrieve their council member. She hoped it would not go that far but doubt grew with every hour that passed.

Another thought lingered in the back of her mind and try as she had she could not dismiss it. She had not completely conquered her attraction to Maximillian, and the young man was aware of her weakness. Before she had left Guttenhamm, she had spoken with Hubert confessing that she felt partly to blame for the obsession their enemy had with her and that she had childishly flirted with him in Briasburg. The king assured the lady that Maximillian was evil before she ever stepped foot within Aikerlan, and that although his fascination with her was not good, she was not responsible for his actions. The statements Josephine had made that evening concerning marriage to her enemy frightened her through and through, and although it brought a small measure of comfort to know Maximillian did not want to hurt her, she wondered how long her luck would hold out. There would come a point when he would want more than she was willing to give and she certainly did not want to return with him to Aikerlan to be his wife nor spend the rest of her life with him.

She shivered and her mind returned to her current dilemma of how to keep warm. *Oh God, how am I going to make it through the night?* She began to pray not only because she was chilled already, but she needed direction about what to do next, especially if she was put on a horse headed for Aikerlan at first light. It didn't take very long for Josephine to nod off and wake herself as she began to sway. Reluctantly, she stretched out on the ground and a few minutes later was sound asleep. She wasn't sure how long she was out before she awoke to a whimpering sound and then suddenly felt something cold and wet against her face. She opened her eyes and in the pale moonlight could see the dark shadow of a dog hovering over her and heard it whimper once more. Slowly, she reached to pet the animal, and as she did, she felt the nudge of its companion against her back. She rolled to where she could pet both dogs, and to her surprise, they laid down on either side, resting their heads happily upon her. Josephine had to smile for the animals were terribly warm compared to her, and instantly she knew her prayers had been heard. God had not forsaken her even in the midst of her enemies. He had made a way for her to keep warm that night, and she knew He would help her know what to do the next morning.

Josephine awoke to Otto twitching, followed by a whimper. As she sat up she had to smile for the dog was dreaming. The pre-dawn air was heavy with fog and there was just enough light to see the outline of trees. Suddenly she realized she needed to use one and desperately so. As she crawled to her feet, the dogs sat up to watch her stretch her achy body. All in all, she felt ten times better than she had the evening before, and despite being on the ground, she had slept well. She had only taken a few steps when a shadow appeared before her. To no surprise, it was Maximillian who quietly bid her good morning and then asked where she was going.

"Urgent business needs attending," she replied in a whisper. She attempted to step around him, but he blocked her path and took hold of her hand. "A little privacy is needed." He moved closer to her.

"It's not safe to be alone in the woods," he replied.

"I was not planning on being alone. Otto and Fran were going with me." At which the dogs as if on cue, came to her side and sat leaning against her legs awaiting her command.

"So I see," the king said. Josephine could tell by his voice that he was amused by the dogs' need for the lady's attention. "But the woods can be dangerous." He reached for the lady's hair. As he lifted a strand, Josephine found herself annoyed by the habit he had formed, and she had a mind to braid it back out of his reach the moment she got the chance.

"The only dangerous thing in these parts is missing her dagger," she replied.

"At least you didn't have your sword or none of my men would be alive to tell about it," he stated, causing the lady to ask what he meant. Her victory at the corral had made it to his ears, and although he congratulated Josephine on her skill, he again criticized the princes for putting no more value on the lady's life than to allow her to compete against the soldiers.

"I grow tired of hearing how my every move has been watched," Josephine fumed. "Can you afford me fifteen minutes alone? And . . ." she said, making a bold request, "point me in the direction of water so I can wash my leg wound." Although there was not much light, she could see a smile spread upon Maximillian's face, and he leaned closer until he was only inches from hers. She knew what he was about to do, and her mind went straight to the dagger that was still strapped to her right leg. She could envision using it, but resisted the temptation. She would have to let him do as he wanted for now in order to be allowed to go into the woods alone. Maximillian continued to stoke her hair as he touched her cheek with his nose as if testing to see if Josephine would draw back from him. When she didn't, he kissed her. Keeping her eyes closed, she endured the embrace, reminding herself not to lose focus.

When their lips parted, Maximillian whispered, "Beyond the horses, about a hundred paces is a small stream. In half an hour, I will come looking for you."

The last words were meant as a warning, but appealing to his desires, Josephine replied, "I would expect nothing less." And to taunt him a little more, she laid her hands upon the lapel of his jacket and slid her fingers over the trim. "Your jacket, please." It worked for the king let out a long sigh, and for a moment, Josephine worried that she had done too much for she felt his other hand come to rest upon the small of her back. The pressure reminded her of her need. "If I may, my uhmm . . . business is growing urgent." Without further delay, the man surrendered his coat and the lady called softly for the hounds to follow. As she passed the horses, very discreetly she lifted a lasso of rope from a saddle horn and tucked it under the jacket. Should the need arise she would tie Otto and Fran to a tree rather than to have them slain for interfering with her plan.

The stream was not five minutes away, and after Josephine was finished with her tasks, she immediately headed north to retrace the route Maximillian had carried her to the camp. As disheartened as she had been the night before that she had not been rescued, she had awoke with a single purpose on her mind, and Wilhelm's words echoed, "I have to have opportunity—we cannot afford another miss." She had hoped the princes were close to the camp during the evening, but she was sure Otto and Fran would have alerted them if it had been so. In reality, she knew Wilhelm would stop short rather than run the risk of his presence being known and have to pursue in the darkness. If she backtracked she was bound to stumble upon the princes and more than likely Maximillian would be upon her heels, alone as her last words to him had suggested. If he caught up to her before the princes did, she would feign that her search for her beloved grandmother's necklace had caused her to stray. When she was far enough away from the camp so as not to be heard, Josephine began to mimic the call of a wren. Dawn had come and she could see Otto and Fran's ears perk up as they looked at her, but she kept hold of them by the makeshift leash and continued to walk. She gave a smile as she remembered the first time the prince had shown her the bird whose sound he so often used. The Schneekonig or Snow King was what Wilhelm called it. Josephine knew she gave a poor imitation of the animal, but it would serve the purpose to attentive ears and all she needed was to find one of the princes in the woods for she had already found the king. Every few minutes, she would whistle as she walked but without a response from neither the woods nor the hounds. About twenty minutes after she had left the stream, she saw the dogs' ears twitch and they became excited and pulled at the rope. She reminded them to stay with her and wondered if their reaction meant it was friend or foe drawing near. Her answer came not a minute later as they began to growl. She pulled up the slack and quickened her pace. She whistled again, and this time the dogs were even more excited, jumping as they pulled against the rope and growled louder. She commanded them to be still and to stay with her as she continued to walk, hoping that she was not being tracked by a bear or mountain lion but that it was in fact her rescuers that the hounds were sensing. She had just come to the base of the hill where Tolner had knocked her to the ground and was contemplating whether to climb it or remain, when she heard the chirping of a bird. She listened but heard nothing and was about to dismiss it to her imagination, when she saw the dogs' ears twitching again as they too were listening intently. Excited she looked toward the woods and then remembering her plan began to walk about as if searching for her necklace. It had been much longer than a half hour and she had to prepare for Maximillian to appear at any moment. As she shuffled a pile of leaves with her foot, she whistled again as loud as she could. This time the sound of a wren could clearly be heard in the distance, and her heart leapt for joy. For a moment doubt crept in as she wondered if it was in fact Maximillian answering her call, but her thought was disrupted when she heard another bird whistling in a different direction. If it was her enemy, he was not alone, but she couldn't think about that now as the hounds were on full alert and growling viciously. She knelt and called them to her, rubbing them and speaking to them in a soothing voice to calm them down. So far they had obeyed the lady in every command she had given even though she knew the moment she let loose of the rope, they would be headed in a dead run for the intruder. Even now, they had stopped pulling to get free but had only lowered their growls to a grumble and sat anxiously shifting on their haunches as they watched the woods in every direction. Josephine had just risen to her feet when she saw Maximillian coming through the woods in the distance. The lady reached down and gave each of the dogs a pat on the head and then called out in a loud voice.

"*You* are late," Josephine gave a confident smile as the man came closer.

"I had not decided whether it was an invitation or you were just out to try my patience," he said, stopping more than a dozen paces away.

"Both," the lady replied. "You came alone?"

"You are my burden to bear," the king said with a grin and took a step closer. "The last time someone else was sent, you were hurt." He took another step and added with a tease, "I will be the only man wrestling you to the ground." Josephine felt her pulse quicken at his words, but she was determined not to be intimidated nor think of what he would do if he had the chance. He was so captivated by the lady that he was not paying any mind as his own pets warned him that danger was near.

"Perhaps you should reconsider," Josephine replied boldly. "In fact, you should know that I will not be returning with you to Aikerlan." Maximillian threw his head back and gave a deep laugh, not believing what she said.

"Oh, is that so?" And you think I will let you go? I think not," he said with a grin.

Wilhelm, where are you? Josephine thought. For a moment, panic started to overwhelm the lady's mind as her enemy took another step toward her.

"I think . . . that you will not have a choice in the matter," she said very seriously.

"Surely, you are intelligent enough to know that you cannot resist me," he quipped.

"You are right, that I am intelligent." Josephine glared as she took hold of the dogs by their collars and tied them to a nearby tree. Just as she turned to face Maximillian again, she heard the cry of a wren and with confidence began to speak. "Do you honestly think that I am ignorant enough to travel virtually unguarded to Frive when the king of Andervan offered hundreds of soldiers for my disposal?" The lady took a few steps back toward Maximillian as she continued as if giving a speech. "Or that I would allow myself to be so easily captured without a fight?" She gave a smile and then used his words against him. "After all, I am skilled with a sword, so why would my blade be left in Guttenhamm? And . . ." She paused to take a few more steps as she gloated. "Even now, do you think I would invite you into the woods to have your way with me if I were truly alone?" Maximillian's countenance had grown sober yet she could see signs of agitation. "Am I alone?" she said sarcastically, but before he could answer, she added, "Not at all. Yes, in light of the circumstances, I will not be going with you and *you*, have just walked into a trap." The look the king returned to Josephine made a chill run down her spine, but it proved that her words had cut deep. "Is that fear that I see in your eyes?"

"Oh, my darling Josephine . . . You have much to learn," Maximillian said as he slowly began to walk toward the lady. The way he moved and the devilish look he wore frightened the lady terribly, but she clung to the hope that any second she would be rescued. Nervously, she shifted on her feet trying to control the urge to take a step back as he advanced toward her.

"Your reign is coming to an end," she threatened.

"I think not," he replied as he stared her down.

"Your family is gone. I will not be your queen. Your men despise you and listen, for even your pets have turned against you," Josephine added as Otto and Fran were pulling against the rope and growling louder as the king approached. Maximillian was now only a few arm lengths away from the lady, and Josephine prepared for him to grab her.

"I will teach you submission, my love." As he spoke, the lady heard a familiar whistle and couldn't help but smile from ear to ear with relief. A puzzled look crossed Maximillian's face, but the next second, a shout was heard and Wilhelm knocked the man to the ground. Otto and Fran went wild, and it took every ounce of strength Josephine could muster to secure the rope tighter around the tree. She looked up in time to see Wilhelm rising to his feet as Maximillian lay upon the ground not moving. Leopold was a few paces away, and she could now see guardsmen in the woods around them. The dogs secured, Josephine ran toward Wilhelm but was met halfway as he took her into his arms.

"Are you all right?" she asked.

"I am now." He kissed the lady's forehead. Otto barked causing the pair to look up. "We have affairs to finish," he said to his brother who was standing guard over their enemy's body. Wilhelm let loose of Josephine and went to Leopold's side. "We have thought this man to be dead before and I will not suffer that mistake again." His brother nodded in agreement and then turned to the lady who was now at his elbow.

"Step away."

"Sorry, but as councilwoman, I will be witness to the beheading of Maximillian Brias for crimes he has committed against the kingdom of Gutten." Leopold wrapped his arm over Josephine's shoulder and drew her near as his brother rolled Maximillian's body over with his foot and raised his sword. As he brought his weapon down, Josephine turned her face toward Leopold's shoulder for she could not bear the sight. When the deed was done, Leopold handed the lady into his brother's arms while he directed the guardsmen to prepare the body to be taken back with them. Quickly Josephine pleaded for mercy for the other men of Aikerlan and explained how their families had been leverage for their loyalty. It was agreed that surrender would be offered before swords would be used. As the guardsmen headed on, Wilhelm reached into his pocket.

"I believe this belongs to you," he said as he held up Josephine's necklace. "And this." He handed over the dagger he had retrieved from Maximillian's belt.

"Anything else of mine that you found along the way?" the lady asked as the prince drew her closer until his chin rested against her forehead.

"If I heard correctly yesterday . . . your heart?" he said, leaning back to watch the smile spread across her face. Josephine blushed as she had finally admitted to what she had hoped was happening for so many months. She glanced down at his shirt and nodded. "And what should we do about that, my lady?" He leaned to gently kiss her temple. "Ah, may I suggest sending someone to fetch your father and mother." The words caused Josephine to look up at the prince in surprise. "I asked your father for your hand, with your grandmother's blessing, the night before she passed." Josephine was speechless, but her heart raced with excitement. "I wanted to ask long before now but have not had the liberty until our enemy was defeated. I love you, Josephine Armand. Will you marry me?"

About the Author

Robin and her husband, Matt, reside in the beautiful Ozark hills of Missouri. They have raised two daughters in small town America where friendly smiles are abundant and neighbors still look out for each other. She loves to sing and play the piano in church and is active in youth ministries. The highlight of her summer vacation is serving as a counselor at youth camp.